Bonus Book!

**For your enjoyment,
we've added in this volume *Solid Soul*,
a classic book by Brenda Jackson!**

**Selected praise for
New York Times and *USA TODAY*
bestselling author Brenda Jackson**

BRENDA JACKSON

is a die "heart" romantic who married her childhood sweetheart and still proudly wears the "going steady" ring he gave her when she was fifteen. Because she's always believed in the power of love, Brenda's stories always have happy endings. In her real-life love story, Brenda and her husband of thirty-eight years live in Jacksonville, Florida, and have two sons.

A *New York Times* bestselling author of more than seventy-five romance titles, Brenda is a recent retiree who now divides her time between family, writing and traveling with Gerald. You may write Brenda at P.O. Box 28267, Jacksonville, Florida 32226, by email at WriterBJackson@aol.com or visit her website at www.brendajackson.net.

BRENDA JACKSON

THE PROPOSAL
&
SOLID SOUL

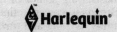

Harlequin®

Desire

ISBN-13: 978-0-373-83764-9

THE PROPOSAL & SOLID SOUL

Copyright © 2010 by Harlequin Books S.A.

Recycling programs for this product may not exist in your area.

The publisher acknowledges the copyright holder of the individual works as follows:

THE PROPOSAL
Copyright © 2011 by Brenda Streater Jackson

SOLID SOUL
Copyright © 2006 by Brenda Streater Jackson

www.Harlequin.com

Printed in U.S.A.

CONTENTS

Dear Reader,

This is it! *The Proposal* is the twentieth book in
The Westmorelands series and the fifth book about those
Denver Westmorelands. For those two reasons alone I
knew this story was special from the moment I began
writing it.

I always thought of Jason Westmoreland as the quiet
storm. He was that one Westmoreland who didn't have a
lot to say and wouldn't have a lot to say...until it was his
time to take center stage. Now it is his time.

I love writing about family, and I'm pleased to announce
that also included in this book is the first book of my
Steele Family series, Chance Steele's story. Including
this story is our way to introduce you to another one of
my families of strong, too-good-to-be-true, irresistible
and handsome men.

In *Solid Soul,* a single mother and a single father get
caught in a web that is woven just for them by their
matchmaking offspring. This is definitely my version of
The Parent Trap.

Sit back and enjoy both Jason Westmoreland and Chance
Steele's stories. And with every Brenda Jackson book, it
is suggested you have a cold drink ready. These stories
are hot!

Happy reading!

Brenda Jackson

THE PROPOSAL

* * *

To Gerald Jackson, Sr. My one and only.

To all my readers who enjoy reading about the Westmorelands, this book is especially for you!

To my Heavenly Father. How Great Thou Art. He hath made everything beautiful in his time.
—*Ecclesiastes* 3:11 KJV

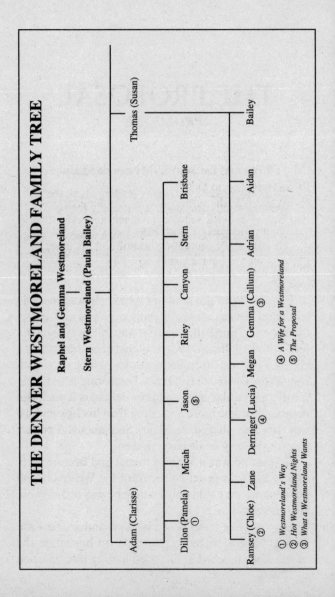

THE DENVER WESTMORELAND FAMILY TREE

Raphel and Gemma Westmoreland

Stern Westmoreland (Paula Bailey)

Adam (Clarisse)   Thomas (Susan)

Dillon (Pamela) ①   Micah   Jason ⑤   Riley   Canyon   Stern   Brisbane

Ramsey (Chloe) ②   Zane   Derringer (Lucia) ④   Megan   Gemma (Callum) ③   Adrian   Aidan   Bailey

① *Westmoreland's Way*
② *Hot Westmoreland Nights*
③ *What a Westmoreland Wants*
④ *A Wife for a Westmoreland*
⑤ *The Proposal*

PROLOGUE

"HELLO, MA'AM, I'M JASON Westmoreland and I'd like to welcome you to Denver."

Even before she turned around, the deep, male voice had Bella Bostwick's stomach clenching as the throaty sound vibrated across her skin. And then when she gazed up into his eyes she had to practically force oxygen into her lungs. He had to be the most gorgeous man she'd ever seen.

For a moment she couldn't speak nor was she able to control her gaze from roaming over him and appreciating everything she saw. He was tall, way over six feet, with dark brown eyes, sculpted cheekbones and a chiseled jaw. And then there was his skin, a deep, rich chocolate-brown that had her remembering her craving for that particular treat and how delicious it was. But nothing could be more appealing than his lips and the way they were shaped. Sensuous. Sumptuous. A perfect pair for the sexy smile curving them.

He said he was a Westmoreland and because this charity ball was given on behalf of the Westmoreland Foundation, she could only assume he was one of *those* Westmorelands.

She took the hand he'd extended and wished she hadn't when a heated sizzle rode up her spine the moment she touched it. She tried forcing the sensation away. "And I'm Elizabeth Bostwick, but I prefer just Bella."

The smile curving his lips widened a fraction, enough to send warm blood rushing through her veins. "Hi, Bella."

The way he pronounced her name was ultrasexy. She thought his smile was intoxicating and definitely contagious, which was the reason she could so easily return it. "Hi, Jason."

"First, I'd like to offer my condolences on the loss of your grandfather."

"Thank you."

"And then I'm hoping the two of us could talk about the ranch you inherited. If you decide to sell it, I'd like to put in my bid for both the ranch and Hercules."

Bella drew in a deep breath. Her grandfather Herman Bostwick had died last month and left his land and prized stallion to her. She had seen the horse when she'd come to town for the reading of the will and would admit he was beautiful. She had returned to Denver from Savannah only yesterday to handle more legal matters regarding her grandfather's estate. "I haven't decided what I plan on doing regarding the ranch or the livestock, but if I do decide to sell I will keep your interest in mind. But I need to make you aware that according to my uncle Kenneth there are others who've expressed the same interest."

"Yes, I'm sure there are."

He had barely finished his sentence when her uncle suddenly appeared at her side and spoke up. "Westmoreland."

"Mr. Bostwick."

Bella immediately picked up strong negative undercurrents radiating between the two men and the extent of it became rather obvious when her uncle said in a curt tone, "It's time to leave, Bella."

She blinked. "Leave? But we just got here, Uncle Kenneth."

Her uncle smiled down at her as he tucked her arm underneath his. "Yes, dear, but you just arrived in town yesterday and have been quite busy since you've gotten here taking care of business matters."

She arched a brow as she stared at the great-uncle she only discovered she had a few weeks ago. He hadn't been concerned with how exhausted she was when he'd insisted she accompany him here tonight, saying it was her place to attend this gala in her grandfather's stead.

"Good night, Westmoreland. I'm taking my niece home."

She barely had time to bid Jason farewell when her uncle escorted her to the door. As they proceeded toward the exit she couldn't help glancing over her shoulder to meet Jason's gaze. It was intense and she could tell he hadn't appreciated her uncle's abruptness. And then she saw a smile touch his lips again and she couldn't help reciprocate by smiling back. Was he flirting with her? Was she with him?

"Jason Westmoreland is someone you don't want to get to know, Bella," Kenneth Bostwick said in a gruff tone, apparently noticing the flirtatious exchange between them.

She turned to glance up at her uncle as they walked out into the night. People were still arriving. "Why?"

"He wants Herman's land. None of the Westmorelands are worth knowing. They think they can do whatever the hell they please around these parts." He interrupted her thoughts by saying, "There're a bunch of them and they own a lot of land on the outskirts of town."

She lifted an arched brow. "Near where my grandfather lived?"

"Yes. In fact, Jason Westmoreland's land is adjacent to Herman's."

"Really?" She smiled warmly at the thought that Jason Westmoreland lived on property that connected to the land she'd inherited. Technically that made her his neighbor. *No wonder he wants to buy my land,* she thought to herself.

"It's a good thing you're selling Herman's land, but I wouldn't sell it to him under any circumstances."

She frowned when he opened the car for her to get in. "I haven't decided what I plan to do with the ranch, Uncle Kenneth," she reminded him.

He chuckled. "What is there to decide? You know nothing about ranching and a woman of your delicacy, breeding and refinement belongs back in Savannah and not here in Denver trying to run a hundred-acre ranch and enduring harsh winters. Like I told you earlier, I already know someone who wants to buy the ranch along with all the livestock—especially that stallion Hercules. They're offering a lot of money. Just think of all the shoes, dresses and hats you'll be able to buy, not to mention a real nice place near the Atlantic Ocean."

Bella didn't say anything. She figured this was probably not the time to tell him that as far as she was concerned there was a lot to decide because none of those things he'd mentioned meant anything to her. She refused to make a decision about her inheritance too hastily.

As her uncle's car pulled out of the parking lot,

she settled back against the plush leather seats and remembered the exact moment her and Jason Westmoreland's eyes had met.

It was a connection she doubted she would ever forget.

CHAPTER ONE

One month later

"DID YOU HEAR HERMAN BOSTWICK's granddaughter is back in Denver and rumor has it she's here to stay?"

Jason Westmoreland's ears perked up on the conversation between his sister-in-law Pam and his two cousins-in-law Chloe and Lucia. He was at his brother Dillon's house, stretched out on the living room floor playing around with his six-month-old nephew, Denver.

Although the ladies had retired to the dining room to sit at the table and chat, it wasn't hard to hear what they were saying and he thought there was no reason for him not to listen. Especially when the woman they were discussing was a woman who'd captured his attention the moment he'd met her last month at a charity ball. She was a woman he hadn't been able to stop thinking about since.

"Her name is Elizabeth but she goes by Bella," Lucia, who'd recently married his cousin Derringer, was saying. "She came into Dad's paint store the other day and I swear she is simply beautiful. She looks so out of place here in Denver, a real Southern belle amidst a bunch of roughnecks."

"And I hear she intends to run the ranch alone. Her uncle Kenneth has made it known he won't be lifting one finger to help her," Pam said in disgust. "The nerve of the man to be so darn selfish. He was counting on her selling that land to Myers Smith who promised to pay him a bunch of money if the deal went through. It seems everyone would love to get their hands on that land and especially that stallion Hercules."

Including me, Jason thought, as he rolled the ball toward his nephew but kept his ears wide-open. He hadn't known Bella Bostwick had returned to Denver and wondered if she remembered he was interested in purchasing her land and Hercules. He definitely hoped so. His thoughts then shifted to Kenneth Bostwick. The man's attitude didn't surprise him. He'd always acted as if he was entitled, which is probably the reason Kenneth and Herman never got along. And since Herman's death, Kenneth had let it be known around town that he felt the land Bella had inherited should be his. Evidently Herman hadn't seen it that way and had left everything in his will to the granddaughter he'd never met.

"Well, I hope she's cautious as to who she hires to help out on that ranch. I can see a woman that beautiful drawing men in droves, and some will be men who she needs to be leery of," Chloe said.

Jason frowned at the thought of any man drawn to her and didn't fully understand why he reacted that way. Luciá was right in saying Bella was beautiful. He had been totally captivated the moment he'd first seen her. And it had been obvious Kenneth Bostwick hadn't wanted him anywhere near his niece.

Kenneth never liked him and had envied Jason's relationship with old man Herman Bostwick. Most people around these parts had considered Herman mean, ornery and craggy, but Jason was not one of them. He would never forget the one time he had run away from home at eleven and spent the night hidden in Bostwick's barn. The old man had found him the next morning and returned him to his parents. But not before feeding him a tasty breakfast and getting him to help gather eggs from the chickens and milk the cows. It was during that time he'd discovered Herman Bostwick wasn't as mean as everyone thought. In fact, Herman had only been a lonely old man.

Jason had gone back to visit Herman often over the years and had been there the night Hercules had been born. He'd known the moment he'd seen the colt that he would be special. And Herman had even told him that the horse would one day be his. Herman had died in his sleep a few months ago and now his ranch and every single thing on it, including Hercules, belonged to his granddaughter. Everyone assumed she would sell the ranch, but from what he was hearing she had moved to Denver from Savannah.

He hoped to hell she had thought through her decision. Colorado's winters were rough, especially in Denver. And running a spread as big as the one she'd inherited wasn't easy for an experienced rancher; he didn't want to think how it would be for someone who knew nothing about it. Granted, if she kept Marvin Allen on as the foreman things might not be so bad, but still, there were a number of ranch hands and some men didn't take kindly to a woman who lacked experience being their boss.

"I think the neighborly thing for us to do is to pay her a visit and welcome her to the area. We can also let her know if there's anything she needs she can call on us," Pam said, interrupting his thoughts.

"I agree," both Lucia and Chloe chimed in.

He couldn't help but agree, as well. Paying his new neighbor a visit and welcoming her to the area was the right thing to do, and he intended to do just that. He might have lost out on a chance to get the ranch but he still wanted Hercules.

But even more than that, he wanted to get to know Bella Bostwick better.

BELLA STEPPED OUT OF the house and onto the porch and looked around at the vast mountains looming before her. The picturesque view almost took her breath away and reminded her of why she had defied her family and moved here from Savannah two weeks ago.

Her overprotective parents had tried talking her out of what they saw as a foolish move on her part mainly because they hadn't wanted her out of their sight. It had been bad enough while growing up when she'd been driven to private schools by a chauffeur each day and trailed everywhere she went by a bodyguard until she was twenty-one.

And the sad thing was that she hadn't known about her grandfather's existence until she was notified of the reading of his will. She hadn't been informed in time to attend the funeral services and a part of her was still upset with her parents for keeping that from her.

She didn't know what happened to put a permanent wedge between father and son, but whatever feud that existed between them should not have included her. She'd had every right to get to know Herman Bostwick and now he was gone. When she thought about the summers she could have spent here visiting him instead of being shipped away to some camp for the summer she couldn't help but feel angry. She used to hate those camps and the snooty kids that usually went to them.

Before leaving Savannah she had reminded her parents that she was twenty-five and old enough to make her own decisions about what she wanted to do with her life. And as far as she was concerned, the trust fund her maternal grandparents had established for her, as well as this ranch she'd now inherited from her paternal grandfather, made living that life a lot easier. It was the first time in her life that she had anything that was truly hers.

It would be too much to ask David and Melissa Bostwick to see things that way and they'd made it perfectly clear that they didn't. She wouldn't be surprised if they were meeting with their attorney at this very moment to come up with a way to force her to return home to Savannah. Well, she had news for them. This was now her home and she intended to stay.

If they'd had anything to say about it she would be in Savannah and getting engaged to marry Hugh Pierce. Most women would consider Hugh, with his tall, dark and handsome looks and his old-money wealth, a prime catch. And if she really thought hard about it, then she would be one of those women who thought so. But that was the problem. She had to think real hard about it. They'd dated a number of times but there was never any connection, any spark and no real enthusiasm on her part about spending time with him. She had tried as delicately as she could to explain such a thing to her parents but that hadn't stopped them from trying to shove Hugh down her throat every chance they got. That only proved how controlling they could be.

And speaking of controlling…her uncle Kenneth had

become another problem. He was her grandfather's fifty-year-old half brother, whom she'd met for the first time when she'd flown in for the reading of the will. He'd assumed the ranch would go to him and had been gravely disappointed that day to discover it hadn't. He had also expected her to sell everything, and when she'd made the decision to keep the ranch, he had been furious and said his kindness to her had ended, and that he wouldn't lift a finger to help and wanted her to find out the hard way just what a mistake she had made.

She sank into the porch swing, thinking there was no way she could have made a mistake in deciding to build a life here. She had fallen in love with the land the first time she'd seen it when she'd come for the reading of the will. And it hadn't taken long to decide even though she'd been robbed of the opportunity to connect with her grandfather in life, she would connect with him in death by accepting the gift he'd given her. A part of her felt that although they'd never met, he had somehow known about the miserable childhood she had endured and was giving her the chance to have a way better adult life.

The extra men she had hired to work the ranch so far seemed eager to do so and appreciated the salary she was paying them which, from what she'd heard, was more than fair. She'd always heard if you wanted good people to work for you then you needed to pay them good money.

She was about to get up to go back into the house to pack up more of her grandfather's belongings when she noticed someone on horseback approaching in the distance. She squinted her eyes, remembering this was Denver and people living on the outskirts of town, in the rural sections, often traveled by horseback, and she was grateful for the riding lessons her parents had insisted that she take. She'd always wanted to own a horse and now she had several of them.

As the rider came closer she felt a tingling sensation in the pit of her stomach when she recognized him. Jason Westmoreland. She definitely remembered him from the night of the charity ball, and one of the things she remembered the most was his warm smile. She had often wondered if he'd been as ruggedly handsome as she recalled. The closer the rider got she realized he was.

And she had to admit that in the three times she'd been to Denver, he was the closest thing to a modern-day cowboy she had seen. Even now he was riding his horse with an expertise and masculinity that had her heart pounding with every step the horse took. His gaze was steady on her and she couldn't help but stare back. Heat crawled up her spine and waves of sensuous sensations swept through her system. She could feel goose bumps form on her skin. He was definitely the first and only man she'd ever been this attracted to.

She couldn't help wondering why he was paying her a visit. He had expressed interest in her land and in Hercules when she'd met him that night at the charity ball. Was he here to convince her she'd made a mistake in moving here like her parents and uncle had done? Would he try to talk her into selling the land and horse to him? If that was the case then she had the same news for him she'd had for the others. She was staying put and Hercules would remain hers until she decided otherwise.

He brought his horse to a stop at the foot of the porch near a hitching post. "Hello, Bella."

"Jason." She gazed up into the dark brown eyes

staring at her and could swear she felt heat radiating from them. The texture of his voice tingled against her skin just as it had that night. "Is there a reason for your visit?"

A smile curved his lips. "I understand you've decided to try your hand at ranching."

She lifted her chin, knowing what was coming next. "That's right. Do you have a problem with it?"

"No, I don't have a problem with it," he said smoothly. "The decision was yours to make. However, I'm sure you know things won't be easy for you."

"Yes, I'm very much aware they won't be. Is there anything else you'd like to say?"

"Yes. We're neighbors and if you ever need my help in any way just let me know."

She blinked. Had he actually offered his help? There had to be a catch and quickly figured what it was. "Is the reason you're being nice that you still want to buy Hercules? If so, you might as well know I haven't made a decision about him yet."

His smile faded and the look on his face suddenly became intense. "The reason I'm being *nice* is that I think of myself as a nice person. And as far as Hercules is concerned, yes, I still want to buy him, but that has nothing to do with my offering my help to you as your neighbor."

She knew she had offended him and immediately regretted it. She normally wasn't this mistrusting of people, but owning the ranch was a touchy subject with her because so many people were against it. He had wanted the land and Hercules but had accepted her decision and was even offering his help when her own uncle hadn't. Instead of taking it at face value, she'd

questioned it. "Maybe I shouldn't have jumped to conclusions."

"Yes, maybe you shouldn't have."

Every cell in her body started to quiver under the
intensity of his gaze. At that moment she knew his offer
had been sincere. She wasn't sure how she knew; she
just did. "I stand corrected. I apologize," she said.

"Apology accepted."

"Thank you." And because she wanted to get back
on good footing with him she asked, "How have you
been, Jason?"

His features relaxed when he said, "Can't complain."
He tilted his Stetson back from his eyes before dis-
mounting from the huge horse as if it was the easiest of
things to do.

And neither can I complain, she thought, watching
him come up the steps of the porch. There was nothing about seeing him in all his masculine form that
any woman could or would complain about. She felt
her throat tighten when moments later he was standing
in front of her. Something she could recognize as hot,
fluid desire closed in on her, making it hard to breathe.
Especially when his gaze was holding hers with the
same concentration he'd had the night of the ball.

Today in the bright sunlight she was seeing things
about him that the lights in the ballroom that night
hadn't revealed: the whiteness of his teeth against his
dark skin, the thickness of his lashes, the smooth texture
of his skin and the broadness of his shoulders beneath
his shirt. Another thing she was seeing now as well as
what she remembered seeing in full detail that night
was the full shape of a pair of sensual lips.

"And what about you, Bella?"

She blinked, realizing he'd spoken. "What about me?" The smile curving his lips returned and in a way that lulled her into thoughts she shouldn't be thinking, like how she'd love kissing that smile on his face.

"How have you been…besides busy?" he asked.

Bella drew in a deep breath and said. "Yes, things have definitely been busy and at times even crazy."

"I bet. And I meant what I said earlier. If you ever need help with anything, let me know."

"Thanks for the offer, I appreciate it." She had seen the turnoff to his ranch. The marker referred to it as Jason's Place. And from what she'd seen through the trees it was a huge ranch and the two-story house was beautiful.

She quickly remembered her manners and said. "I was about to have a cup of tea. Would you like a cup, as well?"

He leaned against the post and his smile widened even more. "Tea?"

"Yes."

She figured he found such a thing amusing if the smile curving his lips was anything to go by. The last thing a cowboy would want after being in the saddle was a cup of tea. A cold beer was probably more to his liking but was the one thing she didn't have in her refrigerator. "I'd understand if you'd rather not," she said.

He chuckled. "A cup of tea is fine."

"You sure?"

He chuckled again. "Yes, I'm positive."

"All right then." She opened the door and he followed her inside.

BESIDES THE FACT JASON thought she looked downright beautiful, Bella Bostwick smelled good, as well. He wished there was some way he could ignore the sudden warmth that flowed through his body from her scent streaming through his nostrils.

And then there was the way she was dressed. He had to admit that although she looked downright delectable in her jeans and silk blouse she also looked out of place in them. But as she walked gracefully in front of him, Jason thought that a man could endure a lot of sleepless nights dreaming about a Southern-belle backside shaped like hers.

"If you'll have a seat, Jason, I'll bring the tea right out."

He stopped walking as he realized she must have a pot already made. "All right."

He watched her walk into the kitchen, but instead of taking the seat like she'd offered, he kept standing as he glanced around taking in the changes she'd already made to the place. There were a lot of framed art pieces on the wall, a number of vases filled with flowers, throw rugs on the wood floor and fancy curtains attached to the windows. It was evident that a woman lived here. And she was some woman.

She hadn't hesitated to get her back up when she'd assumed his visit here was less than what he'd told her. He figured Kenneth Bostwick, in addition to no telling how many others, probably hadn't liked her decision not to sell her land and was giving her pure grief about it. He wouldn't be one of those against her decision.

He continued to glance around the room, noting the changes. There were a lot of things that remained the same, like Herman's favorite recliner, but she'd added a spiffy new sofa to go with it. It was just as well. The old one had seen better days. The old man had claimed he would be getting a new one this coming Christmas, not knowing when he'd said it he wouldn't be around.

Jason drew in a deep breath remembering the last time he'd seen Herman Bostwick alive. It had been a month before he'd died. Jason had come to check on him and to ride Hercules. Jason was one of the few people who could do so mainly because he was the one Herman had let break in the horse.

He glanced down to study the patterns on the throw rug beneath his feet, thinking how unique looking they were when he heard her reenter the room. He looked up and a part of him wished he hadn't. The short, medium-brown curls framing her face made her mahogany colored skin appear soft to the touch and perfect for her hazel eyes and high cheekbones.

There was a refinement about her, but he had a feeling she was a force to be reckoned with if she had to be. She'd proven that earlier when she'd assumed he was there to question her sanity about moving here. Maybe he should be questioning his own sanity for not convincing her to move on and return to where she came from. No matter her best intentions, she wasn't cut out to be a rancher, not with her soft hands and manicured nails.

He believed there had to be some inner conflict driving her to try to run the ranch. He decided then and there that he would do whatever he could to help her succeed. And as she set the tea tray down on the table he knew at that moment she was someone he wanted to get to know better in the process.

"It's herbal tea. Do you want me to add any type of sweetener?" she asked.

"No," he said flatly, although he wasn't sure if he did or not. He wasn't a hot tea drinker, but did enjoy a glass of cold sweet tea from time to time. However, for some reason he felt he would probably enjoy his hot tea like he did his coffee—without anything added to it.

"I prefer mine sweet," she said softly, turning and smiling over at him. His guts tightened and he tried like hell to ignore the ache deep within and the attraction for this woman. He'd never felt anything like this before.

He was still standing and when she crossed the room toward him carrying his cup of tea, he had to forcibly propel air through his lungs with every step she took. Her beauty was brutal to the eyes but soothing to the soul, and he was enjoying the view in deep male appreciation. How old was she and what was she doing out here in the middle of nowhere trying to run a ranch?

"Here you are, Jason."

He liked the sound of his name from her lips and when he took the glass from her hands they touched in the process. Immediately, he felt his stomach muscles begin to clench.

"Thanks," he said, thinking he needed to step away from her and not let Bella Bostwick crowd his space. But he also very much wanted to keep her right there. Topping the list was her scent. He wasn't sure what perfume she was wearing but it was definitely an attention grabber, although her beauty alone would do the trick.

"You're welcome. Now I suggest we sit down or I'm going to get a crick in my neck staring up at you."

He heard the smile in her voice and then saw it on her lips. It stirred to life something inside of him and for a moment he wondered if her smile was genuine or practiced and quickly came to the conclusion it was genuine. During his thirty-four years he had met women who'd been as phony as a four-dollar bill but he had a feeling Bella Bostwick wasn't one of them. In fact, she might be a little too real for her own good.

"I don't want that to happen," he said, easing down on her sofa and stretching his long legs out in front of him. He watched as she then eased down in the comfortable looking recliner he had bought Herman five years ago for his seventy-fifth birthday.

Jason figured this was probably one of the craziest things he'd ever done, sit with a woman in her living room in the middle of the day and converse with her while sipping tea. But he was doing it and at that moment, he couldn't imagine any other place he'd rather be.

BELLA TOOK A SIP OF HER tea and studied Jason over the rim of her cup. Who was he? Why was she so attracted to him? And why was he attracted to her? And she knew the latter was true. She'd felt it that night at the ball and she could feel it now. He was able to bring out desires in her that she'd never felt before but for some reason she didn't feel threatened by those feelings. Instead, although she really didn't know him, she felt he was a powerhouse of strength, tenderness and protectiveness all rolled into one. She knew he would never hurt her.

"So, tell me about yourself Jason," she heard herself say, wanting so much to hear about the man who seemed to be taking up so much space in her living room as well as in her mind.

A smile touched his lips when he said, "I'm a Westmoreland."

His words raised her curiosity up a notch. Was being a Westmoreland supposed to mean something? She hadn't heard any type of arrogance or egotism in his words, just a sense of pride, self-respect and honor.

"And what does being a Westmoreland mean?" she asked as she tucked her legs beneath her to get more comfortable in the chair.

She watched him take a sip of his tea. "There's a bunch of us, fifteen in fact," Jason said.

She nodded, taking in his response. "Fifteen?"

"Yes. And that's not counting the three Westmoreland wives and a cousin-in-law from Australia. In our family tree we've now become known as the Denver Westmorelands."

"Denver Westmorelands? Does that mean there are more Westmorelands in other parts of the country?"

"Yes, there are some who sprung from the Atlanta area. We have fifteen cousins there, as well. Most of them were at the Westmoreland charity ball."

An amused smile touched her lips. She recalled seeing them and remembered thinking how much they'd resembled in looks or height. Jason had been the only one she'd gotten a real good close-up view of, and the only one she'd held a conversation with before her uncle had practically dragged her away from the party that night.

She then decided to bring up something she'd detected at the ball. "You and my uncle Kenneth don't get along."

If her statement surprised him the astonishment was not reflected in his face. "No, we've never gotten along," he said as if the thought didn't bother him, in fact he preferred it that way.

She paused and waited on him to elaborate but he didn't. He just took another sip of tea.

"And why is that?"

He shrugged massive shoulders and the gesture made her body even more responsive to his. "I can't rightly say why we've never seen eye-to-eye on a number of things."

"What about my grandfather? Did you get along with him?"

He chuckled. "Actually I did. Herman and I had a good relationship that started back when I was kid. He taught me a lot about ranching and I enjoyed our chats."

She took a sip of her tea. "Did he ever mention anything about having a granddaughter?"

"No, but then I didn't know he had a son, either. The only family I knew about was Kenneth and their relationship was rather strained."

She nodded. She'd heard the story of how her father had left for college at the age of seventeen, never to return. Her uncle Kenneth claimed he wasn't sure what the disagreement had been between the two men since he himself had been a young kid at the time. David Bostwick had made his riches on the East Coast, first as a land developer and then as an investor in all sorts of moneymaking ventures. That was how he'd met her mother, a Savannah socialite, daughter of a shipping magnate and ten years her senior. The marriage had been based more on increasing their wealth instead of love. She was well aware of both of her parents' supposedly discreet affairs.

And as far as Kenneth Bostwick was concerned, she knew that Herman's widowed father at the age of seventy married a thirty-something-year-old woman and Kenneth had been their only child. Bella gathered from bits and pieces she'd overheard from Kenneth's daughter, Elyse, that Kenneth and Herman had never gotten along because Herman thought Kenneth's mother, Belinda, hadn't been anything but a gold digger who married a man old enough to be her grandfather.

"Finding out Herman had a granddaughter came as a surprise to everyone around these parts."

Bella chuckled softly. "Yes, and it came as quite a surprise to me to discover I had a grandfather."

She saw the surprise that touched his face. "You didn't know about Herman?"

"No. I thought both my father's parents were dead. My father was close to forty when he married my mother and when I was in my teens he was in his fifties already so I assumed his parents were deceased since he never mentioned them. I didn't know about Herman until I got a summons to be present at the reading of the will. My parents didn't even mention anything about the funeral. They attended the services but only said they were leaving town to take care of business. I assumed it was one of their usual business trips. It was only when they returned that they mentioned that Herman's attorney had advised them that I was needed for the reading of the will in a week."

She pulled in a deep breath. "Needless to say, I wasn't happy that my parents had kept such a thing from me all those years. I felt whatever feud was between my father and grandfather was between them and should not have included me. I feel such a sense of loss at not having known Herman Bostwick."

Jason nodded. "He could be quite a character at times, trust me."

For some reason she felt she could trust him…and

in fact, that she already did. "Tell me about him. I want to get to know the grandfather I never knew."

He smiled. "There's no way I can tell you everything about him in one day."

She returned the smile. "Then come back again for tea so we can talk. That is, if you don't mind."

She held her breath thinking he probably had a lot more things to do with his time than to sip tea with her. A man like him probably had other things on his mind when he was with someone of the opposite sex.

"No, I don't mind. In fact, I'd rather enjoy it."

She inwardly sighed, suddenly feeling giddy, pleased. Jason Westmoreland was the type of man who could make his way into any woman's hot and wild fantasies, and he'd just agreed to indulge her by sharing tea with her occasionally to talk about the grandfather she'd never known.

"Well, I guess I'd better get back to work."

"And what do you do for a living?" she asked, without thinking about it.

"Several of my cousins and I are partners in a horse breeding and horse training venture. The horse that came in second last year at the Preakness was one of ours."

"Congratulations!"

"Thanks."

She then watched as he eased his body off her sofa to stand. And when he handed the empty teacup back to her, she felt her body tingle with the exchange when their hands touched and knew he'd felt it, as well.

"Thanks for the tea, Bella."

"You're welcome and you have an open invitation to come back for more."

He met her gaze, held it for a moment. "And I will."

CHAPTER TWO

ON TUESDAY OF THE FOLLOWING week, Bella was in her car headed to town to purchase new appliances for her kitchen. Buying a stove and refrigerator might not be a big deal to some, but for her it would be a first. She was looking forward to it. Besides, it would get her mind off the phone call she'd gotten from her attorney first thing this morning.

Not wanting to think about the phone call, she thought about her friends back home instead. They had teased her that although she would be living out in the boondocks on a ranch, downtown Denver was half an hour away and that's probably where she would spend most of her time—shopping and attending various plays and parties. But she had discovered she liked being away from city life and hadn't missed it at all. She'd grown up in Savannah, right on the ocean. Her parents' estate had been minutes from downtown and was the place where lavish parties were always held.

She had talked to her parents earlier today and found the conversation totally draining. Her father insisted she put the ranch up for sale and come home immediately. When the conversation ended she had been more determined than ever to keep as much distance between her and Savannah as possible.

She had been on the ranch for only three weeks and

already the taste of freedom, to do whatever she wanted whenever she wanted, was a luxurious right she refused to give up. Although she missed waking up every morning to the scent of the ocean, she was becoming used to the crisp mountain air drenched in the rich fragrance of dahlias.

Her thoughts then shifted to something else, or more precisely, someone else. Jason Westmoreland. Good to his word he had stopped by a few days ago to join her for tea. They'd had a pleasant conversation, and he'd told her more about her grandfather. She could tell Jason and Herman's relationship had been close. Part of her was glad that Jason had probably helped relieve Herman's loneliness.

Although her father refused to tell her what had happened to drive him away from home, she hoped to find out on her own. Her grandfather had kept a number of journals and she intended to start reading them this week. The only thing she knew from what Kenneth Bostwick had told her was that Herman's father, William, had remarried when Herman was in his twenties and married with a son of his own. That woman had been Kenneth's mother, which was why he was a lot younger than her father. In fact, her father and Kenneth had few memories of each other since David Bostwick had left home for college at the age of seventeen.

Jason had also answered questions about ranching and assured her that the man she'd kept on as foreman had worked for her grandfather for a number of years and knew what he was doing. Jason hadn't stayed long but she'd enjoyed his visit.

She found Jason to be kind and soft-spoken and whenever he talked in that reassuring tone she would feel safe, protected and confident that no matter what decisions she made regarding her life and the ranch, it would be okay. He also gave her the impression that she could and would make mistakes and that would be okay, too, as long as she learned from those mistakes and didn't repeat them.

She had gotten to meet some of his family members, namely the women, when they'd all shown up a couple of days ago with housewarming goodies to welcome her to the community. Pamela, Chloe and Lucia had married into the family, and Megan and Bailey were Westmorelands by birth. They told her about Gemma, who was Megan and Bailey's sister and how she had gotten married earlier that year, moved with her husband to Australia and was expecting their first child.

Pamela and Chloe had brought their babies and being in their presence only reinforced a desire Bella always had of being a mother. She loved children and hoped to marry and have a houseful one day. And when she did, she intended for her relationship with them to be different than the one she had with her own parents.

The women had invited her to dinner at Pamela's home Friday evening so that she could meet the rest of the family. She thought the invitation to dinner was a nice gesture and downright neighborly on their part. They were surprised she had already met Jason because he hadn't mentioned anything to them about meeting her.

She wasn't sure why he hadn't when all the evidence led her to believe the Westmorelands were a close-knit group. But then she figured men tended to keep their activities private and not share them with anyone. He said he would be dropping by for tea again tomorrow and she looked forward to his visit.

It was obvious there was still an intense attraction between them, yet he always acted honorably in her presence. He would sit across from her with his long legs stretched out in front of him and sip tea while she talked. She tried not to dominate the conversation but found he was someone she could talk to and someone who listened to what she had to say. She could see him now sitting there absorbed in whatever she said while displaying a ruggedness she found totally sexy.

And he had shared some things about himself. She knew he was thirty-four and a graduate of the University of Denver. He also shared with her how his parents and uncle and aunt had been killed in a plane crash when he was eighteen, leaving him and his fourteen siblings and cousins without parents. With admiration laced in his voice he had talked about his older brother Dillon and his cousin Ramsey and how the two men had been determined to keep the family together and how they had.

She couldn't help but compare his large family to her smaller one. Although she loved her parents she couldn't recall a time she and her parents had ever been close. While growing up they had relinquished her care to sitters while they jet-setted all over the country. At times she thought they'd forgotten she existed. When she got older she understood her father's obsession with trying to keep up with his young wife. Eventually she saw that obsession diminish when he found other interests and her mother did, as well.

That was why at times the idea of having a baby without a husband appealed to her, although doing such a thing would send her parents into cardiac arrest. But she couldn't concern herself with how her parents would react if she chose to go that route. Moving here was her first stab at emancipation and whatever she decided to do would be her decision. But for a woman who'd never slept with a man to contemplate having a baby from one was a bit much for her to absorb right now.

She pulled into the parking lot of one of the major appliance stores. When she returned home she would meet with her foreman to see how things were going. Jason had said such meetings were necessary and she should be kept updated on what went on at her ranch.

Moments later as she got out of her car she decided another thing she needed to do was buy a truck. *A truck.* She chuckled, thinking her mother would probably gag at the thought of her driving a truck instead of being chauffeured around in a car. But her parents had to realize and accept her life was changing and the luxurious life she used to have was now gone.

As soon as she entered the store a salesperson was right on her heels and it didn't take long to make the purchases she needed because she knew just what she wanted. She'd always thought stainless steel had a way of enhancing the look of a kitchen and figured sometime next year she would give the kitchen a total makeover with granite countertops and new tile flooring, as well. But she would take things one step at a time.

"Bella?"

She didn't have to turn to know who'd said her name. As far as she was concerned, no one could pronounce it in the same rugged yet sexy tone as Jason. Although she had just seen him a few days ago when he'd joined her for tea, there was something about seeing him now that sent sensations coursing through her.

She turned around and there he stood, dressed in a pair of jeans that hugged his sinewy thighs and long, muscular legs, a blue chambray shirt and a lightweight leather jacket that emphasized the broadness of his shoulders.

She smiled up at him. "Jason, what a pleasant surprise."

IT WAS A PLEASANT SURPRISE for Jason, as well. He had walked into the store and immediately, like radar, he had picked up on her presence, and all it took was following her scent to find her.

"Same here. I had to come into town to pick up a new hot water heater for the bunkhouse," he said, smiling down at her. He shoved his hands into his pockets; otherwise, he would have been tempted to pull her to him and kiss her. Kissing Bella was something he wanted but hadn't gotten around to doing. He didn't want to rush things and didn't want her to think his interest in her had anything to do with wanting to buy Hercules, because that wasn't the case. His interest in her was definitely one of want and need.

"I met the ladies in your family the other day. They came to pay me a visit," she said.

"Did they?"

"Yes."

He'd known they would eventually get around to doing so. The ladies had discussed a visit to welcome her to the community.

"They're all so nice," she said

"I think they are nice, too. Did you get whatever you

needed?" He wondered if she would join him for lunch if he were to ask.

"Yes, my refrigerator and stove will be delivered by the end of the week. I'm so excited."

He couldn't help but laugh. She was genuinely excited. If she got that excited over appliances he could imagine how she would react over jewelry. "Will you be in town for a while, Bella?"

"Yes. I have a meeting with Marvin later this evening."

He raised a brow. "Is everything all right?"

She nodded, smiling. "Yes. I'm just having a weekly meeting like you suggested."

He was glad she had taken his advice. "How about joining me for lunch? There's a place not far from here that serves several nice dishes."

She smiled up at him. "I'd love that."

Jason knew he would love it just as much. He had been thinking about her a lot, especially at night when he'd found it hard to sleep. She was getting to him. No, she had gotten to him. He didn't know of any other woman that he'd been this attracted to. There was something about her. Something that was drawing him to her on a personal level that he could not control. But then a part of him didn't want to control it. Nor did he want to fight it. He wanted to see how far it would go and where it would stop

"Do you want me to follow you there, Jason?"

No, he wanted her in the same vehicle with him. "We can ride in my truck. Your car will be fine parked here until we return."

"Okay."

As he escorted her toward the exit, she glanced up at him. "What about your hot water heater?"

"I haven't picked it out yet but that's fine since I know the brand I want."

"All right."

Together they walked out of the store toward his truck. It was a beautiful day in May but when he felt her shiver beside him, he figured a beautiful day in Savannah would be a day in the eighties. Here in Denver if they got sixty-something degree weather in June they would be ecstatic.

He took his jacket off and placed it around her shoulders. She glanced up at him. "You didn't have to do that."

He smiled. "Yes, I did. I don't want you to get cold on me." She was wearing a pair of black slacks and a light blue cardigan sweater. As always she looked ultrafeminine.

And now she was wearing his jacket. They continued walking and when they reached his truck she glanced up and her gaze connected with his and he could feel electricity sparking to life between them. She looked away quickly, as if she'd been embarrassed that their attraction to each other was so obvious.

"Do you want your jacket back now?" she asked softly.

"No, keep it on. I like seeing you in it."

She blushed again and at that moment he got the most ridiculous notion that perhaps this sort of intense attraction between two people was sort of new to Bella. He wouldn't be surprised to discover that she had several innocent bones in her body; enough to shove him in another direction rather quickly. But for some reason he was staying put.

She nibbled on her bottom lip. "Why do you like seeing me in it?"

"Because I do. And because it's mine and you're in it."

He wasn't sure if what he'd said made much sense or if she was confused even more. But what he *was* sure about was that he was determined to find out just how much Bella Bostwick knew about men. And what she didn't know he was going to make it his business to teach her.

BELLA WAS CONVINCED there was nothing more compelling than the feel of wearing the jacket belonging to a man whose very existence represented true masculinity. It permeated her with his warmth, his scent and his aura in every way. She was filled with an urge to get more, to know more and to feel more of Jason Westmoreland. And as she stared at him through the car's window as he pulled out his cell phone to make arrangements for their lunch, she couldn't help but feel the hot rush of blood in her veins while heat churned deep down inside of her.

And there lay the crux of her problem. As beguiling as the feelings taking over her senses, making ingrained curiosity get the best of her, she knew better than to step beyond the range of her experience. That range didn't extend beyond what the nuns at the private Catholic schools she'd attended most of her life had warned her about. It was a range good girls just didn't go beyond.

Jason was the type of man women dreamed about. He was what fantasies were made of. She watched him ease his phone back into the pocket of his jeans, walk around the front of his truck to get in. He was the type of man a woman would love to snuggle up with on a cold Colorado winter night…especially the kind her parents and uncle had said she would have to endure. Just the thought of being with him in front of a roaring fire that blazed in a fireplace would be an unadulterated fantasy come true for any woman…. And her greatest fear.

"You're comfortable?" he asked, placing a wide-brimmed Stetson on his head.

She glanced over at him and she held his gaze for a moment and then nodded. "Yes, I'm fine. Thanks."

"You're welcome."

He backed up the truck and then they headed out of the parking lot in silence, but she was fully aware of his hands that gripped the steering wheel. They were large and strong hands and she could imagine those same hands gripping her. That thought made heat seep into every cell and pore of her body, percolating her bones and making her surrender to something she'd never had before.

Her virginal state had never bothered her before and it didn't really bother her now except the unknown was making the naughtiness in her come out. It was making her anticipate things she was better off not getting.

"You've gotten quiet on me, Bella," Jason said.

She glanced over at him and again met his gaze thinking, yes she had. But she figured he didn't want to hear her thoughts out loud and certain things she needed to keep to herself.

"Sorry," she said. "I was thinking about Friday," she decided to say.

"Friday?"

"Yes. Pamela invited me to dinner."

"She did?"

Bella heard the surprise in his voice. "Yes. She said it would be the perfect opportunity to meet everyone. It seems all of my neighbors are Westmorelands. You're just the one living the closest to me."

"And what makes you so preoccupied about Friday?"

"Meeting so many of your family members."

He chuckled. "You'll survive."

"Thanks for the vote of confidence." Then she said, "Tell me about them." He had already told her some but she wanted to hear more. And the ladies who came to visit had also shared some of their family history with her. But she wanted to hear his version just to hear the husky sound of his voice, to feel how it would stir across her skin and tantalize several parts of her body.

"You already met the ones who think they run things, namely the women."

She laughed. "They don't?"

"We let them think that way because we're slowly getting outnumbered. Although Gemma is in Australia she still has a lot to say and whenever we take a vote about anything, of course she sides with the women."

She grinned. "You all actually take votes on stuff?"

"Yes, we believe in democracy. The last time we voted we had to decide where Christmas dinner would be held. Usually we hold everything at Dillon's because he has the main family house, but his kitchen was being renovated so we voted to go to Ramsey's."

"All of you have homes?"

"Yes. When we each turned twenty-five we inherited one hundred acres. It was fun naming my own spread."

"Yours is Jason's Place, right?"

He smiled over at her. "That's right."

While he'd been talking her body had responded to the sound of his voice as if it was on a mission to capture each and every nuance. She inhaled deeply and they began chatting again but this time about her family. He'd been honest about his family so she decided to be honest about hers.

"My parents and I aren't all that close and I can't remember a time that we were. They didn't support my move out here," she said and wondered why she'd wanted to share that little detail.

"Is it true that Kenneth is upset you didn't sell the land to Myers Smith?" he asked.

She nodded slowly. "Yes, he told me himself that he thinks I made a mistake in deciding to move here and is looking forward to the day I fail so he can say, 'I told you so.'"

Jason shook his head, finding it hard to believe this was a family member who was hoping for her failure. "Are he and your father close?"

Bella chuckled softly. "They barely know each other. According to Dad he was already in high school when Kenneth was born, although technically Kenneth is my father's half uncle. My father's grandfather married Kenneth's mother who was twenty-five years his junior."

"Do you have any other family, like cousins?"

She shook her head. "Both my parents were the only children. Of course, Uncle Kenneth has a son and daughter but they haven't spoken to me since the reading of the will. Uncle Kenneth only spoke to me when he thought I'd be selling the ranch and livestock to his friend."

By the time he had brought the truck to a stop in front

of a huge building, she had to wipe tears of laughter from her eyes when he'd told her about all the trouble the younger Westmorelands had gotten into.

"I just can't imagine your cousin Bailey—who has such an innocent look about her—being such a hell-raiser while growing up."

Jason laughed. "Hey, don't let the innocent act fool you. The cousins Aiden and Adrian are at Harvard and Bane joined the navy. We talked Bailey into hanging around here to attend college so we could keep an eye on her."

He chuckled and then added, "It turned out to be a mistake when she began keeping an eye on us instead."

When he turned off the truck's engine she glanced through the windshield at the building looming in front of them and raised a brow. "This isn't a restaurant."

He glanced over at her. "No, it's not. It's the Blue Ridge Management, a company my father and uncle founded over forty years ago. After they were killed Dillon and Ramsey took over. Ramsey eventually left Dillon in charge to become a sheep rancher and Dillon is currently CEO."

He glanced out the windshield to look up at the forty-story building with a pensive look on his face and moments later added, "My brother Riley holds an upper management position here. My cousins Zane and Derringer, as well as myself, worked for the company after college until last year when we decided to join the Montana Westmorelands in the horse training and breeding business."

He smiled. "I guess you can say that nine-to-five

gig was never our forte. Like Ramsey, we prefer being outdoors."

She nodded and followed his gaze to the building. "And we're eating lunch here?"

He glanced over at her. "Yes, I have my office that I still use from time to time to conduct business. I called ahead and Dillon's secretary took care of everything for me."

A few moments later they were walking into the massive lobby of Blue Ridge Land Management and the first thing Bella noticed was the huge, beautifully decorated atrium with a waterfall amidst a replica of mountains complete with blooming flowers and other types of foliage. After stopping at the security guard station they caught an elevator up to the executive floor.

"I remember coming up here a lot with my dad," Jason said softly, reflecting on that time. "Whenever he would work on the weekends, he would gather us all together to get us out of Mom's hair for a while. Once we got up to the fortieth floor we knew he would probably find something for us to do."

He chuckled and then added, "But just in case he didn't. I would always travel with a pack of crayons in my back pocket."

Bella smiled. She could just imagine Jason and his six brothers crowded on the elevator with their father. Although he would be working they would have gotten to spend the day with him nonetheless. She couldn't ever recall a time her father had taken her to work with him. In fact, she hadn't known where the Bostwick Firm had been located until she was well into her teens. Her mother never worked outside the home but was mainly the hostess for the numerous parties her parents would give.

It seemed the ride to the top floor took forever. A few times the elevator stopped to let people either on or off. Some of them recognized Jason and he took the time to inquire about the family members he knew, especially their children or grandchildren.

The moment they stepped off the elevator onto the fortieth floor Bella could tell immediately that this was where all the executive offices were located. The furniture was plush and the carpeting thick and luxurious-looking. She was quickly drawn to huge paintings of couples adorning the walls in the center of the lobby. Intrigued, she moved toward them.

"These are my parents," Jason said, coming to stand by her side. "And the couple in the picture over there is my aunt and uncle. My father and Uncle Thomas were close, barely fourteen months apart in age. And my mother and Aunt Susan got along beautifully and were just as close as sisters."

"And they died together," she whispered softly. It was a statement not a question since he had already told her what had happened when they'd all died in a plane crash. Bella studied the portrait of his parents in detail. Jason favored his father a lot but he definitely had his mother's mouth.

"She was beautiful," she said. "So was your aunt Susan. I take it Ramsey and Chloe's daughter was named after her?"

Jason nodded. "Yes, and she's going to grow up to be a beauty just like her grandmother."

She glanced over at him. "And what was your mother's name?"

"Clarisse. And my father was Adam." Jason then looked down at his watch. "Come on. Our lunch should have arrived by now."

He surprised her when he took her arm and led her toward a bank of offices and stopped at one in particular with his name on it. She felt her heart racing. Although he hadn't called it as such, she considered this lunch a date.

That thought was reinforced when he opened the door to his office and she saw the table set for lunch. The room was spacious and had a downtown view of Denver. The table, completely set with everything, including a bottle of wine, had been placed by the window so they could enjoy the view while they ate.

"Jason, the table and the view are beautiful. Thanks for inviting me to lunch."

"You're welcome," he said, pulling a chair out for her. "There's a huge restaurant downstairs for the employees but I thought we'd eat in here for privacy."

"That's considerate of you."

And done for purely selfish reasons, Jason thought as he took the chair across from her. He liked having her all to himself. Although he wasn't a tea drinker, he had become one and looked forward to visiting her each week to sit down and converse while drinking tea. He enjoyed her company. He glanced over at her and their gazes connected. Their response to each other always amazed him because it seemed so natural and out of control. He couldn't stop the heat flowing all through his body at that precise moment even if he wanted to.

He doubted she knew she had a dazed look in the depths of her dark eyes or that today everything about her looked soft, feminine but not overly so. Just to the right degree to make a man appreciate being a man.

She slowly broke eye contact with him to lift the lid off the platter and when she glanced back up she was smiling brightly. "Spaghetti."

He couldn't help but return her smile. "Yes. I recall you saying the other day how much you enjoyed Italian food." In fact they had talked about a number of things in the hour he had been there.

"I do love Italian food," she said excitedly, taking ahold of her fork.

He poured wine into their glasses and glanced over and caught her slurping up a single strand of spaghetti through a pair of luscious lips. His gut clenched and when she licked her lips he couldn't help but envy the noodle.

When she caught him staring she blushed, embarrassed at being caught doing something so inelegant. "Sorry. I know that showed bad manners but I couldn't resist." She smiled. "It was the one thing I always wanted to do around my parents whenever we ate spaghetti that I couldn't do."

He chuckled. "No harm done. In fact, you can slurp the rest of it if you'd like. It's just you and me."

She grinned. "Thanks, but I better not." He then watched as she took her fork in her hand, preparing to eat the rest of her spaghetti in the classical and cultured way.

"I take it your parents were strong disciplinarians," he said, taking a sip of his wine.

Her smile slowly faded. "They still are, or at least they try to be. Even now they will stop at nothing to get me back to Savannah so they can keep an eye on me. I got a call from my attorney this morning warning me they've possibly found a loophole in the trust fund my grandparents established for me before they died."

He lifted a brow. "What kind of a loophole?"

"One that says I'm supposed to be married after the first year. If that's true I have less than three months," she said in disgust. "I'm sure they're counting on me returning to Savannah to marry Hugh."

He sipped his wine. "Hugh?"

She met his gaze and he could see the troubled look in hers. "Yes, Hugh Pierce. His family comes from Savannah's old money and my parents have made up their minds that Hugh and I are a perfect match."

He watched her shoulders rise and fall after releasing several sighs. Evidently the thought of becoming Mrs. Hugh Pierce bothered her. Hell, the thought bothered him, as well.

In a way he should be overjoyed, elated, that there was a possibility she was moving back to Savannah. That meant her ranch and Hercules would probably be up for sale. And when they were, he would be ready to make her an offer he hoped she wouldn't refuse. He knew he wasn't the only one wanting the land and no telling how many others wanted Hercules, but he was determined that the prized stallion wouldn't fall into anyone's hands but his.

And yet, he wasn't overjoyed or elated at the thought that she would return to Savannah.

He got the impression her parents were controlling people, or at least they tried to be. He began eating, wondering why her parents wanted to shove this Hugh Pierce down her throat when she evidently wasn't feeling the guy. Would they coerce her to marry someone just because the man came from "old money"?

He forced the thought to the back of his mind, thinking who she ended up marrying was no concern of his. But making sure his name headed the list as a potential buyer for her ranch and livestock was. He glanced over at her. "When will you know what you'll have to do?"

She looked up after taking a sip of her wine. "I'm not sure. I have a good attorney, but I have to admit my parents' attorney is more experienced in such matters. In other words, he's crafty as sin. I'm sure when my grandparents drew up my trust they thought they were looking out for my future because in their social circles, ideally, a young woman married by her twenty-sixth birthday. For her to attend college was just a formality since she was expected to marry a man who had the means to take care of her."

"And your parents have no qualms in forcing you to marry?"

"No, not one iota," she said without pause. "They don't truly care about my happiness. All they care about is that they would be proving once again they control my life and always will."

He heard the trembling in her voice and when she looked down as to study her silverware, he knew her composure was being threatened. At that moment, something inside of him wanted to get up, pull her into his arms and tell her things would be all right. But he couldn't rightly say that. He had no way of knowing they would be for her, given the situation she was in. Actually it was her problem not his. Still another part of him couldn't help regretting that her misfortune could end up being his golden opportunity.

"I thought I'd finally gotten free of my parents' watchful eyes at college, only to discover they had certain people in place, school officials and professors, keeping tabs on me and reporting to them on my behavior," she said, interrupting his thoughts.

"And I thought, I truly believed, the money I'm getting from my trust fund and inheriting the ranch were my way of living my life the way I want and an end to being under my parents' control. I was going to exert my freedom for the first time in my life."

She paused briefly. "Jason. I really love it here. I've been able to live the way I want, do the things I want. It's a freedom I've never had and I don't want to give it up."

They sat staring at each other for what seemed like several mind-numbing moments and then Jason spoke. "Then don't give it up. Fight them for what you want."

Her shoulders slumped again. "Although I plan to try, it's easier said than done. My father is a well-known and powerful man in Savannah and a lot of the judges are his personal friends. For anyone to even try something as archaic as forcing someone to marry is ludicrous. But my parents will do it with their friends' help if it brings me to heel."

Once again Bella fell silent for a moment. "When I received word about Herman and confronted my father as to why he never told me about his life here in Denver, he wouldn't tell me, but I've been reading my grandfather's journals. He claims my father hated living here while growing up. His mother had visited this area from Savannah, met Herman and fell in love and never went back East. Her family disowned her for it. But after college my father moved to Savannah and sought out his maternal grandparents and they were willing to accept him in their good graces but only if he never reminded them of what they saw as their daughter's betrayal, so he didn't."

She then straightened her shoulders and forced a smile to her lips. "Let's change the subject," she suggested. "Thinking about my woes is rather depressing and you've made lunch too nice for me to be depressed about anything."

They enjoyed the rest of their meal conversing about other things. He told her about his horse breeding business and about how he and the Atlanta Westmorelands had discovered they were related through his great-grandfather Raphel Westmoreland.

"Was your grandfather really married to all those women?" she asked after he told her the tale of how Raphel had become a black sheep in the family after running off in the early nineteen hundreds with the preacher's wife and all the other wives he supposedly collected along the way.

He took another sip of wine. "That's what everyone is trying to find out. We need to know if there are any more Westmorelands out there. Megan is hiring a private detective to help solve the puzzle about Raphel's wives. We've eliminated two and now we have two more to check out."

When they finished the main course Jason used his cell phone to call downstairs to say they were ready for dessert. Moments later banana pudding was delivered to them. Bella thought the dessert was simply delicious. She usually didn't eat a lot of sweets but once she'd taken a bite she couldn't help but finish the whole thing.

A short while later, after they'd devoured the dessert

with coffee, Jason checked his watch. "We're right on schedule. I'll take you back in time to get your car so you can make your meeting with Marvin."

Jason stood, rounded the table and reached for her hand. The instant they touched it seemed a rush of heated sensations tore through the both of them at the same time. It was absorbed in their bones, tangled their flesh and he all but shuddered under the impact. The alluring scent of her filled his nostrils and his breath was freed on a ragged sigh.

Some part of his brain told him to take a step back and put distance between them. But then another part told him he was facing the inevitable. There had been this blazing attraction, this tantalizing degree of lust between them from the beginning. For him it had been since the moment he had seen her when she'd entered the ballroom with Kenneth Bostwick. He had known then he wanted her.

They stared at each other and for a second he thought she would avert her gaze from his but she didn't. She couldn't resist him any more than he could resist her and they both knew it, which was probably why, when he took a step closer and began lowering his head, she went on tiptoes and lifted her mouth to meet his.

The moment their lips connected, a low, guttural sound rumbled from deep in his throat and he deepened the kiss the moment she wrapped her arms around his neck. His tongue slid easily into her mouth, exploring one side and then another, as well as all the areas in between before tangling with her own, mating deeply, and when she reciprocated the move sent a jolt of desire all through his bones.

And then it was on.

Holy crap. Hunger the likes of he'd never felt before infiltrated his mind. He felt a sexual connection with her that he'd never felt with any woman before. As his tongue continued to slide against hers, parts of him felt primed and ready to explode at any moment. Never had he encountered such overwhelming passion, such blatant desire and raw primal need.

His mouth was doing a good job tasting her, but the rest of him wanted to feel her, draw her closer into his arms. On instinct he felt her lean into him, plastering their bodies from breast to knee and as Jason deepened the kiss even more, he groaned, wondering if he would never get enough of her.

Bella was feeling the same way about Jason. No man had ever held her this close, taken her mouth this passionately and made sensations she'd never felt before rush through her quicker than the speed of light.

And she felt him, his erection, rigid and throbbing, against her middle, pressing hard at the juncture of her thighs, making her feel sensations there—right there— she hadn't felt before. It was doing more than just tingling. She was left aching in that very spot. She felt like a mass of kerosene and he was a torch set to ignite her, making her explode into flames. He was all solid muscle pressing against her and she wanted it all. She wanted him. She wasn't sure what wanting him entailed but she knew he was the only man who made her feel this way. He was the only man she wanted to make her feel this way.

When at last he drew his mouth away from her, his face remained close. Acting by instinct, she took her tongue and licked around his lips from corner to corner, not ready to relinquish the taste of him. When a guttural sound emitted from his throat, need rammed through her and when she tilted her lips toward his, he took her mouth once again. He eased his tongue into her mouth like it had every right to be there and at the moment she was of the conclusion that it did.

He slowly broke off the kiss and stared into her face for a long moment before caressing his thumb across her lips then running his fingers through the curls on her head.

"I guess we better leave now so you won't miss your meeting," he said in a deep, husky tone.

Unable to utter a single word she merely nodded.

And when he took her hand and entwined her fingers in his, the sensations she'd felt earlier were still strong, nearly overpowering, but she was determined to fight it this time. And every time after that. She could not become involved with anyone, especially someone like Jason. And especially not now.

She had enough on her plate in dealing with the ranch and her parents. She had to keep her head on straight and not get caught up in the desires of the flesh. She didn't need a lover; she needed a game plan.

And as Jason led her out of his office, she tried sorting out all the emotions she was feeling. She'd just been kissed senseless and now she was trying to convince herself that no matter what, it couldn't happen again.

Only problem with that was her mind was declaring one thing and her body was claiming another.

CHAPTER THREE

HE WAS IN SERIOUS TROUBLE.

Jason rubbed his hand across his face as he watched Bella rush off toward her car. He made sure she had gotten inside and driven off before pulling out of the parking lot behind her. The Westmoreland men were known to have high testosterone levels but his had never given him pause until today, and only with Bella Bostwick.

He wouldn't waste his time wondering why he had kissed her since he knew the reason. She was walking femininity at its finest, temptation not too many men could resist and a lustful shot in any man's arms. He had gotten a sampling of all three. And it hadn't been a little taste but a whole whopping one. Now that he knew her flavor he wanted to savor it again and again and again.

When he brought his truck to a stop at a traffic light he checked his watch. Bella wasn't the only one who had a meeting this afternoon. He, Zane and Derringer had a conference call with their partners in Montana in less than an hour. He hadn't forgotten about the meeting but spending time with Bella had been something he hadn't been willing to shorten. Now with the taste of her still lingering in his mouth, he was glad he hadn't.

He shook his head, still finding it hard to believe just

how well they had connected with that kiss, which made him wonder how they would connect in other ways and places…like in the bedroom.

The thought of her naked, thighs opened while he entered her was something he couldn't get out of his mind. He was burning for her and although he'd like to think it was only a physical attraction he wasn't sure that was the case. But then if it wasn't the case, what was it?

He didn't get a chance to think any further because at that moment his cell phone rang. He pulled it off his belt and saw it was his cousin Derringer. The newlywed of just a little over a month had been the last person he'd thought would fall in love with any woman. But he had and Jason could see why. Lucia was as precious as they came and everyone thought she was a great addition to the Westmoreland family.

"Yes, Derringer?"

"Hey, man, where are you? Did you forget about to-day's meeting?"

Jason couldn't help but smile as he remembered how he'd called to ask Derringer the same question since he'd gotten married. It seemed these days it was hard for his cousin to tear himself away from his wife at times.

"No, I didn't forget and I'm less than thirty minutes away."

"Okay. And I hear your lady is joining the family for dinner on Friday night."

He considered that for a moment. Had anyone else made that comment he probably would have gotten irritated by it, but Derringer was Derringer and the two people who knew more than anyone that he didn't have a "lady" were his cousins Derringer and Zane. Knowing that was the case he figured Derringer was fishing for information.

"I don't have a *lady* and you very well know it, Derringer."

"Do I? If that's the case when did you become a tea sipper?"

He laughed as his gaze held steady to the road. "Ah, I see our precious Bailey has been talking."

"Who else? Bella might have mentioned it to the ladies when they went visiting, but of course it's Bailey who's decided you have the hots for the Southern belle. And those were Bailey's words not mine."

"Thanks for clarifying that for me." The hots weren't all he had for Bella Bostwick. Blood was pumping fast and furious in his veins at the thought of the kiss they had shared.

"No problem. So level with me, Jason. What's going on with you and the Southern Bella?"

Jason smiled. The Southern Bella fit her. But then so did the Sensuous Bella. The Sexy Bella. The Sumptuous Bella. "And what makes you think something is going on?"

"I know you."

True. Derringer and Zane knew him better than any of the other Westmorelands because they'd always been close, thick as thieves while growing up. "I admit I'm attracted to her but what man wouldn't be? Otherwise, it's not that serious."

"You sure?"

Jason's hand tightened on his steering wheel—that was the crux of his problem. When it came to Bella the only thing he was sure about was that he wanted her in a way he'd never wanted any other woman. When they'd kissed she kissed him back in a way that had his body heating up just thinking how her tongue had mated with his. He had loved the way her silken curls had felt flowing through his fingers and how perfect their bodies fit together.

He was probably treading on dangerous ground but for reasons he didn't quite understand, he couldn't admit to being sure right now. So instead of outright lying he decided to plead the fifth by saying, "I'll get back to you on that."

Irritation spread all through his gut at the thought that he hadn't given Derringer an answer mainly because he couldn't. And for a man who'd always been decisive when it came to a woman's place in his heart, he could just imagine what Derringer was thinking.

He was trying not to think the same thing himself. Hell, he'd only set out to be a good neighbor and then realized how much he enjoyed her company. And then there had been the attraction he hadn't been able to overlook.

"I'll see you when you get here, Jason. Have a safe drive in," Derringer said without further comment about Bella.

"Will do."

BELLA STOOD STARING out her bedroom window at the mountains. Her meeting with Marvin had been informative as well as a little overwhelming. But she had been able to follow everything the man had said. Heading the list was Hercules. The horse was restless, agitated and it seemed when Hercules wasn't in a good mood everybody knew it.

According to Marvin, Hercules hadn't been ridden

in a while mainly because very few men would go near
him. The only man capable of handling Hercules was
Jason. The same Jason she had decided to avoid from
now on. She recognized danger when she saw it and in
this case it was danger she could feel. Physically.

Even now she could remember Jason mesmerizing her
with his smile, seducing her with his kiss and making
her groan over and over again. And there was the way
his gaze had scanned over her body while in the elevator
as they left his office after lunch, or the hot, lusty look
he gave her when she got out of the truck at the appliance store. That look had her rushing off as if a pack of
pit bulls were nipping at her heels.

And last but not least were Jason's hands on her.
Those big, strong hands had touched her in places that
had made her pause for breath, had made sensations
overtake her and had made her put her guard up in a
way she didn't feel safe in letting down.

Of course she'd known they were attracted to each
other from the first, but she hadn't expected that attraction to become so volatile and explosive. And she'd
experienced all that from just one kiss. Heaven help
them if they went beyond kissing.

If he continued to come around, if he continued to
spend time with her in any way, they would be tempted
to go beyond that. Today proved she was virtually putty
in his hands and she didn't want to think about what
that could mean if it continued. She liked it but then she
was threatened by it. She was just getting to feel free
and the last thing she wanted to be was held in bondage
by anything, especially by emotions she couldn't quite
understand. She wasn't ready to become the other part
of anyone. Jeez, she was just finding herself, enjoying

her newfound independence. She didn't want to give it up before experiencing it fully.

At that moment her cell phone went off and she rolled her eyes when she saw the caller was her mother. She pulled in a deep breath before saying, "Yes, Mother?"

"I'm sure you've heard from your attorney about that little stipulation we found out about in your trust fund. My mother was definitely smart to think of it."

Bella frowned. "Yes, I heard all about it." Of course Melissa Bostwick would take the time to call and gloat. And of course she wanted to make it seem that they had discovered the stipulation by accident when the truth was that they'd probably hired a team of attorneys to look for anything in the trust fund they could use against her to keep her in line. If they had their way she would be dependent on them for life.

"Good. Your father and I expect you to stop this nonsense immediately and come home."

"Sorry, Mom, but I am home."

"No, you're not, and if you continue with this foolishness you will be sorry. With no money coming in, what on earth will you do?"

"Get a job I guess."

"Don't be ridiculous."

"I'm being serious. Sorry you can't tell the difference."

There was a pause and then her mother asked, "Why do you always want to have your way?"

"Because it's my way to have. I'm twenty-five for heaven's sake. You and Dad need to let me live my own life."

"We will but not there, and Hugh's been asking about you."

"That's nice. Is there anything else you wanted, Mom?"

"For you to stop being difficult."

"If wanting to live my life the way I want is being difficult then get prepared for more difficult days ahead. Goodbye, Mom."

Out of respect Bella didn't hang up the phone until she heard her mother's click. And when she did she clicked off and shook her head. Her parents were so sure they had her where they wanted her.

And that possibility bothered her more than anything.

JASON GLANCED AROUND the room. All of his male cousins had Bella to the side conversing away with her. No doubt they were as fascinated by her intellect as well as her beauty. And things had been that way since she'd arrived. More than once he'd sent Zane dirty looks that basically told his cousin to back off. Why he'd done such a thing he wasn't sure. He and Bella weren't an item or anything of the sort.

In fact, to his way of thinking, she was acting rather coolly toward him. Although she was polite enough, no one would have thought he had devoured her mouth the way he had three days ago in his office. And maybe that was the reason she was acting this way. No one was supposed to know. It was their secret. Right?

Wrong.

He knew his family well, a lot better than she did. Their acting like cordial acquaintances only made them suspect. His brother Riley had already voiced his suspicions. "Trouble in paradise with the Southern Bella?"

He'd frowned and had been tempted to tell Riley

there was no trouble in paradise because he and Bella didn't have that kind of relationship. They had kissed only once for heaven's sake. Twice, if you were to take into consideration that he'd kissed her a second time that day before leaving his office.

So, okay, they had kissed twice. No big deal. He drew in a deep breath wondering if it wasn't a big deal, why was he making it one? Why had he come early and anticipated her arrival like a kid waiting for Christmas to get here?

Everyone who knew him, especially his family, was well aware that he dated when it suited him and his reputation with women was nothing like Derringer's had been or Zane's was. It didn't come close. The thought of meeting someone and getting married and having a family was something at the bottom of his list, but at least he didn't mind claiming it was on his list. That was something some of his other single brothers and cousins refused to do.

"You're rather quiet tonight, Jason."

He glanced over and saw his cousin Bailey had come to stand beside him and knew why she was there. She wanted to not just pick his brain but to dissect his mind. "I'm no quieter than usual, Bail."

She tilted her head and looked up at him. "Hmm, I think you are. Does Bella have anything to do with it?"

He took a sip of his wine. "And what makes you think that?"

She shrugged. "Because you keep glancing over there at her when you think no one is looking."

"That's not true."

She smiled. "Yes, it is. You probably don't realize you're doing it."

He frowned. Was that true? Had he been that obvious whenever he'd glanced over at Bella? Of course someone like Bailey—who made it her business to keep up with everything and everyone, or tried to—would notice such a thing.

"I thought we were just having dinner," he decided to say. "I didn't know it was an all-out dinner party."

Bailey grinned. "I remember the first time Ramsey brought Chloe to introduce her to the family. He'd thought the same thing."

Nodding, he remembered that time. "Only difference in that is that Ramsey *brought* Chloe. I didn't bring Bella nor did I invite her."

"Are you saying you wished she wasn't here?"

He hated when Bailey tried putting words into his mouth. And speaking of mouth…he glanced across the room to Bella and watched hers move and couldn't help remembering all he'd done to that mouth when he'd kissed her.

"Jason?"

He then recalled what Bailey had asked him and figured until he gave her an answer she wasn't going anywhere. "No, that's not what I'm saying and you darn well know it. I don't have a problem with Bella being here. I think it's important for her to get to know her neighbors."

But did his brothers and cousins have to stay in her face, hang on to her every word and check her out so thoroughly? He knew everyone who hadn't officially met her had been taken with her the moment Dillon had opened the door for her. She had walked in with a gracefulness and pristine elegance that made every male in the house appreciate not only her beauty but her poise, refinement and charming personality.

Her outfit, an electric-blue wrap dress with a flattering scoop neckline and a hem line that hit just above her knees greatly emphasized her small waist, firm breasts and shapely legs, and looked stylishly perfect on her. He would admit that his heart had slammed hard in his chest the moment she'd entered the room.

"Well, dinner is about to be served. You better hope you get a seat close to her. It won't take much for the others to boot you out of the way." She then walked off.

He glanced back over to where Bella was standing and thought that no one would boot him out of the way when it came to Bella. They better not even try.

BELLA SMILED AT SOMETHING Zane had said while trying not to glance across the room at Jason. He had spoken to her when she'd first arrived but since then had pretty much kept his distance, preferring to let his brothers and cousins keep her company.

You would never know they had been two people who'd almost demolished the mouths right off their faces a few days ago. But then maybe that was the point. Maybe he didn't want anyone to know. Come to think of it, she'd never asked if he even had a girlfriend. For all she knew he might have one. Just because he'd dropped by for tea didn't mean anything other than he was neighborly. And she had to remember that he had never gotten out of the way with her.

Until that day in his office.

What had made him want to kiss her? There had

been this intense chemistry between them from the first, but neither of them had acted on it until that day. Had stepping over those boundaries taken their relationship to a place where it couldn't recover? She truly hoped not. He was a nice person, a charmer if ever there was one. And although she'd decided that distance between them was probably for the best right now, she did want him to remain her friend.

"Pam's getting everyone's attention for dinner," Dillon said as he approached the group. "Let me escort you to the dining room," he offered and tucked Bella's arm beneath his.

She smiled at him. The one thing she noticed was that all the Westmoreland men resembled in some way. "Thank you."

She glanced over at Jason. Their gazes met and she felt it, the same sensations she felt whenever he was near her. That deep stirring in the pit of her stomach had her trying to catch her breath.

"You okay?" Dillon asked her.

She glanced up and saw concern in his deep dark eyes. He'd followed her gaze and noted it had lit on his brother. "Yes, I'm fine."

She just hoped what she'd said was true.

JASON WASN'T SURPRISED to discover he had been placed beside Bella at the dinner table. The women in the family tended to be matchmakers when they set their minds to it, which he could overlook considering three of them were all happily married themselves. The other two, Megan and Bailey, were in it for the ride.

He dipped his head, lower than he'd planned, to ask Bella if she was enjoying herself, and when she turned her head to look at him their lips nearly touched. He came close to ignoring everyone sitting at the table and giving in to the temptation to kiss her.

She must have read his mind and a light blush spread into her cheeks. He swallowed, pulled his lips back. "Are you having a good time?"

"Yes. And I appreciate your family for inviting me."

"And I'm sure they enjoy having you here," he said. Had she expected him to invite her? He shrugged off the thought as wrong. There had been no reason for him to invite her to meet his family. Come to think of it, he had never invited a woman home for dinner. Not even Emma Phillips and they'd dated close to a year before she tried giving him an ultimatum.

The meal went off without a hitch with various conversations swirling around the table. Megan informed everyone that the private investigator she had hired to dig deeper into their great-grandfather Raphel's past was Rico Claiborne, who just happened to be the brother of Jessica and Savannah, who were married to their cousins Chase and Durango. Rico, whom Megan hadn't yet met, was flying into Denver at some point in time to go over the information he'd collected on what was supposed to be Raphel's third wife.

By the time dinner was over and conversations wound down it was close to ten o'clock. Someone suggested given the lateness of the hour that Bella be escorted back home. Several of his cousins spoke up to do the honor and Jason figured he needed to end the nonsense once and for all and said in a voice that brooked no argument, "I'll make sure Bella gets home."

He noticed that all conversation automatically ceased

and no one questioned his announcement. "Ready to go?" he asked Bella softly.

"Yes."

She thanked everyone and openly gave his cousins and brothers hugs. It wasn't hard to tell that they all liked her and had enjoyed her visit. After telling everyone good-night he followed her out the door.

BELLA GLANCED OUT HER rearview mirror and saw Jason was following her at a safe distance. She laughed, thinking when it came to Jason there wasn't a safe zone. Just knowing he was anywhere within her area was enough to rattle her. Even sitting beside him at dinner had been a challenge for her, but thanks to the rest of his family who kept lively conversation going on, she was able to endure his presence and the sexual tension she'd felt. Each time he talked to her and she looked into his face and focused on his mouth, she would remember that same mouth mating with hers.

A sigh of relief escaped her lips when they pulled into her yard. Figuring it would be dark when she returned she had left lights burning outside and her yard was practically glowing. She parked her car and was opening the door to get out when she saw Jason already standing there beside it. Her breathing quickened and panic set in. "You don't need to walk me to the door, Jason," she said quickly.

"I want to," he said simply.

Annoyance flashed in her eyes when she recalled how he'd gone out of his way most of the evening to avoid her. "Why would you?"

He gave her a look. "Why wouldn't I?" Instead of

waiting for her to respond he took her hand in his and headed toward her front door.

Fine! she thought, fuming inside and dismissing the temptation to pull her hand away from his. Because her foreman lived on the ranch, she knew the last thing she needed to do was make a scene with Jason outside under the bright lights. He stood back while she unlocked the door and she had a feeling he intended to make sure she was safely inside before leaving. She was right when he followed her inside.

When he closed the door behind them she placed her hands on her hips and opened her mouth to say what was on her mind, but he beat her to the punch. "Was I out of line when I kissed you that day, Bella?"

The softly spoken question gave her pause and she dropped her hands to her sides. No, he hadn't been out of line mainly because she'd wanted the kiss. She had wanted to feel his mouth on hers, his tongue tangling with her own. And if she was downright truthful about it, she would admit to wanting his hands on her, all over her, touching her in ways no man had touched her before.

He was waiting for her response.

"No, you weren't out of line."

"Then why the coldness today?"

She tilted her chin. "I can be asking you the same thing, Jason. You weren't Mr. Congeniality yourself tonight."

He didn't say anything for a moment but she could tell her comment had hit a mark with him. "No, I wasn't," he admitted.

Although she had made the accusation she was stunned by the admission. It had caught her off guard.

"Why?" She knew the reason for her distance but was curious to know the reason for his.

"Ladies first."

"Fine," she said, placing her purse on the table. "We might as well get this little talk over with. Would you like something to drink?"

"Yes," he said, rubbing his hand down his face in frustration. "A cup of tea would be nice."

She glanced up at him, surprised by his choice. There was no need to mention since that first day when he'd shown up she had picked up a couple bottles of beer and wine at the store to give him more of a choice. Since tea was also her choice she said, "All right, I'll be back in a moment." She then swept from the room.

JASON WATCHED HER LEAVE and felt more frustrated than ever. She was right, they needed to talk. He shook his head. When had things between them gotten so complicated? Had it all started with that kiss? A kiss that was destined to happen sooner or later given the intense attraction between them?

He sighed deeply, wondering how he would explain his coldness to her tonight. How could he tell her his behavior had been put in place as a safety mechanism stemming from the fact that he wanted her more than he'd ever wanted any other woman? And how could he explain that the thought of any woman getting under his skin to the extent she had scared the hell out of him?

Chances were if he hadn't run into her at the appliance store he would have sought out her company anyway. More than likely he would have dropped by later for tea, although he had tried limiting his visits for fear of wearing out his welcome.

Her phone rang and he wondered who would be calling her at this late hour but knew it was none of his business when she picked it up on the second rang. He'd never gotten around to asking if she had a boyfriend or not and assumed she didn't.

Moments later Jason glanced toward the kitchen door when he heard a loud noise, the sound of something crashing on her floor. He quickly moved toward the kitchen to see what had happened and to make sure she was all right.

He frowned when he entered the kitchen and saw Bella stooping to pick up the tray she'd dropped along with two broken cups.

He quickly moved forward. "Are you okay, Bella?" he asked.

She didn't look at him as she continued to pick up broken pieces of the teacups. "I'm fine. I accidentally dropped it."

He bent down toward her. "That's fine. At least you didn't have tea in the cups. You could have burned yourself. I can help you get that up."

She turned to look up at him. "I can do this, Jason. I don't need your help."

He met her gaze and would have taken her stinging words to heart if he hadn't seen the redness of her eyes. "What's wrong?"

Instead of answering she shook her head and averted her gaze, refusing to look at him any longer. Quickly recovering his composure at seeing her so upset, he was pushed into action and wrapped his arms around her waist and assisted her up off the floor.

He stood facing her and drew in a deep, calming

breath before saying, "I want to know what's wrong, Bella."

She drew in her own deep breath. "That was my father. He called to gloat."

Jason frowned. "About what?"

He watched her when she swallowed deeply. "He and his attorney were able to get an injunction against my trust fund and wanted me to know my monthly funds are on hold."

He heard the tremor in her voice. "But I thought you had three months before your twenty-sixth birthday."

"I do, but some judge—probably a close friend of Dad's—felt my parents had grounds to place a hold on my money. They don't believe I'll marry before the trust fund's deadline date."

She frowned. "I need my money, Jason. I was counting on the income to pay my men as well as to pay for all the work I've ordered to be done around here. There were a number of things my grandfather hadn't taken care of around here that need to be done, like repairing the roof on the barn. My parents are deliberately placing me in a bind and they know it."

Jason nodded. He had started noticing a number of things Herman had begun overlooking that had needed to be done. He then shook his head. He'd heard of controlling parents but felt hers were ridiculous.

"Certainly there is something your attorney can do."

She drew in a deep breath. "He sent me a text moments ago and said there's nothing he can do now that a judge has gotten involved. And even if there were, it would take time and my parents know it. It is time they figure I don't have, which will work in their favor. True,

I got this ranch free and clear but it takes money to keep it operational."

He shook his head. "And all because you won't get married?"

"Yes. They believe I was raised and groomed to be the wife of someone like Hugh who already has standing in Savannah's upper-class society."

Jason didn't say anything for a few moments. "Does your trust fund specifically state who you're to marry?"

"No, it just says I have to be a married woman. I guess my grandparents figured in their way of thinking that I would automatically marry someone they would consider my equal and not just anyone."

An idea suddenly slammed into Jason's head. It was a crazy one…but it would serve a purpose in the long run. In the end, she would get what she wanted and he would get what he wanted.

He reached out and took her hand in his, entwined their fingers and tried ignoring the sensations touching her caused. "Let's sit down for a moment. I might have an idea."

Bella allowed him to lead her over to the kitchen table and she sat down with her hands on top of the table and glanced up at him expectantly.

"Promise you'll keep an open mind when you hear my proposal."

"All right, I promise."

He paused a moment and then said, "I think you should do what your parents want and get married."

"What!"

"Think about it, Bella. You can marry anyone to keep your trust fund intact."

He could tell she was even more confused. "I don't understand, Jason. I'm not seriously involved with anyone, so who am I supposed to marry?"

"Me."

CHAPTER FOUR

BELLA'S JAW DROPPED open. "You?"

"Yes."

She stared at Jason for a long moment and then she adamantly shook her head.

"Why would you agree to marry me?" she asked, confused.

"Think about it, Bella. It will be a win-win situation for the both of us. Marriage to me will guarantee you'll keep your trust fund rolling in without your parents' interfering. And it will give me what I want, as well, which is your land and Hercules."

Her eyes widened. "A marriage of convenience between us?"

"Yes." He could see the light shining bright in her wide-eyed innocent gaze. But then caution eased into the hazel depths.

"And you want me to give you my land as well as Hercules?"

"Co-ownership of the land and total ownership of Hercules."

Bella nibbled on her bottom lip, giving his proposal consideration while trying not to feel the disappointment trying to crowd her in. She had come here to Denver to be independent and not dependent. But what he was proposing was not how she had planned things to go.

She was just learning to live on her own without her parents looking over her shoulder. She wanted her own life and now Jason was proposing that he share it. Even if it was on a temporary basis, she was going to feel her independence snatched away. "And how long do we have to remain married?"

"For as long as we want but at least a year. Anytime after that either of us are free to file for a divorce to end things. But think about it, once we send your father's attorney proof we're officially married he'll have no choice but to release the hold on your trust fund."

Bella knew that her parents would always be her parents and although she loved them, she could not put up with their controlling ways any longer. She thought Jason's proposal might work but she still had a few reservations and concerns.

"Will we live in separate households?" she decided to ask.

"No, we will either live here or at my place. I have no problem moving in here but we can't live apart. We don't want to give your parents or anyone a reason to think our marriage isn't the real thing."

She nodded, thinking what he said made sense but she needed to ask another question. This one was of a delicate nature but was one she definitely needed to know the answer to. She cleared her throat. "If we lived in the same house would you expect for us to sleep in the same bed?"

He held her gaze intently. "I think by now it's apparent we're attracted to each other, which is the reason I wasn't Mr. Congeniality tonight as you've indicated. That kiss we shared only made me want more and I think you know where wanting more would have led."

Yes, she knew. And because he was being honest with her she might as well be honest with him. "And the reason I acted 'cold,' as you put it, was that I felt sensations kissing you that I'd never felt before and with everything going on in my life, the last thing I needed to take on was a lover. And now you want me to take on a husband, Jason?"

"Yes, and only because you won't have all those issues you had before. And I would want us to share a bed, but I'll leave the decision of what we do up to you. I won't rush you into doing anything you're not comfortable with doing. But I think you can rightly say with us living under the same roof such a thing is bound to happen eventually."

She swallowed. Yes, she could rightly say that. Marrying him would definitely be a solution to her problem and like he'd said, he would be getting what he wanted out of the deal as well—co-ownership of her land and Hercules. It would be a win-win situation.

But still.

"I need to think about it, Jason. Your proposal sounds good but I need to make sure it's the right answer."

He nodded. "I have an attorney who can draw up the papers so you won't have to worry about everything I'm proposing being legit and binding. Your attorney can look at them as well if you'd like. He will be bound by attorney-client privilege not to disclose the details of our marriage to anyone."

"I still need time to think things through, Jason."

"And I'll give you that time but my proposal won't be out there forever."

"I understand."

And whether or not he believed her, she *did* understand, which was why she needed time to think about it. From his standpoint things probably looked simple and easy. But to her there were several "what ifs" she had to consider.

What if during that year she fell in love with him but he wanted out of the marriage? What if he was satisfied with a loveless marriage and like her parents wanted to be discreet in taking lovers? What if—

"How much time do you think you'll need to think about it?"

"No more than a week at the most. I should have my answer to you by then." And she hoped more than anything it would be the right one.

"All right, that will work for me."

"And you're not involved with anyone?" she asked, needing to know for certain.

He smiled. "No, I'm not. Trust me. I couldn't be involved with anyone and kiss you the way I did the other day."

Bringing up their kiss made her remember how it had been that day, and how easily her lips had molded to his. It had been so easy to feel his passion, and some of the things his tongue had done inside her mouth nearly short-circuited her brain. Even now her body was inwardly shuddering with the force of those memories. And she expected them to live under the same roof and not share a bed? That was definitely an unrealistic expectation on her part. It seemed since their kiss, being under the same roof for any period of time was a passionate time bomb waiting to happen for them and they both knew it.

She glanced across the table at him and her stomach clenched. He was looking at her the same way he'd done that day right before he'd kissed her. And she'd kissed him back. Mated with his mouth and loved every minute doing so.

Even now she recognized the look in his eyes. It was a dark, hungry look that did more than suggest he wanted her and if given the chance he would take her right here, on her kitchen table. And it would entail more than just kissing. He would probably want to sample her the same way she'd done the seafood bisque Pam had served at dinner. And heaven help her but she would just love to be sampled.

She knew what he wanted but was curious to know what he was thinking at this moment. He was staring at her with such intensity, such longing and such greed. Then she thought, maybe it was best that she didn't know. It would be safer to just imagine.

Swallowing hard, she broke eye contact with him and thought changing the subject was a good idea. The discussion of a possible marriage between them was not the way to go right now.

"At least I've paid for the appliances they are delivering next week," she said, glancing over at her stove that had seen better days. "I think that stove and refrigerator were here when my Dad lived here," she added.

"Probably."

"So it was time for new ones, don't you think?"

"Yes. And I think we need to get those broken pieces of the teacups off the floor," he said.

"I'll do it later. It will give me something to do after you leave. I'm going to need to stay busy for a while. I'm not sleepy."

"You sure you won't need my help cleaning it up?"

"Yes, I'm sure" was her response.

"All right."

"I have beer in the refrigerator if you'd like one," she offered.

"No, I'm straight."

For the next ten minutes they continued to engage in idle chatter. Anything else was liable to set off sparks that could ignite into who knows what.

"Bella?"

"Yes."

"It's not working."

She knew just what he meant. They had moved the conversation from her appliances, to the broken teacups, to him not wanting a beer, to the furniture in her living room, to the movie that had made number one at the box office last weekend like either of them really gave a royal flip. "It's not?"

"No. It's okay to feel what we're feeling right now, no matter what decision you make a week from now. And on that note," he said, standing, "if you're sure you don't want me to help clean up the broken teacups, I think I'd better go before…"

"Before what?" she asked when he hesitated in completing the statement.

"Before I try eating you alive."

She sucked in a quick breath while a vision of him doing that very thing filtered through her mind. And then instead of leaving well enough alone, she asked something really stupid. "Why would you want to do something like that?"

He smiled. And the way he smiled had her pulse beating rapidly in several areas of her body. It wasn't a predatory smile but one of those "if you really want to know" smiles. Never before had she been aware of the many smiles a person's lips could convey.

In truth, with the little experience she had when it came to men, she was surprised she could read him at all. But for some strange reason she could read Jason and she could do so on a level that could set off passion fizzing to life inside of her.

Like it was doing now.

"The reason I'd try eating you alive is that the other day I only got a sample of your taste. But it was enough to give me plenty of sleepless nights since then. Now I find that I crave knowing how you taste all over. So if you're not ready for that to happen, come on and walk me to the door."

Honestly, at that moment she wasn't quite sure what she was ready for and figured that degree of uncertainty was reason to walk him to the door. She had a lot to think about and work out in her mind and only a week to do it.

She stood and moved around the table. When he extended his hand to her, she knew if they were to touch it would set off a chain of emotions and events she wasn't sure she was ready for. Her gaze moved away from his hand up to his face and she had a feeling that he knew it, as well. Was this supposed to be a challenge? Or was it merely a way to get her to face the facts of how living under the same roof with him would be?

She could ignore his outstretched hand but doing so would be rude and she wasn't a rude person. He was watching her. Waiting for her next move. So she made it and placed her hand in his. And the instant their hands touched she felt it. The heat of his warmth spread through her and instead of withstanding it she was drawn deeper and deeper into it.

Before she realized his intentions he let go of her hand to slide his fingertips up and down her arm in a caress so light and so mind-bogglingly sensual that she had to clamp down her mouth to keep from moaning.

The look in the dark eyes staring at her was intense and she knew at that moment his touch wasn't the only thing making her come apart. His manly scent was flowing through her nostrils and drawing him to her in a way that was actually making her panties wet.

My goodness.

"Maybe my thinking is wrong, Bella," he said in a deep, husky voice as his fingers continued to caress her arms, making her stomach clench with every heated stroke against her skin.

"Maybe you are ready for me to taste you all over, let my tongue glide across your skin, sample you in my mouth and feast on you with the deep hunger I need assuaged. And while your delicious taste sinks into my mouth, I will use my tongue to push you over the edge time and time again and drown you in a need that I intend to fulfill."

His words were pushing her over the edge just as much as his touch was doing. They were making her feel things. Want things. And increasing her desire to explore. To experience. To exert her freedom this way.

"Tell me you're ready," he urged softly in a heated voice. "Just looking at you makes me hot and hard," he said in a tone that heated her skin. "So please tell me you're ready for me."

BELLA THOUGHT JASON'S words had been spoken in the huskiest whisper she'd ever heard, and they did something to her both physically and mentally. They prodded her to want whatever it was he was offering. Whatever she was supposed to be ready for.

Like other women, sex was no great mystery to her. At least not since she had seen her parents' housekeeper Carlie have sex with the gardener when she was twelve. She hadn't understood at the time what all the moans and groans were about and why they had to be naked while making them. As she got older she'd been shielded from any encounters with the opposite sex and never had time to dwell on such matters.

But there had been a time when she'd become curious so she had begun reading a lot. Her parents would probably die of shame if they knew about all the romance novels Carlie would sneak in to her. It was there between the pages of those novels that she began to dream, fantasize and hope that one day she would fall in love and live happily ever after like the women she read about. Her most ardent desire was to one day find the one man who would make her sexually liberated. She wouldn't press her luck and hold out for love.

She swallowed deeply as she gazed up at Jason, knowing he was waiting for her response, and she knew at that moment what it would be. "Yes, Jason, I'm ready."

He didn't say anything for the longest time; he just stood there and stared at her. For a moment she wondered if he'd heard her. But his darkened eyes, the sound of his breathing alerted her that he had. And his eyes then traveled down the length of her throat and she knew he saw how erratically her pulse was throbbing there at the center.

And then before she could blink, he lowered his head to kiss her. His tongue drove between her lips at the same time his hand reached under her wrap dress. While his tongue relentlessly probed her mouth, his fingers began sliding up her thighs and the feel of his hands on that part of her, a part no other man had touched, made something inside of her uncoil and she released a breathless sigh. She knew at that moment the heat was on. Before she realized he'd done so, he had inched her backward and the cheeks of her behind aligned with the table.

He withdrew his mouth from hers long enough to whisper, "I can't wait to get my tongue inside of you."

His words sent all kinds of sensations swirling around in her stomach and a deep ache began throbbing between her legs. The heat was not just on, it was almost edging out of control. She felt it emitting even more when his fingers moved from her thighs to her panties.

And when he reclaimed her mouth again she moaned at how thoroughly he was kissing her and thinking her brain would overload from all the sensations ramming through her. She tried keeping up as his tongue did a methodical sweep of her mouth. And when she finally thought her senses were partially back under control, he proved her wrong when his fingers wiggled their way beneath the waistband of her panties to begin stroking her in a way that all but obliterated her senses.

"Jason…"

She felt her body being eased back onto the table at the same time her dress was pushed up to her waist. She was too full of emotions, wrapped up in way too many sensations, to take stock in what he was doing, but she got a pretty good idea when he eased her panties down her legs, leaving her open and bare to his sight. And when he eased her back farther on the table and placed her legs over his shoulders to nearly wrap around his neck she knew.

Her breath quickened at the smile that then touched his lips, a smile like before that was not predatory and this time wasn't even one of those "if you really want to know" smiles. This one was a "you're going to enjoy this" smile that curved the corners of his mouth and made a hidden dimple appear in his right cheek.

And before she could release her next breath he lifted her hips to bury his face between her legs. She bit her tongue to keep from screaming when his hot tongue slid between her womanly folds.

She squirmed frantically beneath his mouth as he drove her crazy with passion, using his tongue to coax her into the kind of climax she'd only read about. It was the kind that had preclimactic sensations rushing through her. He shoved his tongue deeper inside her, doing more than tasting her dewy wetness; he was using the hot tip of his tongue to greedily lick her from core to core.

She threw her head back and closed her eyes, as his tongue began making all kinds of circles inside her, teasing her flesh, branding it. But he wouldn't let up and she saw he had no intentions of doing so. She felt the buildup right there at the center of her thighs where his mouth was. Pleasure and heat were taking their toll.

Then suddenly her body convulsed around his mouth and she released a moan from deep within her throat as sharp jolts of sexual pleasure set ripples off in her body. And she moaned while the aftershocks made her body shudder uncontrollably. What she was enduring was unbearably erotic, pleasure so great she thought she would pass out from it.

But she couldn't pass out, not when his tongue continued to thrust inside her, forcing her to give even more. And then she was shoved over the edge. Unable to take anymore, she tightened her legs around his neck and cried out in ecstasy as wave after turbulent wave overtook her.

It was only when the last spasm had eased from her body did he tear his mouth away from her, lower her legs, lean down and kiss her, letting her taste the essence of herself from his lips.

She sucked hard on his tongue, needing it like a lifeline and knowing at that moment he had to be the most sensual and passionate man to walk on the planet. He had made her feel things she'd never felt before, far greater than what she had imagined in any of those romance novels. And she knew this was just the beginning, an introduction to what was out there…and she had a feeling of what was to come.

She knew at that moment, while their tongues continued to mate furiously, that after tonight there was no way they could live under the same roof and not want to discover what was beyond this. How far into pleasure could he take her?

She was definitely going to have to give the proposal he'd placed out there some serious thought.

JASON EASED BELLA'S DRESS back down her thighs before lifting her from the table to stand on her feet. He studied her features and was pleased with what he saw. Her eyes glowed, her lips were swollen and she looked well rested when she hadn't slept.

But more than anything he thought she was the most beautiful woman he'd ever seen. He hoped he'd given her something to think about, something to anticipate, because more than anything he wanted to marry her.

He intended to marry her.

"Come on, walk me to the door," he whispered thickly. "And this time I promise to leave."

He took her hand in his and ignored the sensations he felt whenever he touched her. "Have breakfast with me tomorrow."

She glanced up at him. "You don't intend to make my decision easy, do you?"

A soft chuckle escaped his lips. "Nothing's wrong with me giving you something to think about. To remember. And to anticipate. It will only help you to make the right decision about my proposal."

When they reached her door he leaned down and kissed her again. She parted her lips easily for him and he deepened the kiss, finding her tongue and then enjoying a game of hide-and-seek with it before finally releasing her mouth on a deep, guttural moan. "What about breakfast in the morning at my place?" he asked huskily.

"That's all it's going to be, right? Breakfast and nothing more?" she asked, her voice lower than a whisper.

He smiled at her with a mischievous grin on his face. "We'll see."

"In that case I'll pass. I can't take too much of you, Jason Westmoreland."

He laughed as he pulled her closer into his arms. "Sweetheart, if I have my way, one of these days you're going to take *all* of me." He figured she knew just what he meant with his throbbing erection all but poking at her center. Maybe she was right and for them to share breakfast tomorrow wasn't a good idea. He would be pouncing on her before she got inside his house.

"A rain check, then?" he prompted.

"Um, maybe."

He lifted a brow. "You're not trying to play hard to get, are you?"

She smiled. "You can ask me that after what happened a short while ago in my kitchen? But I will warn you that I intend to build up some type of immunity to your charms by the time I see you again. You can be overwhelming, Jason."

He chuckled again, thinking she hadn't seen anything yet. Leaning over he brushed a kiss across her lips. "Think about me tonight, Bella."

He opened the door and walked out, thinking the next seven days were bound to be the longest he'd ever endured.

Later that night Bella couldn't get to sleep. Her body was tingling all over from the touch of a man. But it hadn't been any man, it had been Jason. When she tried closing her eyes all she could see was how it had been in her kitchen, the way Jason had draped her across the table and proceeded to enjoy her in such a scandalous way. The nuns at her school would have heart failure to know what had happened to her…and to know how much she had enjoyed it.

All her life she'd been taught—it had virtually been drilled into her head—all about the sins of the flesh. It was wrong for a woman to engage in any type of sexual encounter with a man before marriage. But how could something be so wrong if it felt so right?

Color tinted her cheeks. She needed to get to Confessions the first chance she got. She'd given in to temptation tonight and as much as she had enjoyed it, it would be something she couldn't repeat. Those kinds of activities belonged to people who were married and doing otherwise was improper.

She was just going to have to make sure she and Jason weren't under the same roof alone for a long period of time. Things could get out of hand. She was a weakling when it came to him. He would tempt her to do things she knew she shouldn't.

And now she was paying the price for her little indulgence by not being able to get to sleep. There was no doubt in her mind that Jason's mouth should be outlawed. She inwardly sighed. It was going to take a rather long time to clear those thoughts from her mind.

CHAPTER FIVE

"I LIKE BELLA, JASON."

He glanced over at his cousin Zane. It was early Monday morning and they were standing in the round pen with one of the mares while waiting for Derringer to bring the designated stallion from his stall for the scheduled breeding session. "I like her, too."

Zane chuckled. "Could have fooled me. Because you weren't giving her your attention at dinner Friday night. We all felt that it was up to us to make her feel welcome, because you were ignoring the poor girl."

Jason rolled his eyes. "And I bet it pained all of you to do so."

"Not really. Your Southern Bella is a real classy lady. If you weren't interested in her I'd make a play for her."

"But I *am* interested in her."

"I know," Zane said, smiling. "It was pretty obvious. I intercepted your dirty looks loud and clear. In any case, I hope things get straightened out between you two."

"I hope so, too. I'll find out in five more days."

Zane lifted a curious brow. "Five days? What's supposed to happen in five days?"

"Long story and one which I prefer not to share right now." He had intentionally not contacted Bella over the past two days to give her breathing space from him to think his proposal through. He'd thought it through and it made perfect sense to him. He was beginning to anticipate her answer. It would be yes; it just had to be.

But what if yes wasn't her answer? What if even after the other night and the sample lovemaking they'd shared that she thought his proposal wasn't worth taking the chance? He would be the first to admit that his proposal was a bit daring. But he felt the terms were fair. Hell, he was giving her a chance to be the first to file for a divorce after the first year. And he—

Zane snapped a finger in front of his face. "Hellooo. Are you with us? Derringer is here with Fireball. Are you up to this or are you thinking about mating of another kind?" Zane was grinning.

Jason frowned when he glanced over at Derringer and saw a smirk on his face, as well. "Yes, I'm up to this and it's none of your business what I'm thinking about."

"Fine, just keep Prancer straight while Fireball mounts her. It's been a while since he's had a mare and he might be overly eager," Zane said with a meaningful smile.

Just like me, Jason thought, remembering every vivid detail of Bella spread out on her kitchen table for him to enjoy. "All right, let's get this going. I have something to do later."

Both Zane and Derringer gave him speculative looks but said nothing.

BELLA STEPPED OUT OF the shower and began toweling herself dry. It was the middle of the day but after going for a walk around the ranch she had gotten hot and sticky. Now she intended to slip into something comfortable and have a cup of tea and relax…and think about Jason's proposal.

The walk had done her good and walking her land had made her even more determined to hold on to what was hers. But was Jason's proposal the answer? Or would she be jumping out of the pot and into the fire?

After Friday night and what had gone down in her kitchen, there was no doubt in her mind that Jason was the kind of lover women dreamed of having. And he had to be the most unselfish person she knew. He had given her pleasure without seeking his own. She had read enough articles on the subject to know most men weren't usually that generous. But he had been and her body hadn't been the same since. Every time she thought about him and that night in the kitchen, she had to pause and catch her breath.

She hadn't heard from him since that night but figured he was giving her time to think things through before she gave him her answer. She had talked to her attorney again and he hadn't said anything to make her think she had a chance of getting the hold on her trust fund lifted.

She had run into her uncle yesterday when she'd gone into town and he hadn't been at all pleasant. And neither had his son, daughter and two teenage grandsons. All of them practically cut her with their sharp looks. She just didn't get it. Jason had wanted her land as well but he hadn't been anything but supportive of her decision to keep it and had offered his help from the first.

She understood that she and her Denver relatives didn't have the same bond as the Westmorelands but she would think they wouldn't be dismissing her the way they were doing over some land.

She had dressed and was heading downstairs when something like a missile sailed through her living room window, breaking the glass in the process. "What on earth!" She nearly missed her step when she raced back up the stairs to her bedroom, closing the door and locking it behind her.

Catching her breath she grabbed her cell phone off the nightstand and called the police.

"WHERE IS SHE, MARVIN?" Jason asked, walking into Bella's house with Zane and Derringer on his heels.

"She's in the kitchen," the man answered, moving quickly out of Jason's way.

Jason had gotten a call from Pam to tell him what had happened. He had jumped in his truck and left Zane's ranch immediately with Derringer and Zane following close behind in their vehicles.

From what Pam had said, someone had thrown a large rock through Bella's window with a note tied to it saying, "Go back to where you came from." The thought of anyone doing that angered him. Who on earth would do such a thing?

He walked into the kitchen and glanced around, dismissing memories of the last time he'd been there and his focus immediately went to Bella. She was sitting at the kitchen table talking to Pete Higgins, one of the sheriff's deputies and a good friend of Derringer's.

Everyone glanced up when he entered and the look on Bella's face was like a kick in his gut. He could tell she was shaken and there was a hurt expression in her eyes he'd never seen before. His anger flared at the thought that someone could hurt her in any way. The rock may not have hit her but she'd taken a hit just the same. Whoever had thrown that rock through the window had hit her spirit and left her shaken.

"Jason, Zane and Derringer," Pete said, acknowledging their arrival. "Why am I not surprised to see the three of you here?"

Jason didn't respond as he moved straight toward Bella and, disregarding the onlookers, he reached out to caress the soft skin beneath her ear. "Are you all right?" he whispered in a husky tone.

She held his gaze and nodded slowly. "Yes, I'm fine. I was on my way downstairs when that rock came flying through the window. It scared me more than anything."

He glanced at the rock that someone had placed on the table. It was a huge rock, big enough to hurt her had she been in her living room anywhere near the window. The thought of anyone harming one single hair on her head infuriated him.

He glanced over at Pete. "Do you have any idea who did it?"

Peter shook his head. "No, but both the rock and note have been dusted for fingerprints. Hopefully we'll know something soon."

Soon? He wanted to know something now. He glanced down at the note and read it.

"I was just asking Ms. Bostwick if she knew of anyone who wanted her off this property. The only people she could think of are her parents and possibly Kenneth Bostwick."

"I can't see my parents behind anything like this," Bella said in a soft voice. "And I don't want to think Uncle Kenneth is capable of doing anything like this, either. However, he does want me off the land because he knows of someone who wants to buy it."

Pete nodded. "What about Jason here? I think we

all know he wants your land and Hercules, as well," the deputy said as if Jason wasn't standing right there listening to his every word. "Do you think he'd want you gone, too?"

Bella seemed surprised by the question and moved her gaze from Pete to Jason. Jason figured she saw remnants of passion behind the anger in his eyes.

"No, he'd want me to stay," she said with a soft sigh.

Pete closed his notepad, evidently deciding not to ask why she was so certain of that. "Well, hopefully we'll have something within a week if those fingerprints are identified," he said.

"And what is she supposed to do in the meantime, Pete?" Jason asked in a frustrated tone.

"Report anything suspicious," Pete responded drily. He turned to face Bella. "I'll request that the sheriff beef up security around here starting today."

"Thank you, Deputy Higgins," Bella said softly. "I'd appreciate that tremendously. Marvin is getting the window replaced and I'll be keeping the lights on in the yard all night now."

"Doesn't matter," Jason said. "You're staying at my place tonight."

Bella tilted her head to the side and met Jason's intense gaze. "I can't do that. You and I can't stay under the same roof."

Jason crossed his arms over his chest. "And why not?"

A flush stole into her cheeks when she noted Jason wasn't the only one waiting on her response. "You know why," she finally said.

Jason's forehead bunched up. Then when he remembered what could possibly happen if they stayed overnight under the same roof, he smiled. "Oh, yeah."

"Oh, yeah, what?" Zane wanted to know.

Jason frowned at his cousin. "None of your business."

Pete cleared his throat. "I'm out of here but like I said, Miss Bostwick, the department will have more police checking around the area." He slipped both the rock and note into a plastic evidence bag.

Zane and Derringer followed Pete out the door, which Jason appreciated since it gave him time alone with Bella. The first thing he did was lean down and kiss her. He needed the taste of her to know she was really okay.

She responded to his kiss and automatically he deepened it, drawing her up out of the chair to stand on her feet in the process. He needed the feel of all of her to know she was safe. He would protect her with his life if he had to. He'd aged a good twenty years when he'd gotten that call from Pam telling him what had happened. And speaking of Pam's phone call…

He broke off the kiss and with an irritated frown on his features he looked down at Bella. "Why didn't you call me? Why did I have to hear what happened from someone else?"

She gazed right back at him with an irritated frown of her own. "You've never given me your phone number."

Jason blinked in surprise and realized what she'd said was true. He hadn't given her his phone number.

"I apologize for that oversight," he said. "You will definitely have it from here on out. And we need to talk about you moving in with me for a while."

She shook her head. "I can't move in with you, Jason, and as I said earlier, we both know why."

"Do you honestly think if you gave me an order not to touch you that I wouldn't keep my hands off you?" he asked.

She shrugged delicate shoulders. "Yes, I believe you'd do as I ask, but I'm not sure given that same scenario, in light of what happened in this very kitchen Friday night, that I'd be able to keep my hands off you."

He blinked, stared down at her and blinked again. This time with a smile on his lips. "You don't say?"

"I do say and I know it's an awful thing to admit, but right now I can't make you any promises," she said, rubbing her hands together as if distressed by the very notion.

He wasn't distressed, not even a little bit. In fact, he was elated. For a minute he couldn't say a word and then said, "And you think I have a problem with you not being able to keep your hands off me?"

She nodded. "If you don't have a problem with it then you should. We aren't married. We aren't even engaged."

"I asked you to marry me Friday night."

She used her hand to wave off his reminder. "Yes, but it would be a marriage of convenience, which I haven't agreed to yet since the issue of the sleeping arrangements is still up in the air. Until I do decide I think it's best if you stay under your roof and I stay under mine. Yes, that's the proper thing to do."

He lifted a brow. "The proper thing to do?"

"Yes, proper, appropriate, suitable, fitting—which of those words do you prefer using?"

"What about none of them?"

"It doesn't matter, Jason. It's bad enough that we got carried away the other night in this kitchen. But we can't repeat something like that."

He didn't see why they couldn't and was about to say as much when he heard footsteps approaching and glanced over as Derringer and Zane entered the kitchen.

"Pete thinks he's found a footprint outside near the bushes and is checking it out now," Derringer informed them.

Jason nodded. He then turned back to Bella and his expression was one that would accept no argument on the matter. "Pack an overnight bag, Bella. You're staying at my place tonight even if I have to sleep in the barn."

CHAPTER SIX

BELLA GLARED AT JASON. It was a ladylike glare but a glare nonetheless. She opened her mouth to say something then remembered they had an audience and immediately closed it. She cast a warm smile over at Zane and Derringer. "I'd like a few minutes alone with Jason to discuss a private matter, please."

They returned her smile, nodded and gave Jason "you've done it now" smiles before walking out of the kitchen.

It was then that she turned her attention back to Jason. "Now then, Jason, let's not be ridiculous. You are not sleeping in your barn just so I can sleep under your roof. I'm staying right here."

She could tell he did not appreciate his order not being obeyed when she saw his irritation with her increase. "Have you forgotten someone threw a rock through your window with a note demanding you leave town?"

She nibbled a minute on her bottom lip. "No, I didn't forget the rock or the note attached to it, but I can't let them think they've won by running away. I admit to being a little frightened at first but I'm fine now. Marvin is having the window replaced and I'll keep lights shining around here all night. And don't forget Marvin sleeps in the bunkhouse each night so technically, I won't be here by myself. I'll be fine, but I appreciate your concern."

Jason stared at her for a moment and didn't say anything. He hadn't lied about aging twenty years when he'd gotten that call from Pam. He had walked into her house not knowing what to expect. The thought that someone wanted her gone bothered him, because he knew she wasn't going anywhere and that meant he needed to protect her.

"Fine, you stay inside here and I'll sleep in your barn," he finally said.

She shook her head after crossing her arms over her chest. "You won't be sleeping in anyone's barn. You're going to sleep in your own bed tonight and I intend to sleep in mine."

"Fine," he snapped like he was giving in to her suggestion when he wouldn't do anything of the sort. But if she wanted to think it he would let her. "I need to take you to Pam's to show her and the others you're okay and in one piece."

A smile touched her lips. "They were worried about me?"

She seemed surprised by that. "Yes, everyone was worried."

"In that case let me grab my purse."

"I'll be waiting outside," he said to her fleeing back.

He shook his head and slowly left the kitchen and walked through the dining room to the living room where Marvin and a couple of the men were replacing the window. They had cleaned up all the broken glass but a scratch mark on the wooden floor clearly showed where the rock had landed once it entered the house.

He drew in a sharp breath at the thought of Bella getting hit by that rock. If anything would have happened to her he would have...

At that moment he wasn't sure just what he would do. The thought of anything happening to her sent sharp fear through him in a way he'd never known before. Why? Why were his feelings for her so intense? Why was he so possessive when it came to her?

He shrugged off the responses that flowed through his mind, not ready to deal with any of them. He walked out the front door to where Zane and Derringer were waiting.

"You aren't really going to let her stay here unprotected?" Derringer asked, studying his features.

Jason shook his head. "No."

"And why can't the two of you stay under the same roof?" Zane asked curiously.

"None of your business."

Zane chuckled. "If you don't give me an answer I'm going to think things."

That didn't move Jason. "Think whatever you want." He then checked his watch. "I hate to do this but I'm checking out for the rest of the day. I intend to keep an eye on Bella until Pete finds out who threw that rock through her window."

"You think Kenneth Bostwick had something to do with it?" Derringer asked.

"Not sure, but I hope for his sake he didn't," Jason said in a voice laced with tightly controlled anger.

He stopped talking when Bella walked onto the porch. Not only had she grabbed her purse but she'd also changed her dress. At his curious look, she said, "The dress I was wearing wasn't suitable for visiting."

He nodded and decided not to tell her she looked good now and had looked good then. Whatever she put on her body she wore with both grace and style. He met her in the middle of the porch and slipped her hand in his. "You look nice. And I thought we could grab dinner someplace before I bring you back here."

Her eyes glowed in a way that tightened his stomach and sent sensations rushing through his gut. "I'd like that, Jason."

IT WAS CLOSE TO TEN AT night when Bella returned home. Jason entered her house and checked around, turning on lights as he went from room to room. It made her feel extra safe when she saw a police patrol car parked near the turnoff to her property.

"Everything looks okay," Jason said, breaking into her thoughts.

"Thanks. I'll walk you to the door," she said quickly, heading back downstairs.

"Trying to rush me out of here, Bella?"

At the moment she didn't care what he thought. She just needed him gone so she could get her mind straightened out. Being with him for the past eight hours had taken its toll on her mind and body.

She hadn't known he was so touchy and each time he'd touched her, even by doing something as simple as placing a hand in the center of her back when they'd been walking into the movies, it had done something to her in a way that had her hot and bothered for the rest of the evening.

But she had enjoyed the movies they'd gone to after dinner. She had enjoyed sitting beside him while he held her hand when he wasn't feeding her popcorn.

"No, I'm not trying to rush you, Jason, but it is late," she said. "If your goal this evening was to tire me out then you've done a good job of it. I plan to take a shower and then go to bed."

They were standing facing each other and he wrapped his arms around her and took a step closer, almost plastering his body to hers. She could feel all of him from chest to knee; but especially the erect body part in between.

"I'd love to take a shower with you, sweetheart," he whispered.

She didn't know what he was trying to do, but he'd been whispering such naughty come-ons to her all evening. And each and every one of them had only added to her torment. "Taking a shower together wouldn't be right, Jason, and you know it."

He chuckled. "Trying to send me home to an empty bed isn't right, either. Why don't you just accept my proposal? We can get married the same day. No waiting. And then," he said, leaning closer to begin nibbling around her mouth, "we can sleep under the same roof that night. Just think about that."

Bella moaned against the onslaught of his mouth on hers. She was thinking about it and could just imagine it. Oh, what a night that would be. But then she also had to think about what would happen if he got tired of her like her father had eventually gotten tired of her mother. The way her mother had gotten tired of her father. What if he approached her about wanting an open marriage? What if he told her after the first year that he wanted a divorce and she'd gotten attached to him? She could just imagine the heartbreak she would feel.

"Bella?"

She glanced up at him. "Yes?"

Jason Westmoreland was such a handsome man that it made her heart ache. And at the same time he made parts of her sizzle in desire so thick you could cut it with a knife. She thought his features were flawless and he had to have the most irresistible pair of lips born to any man. Staring at his mouth pushed her to recall the way their tongues would entangle in his mouth while they mated them like crazy. It didn't take much to wonder how things would be between them in the bedroom. But she knew as tempting as it was, there was more to a marriage than just great sex. But could she really ask for more from a marriage of convenience?

"Are you sure you don't want me to stay tonight? I could sleep on the sofa."

She shook her head. Even that would be too close for comfort for her. "No, Jason, I'll be fine. Go home."

"Not before I do this," he said, leaning down and capturing her mouth with his. She didn't have a problem offering him what he wanted and he proved he didn't have a problem taking it. He kissed her deeply, thoroughly and with no reservations about making her feel wanted, needed and desired. She could definitely feel heat radiating from his body to hers and wasn't put off by it. Instead it ignited passion within her so acute she had to fight to keep a level head or risk the kiss taking them places she wasn't ready to go.

Moments later she was the one who broke off the kiss. Desperately needing to breathe, she inhaled a deep breath. Jason just simply stood there staring and waiting, as if he was ready to go another round.

Bella knew she disappointed him when she took a step back. "Good night, Jason."

His lips curved into a too-sexy smile. "Tell me one thing that will be good about it once I walk out that door."

She really wasn't sure what she could say to that, and in those cases she'd always been told it was better not to say anything at all. Instead she repeated herself while turning the knob on the door to open it. "Good night, Jason.

He leaned in, brushed a kiss across her lips and whispered, "Good night, Bella."

BELLA WASN'T SURE WHAT brought her awake during the middle of the night. Glancing over at the clock on her nightstand she saw it was two in the morning. She was restless. She was hot. And she was definitely still bothered. She hadn't known just spending time with a man could put a woman in such an erotic state.

Sliding out of bed she slipped into her robe and house shoes. A full moon was in the sky and its light spread into the room. She was surprised by how easily sleep had come to her at first. But that had been a few hours ago and now she was wide-awake.

She moved over to the windows to look out. Under the moon-crested sky she could see the shape of the mountains in their majestic splendor. At night they were just as overpowering as they were in the daylight.

She was about to move away from the window when she happened to glance down below and saw a truck parked in her yard. She frowned and pressed her face closer to the window to make out just whose vehicle was parked in her yard and frowned when she recognized the vehicle was Jason's.

What was his truck doing in her yard at two in the morning? Was he in it?

She rushed downstairs. He couldn't be in a truck in front of her house at two in the morning. What would Marvin think? What would the police officers cruising the area think? His family?

When she made it to the living room she slowly opened the door and slipped out. She then released a disgusted sigh when she saw he was sitting in the truck. He had put his seat in a reclining position, but that had to be uncomfortable for him.

As if he'd been sleeping with one eye open and another one closed, he came awake when she rounded the truck and tapped on his window. He slowly tilted his Stetson back from covering his eyes. "Yes, Bella?"

She opened her mouth to speak and then closed it. If she thought he was a handsome man before, then he was even more now with the shadow covering his jaw. There was just something ultrasexy about a man who hadn't shaved.

She fought her attention away from his jaw back to his gaze. "What are you doing here? Why did you come back?"

"I never left."

She blinked. "You never left? You mean to tell me you've been out here in the car since I walked you to the door?"

He smiled that sexy smile. "Yes, I've been here since you walked me to the door."

"But why?"

"To protect you."

That simple statement suddenly took the wind out of her sail for just a moment. Merely a moment. That was all the time she needed to be reminded that no one had tried truly protecting her before. She'd always considered her parents' antics more in the line of controlling than protecting.

She then recovered and remembered why he couldn't sit out here protecting her. "But you can't sit out here, Jason. It's not proper. What will your family think if any of them see your car parked in front of my house at this hour? What would those policemen think? What would—"

"Honestly, Bella, I really don't give a royal damn what anyone thinks. I refuse to let you stay here without being close by to make sure you're okay. You didn't want me to sleep in the barn so this is where I am and where I will stay."

She frowned. "You're being difficult."

"No, I'm being a man looking out for the woman I want. Now go back inside and lock the door behind you. You interrupted my sleep."

She stared at him for a long moment and then said, "Fine, you win. Come on inside."

He stared back at her. "That wasn't what this was about, Bella. I recognize the fact just as much as you do that we don't need to be under the same roof alone. I'm fine with being out here tonight."

"Well, I'm not fine with it."

"Sorry about that but there's nothing I can do about it."

She glared at him and seeing he was determined to be stubborn, she threw up her hands before going back into the house, closing the door behind her.

Jason heard the lock click in place and swore he could also hear her fuming all the way up the stairs. She could fume all she wanted but he wasn't leaving. He had been sitting out there for the past four hours thinking, and the more he thought the more he realized something vital to him. And it was something he could not deny or ignore. He had fallen in love with Bella. And accepting how he felt gave his proposal much more meaning than what he'd presented to her. Now he fully understood why Derringer had acted so strangely while courting Lucia.

He had dated women in the past but had never loved any of them. He'd known better than to do so after that fiasco with Mona Cardington in high school. He'd admitted he loved her and when a new guy moved to town weeks later she had dumped him like a hot potato. That had been years ago but the pain he'd felt that day had been real and at seventeen it had been what had kept him from loving another woman.

And now he had fallen head over heels in love with a Southern belle, and for the time being would keep how he felt to himself.

AN HOUR LATER BELLA lay in bed staring up at the ceiling, still inwardly fuming. How dare Jason put her in such a compromising position? No one would think he was sleeping in the truck. People were going to assume they were lovers and he was sleeping in her bed, lying with her between silken sheets with their limbs entwined and mouths fused while making hot, passionate and steamy love.

Her thighs began to quiver and the juncture between her legs began to ache just thinking of how it would probably be if they were to share a bed. He would stroke her senseless with his fingers in her most intimate spot first, taking his time to get her primed and ready for the next stage of what he would do to her.

She shifted to her side and held her legs tightly together, hoping the ache would go away. She'd never craved a man before and now she was craving Jason something fierce, more so than ever since he'd tasted her there. All she had to do was close her eyes and remember being stretched out on her kitchen table with his head between her legs and how he had lapped her into sweet oblivion. The memories sent jolts of electricity throughout her body, making the tips of her breasts feel sensitive against her nightgown.

And the man causing her so much torment and pleasure was downstairs sleeping in his truck just to keep her safe. She couldn't help but be touched that he would do such a thing. He had given up a nice comfortable bed and was sleeping in a position that couldn't be relaxing with his hat over his eyes to shield the brightness of the lights around her yard. Why? Was protecting her that important to him?

If it was, then why?

Deep down she knew the reason and it stemmed from him wanting her land and Hercules. He had been upfront about it from the beginning. She had respected him for it and for accepting the decision was hers to make. So, in other words, he wasn't really protecting her per se but merely protecting his interest, or what he hoped to be his interest. She figured such a thing made sense but…

Would accepting the proposal Jason placed on the table be in her best interest? Did she have a choice if she wanted the hold lifted on her trust fund? Was being legally bound to Jason as his wife for a minimum of a year something she wanted? What about sleeping under the same roof with him and sharing his bed—she'd accepted they would be synonymous—would they be in her best interest? Was it what she wanted to do, knowing in a year's time he could walk away without looking back? Knowing after that time he would be free to marry someone else? Free to make love to someone else the same way he'd make love to her?

And then there was the question of who was responsible for throwing the rock inside her house. Why was someone trying to scare her off? Although she doubted it, could it be her parents' doing to get her to run back home?

She yawned when she felt sleep coming down on her. Although she regretted Jason was sleeping in his truck, she knew she could sleep a lot more peacefully knowing he was the one protecting her.

BELLA WOKE TO THE SOUND of someone knocking on her door and discovered it was morning. She quickly eased out of bed and slid into her bathrobe and bedroom shoes to head downstairs.

"I'm coming!" she called out, rushing to the door. She glanced out the peephole and saw it was Jason. Her heart began beating fast and furiously in her chest at the sight of him, handsome and unshaven with his Stetson low on his brow. Mercy!

Taking a deep breath she opened the door. "Good morning, Jason."

"Good morning, Bella. I wanted to let you know I'm leaving to go home and freshen up, but Riley is here."

"Your brother Riley?" she asked, looking over his shoulder to see the truck parked next to his and the man sitting inside. Riley threw up his hand in a wave, which she returned. She recalled meeting him that night at dinner. Jason was older than Riley by two and a half years.

"Yes, my brother Riley."

She was confused. "Why is he here?"

"Because I'm going home to freshen up." He tilted his head and smiled at her. "Are you awake yet?"

"Yes, I'm awake and I know you said you're going home to change but why does Riley have to be here? It's not like I need a bodyguard or something. A rock got thrown through my window, Jason. Not a scud missile."

He merely kept smiling at her while leaning in her doorway. And then he said, "Has anyone ever told you how beautiful you look in the morning?"

She stood there and stared at him. Not ready for him to change the subject and definitely not prepared for him to say something so nice about how she looked. She could definitely return the favor and ask, had anyone ever told him how handsome he looked in the morning? However, she was certain a number of women already had.

So she answered him honestly. "No one has ever told me that."

"Then let me go on record as being your first."

She drew in a deep breath. He didn't say "the" first but had said "your" first. He had made it personal and exclusive. She wondered what he would think to know she had drifted off to sleep last night with images of him flittering through her mind. Memories of his mouth on her probably elicited pleasurable sighs from her even while she slept.

"Doesn't Riley have to go to work today?" she asked, remembering when he'd mentioned that Riley worked for Blue Ridge Management. She'd even seen his name on one of the doors when they'd exited from the elevator on the fortieth floor.

"Yes, but he'll leave whenever I get back."

She crossed her arms over her chest. "And what about you? Don't you have horses to breed or train?"

"Your safety is more important to me."

"Yeah, right."

He lifted a brow. "You don't believe me? Even after I spent the entire night in my truck?"

"You were protecting your interest."

"And that's definitely you, sweetheart."

Don't even go there. Bella figured it was definitely time to end this conversation. If she engaged in chatter with him too much longer he would be convincing her that everything he was saying was true.

"You will have an answer for me in four days, right, Bella?"

"That's my plan."

"Good. I'll be back by the time you're dressed and we can do breakfast with Dillon and Pam, and then I want to show you what I do for a living."

Before she could respond he leaned in and kissed her on the lips. "See you in an hour. And wear your riding attire."

She sucked in a deep breath and watched as he walked off the porch to his truck to drive away. The man was definitely something else. She cast a quick glance to where Riley sat in his own truck sipping a cup of coffee. There was no doubt in her mind Riley had seen his brother kiss her, and she could only imagine what he was thinking.

Deciding the least she could do was invite him in, she called out to him. "You're welcome to come inside, Riley," she said, smiling broadly at him.

The smile he returned was just as expansive as he leaned his head slightly out the truck's window and said, "Thanks, but Jason warned me not to. I'm fine."

Jason warned him not to? Of course he was just joking, although he looked dead serious.

Instead of questioning him about it, she nodded, closed the door and headed back upstairs. As she entered her bedroom she couldn't ignore the excitement she felt about riding with Jason and checking out his horse training business.

JASON HAD GRABBED HIS Stetson off the rack and was about to head out the door when his cell phone rang. He pulled it off his belt and saw it was Dillon.

"Yes, Dil?"

"Pam wanted me to call and verify that you and Bella are coming for breakfast."

Jason smiled. "Yes, we'll be there. In fact, I'm about to saddle up one of the mares. I thought we'd ride over on horseback. We can enjoy the sights along the way."

"That's a good idea. Everything's okay at her place?"

"Yes, so far so good. The sheriff has increased the patrols around Bella's house and I appreciate it. Thank him the next time the two of you shoot pool together."

Dillon chuckled. "I will. And just so you know, I like Bella. She has a lot of class."

Jason smiled. That meant a lot coming from his older brother. While growing up he'd always thought Dillon was smart with a good head on his shoulders. Jason's admiration increased when Dillon had worked hard to keep the family together.

"And thanks, Dillon."

"For what?"

"For being you. For being there when all of us needed you to be. For doing what you knew Mom and Dad, as well as Uncle Thomas and Aunt Susan would have wanted you to do."

"You don't have to thank me, Jason."

"Yes, I do."

Dillon didn't say anything for a moment. "Then you're welcome. Now don't keep us waiting with Bella. We won't start breakfast until the two of you get here. At least all of us except Denver. He wakes up hungry. Pam has fed him already," Dillon said.

Jason couldn't help but smile, and not for the first time, as he thought of one day having a son of his own. Being around Denver had the tendency to put such thoughts into his head. He enjoyed his nephew immensely.

"We'll get there in good time, I promise," he said before clicking off the phone.

BELLA GLANCED DOWN AT her riding attire and smiled. She wanted to be ready when Jason returned.

Grabbing her hat off the rack she placed it on her head and opened the door to step outside on the porch. Riley had gotten out of the truck and was leaning against it. He glanced over at her and smiled.

"Ready to go riding I see," he said.

"Yes, Jason told me to be ready. We're having breakfast with Dillon and Pam."

"Yes, I had planned to have breakfast with them as well but I have a meeting at the office."

Bella nodded. "You enjoy working inside?"

Riley chuckled. "Yes, I'll leave the horses, dirt and grime to Jason. He's always liked being outdoors. When he worked at Blue Ridge I knew it was just a matter of time before wanderlust got ahold of him. He's good with horses, so are Zane and Derringer. Joining in with the Montana Westmorelands in that horse business was great for them."

Bella nodded again. "So exactly what do you do at Blue Ridge?"

"Mmm, a little bit of everything. I like to think of myself as Dillon's right-hand man. But my main job is PR. I have to make sure Blue Ridge keeps a stellar image."

Bella continued to engage in conversation with Riley while thinking he was another kind Westmoreland man. It seemed that all of them were. But she'd heard Bailey remark more than once that Riley was also a ladies' man, and she could definitely believe that. Like Jason, he was handsome to a fault.

"So, Riley, when will you settle down and get married?" she asked him, just to see what his response would be.

"Married? Me? Never. I like things just the way they are. I am definitely not the marrying kind."

Bella smiled, wondering if Jason wasn't the marrying kind, as well, although he'd given a marriage proposal to her. Did he want joint ownership of her land and Hercules that much? Evidently so.

JASON SMILED AS HE HEADED back to Bella's ranch with a horse he knew she would love riding. Fancy Free was an even tempered mare. In the distance, he could see Bella was standing on the porch waiting for him. He would discount the fact that she seemed to be having an enjoyable conversation with Riley, who seemed to be flirting with her.

He ignored the signs of jealousy seeping into his bones. Riley was his brother and if you couldn't trust your own brother who could you trust? A lightbulb suddenly went off in his head. Hell. Had Abel assumed the same thing about Cain?

He tightened his hands on his horse and increased his pace to a gallop. What was Riley saying to Bella to make her laugh so much anyway? Riley was becoming a regular ladies' man around town. It seemed he was trying to keep up with Zane in that aspect. Jason had always thought Riley's playboy ways were amusing. Until now.

Moments later he brought his horse to a stop by the edge of Bella's porch. He tilted his Stetson back on his head so it wouldn't shield his eyes. "Excuse me if I'm interrupting anything."

Riley had the nerve to grin up at him. "No problem but you're twenty minutes late. You better be glad I enjoy Bella's company."

Jason frowned at his brother. "I can tell."

His gaze then shifted to Bella. She looked beautiful standing there in a pair of riding breeches that fitted her body to perfection, a white shirt and a pair of riding boots. She didn't just look beautiful, she looked hot as sin and a side glance at Riley told him that his brother was enjoying the view as much as he was.

"Don't you need to be on your way to work, Riley?"

His brother gave him another grin. "I guess so. Call

if you need me as Bella's bodyguard again." He then got into his truck and drove off.

Jason watched him leave before turning his full attention back to Bella. "Ready to go riding, sweetheart?"

As BELLA RODE WITH JASON she tried concentrating on the sheer beauty of the rustic countryside instead of the sexiness of the man in the saddle beside her. He was riding Hercules and she could tell he was an expert horseman. And she could tell why he wanted to own the stallion. It was as if he and the horse had a personal relationship. It was evident Hercules had been glad to see him. Whereas the stallion had been like putty in Jason's hands, the horse had given the others grief in trying to handle him. Even now the two seemed in sync.

This was beautiful countryside and the first time she'd seen it. She was stunned by its beauty. The mare he'd chosen for her had come from his stable and was the one he'd rode over to her place. She liked how easily she and the horse were able to take the slopes that stretched out into valleys. The landscape looked majestic with the mountains in the distance.

First they rode over to Dillon and Pam's for breakfast. She had fallen in love with the Westmoreland Estate the first time she had seen it. The huge Victorian-style home with a wide circular driveway sat on three hundred acres of land. Jason had told her on the ride over that as the oldest cousin, Dillon had inherited the family home. It was where most of the family seemed to congregate the majority of the time.

She had met Pam's three younger sisters the other night at dinner and enjoyed their company again around the breakfast table. Everyone asked questions about the rock-throwing incident, and Dillon, who knew the sheriff personally, felt the person or persons responsible would eventually get caught.

After breakfast they were in the saddle again. Jason and Bella rode to Zane's place. She was given a front row seat and watched as Zane, Derringer and Jason exercised several of the horses. Jason had explained some of the horses needed both aerobic and anaerobic training, and that so many hours each day were spent on that task. She could tell that it took a lot of skill as well as experience for any trainer to be successful and achieve the goals they wanted for the horses they trained.

At noon Lucia arrived with box lunches for everyone and Bella couldn't help noticing how much the newlyweds were still into each other. She knew if she decided to marry Jason they would not share the type of marriage Derringer and Lucia did since their union would be more of a business arrangement than anything else. But it was so obvious to anyone around Derringer and Lucia they were madly in love with each other.

Later that day they had dinner with Ramsey and Chloe and enjoyed the time they spent with the couple immensely. Over dinner Ramsey provided tidbits about sheep ranching and how he'd made the decision to move from being a businessman to operating a sheep ranch.

The sun was going down when she and Jason mounted their horses to return to her ranch. It had been a full day of activities and she had learned a lot about both the horse training business and sheep ranching.

She glanced over at Jason. He hadn't said a whole lot since they'd left his brother's ranch and she couldn't help wondering what he was thinking. She also couldn't help wondering if he intended to sleep in his truck again tonight.

"I feel like a freeloader today," she said to break the silence between them.

He glanced over at her. "Why?"

"Your family fed me breakfast, lunch and dinner today."

He smiled. "They like you."

"And I like them."

She truly did. One of the benefits of accepting Jason's proposal would be his family. But what would happen after the year was up and she'd gotten attached to them? Considered herself part of the family?

They had cleared his land and were riding on her property when up ahead in the distance they saw what appeared to be a huge fiery red ball filled with smoke. They both realized at the same time what it was.

Fire.

And it was coming from the direction of her ranch.

CHAPTER SEVEN

BELLA STOOD IN WHAT USED to be the middle of her living room, glanced around and fought the tears stinging her eyes. More than half of her home was gone, destroyed by the fire. And according to the fire marshal it had been deliberately set. If it hadn't been for the quick thinking of her men who begun using water hoses to douse the flames, the entire ranch house would have gone up in smoke.

Her heart felt heavy. Oppressed. Broken. All she'd wanted when she had left Savannah was to start a new life here. But it seemed that was not going to happen. Someone wanted her gone. Who wanted her land that much?

She felt a touch to her arm and without looking up she knew it was Jason. Her body would recognize his touch anywhere. He had been by her side the entire time and watched as portions of her house went up in flames. And he had held her when she couldn't watch any longer and buried her face in his chest and clung to him. At that moment he had become the one thing that was unshakable in a world that was falling down all around her; intentionally being destroyed by someone who was determined to steal her happiness and joy. And he had held her and whispered over and over that everything was going to be all right. And she had tried to believe him and had managed to draw strength from him.

His family had arrived and had given their support as well and had let the authorities know they wanted answers and wanted the person or persons responsible brought to justice. Already they were talking about helping her rebuild and, like Jason had done, assured her that everything would be all right.

Sheriff Harper had questioned her, making inquiries similar to the ones Pete had yesterday when the rock had been thrown through her living room window. Did she know of anyone who wanted her out of Denver? Whoever was responsible was determined to get their message through to her loud and clear.

"Bella?"

She glanced up and met Jason's gaze. "Yes?"

"Come on, let's go. There's nothing more we can do here tonight."

She shuddered miserably and the lungs holding back her sob constricted. "Go? Go where, Jason? Look around you. I no longer have a home."

She couldn't stop the single tear that fell from her eyes. Instead of responding to what she'd said Jason brushed the tear away with the pad of his thumb before entwining his fingers in hers. He then led her away toward the barn for a moment of privacy. It was then that he turned her to face him, sweeping the curls back from her face. He fixed her with a gaze that stirred everything inside of her.

"As long as I have a home, Bella, you do, too."

He then drew in a deep breath. "Don't let whoever did this win. This is land that your grandfather gave you and you have every right to be here if that's what you want.

Don't let anyone run you off your land," Jason said in a husky whisper.

She heard his words, she felt his plea, but like she'd told him, she no longer had a home now. She didn't want to depend on others, become their charity case. "But what can I do, Jason? It takes money to rebuild and thanks to my parents, my trust fund is on hold." She paused and then with sagging shoulders added, "I don't have anything now. The ranch was insured, but it will take time to rebuild."

"You have me, Bella. My proposal still stands and now more than ever you should consider taking it. A marriage between us means that we'll both get what we want and will show the person who did this that you aren't going anywhere. It will show them they didn't win after all and sooner or later they will get caught. And even if it happens to be a member of your family, I'm going to make sure they pay for doing this."

Jason lowered his gaze to the ground for a moment and then returned it to her. "I am worse than mad right now, Bella, I'm so full of rage I could actually hurt someone for doing this to you. Whoever is behind this probably thought you were inside the house. What if you had been? What if you hadn't spent the day with me?"

Bella took a deep breath. Those were more "what ifs" she didn't want to think about or consider. The only thing she wanted to think about right now was the proposal; the one Jason had offered and still wanted her to take. And she decided at that very moment that she would.

She would take her chances on what might or might not happen within that year. She would be the best wife possible and hopefully in a year's time even if he wanted a divorce they could still be friends.

"So what about it, Bella? Will you show whoever did this today that you are a fighter and not a quitter and that you will keep what's yours? Will you marry me so we can do that together?"

She held his gaze, exhaled deeply. "Yes, I'll marry you, Jason."

She thought the smile that touched his lips was priceless and she had to inwardly remind herself he wasn't happy because he was marrying her but because marrying her meant he would co-own her land and get full possession of Hercules. And in marrying him she would get her trust fund back and send a message to whomever was behind the threats to her that they were wasting their time and she wasn't going anywhere.

He leaned down, brushed a kiss across her lips and tightened his hold on her hand. "Come on. Let's go tell the family our good news."

IF JASON'S BROTHERS and cousins were surprised by their announcement they didn't let on. Probably because they were too busy congratulating them and then making wedding plans.

She and Jason had decided the true nature of their marriage was between them. They planned to keep it that way. The Westmorelands didn't so much as bat an eye when Jason further announced they would be getting married as soon as possible. Tomorrow in fact. He assured everyone they could plan a huge reception for later.

Bella decided to contact her parents *after* the wedding tomorrow. A judge who was a friend of the West-

morelands was given a call and he immediately agreed
to perform the civil ceremony in his chambers around
three in the afternoon. Dillon and Ramsey suggested the
family celebrate the nuptials by joining them for dinner
after the ceremony at a restaurant downtown.

The honeymoon would come later. For now they
would spend the night at a hotel downtown. With so
many things to do to prepare for tomorrow, Bella was
able to put the fire behind her and she actually looked
forward to her wedding day. She was also able to put out
of her mind the reason they were marrying in the first
place. Dillon and Pam invited her to spend the night in
their home, and she accepted their invitation.

"Come walk me out to my truck," Jason whispered,
taking her hand in his.

"All right."

When they got to where his truck was parked, he
placed her against it and leaned over and kissed her
in a deep, drugging kiss. When he released her lips he
whispered, "You can come home with me tonight, you
know."

Yes, she knew but then she also knew if she did so,
they would consummate a wedding that was yet to take
place. She wanted to do things in the right order. The
way she'd always dreamed of doing them when she read
all those romance novels.

"Yes, I know but I'll be fine staying with Dillon and
Pam tonight. Tomorrow will be here before you know
it." She then paused and looked up at him, searched
his gaze. "And you think we're doing the right thing,
Jason?"

He smiled, nodding. "Yes, I'm positive. After the
ceremony we'll contact your parents and provide their

attorney with whatever documentation needed to kick your trust fund back in gear. And I'm sure word will get around soon enough for whoever has been making those threats to hear Bella Bostwick Westmoreland is here to stay."

Bella Bostwick Westmoreland. She liked the sound of it already but deep down she knew she couldn't get attached to it. She stared into his eyes and hoped he wouldn't wake up one morning and think he'd made a mistake and the proposal hadn't been worth it.

"Everything will work out for the best, Bella. You'll see." He then pulled her into his arms and kissed her again.

"I NOW PRONOUNCE YOU man and wife. Jason, you may kiss your bride."

Jason didn't waste any time pulling Bella into his arms and devouring her mouth the way he'd gotten accustomed to doing.

He had expected a small audience but every Westmoreland living in Denver was there, except Micah, his brother who was a year older and an epidemiologist with the federal government, as well as his brothers Canyon and Stern who were away attending law school. And of course he missed his cousin Gemma who was living with her husband in Australia, and his younger brother Bane who was in the navy. Jason also missed the twins, Aiden and Adrian. They were away at college.

When he finally released Bella's mouth, cheers went up and he glanced at Bella and knew at that moment just how much he loved her. He would prove the depth of his love over the rest of their lives. He knew she assumed after the first year either of them could file for divorce, but he didn't intend for that to happen. Ever. There would be no divorce.

He glanced down at the ring he'd placed on her finger. He had picked her up at eight that morning, taken her into town for breakfast and from there a whirlwind of activities had begun with a visit to the jeweler. Then to the courthouse to file the necessary papers so they could marry on time. Luckily there was no waiting period in Colorado and he was grateful for that.

"Hey, Jason and Bella. Are the two of you ready for dinner?" Dillon asked, smiling.

Jason smiled back. "Yes, we are." He took Bella's hand in his, felt the sensations touching her elicited and knew that, personally, he was ready for something else, as well.

BELLA CAST A QUICK GLANCE over at Jason as they stepped on the elevator that would take them up to their hotel room in the tower—the honeymoon suite—compliments of the entire Westmoreland family. She realized she hadn't just married the man but had also inherited his entire family. For someone who'd never had an extended family before, she could only be elated.

Dinner with everyone had been wonderful and Jason's brothers and cousins had stood to offer toasts to what everyone saw as a long marriage. There hadn't been anything in Jason's expression indicating they were way off base in that assumption or that it was wishful thinking on their parts.

All of the Westmoreland ladies had given her hugs and welcomed her to the family. The men had hugged her, as well, and she could tell they were genuinely happy for her and Jason.

And now they were on the elevator that would carry them to the floor where their room was located. They would be spending the night, sleeping under the same roof and sharing the same bed. They hadn't discussed such a thing happening, but she knew it was an unspoken understanding between them.

Jason had become quiet and she wondered if he'd already regretted making the proposal. The thought that he had sent her into a panic mode made her heart begin to break a piece at a time. Then without warning, she felt his hand touch her arm and when she glanced over at him he smiled and reached for her and pulled her closer to his side, as if refusing to let her stand anywhere by herself…without him. It was as if he was letting her know she would never ever be alone again.

She knew a part of her was probably rationalizing things the way she wished they were, the way she wanted them to be but not necessarily how they really were. But if she had to fantasize then she would do that. If she had to pretend they had a real marriage for the next year then she would do that, too. However, a part of her would never lose sight of the real reason she was here. A part of her would always be prepared for the inevitable.

"You were a beautiful bride, Bella."

"Thank you." Warmth spread through her in knowing that he'd thought so because she had tried so hard to be. She had been determined to make some part of today resemble a real wedding—even if it was a civil one in the judge's chambers. The ladies in the family had insisted that she be turned over to them after securing a license at the Denver County Court House and had promised Jason she would be on time for her wedding.

It had taken less than an hour to obtain the marriage

license and Lucia had been there to pick her up afterward. Bella had been whisked away for a day of beauty
and to visit a very exclusive bridal shop to pick up the
perfect dress for her wedding. Since time was of the essence, everything had been arranged beforehand. When
they had delivered her back to Jason five hours later,
the moment she'd joined him in the judge's chambers
his smile had let her know he thought her time away
from him had been well worth it. She would forever be
grateful to her new in-laws and a part of her knew that
Pam, Chloe, Megan, Lucia and Bailey would also be
friends she could count on for life.

"You look good yourself," she said softly.

She thought that was an understatement. She had
seen him in a suit the night at the charity ball. He had
taken her breath away then and was taking it away now.
Tall, dark and handsome, he was the epitome of every
woman's fantasy and dream. And for at least one full
year, he would be hers.

The elevator stopped on their floor and, tightening
his hand on hers, they stepped out. Her breath caught
when the elevator doors whooshed closed behind them
and they began walking toward room 4501. She knew
once they reached those doors and she stepped inside
there would be no turning back.

They silently strolled side by side holding hands.
Everything about the Four Seasons Hotel spoke of its
elegance and the decorative colors all around were vibrant and vivid.

Jason released her hand when they reached their room
to pull the passkey from the pocket of his suit jacket.
Once he opened the door he extended his hand to her
and she took it, felt the sensations flowing between

them. She gasped when she was suddenly swept off her feet and into his arms and carried over the threshold into the honeymoon suite.

JASON KICKED THE DOOR closed with his foot before placing Bella on her feet. And then he just stood there and looked at her, allowing his gaze to roam all over her. What he'd told her earlier was true. She was a beautiful bride.

And she was his.

Absolutely and positively his.

Her tea-length dress was ivory in color and made of silk chiffon and fitted at her small waist with a rose in the center. It was a perfect match for the ivory satin rose-heeled shoes on her feet. White roses were her favorite flower and she'd used them as the theme in their wedding. Even her wedding bouquet had consisted of white roses.

His chest expanded with so much love for her, love she didn't know about yet. He had a year to win her over and intended to spend the next twelve months doing just that. But now, he needed for her to know just how much she was desired.

He lowered his head and kissed her, letting his tongue tangle with hers, reacquainting himself with the taste of her, a taste he had not forgotten and had so desperately craved since the last time. He kissed her deeply, not allowing any part of her mouth to go untouched. And she returned the kiss with a hunger that matched his own and he was mesmerized by how she was making him feel.

He tightened his hold on her, molding his body to hers, and was certain she could feel the hot ridge of his erection pressing against her. It was throbbing something awful with a need for her that was monumental. He had wanted her for a long time…ever since he'd seen her that night at the ball, and his desire for her hadn't diminished any since. If anything, it had only increased to a level that even now he could feel his gut tighten in desire. Taking her hands he deliberately began slowly lifting her dress up toward her waist.

"Wrap your legs around me, Bella," he whispered and assisted by lifting her hips when she wrapped her legs around him to walk her toward the bedroom. It was a huge suite and he was determined that later, after they took care of business in the bedroom, they would check out all the amenities the suite had to offer; especially the large Jacuzzi bathtub. Already he saw the beauty of downtown Denver from their hotel room window. But downtown Denver was the last thing on his mind right now. Making love to his wife was.

His wife.

He began kissing her again, deeper and longer, loving the way her tongue mated with his over and over again. He placed her on the bed while reaching behind her to unfasten her dress and slide it from her body. It was then that he took a step back and thought he was dreaming. No fantasy could top what he was seeing now.

She was wearing a white lace bra and matching panties. On any other woman such a color would come across as ultrainnocence, but on Bella it became the epitome of sexual desire.

He needed to completely undress her and did so while thinking of everything he wanted to do to her. When she was on her knees in the middle of the bed naked, he could tell from her expression that this was the first time a man had seen her body and the thought sent shivers through him as his gaze roamed over her in male appreciation. A shudder of primal pride flowed through him and he could only stand there and take her all in.

An erection that was already hard got even harder when he looked at her chest, an area he had yet to taste. Her twin globes were firm. His tongue tingled at the thought of being wrapped around those nipples.

No longer able to resist temptation, he moved toward the bed and placed a knee on it and immediately leaned in to capture a nipple in his mouth. His tongue latched on the hard nub and began playing all kinds of games with it. Games she seemed to enjoy if the way she was pushing her breasts deeper into his mouth was anything to go by.

He heard her moan as he continued to torture her nipples, with quick nips followed by sucking motions and when he reached down to let his hands test her to see how ready she was, he found she was definitely ready for him. Pulling back he eased from the bed to remove his clothes as she watched.

"I'm not on the Pill, Jason."

He glanced over at her. "You're not?"

"No."

And evidently thinking she needed to explain further she said, "I haven't been sexually active with anyone."

"Since?"

"Never."

A part of him wasn't surprised. In fact, he had suspected as much. He'd known no other man had performed oral sex on her but hadn't been sure of the depth of any other sexual experience. "Any reason you **hadn't?**"

She met his gaze and held it. "I've been waiting for you."

He drew in a sharp breath and wondered if she knew what she'd just insinuated and figured she hadn't. Maybe she hadn't insinuated anything and it was just wishful thinking on his part. He loved her and would give just about anything for her to love him in return. And until she said the words, he wouldn't assume anything.

"Then your wait is over, sweetheart," he said, sliding on a condom over the thickness of his erection while she looked on. And from the fascinated expression on her face he could tell what she was seeing was another first for her.

When he completed that task he moved to the bed and toward her. "You are so beautifully built, Jason," she said softly, and as if she needed to test her ability to arouse him, she leaned up and flicked out her tongue, licking one of the hardened nubs on his breast like he'd done earlier to her.

He drew in a sharp intake of breath. "You're a quick learner," he said huskily.

"Is that good or bad?"

He smiled at her. "For us it will always be good."

Since this would be her first time he wanted her more than ready and knew of one way to do it. He eased her down on the bed and decided to lick her into an orgasm. Starting at her mouth, he slowly moved downward to her chin, trekked down her neck to her breasts. By the time he'd made it past her midriff to her flat tummy she was writhing under his mouth but he didn't mind. That was a telltale sign of how she was feeling.

"Open your legs, baby," he whispered. The moment she did so he dipped his head to ease his tongue between

the folds of her femininity. He recalled doing this to her
the last time and knew just what spots would make her
moan deep in her throat. Tonight he wanted to do better
than that. He wanted to make her scream.

Over and over again he licked her to the edge of an
orgasm then withdrew his tongue and began torturing
her all over again. She sobbed his name, moaned and
groaned. And then, when she was on the verge of an
explosion he shifted upward and placed his body over
hers.

When he guided his erection in place, he held her
gaze and lowered his body to join with hers, uniting
them as one. She was tight and he kept a level of control as he eased inside her, feeling how firm a hold her
clenched muscles had on him. He didn't want to hurt
her and moved inch by slow inch inside her. When he
had finally reached the hilt, he closed his eyes but didn't
move. He needed to be still for a moment and grasp the
significance of what was taking place. He was making
love to his wife and she was a wife he loved more than
life.

He slowly opened his eyes and met hers and saw she
had been watching…waiting and needing him to finish
what he'd started. So he did. He began moving slowly,
with an extremely low amount of pressure as he began
moving in and out of her. When she arched her back,
he increased the pressure and the rhythm.

The sounds she began making sent him spiraling
and let him know she was loving it. The more she
moaned, the more she got. Several times he'd gone so
deep inside her he knew he had touched her womb and
the thought that he had done so made him crave her that
much more.

She released a number of shuddering breaths as he continued to thrust, claiming her as his while she claimed him as hers. And then she threw her head back and screamed out his name.

That's when he came, filling her while groaning thickly as an orgasm overtook them both. The spasms that rammed through his body were so powerful he had to force himself to breathe. He bucked against her several times as he continued to ride her through the force of his release.

He inhaled the scent of their lovemaking before leaning down to capture her mouth, and knew at that moment the night for them was just beginning.

SOMETIME DURING THE night Jason woke up from the feel of Bella's mouth on him. Immediately his erection began to swell.

"Oh." She pulled her mouth away and looked up at him with a blush on her face. "I thought you were asleep."

His lips curved into a smile. "I was, but there are some things a man can't sleep through. What are you doing down there?"

She raised her head to meet his gaze. "Tasting you the way you tasted me," she said softly.

"You didn't have to wait until I was asleep, you know," he said, feeling himself get even harder. Although he was no longer inside her mouth, it was still close. Right there. And the heat of her breath was way too close.

"I know, but you were asleep and I thought I would practice first. I didn't want to embarrass myself while you were awake and get it wrong," she said, blushing even more.

He chuckled, thinking her blush was priceless. "Baby, this is one of those things a woman can never get wrong."

"Do you want me to stop?"

"What do you think?"

She smiled up at him shyly. Wickedly. Wantonly. "I think you don't. Just remember this is a practice session."

She then leaned closer and slid him back into her mouth. He groaned deep in his throat when she began making love to him this way. Earlier that night he had licked her into an orgasm and now she was licking him to insanity. He made a low sound in the back of his throat when she began pulling everything out of him with her mouth. If this was a practice session she would kill him when it came to the real thing.

"Bella!"

He quickly reached down and pulled her up to him and flipped her onto her back. He moved on top of her and pushed inside of her, realizing too late when he felt himself explode that he wasn't wearing a condom. The thought that he could be making her pregnant jutted an even bigger release from his body into hers.

His entire body quivered from the magnitude of the powerful thrusts that kept coming, thrusts he wasn't able to stop. The more she gave, the more he wanted and when her hips arched off the bed, he drove in deeper and came again.

"Jason!"

She was following him to sweet oblivion and his heart began hammering at the realization that this was lovemaking as naked as it could get, and he clung to it, clung to her. A low, shivering moan escaped his lips and when her thighs began to tremor, he felt the vibration to the core.

Moments later he collapsed on top of her, moaned her name as his manhood buried inside of her continued to throb, cling to her flesh as her inner muscles wouldn't release their hold.

What they'd just shared as well as all the other times they'd made love tonight was so unbearably pleasurable he couldn't think straight. The thought of what she'd been doing when he had awakened sent sensuous chills down his body.

He opened his mouth to speak but immediately closed it when he saw she had drifted off to sleep. She made such an erotic picture lying there with her eyes closed, soft dark curls framing her face and the sexiest lips he'd ever had the pleasure of kissing slightly parted.

He continued to look at her, thinking he would let her get some rest now. Later he intended to wake her up the same way she'd woken him.

CHAPTER EIGHT

THE FOLLOWING MORNING after they'd enjoyed breakfast in bed, Bella figured now was just as good a time as any to let her parents know she was a married woman.

She picked up her cell phone and then glanced over at Jason and smiled. That smile gave her the inner strength for the confrontation she knew was coming. The thought of her outwitting them by marrying—and someone from Denver—would definitely throw her parents into a tizzy. She could just imagine what they would try to do. But just as Jason had said, they could try but wouldn't succeed. She and Jason were as married as married could get and there was nothing her parents could do about it.

Taking a deep breath she punched in their number and when the housekeeper answered she was put on hold, waiting for her father to pick up the line.

"Elizabeth. I hope you're calling to say you've come to your senses and have purchased a one-way plane ticket back home."

She frowned. He didn't even take the time to ask how she was doing. Although she figured her parents had nothing to do with those two incidents this week, she decided to ask anyway. "Tell me something, Dad. Did you and Mom think using scare tactics to get me to return to Savannah would work?"

"What are you talking about?"

"Three days ago someone threw a rock through my living room window with a threatening note for me to leave town, and two days ago someone torched my house. Luckily I wasn't there at the time."

"Someone set Dad's house on fire?"

She'd heard the shock in his voice and she heard something else, too. Empathy. This was the first time she'd heard him refer to Herman as "Dad."

"Yes."

"I didn't have anything to do with that, Elizabeth. Your mother and I would never put you in danger like that. What kind of parents do you think we are?"

"Controlling. But I didn't call to exchange words, Dad. I'm just calling for you and Mother to share my good news. I got married yesterday."

"What!"

"That's right. I got married to a wonderful man by the name of Jason Westmoreland."

"Westmoreland?"

"Yes."

"I went to schools with some Westmorelands. Their land was connected to ours."

"Probably his parents. They're deceased now."

"Sorry to hear that, but I hope you know why he married you. He wants that land. But don't worry about it, dear. It can easily be remedied once you file for an annulment."

She shook her head. Her parents just didn't get it. "Jason didn't force me to marry him, Dad. I married him of my own free will."

"Listen, Elizabeth, you haven't been living out there

even a full month. You don't know this guy. I will not allow you to marry him."

"Dad, I am already married to him and I plan to send your attorney a copy of our marriage license so the hold on my trust fund will be lifted."

"You think you're smart, Elizabeth. I know what you're doing and I won't allow it. You don't love him and he can't love you."

"Sounds pretty much like the same setup you and Mom have got going. The same kind of marriage you wanted me to enter with Hugh. So what's the problem? I don't see where there is one and I refuse to discuss the matter with you any longer. Goodbye, Dad. Give Mom my best." She then clicked off the phone.

"I take it the news of our marriage didn't go over well with your father."

She glanced over at Jason who was lying beside her and smiled faintly. "Did you really expect that it would?"

"No and it really doesn't matter. They'll just have to get over it."

She snuggled closer to him. That was one of the things she liked about Jason. He was his own man. "What time do we have to check out of here?"

"By noon. And then we'll be on our way to Jason's Place."

She had to restrain the happiness she felt upon knowing they would be going to his home where she would live for at least the next twelve months. "Are there any do's and don'ts that I need to know about?"

He lifted a brow. "Do's and don'ts?"

"Yes. My time at your home is limited. I don't want to jeopardize my welcome." She could have sworn she'd seen something flash in his eyes but couldn't be certain.

"You'd never jeopardize your welcome and no, there are no do's and don'ts that will apply to you, unless…"

Now it was her turn to raise a brow. "Unless what?"

"You take a notion to paint my bedroom pink or something."

She couldn't help bursting out in laughter. She calmed down enough to ask, "What about yellow? Will that do?"

"Not one of my favorite colors but I guess it will work."

She smiled as she snuggled even closer to him. She was looking forward to living under the same roof with Jason.

"Bella?"

She glanced up. "Yes?"

"The last time we made love, I didn't use a condom."

She'd been aware of it but hadn't expected him to talk about it. "Yes, I know."

"It wasn't intentional."

"I know that, too," she said softly. There was no reason he would want to get her pregnant. That would only throw a monkey wrench in their agreement.

They didn't say anything for a long moment and then he asked, "Do you like children?"

She wondered why he was asking such a thing. Surely he had seen her interactions with Susan and Denver enough to know that she did. "Yes, I like children."

"Do you think you'd want any of your own one day?"

Was he asking because he was worried that she would use that as a trap to stay with him beyond the one year? But he'd asked and she needed to be honest. "Yes, I'd love children, although I haven't had the best of childhoods. Don't get me wrong, my parents weren't monsters or anything like that but they just weren't affectionate… at least not like your family."

She paused for a moment. "I love my parents, Jason, although I doubt my relationship with them will ever be what I've always wished for. They aren't those kind of people. Displaying affection isn't one of their strong points. If I become a mother I want to do just the opposite. There will never be a day my child will not know he or she is loved." She hadn't meant to say all of that and now she couldn't help wondering if doing so would ruin things between them.

"I think you would make a wonderful mother."

His words touched her. "Thank you for saying that."

"You're welcome, and I meant it."

She drew in a deep breath, wondering how he could be certain of such a thing. She continued to stare at him for a long moment. He would be a gift to any woman and he had sacrificed himself to marry her—just because he'd wanted her land and Hercules. When she thought about it she found it pitiful that it had taken that to make him want to join his life to hers.

He lifted her hand and looked at the ring he'd placed there. She looked at it, too. It was beautiful. More than she'd expected and everyone had oohed and aahed over it.

"You're wearing my ring," he said softly.

The sound of his deep, husky voice made her tummy

tingle and a heated sensation spread all through her. "Yes, I'm wearing your ring. It's beautiful. Thank you."

Then she lifted his hand. Saw the gold band brilliantly shining in the sunlight. "And you're wearing mine."

And then she found herself being kissed by him and she knew that no matter how their marriage might end up, right now it was off to a great beginning.

FOR THE SECOND TIME IN two days Jason carried the woman he loved over the threshold. This time he walked into his house. "Welcome to Jason's Place, sweetheart," he said, placing her on her feet.

Bella glanced around. This was the first time she'd been inside Jason's home. She'd seen it a few times from a distance and thought the two-story dwelling flanked by a number of flowering trees was simply beautiful. On the drive from town he'd given her a little history of his home. It had taken an entire year to build and he had built it himself, with help from all the other Westmorelands. And with all the pride she'd heard when he spoke of it, she knew he loved his home. She could see why. The design was magnificent. The decorating—which had been done by his cousin Gemma—was breathtaking and perfect for the single man he'd been.

Jason's eyes never left Bella's as he studied her reaction to being in his home. As far as he was concerned, she would be a permanent fixture. His heart would beat when hers did. His breath was released the same time hers was. He had shared something with her he had never done with any woman—the essence of himself. For the first time in his life he had made love to a woman without wearing a condom. It had felt wonderful being skin to skin, flesh to flesh with her—but only with her. The wife he adored and intended to keep forever.

He knew he had a job to do where she was concerned and it would be one that would give him the greatest of pleasure and satisfaction. Her pain was his pain, her happiness was his. Their lives were now entwined and all because of the proposal he'd offered and she'd taken.

Without thought he turned her in his arms and lowered his head to kiss her, needing the feel of his mouth on hers, her body pressed against his. The kiss was long, deep and the most satisfying experience he could imagine. But then, he'd had nothing but satisfying experiences with her. And he planned on having plenty more.

"AREN'T YOU GOING TO work today?" Bella asked Jason the following day over breakfast. She was learning her way around his spacious kitchen and loved doing it. They had stayed inside yesterday after he'd brought her here. He had kept her mostly in the bedroom, saying their honeymoon was still ongoing. And she had been not one to argue considering the glow she figured had to be on her face. Jason was the most ardent and generous of lovers.

Her mother had called last night trying to convince her she'd made a mistake and that she and her father would be flying into Denver in a few days to talk some sense into her. Bella had told her mother she didn't think coming to Denver was a good idea, but of course Melissa Bostwick wouldn't listen.

When Bella had told Jason about the latest developments—namely her parents' planned trip to Denver—

he'd merely shrugged and told her not to worry about it. That was easy for him to say. He'd never met her parents.

"No, I'm not going to work today. I'm still on my honeymoon," Jason said, breaking into her thoughts. "You tell me what you want to do today and we'll do it."

She turned away from the stove where she'd prepared something simple like French toast. "You want to spend more time with me?"

He chuckled. "Of course I do. You sound surprised."

She was. She figured as much time as they'd spent in the bedroom he would have tired of her by now. She was about to open her mouth when his house phone rang. He smiled over at her. "Excuse me for a minute while I get that."

Bella figured the caller was one of his relatives. She turned back to the stove to turn it off. She couldn't help but smile at the thought that he wanted to spend more time with her.

A few moments later Jason hung up the phone. "That was Sheriff Harper."

She turned back around to him. "Has he found out anything?"

"Yes, they've made some arrests."

A lump formed in her throat. She crossed the floor to sit down at the table, thinking she didn't want to be standing for this. "Who did it?"

He came to sit across from her. "Your uncle Kenneth's twin grandsons."

Bella's hand flew to her chest. "But they're only four-teen years old."

"Yes, but the footprints outside your window and the

fingerprints on the rock matched theirs. Not to mention that the kerosene can they used to start the fire at your ranch belonged to their parents."

Bella didn't say anything. She just continued to stare at him.

"Evidently they heard their grandfather's grumblings about you and figured they were doing him a favor by scaring you away," Jason said.

"What will happen to them?" she asked quietly.

"Right now they're in police custody. A judge will decide tomorrow if they will be released into the custody of their parents until a court date is set. If they are found guilty, and chances are they will be since the evidence against them is so strong, they will serve time in a detention center for youth for about one or two years, maybe longer depending on any prior arrests."

Jason's face hardened. "Personally, it wouldn't bother me in the least if they locked them up and threw away the key. I'm sure Kenneth is fit to be tied, though. He thinks the world of those two."

Bella shook her head sadly. "I feel so bad about this."

A deep scowl covered Jason's face. "Why do you feel bad? You're the victim and they broke the law."

She could tell by the sound of his voice that he was still upset. "But they're just kids. I need to call Uncle Kenneth."

"Why? As far as I'm concerned this is all his fault for spouting off at the mouth around them about you."

A part of Bella knew what Jason said was true and could even accept he had a right to be angry, but still, the thought that she was responsible for the disruption of so many lives was getting to her. Had she made a mistake in moving to Denver after all?

"Don't even think it, Bella."

She glanced across the table at Jason. "What?"

"I know what's going through your mind, sweetheart. I can see it all over your face and you want to blame yourself for what happened but it's not your fault."

"Isn't it?"

"No. You can't hold yourself responsible for the actions of others. What if you had been standing near the window the day that rock came flying through, or worse yet, what if you'd been home the day they set fire to the house? If I sound mad it's because I still am. And I'm going to stay mad until justice is served."

He paused a moment and then said, "I don't want to talk about Kenneth or his grandsons any longer. Come on, let's get dressed and go riding."

WHEN THEY RETURNED FROM riding and Bella checked her cell phone, she had received a call from her parents saying that they had changed their minds and would not be coming to Denver after all. She couldn't help wondering why, but she figured the best thing to do was count her blessings and be happy about their change in plans.

Jason was outside putting the horses away and she decided to take a shower and change into something relaxing. So far, other than the sheriff, no one else had called. She figured Jason's family was treating them as honeymooners and giving them their privacy.

When her cell phone rang, she didn't recognize the caller but figured it might be one of her parents calling from another number. "Yes?"

"This is all your fault, Bella."

She froze upon hearing her uncle's voice. He was angry. "My grandsons might be going to some youth detention center for a couple of years because of you."

Bella drew in a deep breath and remembered the conversation she and Jason had had earlier that day. "You should not have talked badly about me in front of them."

"Are you saying it's my fault?"

"Yes, Uncle Kenneth, that's exactly what I'm saying. You have no one else to blame but yourself."

"Why you… How dare you speak to me that way. You think you're something now that you're married to a Westmoreland. Well, you'll see what a mistake you made. All Jason Westmoreland wanted was your land and that horse. He doesn't care anything about you. I told you I knew someone who wanted to buy your land."

"And I've always told you my land isn't for sale."

"If you don't think Westmoreland plans to weasel it from you then you're crazy. Just mark my word. You mean nothing to him. All he wants is that land. He is nothing but a controller and a manipulator."

Her uncle then hung up the phone on her.

Bella tried not to let her uncle's words get to her. No one knew the details of their marriage so her uncle had no idea that she was well aware that Jason wanted her land and horse. For what other reason would he have presented her with that proposal? She wasn't the crazy person her uncle evidently assumed she was. She was operating with more than a full deck and was also well aware Jason didn't love her.

She glanced up when Jason walked through the back

door. He smiled when he saw her. "I thought you were going to take a shower."

"I was, but I got a phone call."

"Oh, from who?"

She knew now was not the time to tell him about her uncle's call—especially after all he'd said earlier. So she decided to take that time to tell him about her parents' decision.

"Dad and Mom called. They aren't coming after all."

"What changed their minds?" he asked, taking a seat on the sofa.

"Not sure. They didn't say."

He caught her wrist and pulled her down on the sofa beside him. "Well, I have a lot to say, none of it nice. But the main thing is they've decided not to come and I think it's a good move on their part because I don't want anyone to upset you."

"No one will," she said softly. "I'm fine."

"And I want to make sure you stay that way," he said and pulled her closer into his arms.

She was quiet as her head lay rested against his chest and could actually hear his heart pounding. She wondered if he could hear the pounding of her heart. She still found it strange how attracted they were to each other. Getting married hadn't lessened that any.

She lifted her head to look up at him and saw the intense look that was there in his eyes. It was a look that was so intimate it sent a rush of heat sprinting all through her.

And when he began easing his mouth toward hers, all thoughts left her mind except for one, and that was how much he could make her feel loved even when he was pretending. The moment their lips touched she refused to believe her uncle Kenneth's claim that he was controlling.

Instead she concentrated on how he was making her feel with the way his mouth was mating with hers. And she knew this kiss was just the beginning.

CHAPTER NINE

DURING THE NEXT FEW WEEKS Bella settled into what she considered a comfortable routine. She'd never thought being married would be such a wonderful experience and could only thank Jason for making the transition easy for her.

They shared a bed and made passionate love each night. Then in the morning they would get up early and while he sat at the table drinking coffee she would enjoy a cup of tea while he told her about what horses he would be training that day.

While he was away she usually kept busy by reading her grandfather's journals, which had been upstairs in her bedroom and so were spared by the fire. Because she'd been heavily involved with a lot of charity work while living in Savannah, she'd already volunteered a lot of her time at the children's hospital and the Westmoreland Foundation.

Hercules was now in Jason's stalls and Jason was working with the insurance company on the repairs of her ranch. He had arranged for all the men who'd worked with her before the fire to be hired on with his horse training business.

Although she appreciated him stepping in and taking charge of her affairs the way he'd done, she hadn't been able to put her uncle Kenneth's warning out of her mind.

She knew it was ludicrous to worry about Jason's motivation because he had been honest with her from the beginning and she knew why he'd made the proposal for their marriage. She was well aware that he didn't love her and that he was only married to her for the land and Hercules. But now that he had both was it just a matter of time for him before he tried to get rid of her?

She would be the first to admit he never acted as if he was getting tired of her and still treated her as if he enjoyed having her around. In the afternoons when he returned home from work, the first thing he did after placing his Stetson on the hat rack was to seek her out. Usually he didn't have far to look because she would be right there, close by. Anticipating his return home always put her near the door when he entered the house.

Bella couldn't help noticing that over the past couple of days she had begun getting a little antsy where Jason was concerned because she was uncertain as to her future with him. And to make matters even worse, she was late, which was a good sign she might be pregnant. She hadn't told him of her suspicions because she wasn't sure how he would take the news.

If she were pregnant, the baby would be born within the first year of their marriage. Would he still want a divorce even if she was the mother of his child, or would he want to keep her around for that same reason; because he felt obligated to do so? But an even more important question was, did he even want to become a father? He had questioned her feelings on motherhood but she'd never questioned his. She could tell from his interactions with Susan and Denver that he liked kids, but that didn't necessarily mean he wanted any of his own.

Bella knew she should tell him about the possibility she could be pregnant and discuss her concerns with him now, but each time she was presented with the opportunity to do so, she would get cold feet.

She walked into an empty room he'd converted into an office and sat down at the desk to glance out the window. She would finally admit that another reason she was antsy was that she knew without a shadow of doubt that she had fallen in love with Jason and could certainly understand how such a thing had happened. She could understand it, but would he? He'd never asked for her love, just her land and horse.

She heard the sound of a vehicle door closing and stood from the desk, went to the window and looked down. It was Jason. He glanced up and saw her and a smile touched the corners of his mouth. Instantly she felt the buds of her nipples harden against her blouse. A flush of desire rushed through her and she knew at that moment her panties had gotten wet. The man could turn her on with a single look. He was home earlier than usual. Three hours earlier.

Now that he was here a lot of ideas flowed in her mind on how they could use those extra hours. What she wanted to do first was to take him into her mouth, something she discovered she enjoyed doing. And then he could return the favor by putting that tongue of his to work between her legs. She shuddered at the thought and figured her hormones were on the attack; otherwise, she wouldn't be thinking such scandalous things. They were definitely not things a Miss Prim and Proper lady would think.

He broke eye contact with her to walk up the steps to come into the house and she rushed out of the office to stand at the top of the stairs. She glanced down the moment he opened the door. Jason's dark gaze latched on her and immediately her breath was snatched from her lungs. As she watched, he locked the door behind him and slowly began removing the clothes from his body, first tossing his hat on the rack and then unbuttoning his shirt.

She felt hot as she watched him and he didn't stop. He had completely removed his shirt and she couldn't help admiring the broad shoulders and sinewy muscular thighs in jeans. The masculine sight had blood rushing fast and furious through her veins.

"I'm coming up," he said in a deep, husky voice.

She slowly began backing up when he started moving up the stairs with a look in his eyes that was as predatory as anything she'd ever seen. And there was a deep, intense hunger in his gaze that had her heart hammering like crazy in her chest.

When he cleared the top stair and stepped onto the landing, she breathed in deeply, taking in his scent, while thinking that no man had a right to smell so good, look so utterly male and be so damn hot in a way that would overwhelm any woman's senses.

At least no man but Jason Westmoreland.

"Take off your clothes, Bella," he said in a deep, throaty voice.

She then asked what some would probably think was a dumb question. "Why?"

He moved slowly toward her and it was as if her feet were glued to the spot and she couldn't move. And when he came to a stop in front of her, she tilted back her head to look up at him, saw the hunger in his dark brown gaze. The intensity of that look sent a shudder through her.

He reached out and cupped her face in the palms of his hands and lowered his head slightly to whisper, "I came home early because I need to make love to you. And I need to do it now."

And then he captured her mouth with his, kissing her with the same intensity and hunger she'd seen in his eyes. She returned his kiss, not understanding why he needed to make love to her and why now. But she knew she would give him whatever he wanted and whatever way he wanted it.

He was ravishing her mouth, making her moan deep in her throat. His kiss seemed to be making a statement and staking a claim all at the same time. She couldn't do anything but take whatever he was giving, and she did so gladly and without shame. He had no idea she loved him. How much sharing these past few weeks had meant to her.

And then he jerked his mouth away and quickly removed his boots. Afterward, he carried her into the office and stood her by the desk as he began taking off her clothes with a frenzy that had her head spinning. One part of her wanted to tell him to slow down and to assure him she wasn't going anywhere. But another part was just as eager and excited as he was to get naked, and kept insisting that he hurry up.

Within minutes, more like seconds, spooned between his body and the desk, she was totally naked. The cool air from the air conditioner that swept across her heated skin made her want to cover herself with her hands, but he wouldn't let her. He gently grabbed her wrists in his and held them up over her head, which made her breasts tilt up in perfect alignment to his lips when he leaned down.

On a breathless sigh he eased a nipple into his mouth, sucking it in between his lips and then licking the throbbing tip. She arched her back, felt him gently ease her onto the desk and realized he was practically on the desk with her. The metal surface felt cool to her back, but the warmth of his body felt hot to her front.

He lowered his hand to her sex and the stroke of his fingers on the folds of her labia made her groan out sounds she'd never made before. She'd thought from the first that he had skillful fingers and they were thrumming through her, stirring all kinds of sensations within her. Their lovemaking would often range from gentle to hard and she knew today would be one of those hard times. For whatever reason, he was driven to take her now, without any gentleness of any kind. He was stroking a need within her that wanted it just as fast and hard as he could deliver.

He took a step back and quickly removed his jeans and boxers. When she saw him—in his engorged splendor—a sound of dire need erupted from deep within her throat. He was bringing her to this, this intense state of want and need that was fueled by passion and desire.

"I want to know your taste, baby."

It was on the tip of her tongue to say that as many times as he'd made a meal out of her that he should know it pretty well by now. Instead when he crouched down in front of her body, which was all but spread out on the desk, and proceeded to wrap her legs over his shoulders, she automatically arched her back.

And when she felt his hot mouth close in on her sex, slide his tongue through her womanly folds, she lifted her hips off the table with the intimate contact. And when he began suckling hard, using his tongue to both torture and pleasure, she let out an intense moan as an orgasm tore through her body; sensations started at the soles of her feet and traveled like wildfire all the way to the crown of her head. And then she screamed at the top of her lungs.

Shudders continued to rip through her, made her muscles both ache and rejuvenate. And she couldn't help but lie there while Jason continued to get the taste he wanted.

When her shudders finally subsided, he gave her body one complete and thorough lick before lifting his head and looking up at her with a satisfied smile on his face, and the way he began licking his lips made her feel hot all over again.

He reached out and spread her legs wide and began stroking her again and she began moaning at the contact. "My fingers are all wet, which means you're ready," he said. "Now for me to get ready."

And she knew without looking that he was tearing into a condom packet and soon would be sliding the latex over his erection. After that first time in the hotel he'd never made love to her unprotected again, which gave her even more reason to think he wasn't ready for children. At least not with her, anyway.

From the feel of his erection pressing against her thigh she would definitely agree that at least he was ready for this, probably more ready than any man had a right to be, but she had no complaints.

She came to full attention when she felt his swollen, engorged member easing between her legs, and when he **centered it to begin sliding between the folds of her labia** and then suddenly thrust forward without any preamble, she began shuddering all over again.

"Look at me, baby. I want to be looking in your eyes when you come. I need to see it happen, Bella."

She looked up and met his gaze. He was buried deep inside of her and then holding tight to her gaze, he began moving, holding tight to the hips whose legs were wrapped firmly around him. They began moving together seemingly in perfect rhythm, faultless harmony and seamless precision. With each deep and thorough stroke, she felt all of him…every glorious inch.

"You tasted good and now you feel good," he said in a guttural voice while holding steadfast to her gaze. "Do you have any idea how wonderful you are making me feel?"

She had an idea. If it was anything close to how he was making her feel then the feelings were definitely mutual. And to show him just how mutual, her inner muscles began clamping down on him, milking him. She could tell from the look in his eyes the exact moment he realized what she was doing and the effect it was having on him. The more she milked him the bigger he seemed to get inside of her, as if he intended for her to have it all.

Today she felt greedy and was glad he intended to supply her needs. She dug her nails into his shoulders, at the moment not caring if she was branding him for life. And then he picked up the tempo and pleasure, the likes of nothing she'd experienced before dimming her vision. But through it all, she kept her gaze locked on his and saw how every sound, every move she made, got to him and triggered him to keep it coming.

And then when she felt her body break into fragments,

she screamed out his name and he began pumping into
her as if his very life depended on it. The orgasm that
ripped through her snatched the breath from her lungs
as his intense, relentless strokes almost drove her over
the edge. And when she heard the hoarse cry from his
own lips, saw the flash of something dark and turbulent
in the depths of his eyes, she lost it and screamed again
at the top of her lungs as another orgasm shook the core
of everything inside her body.

And he followed her, pushed over the edge, while he
continued to thrust even deeper. He buried his fingers
into her hair and leaned down and captured her mouth
to kiss the trembles right off her lips. At that moment
she wished she could say all the words that had formed
in her heart, words of love she wanted him to know. But
she couldn't. This was all there was between them. She
had accepted that long ago. And for the moment she was
satisfied and content.

And when the day came that he wanted her gone,
memories like these would sustain her, get her through
each day without him.

And she prayed to God the memories would be
enough.

"SO WHEN CAN WE PLAN your wedding reception?"
Megan asked when the Westmorelands had assembled
around the dinner table at Dillon's place a few weeks
later.

When Bella didn't say anything but looked over at
Jason, he shrugged and said, "Throw some dates out to
see if they will work for us."

Megan began rambling off dates, saying the first
weekend in August would be perfect since all the West-

morelands away at college would be home and Micah, who was presently in Beijing, had sent word he would be back in the States during that time, as well. Gemma, who was expecting, had gotten the doctor's okay to travel from Australia then.

"And," Megan continued, "I spoke with Casey yesterday and she's checked with the other Westmorelands and that will give them plenty of time to make plans to be here, as well. I'm so excited."

Jason glanced over at Bella again thinking he was glad someone was. There was something going on with his wife that he just couldn't put a finger on and whatever it was had put him at a disadvantage. He knew she was upset with the outcome of the Bostwick twins. With all the evidence mounted against the twins, their attorney had convinced their parents to enter a guilty plea in hopes they would get a lesser sentence.

However, given prior mischievous pranks that had gotten the pair into trouble with the law before, the judge was not all that lenient and gave them two years. Bella had insisted on going to the sentencing hearing and he'd warned her against it but she'd been adamant. Things hadn't gone well when Kenneth, who still refused to accept blame for his part in any of it, made a scene, accusing Bella as the one responsible for what had happened to his grandsons. Since that day Jason had noted a change in her and she'd begun withdrawing from him. He'd tried getting her to talk, but she refused to do so.

"So what do the two of you think?" Megan asked, drawing his attention again.

He glanced at Bella. "What do you think, sweetheart?"

She placed a smile on her lips that he knew was

forced. "That time is fine with me, but I doubt Mom and Dad will come either way."

"Then they will miss a good party," Jason replied. He then turned to Megan. "The first weekend in August is fine."

Later, on the ride back to their place, Jason finally found out what was troubling Bella. "I rode over to my ranch today, Jason. Why didn't you tell me work hadn't begun on the house yet?"

"There was no reason to tell you. You knew I was taking care of things, didn't you?"

"Yes. But I assumed work had gotten started already."

"I saw no reason to begin work on the place yet, given we're having a lot of rainy days around here now. It's not a good time to start any type of construction. Besides, it's not like you're going to move into the house or anything."

"You don't know that."

He had pulled into the yard and brought the truck to a stop and turned the ignition off. He glanced over at her. "I don't? I thought I did."

He tilted his hat back from his eyes and stared over at her. "Why would you need to move back into the house?"

Instead of holding his gaze she glanced out the window and looked ahead at his house, which he now considered as their house. "Our marriage is only supposed to last a year and I'm going to need somewhere to live when it ends."

Her words were like a kick in the gut. She was already planning for the time when she would be leaving him? Why? He thought things were going great between them. "What's going on, Bella?"

"Nothing is going on. I just need to be realistic and remember that although we enjoy being bed partners, the reason we married stemmed from your proposal, which I accepted knowing full well the terms. And they are terms we must not forget."

Jason simply looked at her as he swore under his breath. She thought the only thing between them was the fact they were bed partners? "Thanks for reminding me, Bella." He then got out of the truck.

THAT WAS THE FIRST NIGHT they slept in the same bed but didn't make love and Bella lay there hurting inside and wasn't sure what she could do about it. She was trying to protect her heart, especially after the results of the pregnancy test she'd taken a few days ago.

Jason was an honorable man. Just the kind of man who'd keep her around just because she was the mother of his child. She wasn't particularly thinking of herself per se but of her child. She had grown up in a loveless household and simply refused to subject her child to one. Jason would never understand how that could be because he'd grown up with parents who'd loved each other and had set a good example for their children to follow. That was evident in the way his cousins and brother treated the wives they loved. It was easy to see their relationships were loving ones, the kinds that last until death. She didn't expect that kind of long-term commitment from Jason. That was not in the plan and had not been in his proposal.

She knew he was awake by the sound of his breathing but his back was to her as hers was to him. When he had come up to bed he hadn't said anything. In fact, he had barely cast a glance her way before sliding under the covers.

His family was excited about hosting a wedding reception for them but she had been tempted to tell them not to bother. Their year would be up before she knew it anyway. However, she had sat there and listened while plans were being made and fighting the urge to get pulled into the excitement.

The bed shifted and she held her breath hoping that, although she'd given him that reminder, he would still want her. He dashed that hope when instead of sliding toward her he got out of the bed and left the room. Was he coming back to bed or did he plan on sleeping somewhere else tonight? On the sofa? In his truck?

She couldn't help the tears that began falling from her eyes. She only had herself to blame. No one told her to fall in love. She should have known better. She should not have put her heart out there. But she had and now she was paying the price for doing so.

"OKAY, WHAT THE HELL is wrong with you, Jason? It's not like you to make such a stupid mistake and the one you just made was a doozy," Zane stormed. "That's the sheikh's prized horse and what you did could have cost him a leg."

Anger flared up inside of Jason. "Dammit, Zane, I know what I did. You don't have to remind me."

He then glanced over at Derringer and waited to see what he had to say and when he didn't say anything, Jason was grateful.

"Look, guys, I'm sorry about the mistake. I've got a lot on my mind. I think I'll call it a day before I cause another major screwup." He then walked off toward Zane's barn.

He was in the middle of saddling his horse to leave when Derringer walked up. "Hey, man, you want to talk about it?"

Jason drew in a deep breath. "No."

"Come on, Jas, there's evidently trouble in paradise at Jason's Place. I don't profess to be an expert when it comes to such matters, but even you will admit that me and Lucia had a number of clashes before we married."

Jason glanced over at him. "What about *after* you married?"

Derringer threw his head back and laughed. "Want a list? The main thing to remember is the two of you are people with different personalities and that in itself is bound to cause problems. The most effective solution is good, open communication. We talk it out and then we make love. Works every time. Oh, and you need to remind her every so often how much you love her."

Jason chuckled drily. "The first two things you said I should do are things I can handle but not the latter."

Derringer raised a brow. "What? You can't tell your wife you love her?"

Jason sighed. "No, I can't tell her."

Derringer looked confused. "Why? You do love her, don't you?"

"Yes, more than life."

"Then what's the problem?"

Jason stopped what he was doing and met Derringer's gaze. "She doesn't love me back."

Derringer blinked and then drew back slightly and said, "Of course she loves you."

Jason shook his head. "No, she doesn't." He paused for a moment and then said, "Our marriage was based on a business proposition, Derringer. She needed a husband to retain her trust fund and I wanted her land—at least co-ownership of her land—and Hercules."

Derringer stared at him for a long moment and then said, "I think you'd better start from the beginning."

IT TOOK JASON LESS THAN ten minutes to tell Derringer everything, basically because his cousin stood there and listened without asking any questions. But once he'd finished the questions had begun…as well as the observations.

Derringer was certain Bella loved him because he claimed she looked at Jason the way Lucia looked at him, the way Chloe looked at Ramsey and the way Pam looked at Dillon—when they thought no one was supposed to be watching.

Then Derringer claimed that given the fact Jason and Bella were still sharing the same bed—although no hanky-panky had been going on for almost a week now—had significant meaning.

Jason shook his head. "If Bella loves me the way you think she does then why hasn't she told me?"

Derringer crossed his arms over his chest. "And why haven't you told her?" When Jason couldn't answer, Derringer smiled and said, "I think the two of you have a big communication problem. It happens and is something that can easily be corrected."

Jason couldn't help but smile. "Sounds like you've gotten to be a real expert on the subject of marriage."

Derringer chuckled. "I have to be. I plan on being a married man for life so I need to know what it takes to keep my woman happy and to understand that when wifey isn't happy, hubby's life can be a living hell."

Derringer then tapped his foot on the barn's wooden floor as if he was trying to make up his mind about something. "I really shouldn't be telling you this because it's something I overheard Chloe and Lucia discussing yesterday and if Lucia found out I was eavesdropping she—"

"What?"

"Maybe you already know but just hadn't mentioned anything."

"Dammit, Derringer, what the hell are you talking about?"

A sly smile eased across Derringer's lips. "The ladies in the family suspect Bella might be pregnant."

BELLA WALKED OUT OF THE children's hospital with a smile on her face. She loved kids and being around them always made her forget her troubles, which was why she would come here a couple of days a week to spend time with them. She glanced at her watch. It was still early yet and she wasn't ready to go home.

Home.

She couldn't help but think of Jason's Place as her home. Although she'd made a stink with Jason about construction on her ranch, she didn't relish the thought of going back there to live. She had gotten accustomed to her home with Jason.

She was more confused than ever and the phone call from her mother hadn't helped. Now her parents were trying to work out a bargain with her—another proposal of a sort. They would have their attorney draw up a legal document that stated if she returned home they would give her the space she needed. Of course they wanted her to move back onto their estate, although she would be given the entire east wing as her own. They claimed they no longer wanted to control her life, but just wanted to make sure she was living the kind of life she was entitled to live.

Their proposal sounded good but she had gotten into enough trouble accepting proposals already. Besides, even if things didn't work out between her and Jason, he deserved to be around his child. When they divorced, at least his son or daughter would be a stone's throw away.

She was crossing the parking lot to her car when she heard someone call her name. She turned and cringed when she saw it was her uncle Kenneth's daughter, who was the mother of the twins. Although Uncle Kenneth had had an outburst at the trial, Elyse Bostwick Thomas had not. She'd been too busy crying.

Drawing in a deep breath Bella waited for the woman to catch up with her. "Elyse."

"Bella. I just wanted to say how sorry I was for what Mark and Michael did. I know Dad is still bitter and I've tried talking to him about it but he refuses to discuss it. He's always spoiled the boys and there was nothing I could do about it, mainly because my husband and I are divorced. My ex moved away, but I wanted a father figure in their lives."

Elyse didn't say anything for a moment. "I hope Dad will eventually realize his part in all this, and although I miss my sons, they were getting too out of hand. I've been assured the place they are going will teach them discipline. I just wanted you to know I was wrong for listening to everything Dad said about you and when

I found out you even offered to help pay for my sons' attorney I thought that was generous of you."

Bella nodded. "Uncle Kenneth turned down my offer."

"Yes, but just the thought touched me deeply, considering everything. You and I are family and I hope that one day we can be friends."

A smile touched Bella's lips. "I'd like that, Elyse. I really would."

"BELLA, ARE YOU SURE you're okay? You might want to go see the doctor about that stomach virus."

Bella glanced over at Chloe. On her way home she had dropped by to visit with her cousin-in-law and little Susan. Bella had grown fond of the baby who was a replica of both of her parents. The little girl had Ramsey's eyes and skin tone and Chloe's mouth and nose. "Yes, Chloe, I'm fine."

She decided not to say anything about her pregnancy just yet until after she figured out how and when she would tell Jason. Evidently Chloe had gotten suspicious because Bella had thrown up the other day when Chloe had come to deliver a package to Jason from Ramsey.

Bella knew from the bits and pieces of the stories she'd heard from the ladies that Chloe was pregnant when she and Ramsey had married. However, Bella doubted that was the reason Ramsey had married her. Anyone around the pair for any period of time could tell how in love they were.

Bella never had a best friend, no other woman to share her innermost feminine secrets with. That was one of the reasons she appreciated the bond she felt toward all the Westmoreland women. They were all friendly, understanding and supportive. But she was hoping that because Chloe had been pregnant when she'd married Ramsey, her in-law could help her understand a few things. She had decisions to make that would impact her baby's future.

"Chloe, can I ask you something?"

Chloe smiled over at her. "Sure."

"When you found out you were pregnant were you afraid to tell Ramsey for fear of how he would react?"

Chloe placed her teacup down on the table and her smile brightened as if she was recalling that time. "I didn't discover I was pregnant until Ramsey and I broke up. But the one thing I knew was that I was going to tell him because he had every right to know. The one thing that I wasn't sure about was when I was going to tell him. One time I thought of taking the coward's way out and waiting until I returned to Florida and calling him from there."

Chloe paused for a moment and then said, "Ramsey made things easy for me when he came to me. We patched up things between us, found it had been nothing more than a huge misunderstanding and got back together. It was then that I told him about my pregnancy and he was happy about it."

Bella took a sip of her tea and then asked, "When the two of you broke up did you stay apart for long?"

"For over three weeks and they were the unhappiest three weeks of my life." Chloe smiled again when she added, "A Westmoreland man has a tendency to grow on you, Bella. They become habit-forming. And when it comes to babies, they love them."

There was no doubt in Bella's mind that Jason loved children; that wasn't what worried her. The big question was if he'd want to father any with her considering the nature of their marriage. Would he see that as a noose around his neck? For all she knew he might be counting the days until their year would be up so he could go his way and she go hers. A baby would definitely change things.

She glanced back over at Chloe. "Ramsey is a wonderful father."

Chloe smiled. "Yes, and Jason would be a wonderful father, as well. When their parents died all the Westmorelands had to pitch in and raise the younger ones. It was a team effort and it wasn't easy. Jason is wonderful with children and would make any child a fantastic father."

Chloe chuckled. "I can see him with a son while teaching him to ride his first pony, or a daughter who will wrap him around her finger the way Susan does Ramsey. I can see you and Jason having a houseful of kids."

Bella nodded. Chloe could only see that because she thought she and Jason had a normal marriage.

"Don't ever underestimate a Westmoreland man, Bella."

Chloe's words interrupted her thoughts. "What do you mean?"

"I mean that from what I've discovered in talking with all the other wives, even those spread out in Montana, Texas, Atlanta and Charlotte, a Westmoreland man is loyal and dedicated to a fault to the woman he's chosen as a mate. The woman he loves. And although they can be overly protective at times, you can't find a man more loving and supportive. But the one thing they don't care too much for is when we hold secrets from them. Secrets that need to be shared with them. Jason is special, and I believe the longer you and he are married, the more you will see just how special he is."

Chloe reached out and gently touched Bella's hand. "I hope what I've said has helped in some way."

Bella returned her smile. "It has." Bella knew that she needed to tell Jason about the baby. And whatever decision he made regarding their future, she would have to live with it.

CHAPTER TEN

JASON DIDN'T BOTHER riding his horse back home after his discussion with Derringer. Instead he borrowed Zane's truck and drove home like a madman only to discover Bella wasn't there. She hadn't mentioned anything at breakfast about going out, so where was she? But then they hadn't been real chatty lately, so he wasn't really surprised she hadn't told him anything.

He glanced around his home—their home—and took in the changes she'd made. Subtle changes but changes he liked. If she were to leave his house—their house—it wouldn't be the same. He wouldn't be the same.

He drew in a deep breath. What if the ladies' suspicions were true and she was pregnant? What if Derringer's suspicions were true and she loved him? Hell, if both suspicions were true then they had one hell of a major communication problem between them, and it was one he intended to remedy today as soon as she returned.

He walked into the kitchen and began making of all things, a cup of tea. Jeez, Bella had definitely rubbed off on him but he wouldn't have it any other way. And what if she was really pregnant? The thought of her stomach growing big while she carried his child almost left him breathless. And he could recall when it happened.

It had to have been their wedding night spent in the

honeymoon suite of the Four Seasons. He had awakened to find her mouth on him and she had driven him to more passion than he'd ever felt in his entire life. He'd ended up flipping her on her back and taking her without wearing a condom. He had exploded the moment he'd gotten inside her body. Evidently she had been good and fertile that night.

He certainly hoped so. The thought of her having his baby was his most fervent desire. And no matter what she thought, he would provide both her and his child with a loving home.

He heard the sound of the front door opening and paused a moment not to rush out and greet her. They needed to talk and he needed to create a comfortable environment for them to do so. He was determined that before they went to bed tonight there would be a greater degree of understanding between them. With that resolution, he placed the teacup on the counter to go greet his wife.

BELLA'S GROOMING AND social training skills had prepared her to handle just about anything, but now that she was back at Jason's Place she was no longer sure of her capabilities. So much for all the money her parents had poured into those private schools.

She placed her purse on the table thinking at least she'd had one bright spot in her day other than the time spent with the kids. And that was her discussion with Elyse. They had made plans to get together for tea later in the week. She could just imagine how her uncle would handle it when he found out she and Elyse had decided to be friends.

And then there had been her conversation with Chloe.

It had definitely been an eye-opener and made her realize she couldn't keep her secret from Jason any longer. He deserved to know about the baby and she would tell him tonight.

"Bella. You're home."

She was pulled from her reverie by the pure masculine tone of Jason's voice when he walked out of the kitchen. Her pulse hammered in the center of her throat and she wondered if he would always have this kind of effect on her. She took a second or two to compose herself, before she responded to him. "Yes, I'm home. I see you have company."

He lifted a brow. "Company?"

"Yes. Zane's truck is parked outside," she replied, allowing her gaze to roam over her husband, unable to stop herself from doing so. He was such a hunk and no matter what he wore it only enhanced his masculinity. Even the jeans and chambray shirt he was wearing now made him look sexy as hell.

"I borrowed it. He's not here."

"Oh." That meant they were alone. Under the same roof. And hadn't made love in almost a week. So it stood to reason that the deep vibrations of his voice would stir across her skin and that turn-you-on mouth of his would make her panties start to feel damp.

She met his gaze and something akin to potent sexual awareness passed between them, charging the air, electrifying the moment. She felt it and was sure he felt it, as well. She studied his features and knew she wanted a son or daughter who looked just like him.

She knew she needed to break into the sensual vibe surrounding them and go up the stairs, or else she would be tempted to do something crazy like cross the room and throw herself in his arms and beg him to want her, to love her, to want the child they had conceived together.

"Well, I guess I'll go upstairs a moment and—"

"Do you have a moment so we can talk, Bella?"

She swallowed deeply. "Talk?"

"Yes."

That meant she was going to have to sit across from him and watch that sensual mouth of his move, see his tongue work and remember what it felt like dueling nonstop with hers and—

"Bella, could we talk?"

She swallowed again. "Now?"

"Yes."

"Sure," she murmured and then she followed him toward the kitchen. Studying his backside she could only think that the man she had married was such a hottie.

JASON WASN'T SURE WHERE they needed to begin but he did know they needed to begin somewhere.

"I was about to have a cup of tea. Would you like a cup, as well?"

He wondered if she recalled those were the exact words she had spoken to him that first time she had invited him inside her house. They were words he still remembered to this day. And from the trace of amusement that touched her lips, he knew that she had recalled them.

"Yes, I'd love a cup. Thank you," she said, sitting down at the table, unintentionally flashing a bit of thigh.

He stepped back and quickly moved to the counter, trying to fight for control and to not remember this is the woman whom he'd given her first orgasm, the woman who'd awakened him one morning with her mouth on him, the first woman he'd had unprotected sex with, the only woman he'd wanted to shoot his release inside of, but more than anything, this was the woman he loved so very much.

Moments later when he turned back to her with cups of tea in his hands, he could tell she was nervous, was probably wondering what he wanted to talk about and was hoping he would hurry and get it over with.

"So, how was your day today?" he asked, sitting across from her at the table.

She shrugged those delicate shoulders he liked running his tongue over. She looked so sinfully sexy in the sundress she was wearing. "It was nice. I spent a lot of it at the children's hospital. Today was 'read-a-story' day and I entertained a bunch of them. I had so much fun."

"I'm glad."

"I also ran into Uncle Kenneth's daughter, Elyse."

"The mother of the twins, right?"

"Yes."

"And how did that go?" Jason asked.

"Better than I expected. Unlike Uncle Kenneth, she's not holding me responsible for what happened to her sons. She says they were getting out of hand anyway and is hoping the two years will teach them discipline," Bella said.

"We can all hope for that" was Jason's response.

"Yes, but in a way I feel sorry for her. I can only imagine how things were for her having Kenneth for a father. My dad wouldn't get a 'Father of the Year' trophy, either, but at least I had friends I met at all those schools they shipped me off to. It never bothered me when I didn't go home for the holidays. It helped when I went home with friends and saw how parents were supposed to act. Not as business partners but as human beings."

Bella realized after she'd said it that in a way Jason was her business partner, but she'd never thought of him that way. From the time he'd slipped a ring on her finger she had thought of him as her husband—for better or worse.

The kitchen got silent as they sipped tea.

"So what do you want to talk about, Jason?"

Good question, Jason thought. "I want to talk about us."

He saw her swallow. "Us?"

"Yes, us. Lately, I haven't been feeling an 'us' and I want to ask you a question."

She glanced over at him. "What?"

"Do you not want to be married to me anymore?"

She broke eye contact with him to study the pattern design on her teacup. "What gave you that idea?"

"Want a list?"

She shot her gaze back to him. "I didn't think you'd notice."

"Is that what this is about, Bella, me not noticing you, giving you attention?"

She quickly shook her head. Heaven help her or him if he were to notice her any more or give her more attention than she was already getting. To say Jason Westmoreland was all into her was an understatement. Unfortunately he was all into her, literally. And all for the wrong reasons. Sex was great but it couldn't hold a marriage together. It couldn't replace love no matter how many orgasms you had a night.

"Bella?"

"No, that's not it," she said, nervously biting her bottom lip.

"Then what is it, sweetheart? What do you need that I'm not giving you? What can I do to make you happy? I need to know because your leaving me is not an option. I love you too much to let you go."

The teacup froze midway to her lips. She stared over at him in shock. "What did you just say?"

"A number of things. Do I need to repeat it all?"

She shook her head, putting her cup down. "No, just the last part."

"About me loving you?"

"Yes."

"I said I loved you too much to let you go. Lately you've been reminding me about the year I mentioned in my proposal, but there isn't a year time frame, Bella. I threw that in as an adjustment period to not scare you off. I never intended to end things between us."

He saw the single tear flow from her eyes. "You didn't?"

"No. I love you too much to let you go. There, I've said it again and I will keep saying it until you finally hear it. Believe it. Accept it."

"I didn't know you loved me, Jason. I love you, too. I think I fell in love with you the first time I saw you at your family's charity ball."

"And that's when I believe I fell in love with you, as well," he said, pushing the chair back to get up from the table. "I knew there was a reason every time we touched a part of my soul would stir, my heart would melt and my desire for you would increase."

"I thought it was all about sex."

"No. I believe the reason the sex between us was so

good, so damn hot, was that it was fueled by love of the most intense kind. More than once I wanted to tell you I loved you but I wasn't sure you were ready to hear it. I didn't want to run you off."

"And knowing you loved me is what I needed to hear," she said, standing. "I've never thought I could be loved and I wanted so much for you to love me."

"Sweetheart, I do. I love every single thing about you."

"Oh, Jason."

She went to him and was immediately swept up into his arms, held tight. And when he lowered his head to kiss her, her mouth was ready, willing and hungry. That was evident in the way her tongue mated with his with such intensity.

Moments later he pulled back and swept her off her feet and into his arms then walked out of the kitchen.

SOMEHOW THEY MADE IT upstairs to the bedroom. And there in the middle of the room, he kissed Bella again with a hunger that she greedily returned. He finally released her mouth to draw in a deep breath, but before she could draw in one of her own, he flipped her dress up to her waist and was pulling a pair of wet panties down her thighs. She barely had time to react before he moved to her hips to bury his head between her legs.

"Jason!"

She came the moment his tongue whipped inside of her and began stroking her labia, but she quickly saw that wouldn't be enough for him. He sharpened the tip of his tongue and literally stabbed deep inside of her and proceeded to lick circles around her clitoris before drawing it in between his lips.

Her eyes fluttered closed as he then began suckling her senseless as desire, more potent than any she'd ever felt, started consuming her, racing through every part of her body and pushing her toward another orgasm.

"Jason!"

And he still didn't let up. She reached for him but couldn't get a firm hold as his tongue began thrusting inside her again. His tongue, she thought, should be patented with a warning sign. Whenever he parted this life it should be donated to the Smithsonian.

And when she came yet again, he spread her thighs wide to lap her up. She moaned deep in her throat as his tongue and lips made a plaything of her clitoris, driving her demented, crazy with lust, when sensation after earth-shattering sensation rammed through her.

And then suddenly he pulled back and through glazed eyes she watched as he stood and quickly undressed himself and then proceeded to undress her, as well. Her gaze went to his erection.

Without further ado, he carried her over to the bed, placed her on her back, slid over her and settled between her legs and aimed his shaft straight toward the damp folds of her labia.

"Yes!" she almost screamed out, and then she felt him, pushing inside her, desperate to be joined with her.

He stopped moving. Dropped his head down near hers and said in a sensual growl, "No condom tonight."

Bella gazed up at him. "No condom tonight or any other night for a while," she whispered. "I'll tell you why later. It's something I planned to tell you tonight **anyway." And before she could dwell too much on just** what she had to tell him, he began thrusting inside of her.

And when he pushed all the way to the hilt she gasped for breath at the fullness of having him buried so deep inside her. Her muscles clung to him, she was holding him tight and she began massaging him, milking his shaft for everything she had and thought she could get, while thinking a week had been too long.

He widened her legs farther with his hands and lifted her hips to drive deeper still and she almost cried when he began a steady thrusting inside of her, with relentless precision. This was the kind of ecstasy she'd missed. She hadn't known such degrees of pleasure existed until him and when he lifted her legs onto his shoulders while thrusting back and forth inside her, their gazes met through dazed lashes.

"Come for me, baby," he whispered. "Come for me now."

Her body complied and began to shudder in a climax so gigantic she felt the house shaking. She screamed. There was no way she could not, and when he began coming inside her, his hot release thickened by the intensity of their lovemaking, she could only cry out as she was swept away yet again.

And then he leaned up and kissed her, but not before whispering that he loved her and that he planned to spend the rest of his life making her happy, making her feel loved. And she believed him.

With all the strength she could muster, she leaned up to meet him.

"And I love you so very much, too."

And she meant it.

"Why don't I have to wear a condom for a while?" Jason asked moments later with her entwined in his arms, their limbs tangled as they enjoyed the aftermath of their lovemaking together. He knew the reason, but he wanted her to confirm it.

She lifted her head slightly, met his gaze and whispered, "I'm having your baby."

Her announcement did something to him. Being given confirmation that a life they had created together was growing inside her made him shudder. He knew she was waiting for him to say something.

He planned to show her he had taken it well. She needed to know just how happy her announcement had made him. "Knowing that you are pregnant with my child, Bella, is the greatest gift I could ever hope to receive."

"Oh, Jason."

And then she was there, closer into his arms with her arms wrapped around his neck. "I was afraid you wouldn't be happy."

"You were afraid for nothing. I am ecstatic, overjoyed at the prospect of being a father. Thank you for everything you've done, all the happiness you've brought me."

She shook her head. "No, it's I who needs to thank you for sharing your family with me, for giving me your support when my own family tried to break me down. And for loving me."

And then she leaned toward his lips and he gave her what she wanted, what he wanted. He knew at that moment the proposal had worked. It had brought them together in a way they thought wasn't possible. And he would always appreciate and be forever thankful that Bella had come into his life.

TWO DAYS LATER THE Westmorelands met at Dillon's for breakfast to celebrate. It seemed everyone had announcements to make and Dillon felt it was best that they were all made at the same time so they could all rejoice and celebrate.

First Dillon announced he'd received word from Bane that he would be graduating from the naval academy in a few months with honors. Dillon almost choked up when he'd said it, which let everyone know the magnitude of Bane's accomplishments in the eyes of his family. They knew Bane's first year in the navy had been hard since he hadn't known the meaning of discipline. But he'd finally straightened up and had dreams of becoming a SEAL. He'd worked hard and found favor with one of the high-ranking chief petty officers who'd recognized his potential and recommended him for the academy.

Zane then announced that Hercules had done his duty and had impregnated Silver Fly and everyone could only anticipate the beauty of the foal she would one day deliver.

Ramsey followed and said he'd received word from Storm Westmoreland that his wife, Jayla, was expecting and so were Durango and his wife, Savannah. Reggie and Libby's twins were now crawling all over the place. And then with a huge smile on his face Ramsey announced that he and Chloe were having another baby. That sent out loud cheers and it seemed the loudest had come from Chloe's father, Senator Jamison Burton of Florida, who along with Chloe's stepmother, had arrived the day before to visit with his daughter, son-in-law and granddaughter.

Everyone got quiet when Jason stood to announce that he and Bella would be having a baby in the spring, as well. Bella's eyes were glued to Jason as he spoke and she could feel the love radiating from his every word.

"Bella and I are converting her grandfather's ranch into a guest house and combining our lands for our future children to enjoy one day," he ended by saying.

"Does that mean the two of you want more than one child?" Zane asked with a sly chuckle.

Jason glanced over at Bella. "Yes, I want as many children as my wife wants to give me. We can handle it, can't we, sweetheart?"

Bella smiled. "Yes, we can handle it." And they would because what had started out as a proposal had ended up being a whole lot more and she was filled with overflowing joy at how Jason and his family had enriched her life.

He reached out his hand to her and she took it. Hers felt comforting in his and she could only be thankful for her Westmoreland man.

EPILOGUE

"WHEN I FIRST HEARD you'd gotten married I wondered about the quickness of it, Jason, but after meeting Bella I understand why," Micah said to his brother. "She's beautiful."

"Thanks." Jason smiled as he glanced around the huge guest house on his and Bella's property. The weather had cooperated and the construction workers had been able to transform what had once been a ranch house into a huge fifteen room guest house for family, friends and business associates of the Westmorelands. Combining the old with the new, the builder and his crew had done a fantastic job and Jason and Bella couldn't be more pleased.

He glanced across the way and saw Dillon was talking to Bane who'd surprised everyone by showing up. It was the first time he'd returned home since he had left nearly three years ago. Jason had gotten the chance to have a long conversation with his youngest brother. He was not the bad-assed kid of yesteryears but standing beside Dillon in his naval officer's uniform, the family couldn't be more proud of the man he had become. But there still was that pain behind the sharpness of Bane's eyes. Although he hadn't mentioned Crystal's name, everyone in the family knew the young woman who'd been Bane's first love, his fixation probably since puberty, was still in his thoughts and probably had a permanent place in his heart. He could only imagine the conversation Dillon was having with Bane since they both had intense expressions on their faces.

"So you've not given up on Crystal?" Dillon asked his youngest brother.

Bane shook his head. "No. A man can never give up on the woman he loves. She's in my blood and I believe that no matter where she is, I'm in hers." Bane paused a moment. "But that's the crux of my problem. I have no idea where she is."

Bane then studied Dillon's features. "And you're sure that you don't?"

Dillon inhaled deeply. "Yes, I'm being honest with you, Bane. When the Newsomes moved away they didn't leave anyone a forwarding address. I just think they wanted to put as much distance between you and them as possible. But I'll still go on record and say that I think the time apart for you and Crystal was a good thing. She was young and so were you. The two of you were headed for trouble and both of you needed to grow up. I am proud of the man you've become."

"Thanks, but one day when I have a lot of time I'm going to find her, Dillon, and nobody, her parents or anyone, will keep me from claiming what's mine."

Dillon saw the intense look in Bane's face and only hoped that wherever Crystal Newsome was that she loved Bane just as much as Bane still loved her.

JASON GLANCED OVER AT Bella who was talking to her parents. The Bostwicks had surprised everyone by flying in for the reception. So far they'd been on their best behavior, probably because they were still in awe by the fact that Jason was related to Thorn Westmoreland—racing legend; Stone Westmoreland—aka Rock Mason, *New York Times* bestselling author; Jared Westmoreland, whose reputation as a divorce attorney was renowned; Senator Reggie Westmoreland, and that Dillon was the CEO of Blue Ridge. Hell, they were even speechless when they learned there was even a sheikh in the family.

He saw that Bella was pretending to hang on to her parents' every word. He had discovered she knew how to handle them and refused to let them treat her like a child. He hadn't had to step in once to put them in their place. Bella had managed to do that rather nicely on her own. They had opted to stay at a hotel in town, which had been fine with both him and Bella. There was only so much of her parents that either of them could take.

He inwardly smiled as he studied Bella's features and could tell she was ready to be rescued. "Excuse me a minute, Micah, I need to go claim my wife for a second." Jason moved across the yard to her and as if she felt his impending presence, she glanced his way and smiled. She then excused herself from her parents and headed to meet him.

The dress she was wearing was beautiful and the style hid the little pooch of her stomach. The doctor had warned them that because of the way her stomach was growing they shouldn't be surprised if she was having twins. It would be a couple of months before they knew for sure.

"Do you want to go somewhere for tea…and me," Jason leaned over to whisper close to her ear.

Bella smiled up at him. "Think we'll be missed?"

Jason chuckled. "With all these Westmorelands

around, I doubt it. I don't even think your parents will
miss us. Now they're standing over there hanging on to
Sheikh Jamal Yasir's every word."

"I noticed."

Jason then took his wife's hand in his. "Come on.
Let's take a stroll around our land."

And their land was beautiful, with the valley, the
mountains, the blooming flowers and the lakes. Already
he could envision a younger slew of Westmorelands that
he and Bella would produce who would help take care of
their land. They would love it as much as their parents
did. Not for the first time he felt as if he was a blessed
man, his riches abundant not in money or jewelry but
in the woman walking by his side. His Southern Bella,
his Southern beauty, the woman that was everything to
him and then some.

"I was thinking," he said.

She glanced over at him. "About what?"

He stopped walking and reached out and placed a
hand on her stomach. "You, me and our baby."

She chuckled. "Our babies. Don't forget there is that
possibility."

He smiled at the thought of that. "Yes, our babies.
But mainly about the proposal."

She nodded. "What about it?"

"I suggest we do another."

She threw her head back and laughed. "I don't have
any more land or another horse to bargain with."

"A moot point, Mrs. Westmoreland. This time the
stakes will be higher."

"Mmm, what do you want?"

"Another baby pretty soon after this one."

She chuckled again. "Don't you know you never

mention having more babies to a pregnant woman? But I'm glad to hear that you want a house filled with children because I do, too. You'll make a wonderful father."

"And you a beautiful mother."

And then he kissed her with all the love in his heart, sealing yet another proposal and knowing the woman he held in his arms would be the love of his life for always.

* * * * *

SOLID SOUL

To Gerald Jackson, Sr., my husband and hero.
To my sons, Gerald and Brandon,
who constantly make me proud.
To my agent extraordinaire, Pattie Steele Perkins.
To my editor, Mavis Allen, who asked me
to be a part of the Kimani Romance line.
To my readers who have supported me
through forty books.

Beloved, I wish above all things that thou mayest prosper
and be in good health, even as thy soul prospereth.
—3 *John* 1:2

PROLOGUE

"MY MOM NEEDS TO GET a life!"

With a sigh of both anger and frustration, fifteen-year-old Tiffany Hagan dropped down into the chair next to her friend, Marcus Steele.

"I thought you said that the reason you and your mom moved here to Charlotte a few months ago *was* for a better life," sixteen-year-old Marcus said after taking a huge bite of his hamburger as they sat in the school's cafeteria.

Tiffany rolled her eyes. "Yeah, that's what I thought, but now it seems that her idea of a better life is making mine miserable. Just because she got pregnant at sixteen doesn't mean I'd go out and do the same thing. Yeah right! I don't even have a boyfriend and if she keeps up her guard-dog mentality, I never will. She needs a life that doesn't revolve around me."

"Good luck in her getting one," Marcus said, taking a sip of his soda. "My dad is the same way, maybe even worse. He's so hell-bent on me making good grades and getting into an Ivy League college that I barely have time to breathe. If it weren't for my three uncles I probably wouldn't be playing football. Dad sees any extracurricular activities as a distraction."

Tiffany shook her head in disgust. "Parents! They're

so controlling. Can't they see that they're smothering us?"

"Evidently not."

"I wish there was some way that I could shift my mom's attention off of me," Tiffany said, unwrapping her sandwich. "If only she had another interest, like a boyfriend or something. Then she could get all wrapped up in him and give me some breathing space. I don't remember her ever dating anyone."

After taking another bite of his hamburger, Marcus said, "My dad has dated occasionally since my mom died seven years ago, and although I'm sure some of the women have tried, none of them holds his attention for long."

Tiffany laughed. "Then he better not ever meet my mom. One look at her and he'll be a goner for sure. I hate to brag but my mom is hot," she said proudly.

"Hey, my dad doesn't look too bad, either." Marcus grinned. "Maybe we ought to get them together since it seems that neither of them has a life," he added teasingly.

Tiffany was about to bite into her sandwich when Marcus' suggestion sank in. A huge smile curved her lips. "Marcus, that's it!"

He looked at her, baffled. "What's it?"

"My mom and your dad. Both are single, good-looking and desperately in need of something to occupy their time besides us. Just think of the possibilities."

Marcus began thinking. Moments later, he smiled. "Yeah," he agreed. "It just might work."

"It *would* work. Think about it. If we got them together, they would be so into each other that they wouldn't have time to drive us nuts."

"Yeah, but how can we get them together without them getting suspicious about anything?" he asked.

Tiffany smiled mischievously. "Oh, I bet I could think of something...."

CHAPTER ONE

Less than a week later

KYLIE HAGAN REGARDED with keen interest the handsome specimen of a man dressed in a dark business suit, who had just walked into her florist shop. That was *so* unlike her. She couldn't recall the last time a member of the male species had grabbed her attention. Denzel Washington didn't count, since each and every time she saw him on the movie screen it was an automatic drool.

She continued watering her plants, thinking that the woman he was about to buy flowers for was indeed very lucky. The good news was that he had selected her florist shop—she was the newbie in town, and Kylie needed all the business she could get, since she'd only been open for a couple of months. Business was good but she needed to come up with ways to make it even better.

Her heart jumped nervously when, instead of looking around at her vast selection of green plants and floral arrangements, he headed straight for the counter. Evidently he was a man who knew what he wanted and what he needed to woo his woman.

"May I help you?" she asked, thinking that with a face and physique like his, he probably didn't need much

help at all. He stood tall, six-three at least, with a muscular build, a clean-shaven head, chocolate-brown eyes
and a skin tone of the richest cocoa, altogether a striking
combination. The drool she usually reserved only for
Denzel was beginning to make her mouth feel wet. As
she continued to look at him, waiting for his response,
she suddenly noticed that he wasn't smiling. In fact, he
appeared downright annoyed.

"I'm here to see Kylie Hagan."

Kylie lifted her eyebrows and the smile on her face
began fading at his rough and irritated tone of voice.
What business did this man have with her? All her bills
were current, which meant he couldn't be there to collect
anything. And if he was a salesman, with his less than
desirable attitude, she wouldn't be buying whatever it
was he was selling.

"I'm Kylie Hagan."

Surprise flickered in his drop-dead gorgeous eyes.
"You're Kylie Hagan?"

"That's right and who are you?"

"Chance Steele."

The name didn't ring a bell, but then she had only
recently moved to the area. "And what can I do for you,
Mr. Steele?"

He stared at her for a moment, and then he said, "The
only thing you can do for me, Ms. Hagan, is keep your
daughter away from my son."

Kylie froze. The man's words were not what she had
expected. For a long moment she stared back at him,
wondering if she had misunderstood. But all it took
was the deep scowl on his face to let her know she had
not.

"Keep my daughter away from your son?" she repeated when she finally found her voice.

"Yes. I found this note yesterday that evidently dropped out of Marcus's backpack. They were planning on cutting school together on Friday," he said as he pulled a piece of paper out of the pocket of his jacket.

"What!" Kylie shrieked, grabbing the paper out of his hand.

"You heard me and you can read it for yourself," he said, crossing his arms over his chest.

Kylie read, then after the first few lines she wished she hadn't. Three emotions enveloped her: hurt, betrayal and anger. Tiffany had always promised that if she ever got serious about a boy that she would tell her. Granted, she and Tiffany hadn't been that close lately, but a promise was a promise.

"Now can you see why I want your daughter kept away from my son?"

Chance Steele's question sliced through Kylie's tormented mind and grated on her last nerve, deepening her anger. She came from behind the counter to stand directly in front of him. "Don't you dare place all the blame on Tiffany, Mr. Steele. If I read this note correctly, she was merely responding to a note your son had sent asking *her* to cut school. The nerve of him doing such a thing!"

"Look, Ms. Hagan, we can stand here all day and we won't agree who's to blame. But I think we will agree on the fact that your daughter and my son shouldn't even be thinking about cutting school. I have big plans for my son's future that include him attending college."

Kylie glared at him. "And you don't think I have those same plans for my daughter?" she snapped. "Tiffany is a good kid."

"So is Marcus," he snapped back.

Kylie breathed in deeply and closed her eyes in a

concerted effort to calm down before a blood vessel burst in her head. They weren't getting anywhere biting each other's heads off.

"Ms. Hagan, are you all right?"

She slowly opened her eyes to focus on the man looming over her. Concern was evident in his gaze. "Yes, I'm fine."

"Look, I'm sorry I came barging in here like this," he said, the tone of his voice calmer, apologetic. "But after reading that note I got upset."

She nodded. "I can understand why. I'm pretty upset myself."

"Did you know our kids were hung up on each other?" he asked. She could tell that he was trying to maintain a composed demeanor.

"Mr. Steele, until you walked into my shop and dropped your son's name, I had no idea he even existed. Tiffany and I moved here a few months ago from New York State, right before the start of the new school year. I knew she had made some new friends but she's never mentioned anyone's name in particular."

"Okay, so as parents, what do you think we should do?" he asked.

His voice was drenched in wariness and Kylie could tell he was deeply bothered by all of this, but then he wasn't the only one. "The one thing we shouldn't do is demand that they not see each other. Telling them to stay away from each other will only make them want to see each other more. Teenagers will always deliberately do the opposite of what their parents want them to do. And once they start rebelling, it will be almost impossible to do anything."

She didn't have to tell him that she knew firsthand how that worked. Her parents had tried to keep her and

Sam apart, which only made her want him more. The more she and Sam had sneaked around, the more risks they had taken until she had eventually gotten pregnant at sixteen…the same age Tiffany would be in about ten months.

"We have to do something. In confronting Marcus about that letter, I've thrown a monkey wrench into their plans for Friday. But how can we be sure this won't happen again?"

At the sound of Chance's voice, Kylie dragged her thoughts back to the present. "I'll talk to Tiffany and, like I said, she's a good kid."

"Yes, but it appears that my son and your daughter are at the age where overactive hormones cancel out good sense. We need to do what we can to make sure those hormones stay under control."

"I fully agree."

He reached into his pocket and pulled out a business card. "This is how to reach me if you need me to do anything further on my end. I talked to Marcus but things didn't go well. I did the one thing you indicated I should not have done, which was demand that he stay away from Tiffany. I don't think I've ever seen him that angry or rebellious."

Kylie nodded as she took the card from him. She didn't want to think about her upcoming talk with Tiffany. "I appreciate you dropping by and bringing this to my attention."

"Like I said earlier, I apologize that my approach wasn't more subtle. But Marcus's last words to me this morning were that nobody would stop him from seeing Tiffany. I was furious and still riled up when I decided to come over here."

He sighed deeply and then added, "It's not easy raising a teenager these days."

"Don't I know it," Kylie said softly, feeling terribly drained but knowing she would need all her strength when she confronted Tiffany after school.

"Well, I'd better be going."

"Again, thanks for coming by and letting me know what's going on."

He nodded. "There was no way I could *not* let you know, considering what they'd planned to do. Have a good day, Ms. Hagan."

As Kylie watched him walk out of her shop, she knew that as much as she wished it to be so, there was no way that this would be a good day.

THE MOMENT CHANCE GOT into his truck and closed the door, he leaned back against the seat and released a long sigh. If the daughter looked anything like the mother, he was in deep trouble. No wonder his usually smart son had begun acting downright stupid.

Kylie Hagan was definitely a beauty. He had noticed that fact the moment he had walked into the flower shop and headed straight toward the counter. When she had come from behind that same counter and he'd seen that she was wearing a pair of shorts and a T-shirt, he'd thought the outfit fit just right on her curvy, petite body and showed off her shapely legs too perfectly. Braided dark brown hair had been stylishly cut to accent her face. Her creamy chocolate skin complemented a pair of beautiful brown eyes, a perky nose and an incredibly feminine pair of lips.

How in the world could she be the mother of a fifteen-year-old when she looked barely older than twenty herself? She looked more like Tiffany's sister than her mother. Perhaps Tiffany had been adopted. There were a lot of questions circulating around in his mind, but the foremost was what the two of them could do about their kids who seemed hell-bent on starting a relationship that neither was ready for.

He understood Marcus's interest in girls—after all he was a Steele—and Chance could distinctly remember when he was younger. He had fallen in love with Cyndi when he'd been just a few years older than Marcus, and had married her before his twentieth birthday after she had gotten pregnant.

Pregnant.

He would never forget that day when Cyndi had come to him, a mere week before he was to leave for Yale University, to let him know she was having his baby. He had loved her so much he decided not to accept a full college scholarship and leave her alone. Instead, he had married her, gone to work at his father's manufacturing company and attended college at night. It hadn't been easy and it had taken him almost six years to get a degree, but he and Cyndi had made the best of it and he could look back and honestly say that although there were hard years, they had been happy ones.

And then the unthinkable happened. Cyndi had noticed changes in a mole on the side of her neck, a mole that was later determined to be cancerous. Even after surgery and chemo treatments, four years later, on the day Marcus should have been celebrating his ninth birthday, they were in the cemetery putting to rest the one woman who had meant the world to Chance.

He straightened and started up his truck. Although he would never think of marrying Cyndi as a mistake, he couldn't help but remember her plans of attending college; plans that had gotten thrown by the wayside with her pregnancy. If he had it all to do over, he would have been more responsible that night when they had gotten carried away by the moment.

And then on top of everything else, he couldn't forget the promise he had made to Cyndi on her deathbed; a promise that he would make sure that their son got to do everything they hadn't done, and take advantage of every opportunity offered to him, which included one day attending a university that would give him the best education.

That was the reason he was driven to make sure Marcus did well in school. Of course it was Chance's hope for him to one day join the family business, the Steele Corporation, but if Marcus wanted to do something else after finishing college, then he could do so with Chance's blessings.

As he began backing out of the parking lot, he contemplated the emergence of Tiffany Hagan in Marcus's life. He didn't think his son's interest in the girl was going to fade away anytime soon, regardless of what kind of talk Kylie Hagan had with her daughter. That meant Chance needed to have a "Plan B" ready. Under no circumstances would he let Marcus succumb to teen lust and ruin the life he and Cyndi always wanted for him.

His thoughts shifted to Tiffany's mother again, and he felt lust invading his own body. The difference was he was a man and he could handle it.

At least he hoped he could.

AFTER READING THE NOTE, Helena Spears glanced up at the woman who'd been her best friend since high school. "Are you sure Tiffy wrote this, Kylie?"

The two of them had met for lunch and were sitting

at a table in the back of the restaurant. Kylie shook her head. Leave it to Lena to try to wiggle her goddaughter out of any kind of trouble. "Of course I'm sure. I can recognize Tiffany's handwriting when I see it and so can you. Those curls at the end of certain letters give her away and you know it."

Lena shrugged as she handed the note back to Kylie. "Well, the only thing I have to say in defense of my godchild is that if Marcus looks anything like his daddy, then I can see why Tiffy fell for him."

Kylie didn't want to admit that she'd thought the same thing. "You know Chance Steele?"

"Oh, yeah. There are few people living in Charlotte who don't know the Steele brothers. They own a huge manufacturing company, the Steele Corporation. There are four of them who were born and raised here. They're not transplants like the rest of us, and they are very successful, as well as handsome. Chance is the CEO and his brothers have key positions in the corporation. There are also three female cousins, one of which works in the PR Department. The other two chose careers outside of the company, but all three are members of the board of directors."

Lena took a sip of her drink before continuing. "Chance is the oldest and the one I see most often with my charity work. He's a big supporter of the American Cancer Society. His wife died of cancer around seven years ago."

Kylie, who had been putting the note back in her purse, suddenly lifted her head. "He's a widower?"

"Yes, and from what I understand, he's doing a good job raising his son."

Kylie frowned. "Not if his son is enticing girls to cut school with him."

Lena laughed. "Oh, come on, Kylie. You were young once."

"I remember. And that's what I'm afraid of," she said, meeting Lena's gaze with a concerned expression. "You recall how I was all into Sam. I thought I was madly in love. It was like my day wasn't complete until I saw his face. I was obsessed."

Lena shook her head. "Yeah, you did have it bad. You thought you were in love, and nobody could tell you differently."

"And you saw what happened to me. One day of acting irresponsibly changed my entire life. I was pregnant on my sixteenth birthday."

And rejected at sixteen, as well.

She would never forget the day Sam told her that he wanted no part of her or the baby, and that he would get his parents to give her money for an abortion, but that was about all she would ever get from him. He intended to go to college on a football scholarship and under no circumstances would he let her mess up his future with a baby he didn't want. He agreed with his parents that there was no sense in him throwing away a promising career in pro football because of one foolish mistake. So instead of hanging around and doing the right thing, he had split the first chance he got. Even now she could count on one hand the number of times Tiffany had seen her father. Sam did get the football career in the NFL that he'd wanted, at least for a short while before an injury ended things. Now he was living in California, married with a family, and rarely had time for his daughter.

Emotions tightened her throat as she remembered that time she had gotten pregnant. She had hurt her parents something awful. And disappointed them, as well. They had had so many high hopes for her, their only child, including her attending college at their alma mater, Southern University.

She had eventually gotten a college degree but that was only after years of struggling as a single parent and trying to make a life for her and Tiffany. And now to think that her daughter could possibly be traveling down the same path was unacceptable.

"Yes, I did see what happened to you, but look how much you've accomplished since then, Kylie," Lena said. "The only thing you didn't do was allow another man into your life because of Sam's rejection, and I think you were wrong for turning away what I knew were some good men. You never gave yourself the chance for happiness with someone else after Sam. I tried to tell you how arrogant and selfish he was but you wouldn't listen."

Kylie sighed. No, she hadn't wanted to hear anything negative about Sam. She had been too much in love to see his faults and refused to let anyone else talk about them, either. A sickening sensation swelled in her stomach at the thought that history was about to repeat itself with her child. "That's why I can't let Tiffany make the same mistake I did, Lena."

"Don't you think you and Chance might be overreacting just a little? It's not like Tiffy and Marcus planned to cut the entire day of school. They were skipping the last two classes to go somewhere, probably to the mall," Lena pointed out.

"And that's supposed to be okay?" Kylie's nerves were screaming in frustration and anger each and every time she thought about what her daughter had planned on doing. She remembered when she had cut school with Sam. Instead of going to the movies like the two of them

planned, he had taken her to his house, where they had
spent the entire day in his bedroom doing things they
shouldn't have been doing and things neither of them
had been prepared for. But all she could think about
was that Sam Miller, the star player on the Richardson
High School football team, was in love with her. Or so
she'd thought. Silly her.

"You need to calm down before you talk to Tiff,
Kylie. I understand you're upset, but your anger won't
help. You know how headstrong she is. She's just like
you when you were her age."

Kylie sighed deeply. Again, that was the last thing
she wanted to hear. "She broke her promise to me, Lena.
We've had a lot of talks. She had promised me that she
would let me know when she was interested in boys."

"And had she come and told you about Marcus,
then what? Would you have given her your blessings
or locked her up for the rest of her life? Girls like boys,
Kylie. That's natural. And you've had so many talks with
Tiffy that she probably knows your speech by heart.
Has it ever occurred to you that maybe you're laying
things on a little too thick? Tiffy is a good kid, yet you're
judging her by the way you lived your life, by your own
past mistakes. It's important to you that she 'be good'
because you don't think that you were."

Kylie's eyes began filling with tears. "I only want
what's best for her, Lena. I made a foolish and stupid
mistake once and I'll do anything within my power to
keep her from making the same one."

Lena got up, came around the table and hugged her
friend. "I know. Tiffy is going to be fine. I'll be here to
help you any way that I can. You know that. I just don't
want you to build this brick wall between you and her.
That same kind of wall your mother built with you."

Kylie wiped away a tear from her cheek. Although she and her mother had a fairly decent relationship now, Kylie would never forget when Olivia Hagan had let down her only daughter by upholding her belief that by getting pregnant out of wedlock, Kylie had committed the worst possible sin.

"I'll never let that happen," Kylie vowed quietly.

CHAPTER TWO

"THAT'S THE CRISIS you called this meeting for?" Sebastian Steele asked, turning away from the window and looking across the office at his brother with both amazement and amusement on his face.

Chance glared first at Sebastian, and then at his other two brothers, Morgan and Donovan. They were sitting in front of his desk and looking at him with the same expressions. "Your nephew is putting a pretty face before his studies and that doesn't add up to a crisis to any of you?"

When all three chimed the word *no* simultaneously, Chance knew talking to them had been a waste of his time.

At the age of thirty-six, Chance was the oldest of the group. Next was Sebastian, fondly called Bas, who was thirty-four. Morgan was thirty-two, and Donovan was thirty. Of the four, Chance was the only one who had ever been married. Bas was presently engaged, but the other two claimed they enjoyed their bachelor status too much to settle down anytime soon.

"Look, Chance," Morgan said as he stood up. "It's normal for boys Marcus's age to like girls. So what's the problem?"

Chance rolled his eyes heavenward. "The problem

is that the girl is only fifteen and they were planning to cut school together and—"

"No," Sebastian interrupted. "They planned to cut a couple of classes, not school. There is a difference."

"And he of all people should know," Donovan said, grinning. "Considering the number of times he used to play hooky. I understand they still have a desk in Mr. Potter's math class that says, 'Sebastian Steele never sat here.'"

"I don't find any of this amusing," Chance said.

Morgan wiped the grin off his face. "Then maybe you should, before you alienate your son."

"How about chilling here, Chance," Sebastian interjected. "You act as if Marcus committed some god-awful sin. We know the promise you made to Cyndi, but there is more to life for a teenager than hitting the books. He's a good kid. He makes good grades. Marcus is going to go to college in a couple of years, we all know that. One girl isn't going to stop him."

"You haven't seen this girl."

Morgan raised a brow. "Have you?"

"No, but I've seen her mother, and if the daughter looks anything like the mother then I'm in trouble."

"I still think you're blowing things out of proportion," Morgan countered. "If you make a big deal out of it, Marcus will rebel. You remember what happened last year when you didn't want him to play football."

Yes, Chance did remember, although he wished he could forget. He rubbed his hand down his face. Regardless of what his brothers said, he needed to talk to Marcus again. He didn't have any problems with his son being interested in girls, he just didn't want Marcus losing his head over one this soon.

KYLIE WAS WAITING IN the living room the moment Tiffany walked through the door. She took one look at her daughter's expression and realized Tiffany knew the conversation that was about to take place. Kylie tried not to show her anger, as well as a few other emotions, when she said, "We need to talk."

Tiffany met her mother's stare. "Look, Mom, I know what you're going to say and I don't think I did anything wrong."

So much for not showing her anger, Kylie thought. "How can you say that? You planned to cut classes with a boy and you don't consider that wrong?"

Tiffany rolled her eyes. "My last two classes of the day are boring anyway, so we—"

"Boring? I don't care how boring they are, you're supposed to be in them and you *will* be in them anytime that bell sounds. Understood?"

Tiffany glared at her. "Yes, I understand."

Kylie nodded. "Now, about Marcus Steele."

Tiffany straightened her spine and immediately went on the defensive. "What about Marcus?"

"Why didn't you tell me about him?"

"Why? So you could find some reason for me not to like him, Mom? Well, it won't work because I do like him. You're the one who wanted to leave Buffalo and move here. And I'm the one who was forced to go to another school and make new friends. Not all of the kids at school like me. They say I talk funny. Marcus has been nice to me. Extremely nice. He asked me to be his girlfriend and I said yes."

"You're not old enough to have a boyfriend, Tiffany."

"That's your rule, Mom."

"And one you will abide by, young lady."

"Why? Because you think I'll get pregnant like you did? That's not fair."

"It's not about that, Tiffany. It's about such things as keeping your reputation intact and not getting involved in anything you aren't ready for."

"It *is* about what happened to you when you were sixteen, Mom. And how do you know what I am or am not ready for? You want to shelter me and you can't. You've talked to me, but the choice of what I do is ultimately mine."

"No, it's not," Kylie bit out. "As long as you're living under my roof, I make the rules and you will abide by them."

"I can't, Mom. I care too much for Marcus and we have news for you and Mr. Steele. We are madly in love!" she almost shouted. "And nothing either of you say is going to make us not be together, whether it's at school or someplace else."

"What's that supposed to mean?"

"It means," Tiffany said stalking off to her room, "that I don't want to talk anymore."

CHANCE LEAPED TO HIS feet. The sound of his chair crashing to the floor echoed loudly in the kitchen. "What do you mean you might not go to college but stay in Charlotte to be closer to Tiffany Hagan?" he shouted. His anger had clearly reached the boiling point.

"There's no reason to get upset, Dad. What's the big deal if I decided to hang around here and go to college? One university is just as good as another."

Chance rubbed his hand down his face, trying to fight for composure, and quickly decided to use another approach. "Marcus," he said calmly, "I'm sure Tiffany Hagan is a nice girl, but you're only sixteen. In another couple of years you'll finish high school and go to college where you will meet plenty of other nice girls. You have such a bright future ahead of you. I'd hate to see you get too serious about any girl now."

A stubborn expression settled on Marcus's face. "She's not just any girl, Dad. Tiffany is the girl I plan to marry one day."

"Marry!" Chance nearly swallowed the word in shock. "How did marriage get into the picture? You're only sixteen! I know you think you really care for this girl and—"

"It's more than that, Dad, and the sooner you and Tiffany's mother realize it, the better. Tiffany and I are madly in love and we want to be together forever. There's nothing either of you can say or do to stop us, so you may as well accept it."

"Like hell I will."

"I'm sorry to hear that," Marcus said as he walked out of the kitchen toward his bedroom.

Total shock kept Chance from going after his son and wringing his neck.

KYLIE PACED THE FLOOR. Her nerves were stretched to the breaking point. Tiffany hadn't come out of her room yet, which was probably the best thing.

Love!

At fifteen her daughter thought she was in love. Madly in love at that! Kylie swallowed a thickness in her throat when she realized how her mother must have felt sixteen years ago, dealing with her when she'd been obsessed with Sam Miller.

She paused when she heard the phone ring and quickly crossed the room to pick it up, thinking it was probably Lena checking to see how things with Tiffany had gone. "Hello."

"We need to talk, Ms. Hagan."

Kylie blinked at the sound of the ultrasexy male voice. It didn't take a rocket scientist to figure out who the caller was, or to know he'd evidently had another talk with his son. She sighed. Yes, they did need to talk. "You name the place and I'll be there."

"All right." After a quiet pause, he said. "They *think* they're in love. Madly in love."

Kylie shook her head. "So I heard. Louder than I really cared to, in fact."

"Same here. Do you know where the Racetrack Café is?"

"Yes."

"Can you meet me there around noon tomorrow?"

Considering what was going on with Tiffany and his son, she really didn't have a choice. Hopefully, together they could devise a way to stop the young couple before they got into more trouble than they could handle. "Yes, I can meet you there."

"Fine, I'll see you then."

CHANCE ARRIVED AT THE restaurant early to make sure they got a table. Jointly owned by several race car drivers on the NASCAR circuit, the Racetrack Café was a popular eatery in town. He hadn't been seated more than five minutes when he glanced over at the entrance to see Kylie Hagan walk in.

He had hoped his mental picture of her from yesterday had been wrong, but it hadn't. Kylie Hagan was an attractive woman. Every man in the place apparently thought so, too, judging by the looks they gave her. Not for the first time he wondered about her age and how someone who looked so young could have a fifteen-year-old daughter.

He watched her glance around before she spotted him. There wasn't even a hint of a smile on her face as she walked toward him. But, he quickly decided, it didn't matter. Smiling or not, she looked gorgeous dressed in a pair of black slacks and a blue pullover sweater. And those same curves that he'd convinced himself had to be a figment of his imagination made her slacks a perfect fit for her body. Even her walk was mesmerizing and sexy.

When she got closer, he saw the wariness around her eyes, which led him to believe that she'd probably gone a round or two with her daughter sometime during that day, as he'd done with Marcus. He wondered if the discussion had been about the "his and hers" tattoos Marcus had indicated he and Tiffany were thinking about getting.

Chance stood when she reached the table. "Ms. Hagan."

"Mr. Steele."

He thought they were overdoing the formality, but felt it was best to keep things that way for now. After all, this was nothing more than a business meeting, and the only item on the agenda was a discussion about their children.

After they had taken their seats, he asked, "Would you like to order anything? They have the best hamburgers and French fries in town."

A small smile touched Kylie's lips. "So I've heard. But no, I'm fine, you go ahead and order something if you'd like. It's just that my most recent conversation with Tiffany has killed my appetite."

Chance heard the quiver in her voice and recalled

his own conversation with Marcus that morning before he'd left for school. "I take it Tiffany told you about the tattoo."

He watched her nostrils flare as she drew in a silent breath. "Yes, she told me. Matching lovebirds on their tummies right above their navels, I understand."

"That's my understanding, as well." A soft chuckle erupted from his throat. There was a cloud hanging over his head that refused to go away and he had to find amusement anywhere he could to keep his sanity. But he had to believe this was just one part of parenthood that he would get through, and for some reason it was important to him for Kylie Hagan to believe that, as well.

"Things are going to be all right, Ms. Hagan," he said soothingly. "That's why we're meeting today, to make sure of it." He flashed her a smile.

She glanced up and met his gaze. "I want to believe that," she said quietly. "Under the circumstances I think we should forgo formality. Please call me Kylie."

"Okay, and I'm Chance." After a pause he said, "Kylie, I want you to believe things will work out. We have to think positively that we'll get through this particular episode in our children's lives. We have good kids—they're just a little headstrong and stubborn. But I believe with some parental guidance they'll be fine."

"I hope so. Otherwise, if they continue with the route they're going, they're bound to make a mistake."

Chance raised a brow. "By mistake you mean…?"

"Taking their relationship to a level they aren't ready for, Chance."

He liked the way his name easily flowed from her lips. "I take it you mean sex."

"Yes, that's precisely what I'm talking about. Over

the years, I've had the mother-daughter talks with Tiffany, but when teenagers are in love, or think they're in love, they believe that sex is just another way to show how much they care."

They paused in their conversation when a waitress came to give Chance his beer, hand them menus and fill their water glasses.

"And you think that's going to be on their minds?" he asked.

"Of course. Raging teenage hormones are the worst kind."

He picked up his glass to take a sip of beer. "Are they?"

"Yes, trust me, I know. I had Tiffany when I was sixteen."

Chance's glass stopped midway to his lips. His mouth opened in surprise. "Sixteen?"

"Yes. So I hope you can understand why I'm upset with all of this. I don't want Tiffany to make the same mistake I made as a teenager."

Chance nodded. That explained the reason Kylie didn't look old enough to have a fifteen-year-old daughter. That meant she was around thirty-one, but still she didn't look a day over twenty-five. "Did you and Tiffany's father get married?"

Her laugh was bitter. "Are you kidding? He had to make a choice between me and a football scholarship to Hampton University. He chose college."

"I didn't."

Kylie glanced up from studying her water glass. "You didn't what?"

"I was faced with the same decision as Tiffany's father. My girlfriend, Marcus's mother, got pregnant when we were seniors in high school. We were both eighteen and had plans for college. We acknowledged our mistake and felt that no matter what, we loved each other and loved the child we had made. Instead of going to college, we got married, remained here in Charlotte and made the best of things. I later went to college at night. My wife died of cancer when Marcus was nine."

Chance finished his beer. A part of him regretted that the man who had gotten Kylie pregnant hadn't done the responsible thing. "It must have been hard for you, pregnant at sixteen," he said.

"It was." He could tell by the way her lips were quivering their conversation was bringing back painful memories for her. "I disappointed my parents tremendously, embarrassed them. When it was determined that the father didn't want me or his child as part of his future, my parents tried talking me into giving up my baby for adoption, but I refused. That caused friction between us the entire nine months. Things got so bad at home that I had to go live with my best friend and her mother the last couple months of my pregnancy."

After taking a sip of water, she said, "The day the nurse brought Tiffany to me for the first time after I'd given birth to her, I gazed down at my beautiful daughter and knew I had made the right decision, no matter how my parents felt."

"Did they eventually come around to your way of thinking?"

"Years later when they realized they were denying themselves the chance to get to know their granddaughter. But at first they wanted me to know what a mistake I'd made in keeping her. They'd intended to teach me a lesson. I couldn't move back home so I continued to live with my friend's family until I was able to get an apartment at seventeen. I finished high school at night while working at a grocery store as a cashier during the day. My best friend, who also became Tiffany's godmother, kept her at night so I could finish school. It was hard but I was determined to make it work. After high school, I went to college and I struggled for years as a single parent before I finally earned a degree. I got a management position and later purchased a modest home for me and Tiffany."

"What made you decide to move here?"

"The company where I worked as a supervisor decided to downsize. My position was no longer needed so they gave me a pretty nice severance package. Instead of seeing losing my job as the end of the world, I decided to turn it into an opportunity to do something I'd always wanted to do."

"Open up a florist shop?"

"Yes. The reason I decided on Charlotte was that Lena had moved here after college and I liked the area the couple of times I'd come to visit her."

"Lena?"

"Helena Spears, my best friend from high school."

Chance smiled. "Helena Spears? I've met her on several occasions. She's a Realtor in town and is very active with the Cancer Society. I think her father died of the disease some years ago."

"He did, when Lena was fourteen. In recent years her mother has taken ill. I admire Lena for taking on the responsibility of her mother's care the way she has."

Kylie leaned back in her chair. "So knowing my history, Chance, I hope you can understand why I don't want Tiffany to make the same mistakes I did. I don't have anything against your son personally. I'm sure he's a fine young man. I just don't think he and Tiffany are ready for any sort of a relationship just yet."

"And I totally agree. So what do you think we should do?"

"I think we should meet with them, tell them our feelings, let them know we understand how they feel, or how they think they feel, since we were young once. But we should try to do whatever we can to slow down things between them. They're moving too fast. One day I didn't even know Marcus existed and now my daughter is claiming to be madly in love with him."

When the waitress came back to take their order, Chance glanced over at Kylie. "You're still not hungry?"

Kylie smiled. "Yes, in fact I think I'm going to try a hamburger and fries."

Chance returned her smile. "I think I will, too."

"I'M GLAD WE HAD OUR little talk," Chance said as he walked Kylie to her car an hour or so later.

"So am I," she said honestly, although the whole time she'd sat across from him she'd had to fight back her drool. She was amazed at the thoughts that had crept into her mind. Thoughts of how Chance Steele had to have one of the sexiest mouths she'd ever seen. And the type of physique that drew feminine attention. Watching him eat had been quite an ordeal. She'd had to fight the urge to squirm in her seat each time he bit into his hamburger. Her attraction to him was truly bizarre, considering the real problem was finding a way to keep their kids in line.

But she would be crazy not to acknowledge that she was drawn to him in a way she hadn't been drawn to a man in years. Sexual longings were something she hadn't had to deal with for quite some time. Being in Chance's company she had been reminded of just how long it had been.

"So we've decided that I'm to bring Marcus over to your place for Sunday dinner so the four of us can sit down and talk," he said when they reached her car.

"Yes, that's the plan."

"And I think it's a good one. We need to talk to them, but even more importantly, we need to let them talk to us. And no matter what, we're going to have to keep our cool, even when we'd like nothing better than to ring their little necks. The situation we're dealing with calls for strategy and tact, not anger."

She tilted her head up and looked at him. "Strategy and tact I can handle, but it's going to be hard keeping my anger in check," she said, thinking of the conversation she'd had with Tiffany that morning before the girl had left for school. Her daughter was intent on being stubborn, no matter what.

"We'll not only get through it, we'll succeed," Chance said.

Kylie knew he was trying to alleviate some of her worries and she appreciated it. "Okay, then I'll see you and Marcus on Sunday. I'm looking forward to meeting him."

"And I'm looking forward to meeting Tiffany, as well." As he held the car door for her he shook his head and laughed. "Matching lovebird tattoos. Have you ever heard of anything so ridiculous?"

Chance drew Kylie into his amusement. "No, and what's really crazy is that Tiffany is petrified of needles."

"Well, it's been said that love makes you do foolish things."

LATER THAT NIGHT CHANCE swore as he got out of bed. For the first time in eight years, a woman other than his wife had invaded his dreams. Every time he'd closed his eyes, he'd seen Kylie Hagan's face.

It seemed as if he couldn't keep his mind from dredging up memories of her. First there was her appearance yesterday when a T-shirt and a pair of shorts covered her shapely body. And today, at the café, the slacks and sweater she'd been wearing had made him appreciate the fact that he was a male.

And then there were the times she would do something as simple as drink water from her glass. He couldn't help but watch the long, smooth column of her throat as water passed down it. He had wanted to kiss every inch of her neck and had wondered how it would feel for her to grip him the way she was gripping her glass.

Chance dragged a hand down his face thinking it had been a long time for him. Way too long. Sexual cravings were something he'd barely had to deal with, but now he was having several sharp attacks. In addition to the lust he was feeling for her, he also felt a deep sense of admiration.

She had given birth to a child at sixteen, hadn't given in to her parents' demand that she give the child up for adoption, and had struggled the past fifteen years as a single parent who'd gotten a college education and had provided for herself and her daughter. He considered what she'd done a success story. What he really appreciated was the fact that her past experiences enabled her to foresee what could be a potentially dangerous situation for Tiffany and Marcus. It was clear as glass that she didn't want them to make the same mistake she'd made.

As he left the bedroom and headed for the kitchen, he

thought about his own situation with Cyndi. They had been blessed in that both sets of parents had been supportive of their decision to keep their child and marry. And when Marcus was born, there was no doubt in Chance's mind that Cyndi's parents, as well as his own, loved their first grandchild unconditionally. His heart went out to both Kylie and Tiffany when he thought about what they had been denied.

His pulse began racing when he thought about dinner at Kylie's place on Sunday when he would be seeing her again. That was one dinner engagement that he was looking forward to.

KYLIE AWOKE WITH A START, finding that she was drenched in sweat…or heat, since what had awakened her was an erotic dream.

Chance Steele had kissed her, touched her, made love to her. At first she had moaned in protest but then they'd become moans of pleasure. But at the exact moment he was about to do away with all the mind-blowing foreplay and enter her body to take total possession, she had awakened.

She pulled herself into a sitting position and struggled to calm her ragged breath. Perspiration cloaked her body, a sign of just how long she had been in denial. For a brief moment, everything had seemed real, including the way his skin felt beneath her palms, how thick and solid his muscles were against her body and just how good those same muscles felt melding into hers.

With a deep sigh of disgust, she threw the covers back and got out of bed. Why, after fifteen years, did she finally become attracted to a man who just happened to be the father of the boy who could become her worst nightmare? On the way to the bathroom, she inwardly cursed for finding Chance so damn handsome.

As she turned on the shower and began stripping out of her damp nightclothes, she thought about how her life had been over the past fifteen years. Sam was the first and only man she had slept with. Once Tiffany had been born, her precious little girl had become the most important thing to her, her very reason for existing, and the years that followed had been busy ones as a single parent. Although a number of men had shown interest, a relationship with any of them had taken a backseat. It was either bad timing or a lack of desire on her part to share herself with anyone other than Tiffany. In essence, she had placed her needs aside to take care of the needs of her child.

But now it seemed that those needs were catching up with her. Something sharp, unexpected and mind-blowingly stimulating was taking its toll. For years she had been able to keep those urges under control, but now it seemed a losing battle. It was as if her body was saying, *I won't let you deny me any longer.*

As she stepped into the shower and stood beneath the spray of water, she knew that she was in deep trouble. Not only did she have to deal with the situation going on with Tiffany and Marcus, but she had to deal with her own attraction to Chance. It was sheer foolishness to become this enamored with a man she had only met a couple of days ago, and the very thought that she had gone so far as to dream about him making love to her was totally unacceptable.

No matter how intense the sexual longings invading her body, she had to get a grip. And more than anything, she had to remember that men couldn't be depended on to always do the right thing. Sam had proven that to her in a big way, and so had her father. He had let her down when he'd meekly gone along with her mother's treatment of her when she'd gotten pregnant.

Moments later when she stepped out of the shower, dried off and donned a fresh nightgown, she had to concede that the water hadn't washed any thoughts of Chance from her mind. She had a feeling that even when she went back to bed she wouldn't experience anything close to a peaceful sleep.

CHAPTER THREE

"You actually invited Marcus and his father for dinner on Sunday!"

Kylie lifted a brow as she washed her hands in the kitchen sink. Surprised at the excitement she heard in her daughter's voice, she turned to meet her gaze. "I take it that you don't have a problem with it."

The enthusiasm in Tiffany's voice dropped a degree when she shrugged her shoulders and said, "No, why should I? Just as long as you and Mr. Steele aren't going to try and break us up, because it won't happen. Marcus and I are—"

"Madly in love," Kylie rushed in to finish, stifling her anger as she dried her hands. "I know." If she heard her daughter exclaim the depth of her love for Marcus Steele one more time she would scream.

"I thought it would be a good idea for me to finally meet Marcus, considering how you feel about him," Kylie said.

"Why is Mr. Steele coming?"

"Because he's Marcus's father and, like me, he wants what's best for his child."

"Oh, then he won't have to worry about a thing because I am the best."

Kylie rolled her eyes thinking her daughter was getting conceited lately—another of Sam's traits rearing its ugly head.

"So the two of you have been talking a lot?"

Kylie frowned as she began making the pancakes for breakfast. "The two of who?"

"You and Mr. Steele."

"More than we've wanted to, I'm sure," Kylie said with forced calmness. The last thing her daughter needed to know was just what an impact Chance Steele was having on her. Just as she'd figured last night, she hadn't been able to go back to sleep without visions of him dancing around in her head.

"How does he look?"

Many of the descriptive words that came to mind she couldn't possibly share with her daughter. "He's handsome, so I take it that Marcus is handsome, too."

Tiffany beamed. "Yes, of course." Then seconds later she said, "I heard Mr. Steele is nice."

Kylie expelled a deep breath. "I don't know him well enough to form an opinion but I have no reason to think that he's not." Although she pretended nonchalance, she couldn't stop herself from glancing over at Tiffany and asking, "Who told you he was nice?"

"Marcus. He thinks the world of his father."

Kylie's first reaction at hearing that statement was to ask why, if Marcus thought the world of his dad, he was causing Chance so much grief.

"He doesn't date much."

"Who?"

"Mr. Steele."

With his good looks and fine body, Kylie found that hard to believe. "Don't you think you need to start getting dressed for school?" she prompted, not wanting to discuss Chance any longer.

Tiffany nodded. "I'll be back in time for pancakes," she said as she rushed out of the kitchen.

When she was gone, Kylie leaned against the counter wondering why Chance had dominated their conversation. Was there a possibility that Tiffany was nervous about meeting Marcus's father? She couldn't help but remember the first time Sam had taken her to meet his parents. They hadn't been impressed with her and hadn't wasted any time letting her and Sam know they thought the two of them were too young to be involved.

Too bad she hadn't taken the Millers's opinion seriously. How differently things would have turned out if she had. But then she could never regret having Tiffany in her life, even now when her daughter was determined to make her hair gray early.

So, she thought as she pulled the orange juice out of the refrigerator, Chance didn't date often. Rather interesting...

CHANCE LEANED BACK IN the chair and stared out his office window. Instead of reading the report from the research-and-development department, he was sitting at his desk thinking of a reason to call Kylie Hagan. After that dream last night, he had awoken obsessed with hearing her voice.

Gut-twisting emotions clawed through him. It was bad enough that his son was totally besotted with the daughter, now it seemed he was becoming obsessed with the mother. He hadn't even managed to brush his teeth this morning without Kylie consuming his thoughts. He gritted those same teeth, not liking the position he was in one damn bit.

It wasn't as if he hadn't dated since Cyndi's death. But he quickly admitted that Kylie was different from any woman he'd taken out. She had a strong, independent nature that he admired. She had raised her child alone and when times had gotten tough with the downsizing of her job, she had made what she'd felt were the best decisions for the both of them. Even considering all of that, he still wondered what about her had not only grabbed his attention but was holding it tight. Could it be that now that he was getting older with a son who would be leaving for college in a couple of years, the thought of being alone scared him? Of course, he had his brothers, but they had their own lives.

Sebastian was the corporation's problem solver and troubleshooter. The Steele Corporation was more than just a company to Bas; it was his lifeline. Bas had been the last brother to join the company, and of the four, he had been the one to give their parents the most grief while growing up. Cutting school on a regular basis had been minor considering the other things he'd done. His reputation for getting into mischief was legendary. Trouble had seemed to find Bas, even when he wasn't looking for it. His engagement had mystified his brothers since he was the last Steele anyone would have thought would want to tie the knot.

Then there was Morgan, who headed R & D. Although he dated, everyone teased Morgan about holding out for the perfect woman. So far he hadn't found a woman who qualified for the role, although he was convinced one existed.

Last but not least was Donovan, who women claimed could seduce them with his voice alone. The youngest of the Steele brothers headed product administration, but unlike Bas, who was married to the corporation, Donovan always managed to carve out some playtime.

"It doesn't look like you're busy, big brother, so I'll just come in."

Chance turned his head and watched as Bas entered his office. He sat up, a little surprised that anyone, including his brother, had made it past his secretary without being announced. "Where's Joanna?" he asked. It was a rare occurrence for Joanna Cabot to leave her post without advising him.

Bas smiled. "Just where is your mind today, Chance? Have you forgotten that Robert Parker is retiring and today's his last day in sales? We were all at the celebration downstairs and wondering where you were. I made an excuse for you by telling everyone you probably had gotten detained on an important call."

Chance muttered a low curse. He had forgotten about Robert's retirement party. Robert had been part of the Steele Corporation when their father, Lester Steele, had run things. Now their retired parents were living the life in the Keys, doing all the things they'd always dreamed of doing, and had left the family business in the hands of their capable sons and niece.

"Yes, I'd forgotten about it."

Bas leaned against the closed door. "Umm, and you were just talking about it yesterday, which makes me wonder what's weighing so heavily on your mind."

Chance stood and quickly slipped into his suit jacket. "Trust me, you don't want to know."

Bas scowled. "You aren't losing sleep over that Marcus affair, are you? You are chilling like we told you to do, right?"

Chance decided not to tell Bas that the Marcus affair had conveniently become his own personal affair, thanks to Tiffany Hagan's mother. "Yes, I'm chilling."

Bas laughed. "You wouldn't know how to chill if your life depended on it."

Chance rolled his eyes, grinning. "Look who's talking."

It was a couple of hours later that Chance arrived back in his office. A part of him was still obsessed with hearing Kylie's voice. Deciding not to fight it any longer, he pulled out his wallet to find the business card she had given him the other day at the café. He picked up the phone, then put it back down. Damn, he wanted to do more than talk to her. He wanted to see her.

He reached for the phone and punched in the number to connect with his secretary. "Ms. Cabot, I'm leaving early today. If an emergency comes up you can reach me on my cell phone."

Strategy and tact were the methods he'd mentioned to Kylie for bringing their children around. Little did she know he was about to apply that same technique on her.

KYLIE TURNED AT THE SOUND of the shop door opening with a smile of greeting on her lips. The smile quickly faded when she saw it was the one man who had invaded her dreams last night.

She took a calming breath, remembering her reaction the first time she'd seen him when he'd walked through her door two days ago. Nothing had changed. Dressed in another powerhouse business suit, he looked drop-dead gorgeous.

She tried not to stare at him like a love-struck teen-ager, but found she was helpless in doing so. Chance Steele wasn't just any man. He was the one man who had started her blood circulating again in some very intimate places. He was definitely a man who was the very epitome of everything male.

"Hi," she said, deciding to break the silence when they just stood there staring at each other.

"Hi." He then glanced around. "You're not busy."

"No, the lunch crowd has come and gone."

"Oh. Would you like to go out?"

She raised a brow. "Out where?"

"To lunch."

Surprise flickered in the depths of Kylie's dark eyes. "To lunch?"

"Yes," he said, giving her a smile that made her stomach clench. "Would you go to lunch with me?"

"Why? Do we need to talk about the kids again?"

"No."

That single word sent her mind into a spin. He wanted to take her out but not to talk about the kids. Then what on earth would they talk about?

Chance must have seen the question in her eyes because he said, "I discovered something very important yesterday at the café, Kylie."

"What?"

"I enjoyed your company a lot. A whole lot." Then as an afterthought, he added, "I don't date often."

His confession was the same as Tiffany had said that very morning. Although she knew it probably wasn't good manners, Kylie couldn't help asking, "Why?"

He shrugged. "For a number of reasons, but I can probably sum it up in one rationale."

"Which is?"

"Lack of interest."

Kylie knew all about lack of interest. She'd been dealing with it for over fifteen years. She hadn't wanted the drama of getting into a hot and heavy relationship with someone, nor had she wanted to expose Tiffany to the drama, either. "Oh, I see."

"Do you?"

Nervously, Kylie stared down at her hands, confused by a lot of questions, the main one being why she was more attracted to Chance than any other man. She lifted her head. "Then maybe I don't see after all."

Her heart began racing when he started crossing the room. When he came to a stop directly in front of her, he placed his finger under her chin, lifting her gaze to meet his. "In that case, for us to go to lunch together is a rather good idea."

She was warmed by his touch. "Why would you think that?"

"Because it would make things easier for us on Sunday if we were honest with ourselves about a few things now."

Kylie's eyes clung to his, knowing he was right. There was no need to play dumb. There was something happening between them that she didn't need or want, but it was happening anyway. And they needed to get it out in the open, talk about it and put a stop to it before it went any further. How could they help their kids battle lust when they'd found themselves in the same boat?

She drew in a deep breath. "All right, if you'll give me a second, I need to close up and put the Out to Lunch sign on the door."

He nodded. "Take your time. I'm not going anywhere."

Chance stood to the side while Kylie went about closing her shop. His eyes roamed over her with more than mild intensity. For some reason, today she looked even younger than she had the other days. She was wearing shorts and a top again, and he thought her legs were just as shapely as he remembered and her body just as curvy.

He couldn't help the desire that quickly escalated to extreme hunger and hit him in the gut. For one intense moment, he felt a burning desire to walk across the room and take her mouth with his. The need to taste her was driving him insane.

"I'm ready."

He blinked, realizing she had spoken. He inhaled a calming breath and fought for composure. He was ready, too, but doubted they were ready for the same thing.

"ONE OF THESE DAYS I'LL take you to a place that serves something other than hamburgers and fries."

Kylie smiled as he led the way to their table. To save time they had decided to grab a quick lunch at Burger King. "I don't mind," she said, as butterflies began floating around in her stomach. Did he realize he'd just insinuated that he would be taking her out again?

"It's not too crowded," he said, pulling the chair out for her.

"No, I guess the lunch crowd has come and gone."

"Which is fine with me. Before I go order, I think I need to do this." He pulled off his tie and stuffed it into the pocket of his jacket. Then he reached for the top of his shirt and worked a couple of buttons through their holes. "I'm a little too overdressed for this place."

Kylie watched as he walked off toward the counter, thinking that an overdressed Chance was the last thing on her mind. Thoughts of an undressed Chance seemed to be cemented into her brain. In a suit he looked handsome, professional and suave. And she would bet that even in a pair of jeans and a shirt he would look rugged and sexy. She didn't want to think about how he would look without any clothes on at all. But she had, several times, day and night, and that wasn't good.

It didn't take long for him to return and they began digging into their food. It was only when they were halfway through their meal that Chance spoke. He leaned in close, smiled and said, "I was wondering about something."

"What?"

"Since we've assigned ourselves the task of monitoring our kids' behavior, to make sure they stay out of trouble, whom should we assign to do the same thing for us?"

CHAPTER FOUR

THAT WAS A GOOD QUESTION, Kylie thought as she held Chance's gaze from across the table. Who would make sure the two of them stayed out of trouble?

The smile on Chance's lips matched the one in his eyes. Still, she knew that, like her, Chance realized this was a serious discussion. A part of her wished she could forget that he was Marcus's father and that they'd met because of their children. But she couldn't forget, even while her attention focused on nothing but the shape of his mouth. It taunted her to lean in and cop a taste.

She drew in a deep breath, trying to regain control, and got a sniff of his cologne. The manly scent of him was unnerving, totally sexy.

"Don't look at me like that, Kylie."

She blinked and saw more than a bare hint of challenge in his eyes. She didn't have to wonder just how she'd been looking at him. The throb between her legs told the whole story and then some. It was a deep ache and it was all she could do to keep from asking him to relieve her of her pain.

She was astounded with her lack of strength where Chance was concerned and wished she could ignore how he made her feel, dismiss the longings he stirred inside of her. But at the moment she couldn't. At least not while her heart was beating a mile a minute and the heat was taking her body to an intolerable degree.

Regardless, she knew she had to fight temptation and take control. She wasn't a lustful teenager. She was a grown woman of thirty-one. A woman with a teenage daughter she should be concerned about. Tiffany was important. Tiffany was the only thing that mattered.

With all the strength she could muster, she broke eye contact and busied herself with pulling napkins out of the holder. "I don't want this, Chance," she said, knowing he knew full well what she meant.

He nodded. "To be honest with you, I don't want it, either, Kylie. So tell me how we can stop it."

She shrugged. It wasn't as if she had any answers. She was definitely lurking in uncharted territory. The only thing she knew was that around him she had the tendency to feel things she'd never felt before. No man had ever made her breathless, excited and hot. When it came to the opposite sex, she felt just as inexperienced as her daughter. Oh, sure, she'd engaged in sex before, and at the time she'd thought it was pretty good, once she'd gotten beyond the pain. But Sam had been just as young and inexperienced as she had been, and she figured what she'd always thought of as satisfaction was nothing more than an appeasement of her curiosity and the elation of finally reaching womanhood at the hands of someone she thought she loved.

But she wanted more than that for Tiffany. More than teenage lust eroding what could be a wonderful experience with the man she married. That was the reason she was sitting here, a little past one, with the sexiest man alive. It wasn't about them. It was about their children. They needed to realize that and get back on track.

"I think the first thing we should do is to remember

the reason we're here in the first place. You have a business to run and so do I, but our kids take top priority. Nothing else. My wants and needs have always come second to my daughter's and things will continue to be that way, Chance."

She paused briefly before she continued. "It's going to take the two of us working together to keep things from going crazy between Tiffany and Marcus. Shifting our concentration from them to us will not only make us lose focus, but will have us making some of the same mistakes they'd be making."

"So, you're suggesting that we pretend we don't have urges and that we aren't attracted to each other? You think it will be that easy?" he asked.

The frustration in his tone matched her own feelings. "No, it won't be easy, Chance. To be quite honest with you, it will probably be the hardest thing I've had to do in fifteen years."

She thought about the men in her past who had shown interest in her and how she'd sent them away without a moment's hesitation. There had been that new guy at work who tried hitting on her several times; then there was that guy who worked at the post office who had enjoyed flirting with her. Not to mention that handsome man at the grocery store who gave her that "I want to get to know you" smile. But none of them had piqued her interest like Chance had. None of them had offered any temptation. Chance was too incredibly sexy for his own good. Even worse, he was a pretty nice guy.

"We have to keep our heads," she said. "Or the kids will take advantage without us realizing it." Kylie hoped—prayed—that he wouldn't give her any hassles. They needed to be in accord. They needed to be a team with one focus.

He leaned over the table, closer to her. "I know you're right but…"

She lifted an arched brow. "But what?"

"At this very moment, the only thing I want is to kiss you."

His blatant honesty, as well as the heat of his gaze, burned her. She could actually feel the flame. His softly uttered words only intensified the throbbing between her legs, and made fiery sensations rip through her stomach. It wouldn't take much for her to lean in to him and mesh her lips with his, satisfy at least one craving they evidently both had. And without any control, her body began doing just that, leaning closer…

They jumped apart at the sound of a car backfiring. Kylie's eyes widened and her cheeks tinted with embarrassment. They were sitting in the middle of Burger King thinking of sharing a kiss, for heaven's sake!

"Are you ready to go?" Chance asked.

Kylie drew in a deep breath. Yes, she was ready. The sooner she got back to the shop the better. There, she could regain her sensibilities, take back control of her mind. No doubt Chance had more experience dealing with this sort of thing than she did. Regardless, she knew she couldn't depend on him to keep things in perspective. An affair with Chance was the last thing she wanted. No matter what, she had to remember that.

"THANKS FOR LUNCH, CHANCE," Kylie said to him as he backed out of Burger King's parking lot.

"You're welcome. I enjoyed it."

For the next few minutes they shared pleasant conversation in which he told her about his parents retiring to Florida and about his three brothers and three female cousins. It wasn't hard to tell that the Steele family was close.

"So how is your flower business?"

She appreciated him asking. It was a good idea to stick to general conversation. "So far business is good. Before moving here I did my research, made sure adding another florist wasn't overcrowding the market."

"You have a good location since it's an area ripe for development."

"Yes, and I owe it all to Lena. She put her real estate skills to work and gave me a call one day. It was just what I was looking for, exactly what I needed. I grow a lot of my own plants in the greenhouse out back. Those I don't grow I get from a pretty good supplier."

She paused briefly as he glanced over at her. He hadn't put back on his jacket or tie, which made her wonder if he planned to go back to the office or just chill the rest of the day. She scolded herself when she realized what Chance did was really none of her business.

"If you don't mind, I need to make a stop. It won't take but a couple of minutes. I promise to get you back to your shop before two."

"All right."

She blinked seconds later when he pulled up to a car wash. She thought his SUV looked pretty clean. It was definitely in better condition than her car.

"I have those pesky bugs on my fender," Chance said, as he eased his truck into the bay.

The automatic equipment began moving around the truck, blasting water over it and hiding them from the outside world in a cocoonlike waterfall. The insides of the truck suddenly got dark, intimate, warm.

She didn't want to but she couldn't help but glance

over at Chance. Seeing the seductive look in his eyes, she knew this was no coincidence. Coming here had been deliberate on his part.

"This is the first time I've done this. I've never brought a woman with me to get my truck washed," he said in a husky voice. "But I want to kiss you, Kylie."

Kylie swallowed at the passion she heard in his voice. She hated admitting it but she wanted to kiss him, as well. But still…

"Chance, I thought we decided that—"

"Please." His tone vibrated with a need that touched her when she knew it shouldn't. "Ten minutes is all I ask."

Kylie blinked. *Ten minutes? A car wash took that long?* As if reading the question in her eyes, he said, "I'm getting a heavy-duty wash."

"Oh." Still, she'd never been kissed for ten minutes.

"Come here, Kylie. Please."

The knot in her throat thickened. She knew he wanted her to slide over to him, and heaven help her but she wanted it, too. Without stopping to question the wisdom of her actions, she unsnapped her seat belt and scooted toward him. When she got close enough he pushed back the seat and pulled her into his lap. His arms automatically closed around her shoulders as he held her in a warm embrace.

"Thank you," he said huskily, before sweeping his tongue across her lips and taking her mouth, hungrily, thoroughly. The first touch of his mouth on hers had her automatically parting her lips. And now with the insertion of his tongue, he brought out a responsive need in her so deep, she began to intimately stroke his tongue with hers.

She had never been kissed this way, had never known that such a way was possible. But it was clear as glass that Chance had a special, skillful technique. His tongue was stroking the top of her mouth, sliding over her teeth, entwining his tongue with hers, sucking relentlessly on it.

Her breasts, pressing against his chest, felt full, sensitive and tight. Instinctively, she wrapped her arms around his neck as they greedily consumed each other. She tasted every inch of his mouth while pressed against him, feeling the way his body had hardened beneath her bottom.

The kiss went on and on as his mouth continued to take hers, skillfully, thoroughly, tantalizing every bone in her body and making her conscious of just what a master he was at igniting sensations.

And they were ignited—by sensations she had never felt before. She was experiencing the emotions of a woman and not a sixteen-year-old girl. In reality, this was her first taste of passion and Chance was delivering it in grand style.

There was a need hammering deep within her that she didn't understand, but evidently Chance did, since he seemed to sense just what she wanted, just what she needed, even if she wasn't certain. The only thing she was sure about was that he had taken their kiss to a level she hadn't known possible.

The sound of a car door slamming made her remember where they were and what they were doing. The honking of a horn indicated that someone was behind them waiting for their vehicle to move. Still, Chance took his time easing his mouth from hers. She could barely think. She could barely breathe. And she could barely break the connection of the dark eyes locked with hers.

"I think the truck is clean enough now, don't you?" he asked throatily against her moist lips with a sound that sent sensuous chills down her body.

Kylie didn't trust herself to speak at the moment. When he released her, she slid out of his lap and back across the seat. She'd read about women being kissed senseless but never in her wildest dreams had she thought such a thing was possible. Boy, had she been wrong.

She snapped her seat belt back in place as she felt the truck move forward. When they were back in the sunlight, a dose of reality struck. They'd been in the midst of making out in his truck like teenagers. She inhaled deeply, wondering how she could have let things get so out of hand.

"It was inevitable, Kylie."

She glanced over at him. Just because what he said was true didn't mean she liked hearing it.

"Please don't have any regrets," he said softly.

How could she have regrets when she had been a willing participant, just as much into the kiss as he had been? However, she did intend to have her say. "We need to have more control, Chance. How can we expect our kids to have control if we don't?"

He pulled the truck to the side and parked it, and then glanced over at her. "They're kids, but we're adults, Kylie. Our wants and needs are more defined than theirs. And a lot more profound."

"Sounds like a double standard to me."

"It's not. That kiss we shared has nothing to do with our kids. That was strictly personal, between me and you."

She stared at him, hoping he understood what she was about to say. "I don't have any regrets about the kiss but it can't happen again, Chance."

A slow smile played across his lips. "That's easier said than done, Kylie. I tasted your response. You're a very passionate woman, more so than you even know. You've denied yourself pleasure for a long time and now that your body has savored just a sampling, it's going to want more."

She didn't like what he was insinuating. Okay, so she had been a little greedy back there, but still, she had her morals.

"And your principles have nothing to do with it," he said as if he'd read her mind. "So don't even think it. It's about needs that are as old and primitive as mankind. I have them and you have them, too."

She frowned. "And I'm supposed to jump into bed with any man just to appease him?"

"No. Only with me."

He evidently saw the startled look in her face, because he then added, "But I'm willing to wait until you're ready."

Kylie inhaled and decided it would be a waste of her time to tell him that no matter how much she had enjoyed their kiss, when it came to an affair, she would never be ready. Especially not with him.

ANOTHER NIGHT AND CHANCE couldn't sleep a wink. But at least tonight he wasn't being kept awake wondering how it would be to kiss Kylie since he'd gotten a real down-to-earth experience earlier that day.

And it had been better than he'd imagined.

The moments their lips had connected he had felt a slow sizzle all the way to his toes. The more he'd kissed her, the more she had wiggled closer for a better connection, and while his truck was getting the wash it really hadn't needed, he was inside with her locked in his arms, and getting hotter by the second.

She had felt like she belonged in his arms and the firm breasts that had been pressed against his chest had felt like they were meant to touch him that way. More than once he had been tempted to ease his hand under her blouse and cup her breasts, massage them, lift her blouse and lower his head and actually taste them.

The only reason he had finally lifted his mouth from hers had been to breathe in some air. He had heard the car behind them blowing the horn but he would have stayed right there and ignored the sound if he hadn't needed to breathe. What he'd told her was true. She was one responsive woman but he hadn't meant it as a bad thing. He was beginning to realize that everything about Kylie Hagan was all good.

He glanced over at the clock. It was a few minutes past eleven. He wondered if she was still awake. He reached for the phone, deciding there was only one way to find out.

TRYING TO GET TO SLEEP that night was torture for Kylie. The vivid memory of their kiss in Chance's truck, her sitting in his lap while his tongue stroked her mouth into sweet heaven, kept her wide awake.

She remembered the feel of her breasts, their fullness, their sensitivity, and how at one point she had wanted his lips to bestow the same magic on them that he was giving her mouth. Then there was the feel of his body growing hard beneath her bottom. She would have given anything to feel that same erection cradled into the V of her thighs.

Feeling frustrated in the worst possible way, she was about to get out of bed when her telephone rang. She reached over and picked it up. "Hello."

"I just wanted to hear your voice one more time tonight."

Kylie breathed deeply at the seductiveness of Chance's tone. She had wanted to hear his voice again, too, but hadn't had the nerve to call him. He was definitely bolder than she.

"Kylie?"

She swallowed hard before saying, "I'm here."

"Yes, but I wish you were here."

She shook her head. "That's not a good idea."

"Your opinion and not mine."

"We all have opinions."

"Yes, and we all have the capability of getting a good night's sleep. At least some of us do."

She lifted her eyebrows. Was he having trouble sleeping as well? "Try counting sheep."

"I tried that and it didn't work. Any more suggestions?"

She pulled herself up in bed and relaxed against the huge pillow. "We could talk."

"About what?"

"Anything you want to talk about—except what happened this afternoon."

There was a pause, and then he said, "Okay, fair enough. I'll let you choose the topic."

"All right. Tell me about Marcus. Whenever I ask Tiffany about him the only words she can fix her mouth to say are, 'Oh, he's simply wonderful.'"

Chance chuckled. "Hey, I'm the kid's father. Do you expect me to admit to any of his flaws? If she thinks he's wonderful, then who am I to disagree?"

"Be serious, Chance."

Evidently there was something he sensed in her voice that let him know she needed to know about Marcus before actually meeting him on Sunday.

"On a scale of one to ten with ten being exceptional, I'll give Marcus a nine. He isn't perfect but for the past sixteen years he has been a son any father would be proud to claim. He's smart, and he's also sensitive, something he inherited from his mother. Cyndi was a warm, loving and sensitive person."

The undisguised love she heard in his voice let her know that he had cared for his wife very much. "How old was Marcus when his mother died?"

"He was nine and he took her death hard. Thankfully, he had my parents, Cyndi's parents and my brothers and cousins. Still, there were times when I worried about him. I made Cyndi a promise the day before she died that I would do everything within my power to make sure that Marcus had all the opportunities that we either didn't have or didn't take advantage of, especially when it came to college."

She nodded. No wonder he was so intense about his son staying focused to get into a good university.

"Marcus knew of his mother's dreams for him and after she died it was as if he was trying to honor her memory by doing everything that she'd wanted. He was always at the top of his class, and I never had to remind him to do homework. He tried so hard to please me because I think in his mind, pleasing me meant pleasing his mom, as well."

"And then here comes Miss Tiffany.…"

Chance chuckled again and in her mind she could actually see a smile lighting up his eyes. "Ahh, yes, here comes Miss Tiffany. But before Tiffany came football.

I hadn't wanted him to play. I had played in school and I knew how grueling practice could be. I wasn't sure Marcus could handle it and still keep his grades up. I think that was the first time the two of us butted heads."

After a pause he said, "Luckily he had his uncles on his side. It took my brothers to make me see that I was being unrealistic and that it wasn't all about making good grades. Marcus has a few more years in high school to go, and kids these days need to be well-rounded, and I was keeping him from being that."

"So he started playing football?"

"Yes, and the girls started calling...and calling and calling. My phone was a regular hotline. But I think they annoyed him more than captivated his interest. At least until Tiffany."

"Tiffany used to call your house all the time?" Kylie asked, somewhat surprised.

"No, and that's what's so strange. I can't recall her ever calling. That's why I was taken aback when I found that note and was stumped further when Marcus told me, in no uncertain terms, just how he felt about her. It was as if she appeared one day out of the clear blue sky."

Kylie nodded. It was as if Marcus had appeared out of the clear blue sky, as well. He'd definitely been one well-kept secret.

"Now it's your turn."

"My turn?" Kylie echoed.

"Yes, to tell me all about Tiffany so I can be prepared."

Kylie's lips tilted into a smile. "I don't think anyone can ever get fully prepared for Tiffany. She's smart, funny and extremely outgoing. An extrovert if you've ever seen one. I think that's why she's having trouble making friends at school since we moved here. I don't think the kids know how to take her. They see her genuinely exuberant nature as being insincere and phony."

Kylie's smile then widened. "There is, however, something that I do think you should know."

"What?"

"I told Tiffany that as Marcus's father you would want what was best for him."

"And?"

"And she feels certain that you're going to like her when the two of you meet because she is definitely the best."

Chance laughed. "Sounds like a person with a lot of confidence."

"A little too much at times. It comes from her dad's side of the family."

"Hey, there's nothing wrong with having an over-abundance of confidence."

"Remember you said that when you meet her on Sunday."

There was a hint of amusement in Chance's voice when he said, "I will. And by the way, is there anything you need for me to bring?"

"Yes, a lot of prayer just in case Tiffany and Marcus don't want to go along with our plans for them."

"HELLO."

"Marcus, are you awake?"

Marcus clutched the phone as he buried his head back underneath his pillow. "Tiffany, it's Saturday morning. Nobody gets up before eight on Saturdays."

"I do. Some of us have chores to do and the earlier they get done the better. I only called this time of the

morning because you said your dad always plays basketball every Saturday morning with his brothers, and
you told me to call if I had anything to report."

Marcus removed the pillow. She had gotten his attention. "And you have something to report?"

"Yes. Your dad called here last night. And it was
late."

Marcus lifted a curious eyebrow. "How do you
know?"

"Your phone number showed up on our caller ID this
morning and it showed the time as close to midnight.
That means our parents are talking after-hours. That's
a good sign."

"But what if he just called to get directions to your
house or something?"

"At midnight? Think positive, Marcus."

"Okay. But we should be able to tell if anything
is going on when we see them together tomorrow,
right?"

"I hope so, Marcus."

"Yeah, I hope so, too, considering how much of a pain
in the butt I've been to my dad over the past week."

CHAPTER FIVE

BY THE TIME CHANCE AND Marcus arrived at Kylie's home on Sunday evening, Chance was chomping at the bit to see her again.

The moment they pulled into her driveway, he saw her standing in the backyard in front of a barbecue grill. Kylie looked up the moment she heard his truck and their gazes connected. His gut clenched when an irrepressible smile lit her face.

"Wow! Tiffany was right. Her mom is a knockout," Marcus said with such profound amazement that Chance sharply turned his head to look at his son.

Marcus's gaze was glued to Kylie, so Chance let himself stare at her, too, letting his eyes roam over her features. Kylie was a beautiful woman, and that was the main reason he—a man known to have good self-control—had been in such a bad way since meeting her. She was wearing a sundress and the turquoise color flattered her.

"Isn't she pretty, Dad?"

Chance swallowed. In his book she was more than pretty, or beautiful, or even gorgeous. There wasn't a word he had to define just what she was, although the word *perfection* came pretty close. And not for the first time he wondered how she'd succeeded in keeping men at bay all these years.

"Dad?"

He knew his son was waiting on his response but he dared not look at Marcus for fear of him recognizing the lust in his eyes. "Yes, she's pretty."

Moments later, Marcus asked, "Aren't we going to get out?"

Feeling a lot more confident that he had regained a semblance of control, Chance glanced over at Marcus. "You sound rather anxious."

Marcus chuckled. "I am. I want you to meet Tiffany. She's really something else."

Chance nodded as he opened the door to the truck, thinking that, evidently, it ran in the family, because he thought Kylie was something else, as well.

As Kylie watched Chance get out of the truck, she could no more stop the flash of desire and excitement that raced through her body than she could have denied her next breath. And to make matters worse, Chance's eyes were glued to her and she knew he was remembering their kiss as much as she was.

She had thought about it a dozen times since it had happened. Her response to him had surprised her, overwhelmed her, until she'd come to grips with the fact that Chance Steele wasn't your typical man.

Today he was wearing a pair of jeans and a crisp white shirt, and it was the first time she'd seen him dressed in anything other than a suit. He looked the epitome of masculinity, fine and sexy.

She forced her gaze from him to the young man walking by his side. So this was Marcus, the potential root of her troubles. He favored Chance and was almost as tall. He had the look of youth, but like his father, Marcus's features were sharp and well-defined. And she was glad to see that he eschewed the popular baggy pants and was dressed neatly in a pair of shorts and a shirt. It wasn't lost on her that he was checking her out with as much curiosity as she was him.

"I hope we aren't too early," Chance said, breaking into Kylie's thoughts when they reached her.

They *were* early; a good thirty minutes to be exact, but she didn't have any complaints. "No, Mr. Steele, you're right on time," she said, addressing him formally. They had decided not to let the kids know they had been in constant communication with each other. They didn't want to run the risk of Marcus and Tiffany thinking they were gaming and plotting behind their backs, even if they were.

"Tiffany is inside getting dressed and I was setting up the grill. I hope hamburgers and hot dogs sound okay."

Chance chuckled. "You aren't trying to pay me back with the hamburgers, are you?"

"Pay you back for what?" Marcus asked.

Both Chance and Kylie glanced at him. "Nothing," Chance said quickly, clearing his throat. She knew he hadn't meant to let that slip.

"You must be Marcus," she said and then gave him her full attention and offered him her hand.

His grin was unrepentant as he took it. "Yes, ma'am. And you've got to be Tiffany's mom. You're pretty, just like her."

Kylie smiled. This kid was a real charmer and before the evening was over she intended to see if his charm was the real thing or not. "Thanks."

"Do you need our help with anything, Ms. Hagan?" Chance asked, glancing around at her big backyard.

Kylie looked up at him and smiled. "I think it would

be fitting if you called me Kylie, that is if you don't mind me calling you Chance."

He smiled. "No, I don't mind at all."

"In that case, Chance, there is this one little thing I might need help with. Tiffany thought it would be a good idea to put up the volleyball net in case anyone was interested in playing after dinner. If I can get you and Marcus to set it up, that would be wonderful."

"Consider it done. Just tell us where it is and where you want it to go."

"It's over there and I think that would be a good spot," she said, turning to point to an area of her yard.

"I think so, too. That should be fun. I haven't played volleyball in years."

"Should I be worried about that, Dad? I don't think we have anything for sore, aching muscles at home," Marcus said, grinning.

Chance's mouth curved into a smile as he glanced over at his son. "I might be a lot older than you, Marcus Pharis Steele, but I think I can still manage to hit a ball or two over a net."

That's not all he's capable of doing, Kylie thought, shifting her gaze from Chance to Marcus. No matter what disagreements they might have had since Tiffany had appeared on the scene, it was rather obvious that Chance and his son had a close relationship.

"You're going to have to prove that big-time, Dad."

"Hey, kid, you're on," Chance countered and then turned his attention to Kylie. "What do you think?"

"I think that this I got to see," she told him, laughing.

"You'll more than see it. I want your participation, as well. The young against what this pup considers as 'the old'. I think we need to show our children just what we're made of. How about it, Kylie?"

She grinned. "I'm game if you are."

"MR. STEELE?"

Chance cast a quick glance over his shoulder, blinked and did a double take. He turned around and blinked again, shaking his head in disbelief. He looked into the face of what had to be a younger version of Kylie. Her daughter looked so much like her it was uncanny. He watched as her mouth curved into the same type of smile Kylie wore.

He automatically smiled back. "Yes, and you must be Tiffany," he said, taking the hand she offered. "Marcus has told me a lot about you."

"And it was all good, right?"

Chance chuckled, remembering what Kylie had said about her daughter's high confidence level. "Yes, it was all good."

She glanced around. "And where is Marcus?"

"I sent him to the store to pick up some more sodas."

"Oh. Mom told me to tell you that she'll be back outside in a minute. She's finishing up the potato salad and thought I should come out and keep you company."

He smiled. "That would be nice since I'd like to get to know you. So what are your plans for the future?" he asked as he leaned against the stone post holding up the covered patio. Kylie had assigned him the task of cooking the hamburgers and hot dogs, something he had convinced her he was pretty good at.

Tiffany laughed. "You don't have to worry about me and Marcus rushing off doing anything stupid when we become of age, like getting married or something."

Chance grimaced. God, he hoped not. "That's good to hear. What about the two of you making plans to cut school again?"

She grinned. "Okay, I admit that wasn't a smart idea, but like I told Mom, our last two periods of the day are boring."

Chance folded his arms across his chest and regarded her directly. "And I'm sure your mom told you that it doesn't matter how boring the classes are, you and Marcus belong in school."

Tiffany's expressive eyes filled with remorse. "Yes, sir, and Marcus and I talked about it. We didn't intend to get you and my mom upset with us, but Mom thinks I'm too young to start dating and you—"

When it seemed that she had encountered some difficulty in finishing what she was about to say, Chance lifted an eyebrow. "I'm what?"

She leaned in closer and squinted her eyes against the smoke coming from the grill. "Don't take this personally, Mr. Steele, and Marcus says you're a nice dad and everything, but at times you can be too overbearing where his education is concerned."

Chance couldn't help but laugh. He was being told that he was overbearing by a fifteen-year-old girl! She might have inherited her high confidence level from her father but her directness had definitely come from her mother. "Marcus thinks I'm overbearing, does he?"

"Yes, and you don't have to be, you know. Marcus is one of the smartest guys I know. In fact, the way we became such good friends is because the teacher had him help me on a class assignment that I was having problems with. He wants to go to the best college one day, just like you want him to. You're just going to have to trust him to do the right thing. And he will because he wants those things for himself as well as for you."

Chance's smile widened. Tiffany's expressive eyes had gone from being filled with remorse to being filled with sincerity and he liked that. He also liked what she was saying, and had to admit that his curiosity was piqued about something. "And where will all this leave you, Tiffany?"

"Me?"

"Yes, you. Where will that leave you when Marcus goes off to college two years from now?" Assuming your relationship lasts that long, he wanted to add.

Tiffany shrugged. "When he leaves I'll have another year of school to complete and then I'll be leaving for college myself. I doubt it will be to the same college Marcus will be attending since my grades aren't nearly as good as his, but it won't matter. Marcus and I have decided that the best thing for us to do is to make sure we both get a good college education. Then we will return home afterward and be together."

Chance's eyebrows drew together in surprise. The last time he and Marcus had talked, his son had threatened to hang around Charlotte and go to a local college. He released a satisfied sigh. He was certainly glad to hear this recent turn of events and was about to tell her so when they heard his truck pulling into the driveway, which meant Marcus had returned.

"Mr. Steele, Marcus and I can finish cooking if you want to go into the house and keep my mom company. I'm sure she's bored making the potato salad."

Thoughts of being inside the house alone with Kylie had his mind reeling. "You think so?"

"Yes."

He rubbed his chin thoughtfully. "Have you told your

mom what you and Marcus have decided about your futures?"

"No, not yet."

"Do you mind if I do?"

"No, I don't mind. It's not like me and Marcus won't be girlfriend and boyfriend until he leaves for college, because we will. But we won't let anything interfere with him going away to a good university, I can assure you of that. We want what's best for our future." Then with a smile on her face she said, "I'll go help Marcus with the sodas."

Chance watched her walk away, thinking he really liked Tiffany Hagan.

"SO WHAT DO YOU THINK?" Tiffany whispered to Marcus while helping him unload the soda from the truck.

Marcus grinned. "I think my dad likes your mom. In fact, I have a feeling that they may have seen each other another time in addition to that day he visited her flower shop."

"What makes you think that?"

"Because they're too friendly with each other to have met only that one time. And then there was this private joke they shared."

"What private joke?"

"It had something to do with hamburgers."

"Hamburgers?" Tiffany raised a confused brow. "So you think he likes her?"

"He definitely notices that she's a woman, which is more attention than he's given other ladies, including those at church who are always vying for his and my uncle Morgan's and my uncle Donovan's attention. They know it's a lost cause with Uncle Bas since he's already engaged."

After placing the soda cans in the cooler, Marcus continued. "When we pulled up today and I saw your mom for the first time, I commented on how pretty she was and he agreed with me. And he kept staring at her with this funny look on his face. He's been smiling a lot since he got here. I don't recall ever seeing my dad smile this much."

Marcus then gave Tiffany a questioning glance. "You do think we're doing the right thing, don't you? Making our parents think something is going on between us so we can get them interested in each other?"

Tiffany nodded her head. "Yes, I think we're doing the right thing. I have to admit that at first I was doing it just to get Mom off my back because I thought she needed a life, but today she was actually humming. She was humming because she's in a good mood, and I think the reason she's in a good mood is because of you and your dad's visit. Seeing her that way made me realize just how lonely my mom probably has been. All she's ever had is me. Like I told you, I don't ever recall her dating anyone. In a few years I'll be leaving for college and she'll be all alone if she doesn't meet someone and get serious about him."

Marcus nodded. "Yeah, Dad will be all alone when I leave for college, too, in two years. He has his parents and his brothers and cousins but it won't be the same. He needs to get involved with a nice lady like your mom. I really like her."

When they reached the backyard, Marcus glanced around. "Speaking of our parents, where are they?"

Tiffany's face glowed with excitement when she said, "My mom is inside making the potato salad, and I suggested to your dad that he go inside and keep her company, and that you and I were capable of doing the cooking."

Marcus smiled down at her. "It seems our plan just might be working."

Tiffany tipped her head back and looked up at him, returning his smile. "Yes, it certainly appears that way. Now it's going to be up to us to make sure they get to spend more and more time together."

CHANCE STRODE INTO KYLIE's house, rounded the corner that led from the utility room to the kitchen and stopped dead in his tracks. For the first time in his life, he forgot how to breathe.

Kylie was standing on a stool trying to get something out of a top cabinet. Stretching upward, the sundress she was wearing had raised, showing off a pair of luscious hips and those legs of hers that he admired so much.

His conscience gave him a hard kick. He shouldn't be standing in the middle of her kitchen ogling her this way. The truth of the matter was that he couldn't help it. The tantalizing sight of her had captured his attention and wouldn't let go. Pure, unadulterated hunger filled his gaze, keeping him focused primarily on her. She had a gorgeous body and, with the fantasies playing around in his head, he could just imagine his hands all over it, followed by his mouth.

He inhaled deeply when he felt his body getting hotter by the second. The need to escape back outside suddenly overwhelmed him. He had to get out of there, right now, this very instant, before he went up in flames or—even worse—before he did something outside of his control like cross the room, snatch her off that stool and take her into his arms and kiss her senseless.

KYLIE WASN'T CERTAIN if she'd heard a sound behind her or if her own body had alerted her to the fact that Chance was near. Whichever it was, she turned around so fast that she almost slipped off the step stool and had to fight to regain her balance.

Within an instant she was gathered into strong arms, avoiding a possible fall.

"You okay?"

The soft husky words from Chance's lips that fanned against her temple raised her temperature ten degrees. "Yes, I'm okay. You startled me. I hadn't heard you come in."

Instead of offering her any kind of explanation, he simply nodded as he held her body in his strong arms. For the next couple of seconds her mind questioned the sanity of them standing in her kitchen that way. What if the kids walked in?

She panicked at that possibility. "I'm okay, Chance. You can put me down now," she said, although she knew her voice lacked conviction.

"Are you sure you're okay?" he asked, his tone deep and rich, and his gaze remaining steadily on hers.

No, Kylie thought. She wasn't sure. Desire, the likes of which she'd never encountered before, raced through her, igniting her awareness, her attraction and her fire. Her eyes locked with his and at that instant she felt safe and protected in his arms, even with the feel of his body growing hard beneath her, which reminded her of the kiss they had shared Friday at the car wash.

With her teeth she caught the edge of her bottom lip, thinking she was just where she had dreamed of being last night—in his arms. Would it be so terrible if she stayed there just a little longer?

"Where are the kids?" she asked softly, tilting her head back and not breaking eye contact.

"Outside, cooking the rest of the meat."

"That should take at least five minutes."

"I'm counting on at least ten," he said.

She felt him sliding her down his body, lowering her feet to the floor. But he kept his hand at her waist, not intending for her to go anywhere out of touching distance. When she was standing, her legs automatically parted slightly to gain her balance; ironically it was just enough room for him to pull her close and place his thigh between them. She felt him again, the hardness of his erection that was resting between her legs.

"Why didn't you let me know that you had come inside?" she asked as intense heat shot up her core.

An apologetic smile touched his lips. "I couldn't have spoken even if I had wanted to, Kylie. Seeing you on that stool like that had me barely breathing. Has anyone ever told you that you've got one hell of a nice figure?"

She tried not to be touched by the thought that he liked the way her body looked. "Yes, but it never really mattered."

"Oh."

"Until now."

He bent toward her. "You're sure?"

"Positive."

He intended to be certain of that. Moving his hand to the swell of her hips, he gently pulled her closer as he leaned down and slanted his mouth over hers. She tasted sweeter than he remembered and he was helpless to do anything but deepen the kiss. He knew the exact moment she placed her arms around his neck, bringing their bodies closer into a locked embrace.

What he was sharing with her was a degree of passion

he hadn't shared with any woman in over seven years, and he was desperate for anything and everything she was offering. He suddenly felt it, a primitive need to bind her to him in the most elemental way. But he also knew he wanted more from her than just her body. He wanted her mind and soul, as well.

The sound of their kids' laughter came through the closed window and they parted quickly, but he didn't release her. Resting his forehead against hers, he breathed in deeply, seeing the passionate look in her eyes and knowing it mirrored his own.

He motioned his head toward the back door. "You don't think they're outside burning our dinner, do you?" he asked, making an attempt at gaining control.

"I hope not," she replied, trying to breathe again normally.

"I came inside to keep you company. Tiffany suggested it."

"Did she?"

"Yes. Is that a bad thing?"

"Only if it meant doing so would give her more time alone with Marcus."

Chance gave her an incredibly sexy smile. "I didn't think of that. But I guess there's only so much they can do outside in the open."

Kylie smiled. "Thank heavens for that."

"And she happened to mention something to me that she said she hadn't told you about yet."

"What?" she asked, her voice barely above a whisper, hoping whatever it was would not make her fall dead in a faint. She had asked, and Tiffany, although upset with her for asking, had assured her that she was still a virgin.

Evidently Chance heard the panic in her voice and

an easy smile touched his lips. "Relax, Kylie, that isn't it. Far from it."

"Thank goodness for that."

"I personally don't think they've taken their relationship to that level, which is a good thing. In fact, I'm a little more confused than before by what she said, although it pleases me."

"Dammit, Chance, don't keep me hanging," Kylie said in a near desperate voice. "What did Tiffany tell you?"

"Our kids have decided that although they intend to remain girlfriend and boyfriend, they also intend to further their education by going off to college, after which they'll return here and then decide their future."

Kylie blinked. "Are you sure that's what she said?"

"I'm positive."

She shook her head. "It doesn't make sense. Earlier this week she was ranting and raving about how madly in love they were and nothing and no one would ever break them apart."

"I heard the same thing from Marcus. I guess they sat down and talked about it and in the end decided to take our advice. They were getting too serious way too fast."

"Whatever made them decide to slow things down, I'm extremely grateful for it. Do you think we still need to lay out the rules we came up with?"

Chance nodded. "They may think this way now but it might be a different story tomorrow. Besides, either way, there's plenty of trouble they can get into before Marcus actually leaves for school in two years."

And it was the kind of trouble Kylie was definitely familiar with. She agreed with Chance. It wouldn't hurt to let the kids know exactly where she and Chance stood and how they planned on handling the situation of them being a couple.

"Ready to go outside?" he asked.

"Just about. I just need to find that lid for the bowl of potato salad. That's what I was looking for when you came in."

"Then let me look for it."

Kylie watched as he crossed the room and, not needing a stool, reached up and opened the cabinet. He pulled out several lids. "Will one of these work?"

"Yes."

He placed them on the counter then crossed the room to her. He reached out and caressed his finger against her cheek. "Thanks for the kiss, Kylie. I needed it more than you will ever know."

He really didn't have to thank her. She'd needed it just as much as he had, although she wished she hadn't. "I think we need to get back outside now."

As much as Chance wanted to stay inside with her, a part of him knew she was right. "All right. Is there anything else you need for me to do before I go?"

A smile touched her lips. "No, but it might be a good idea for you to wipe your mouth. You're wearing the same shade lipstick I'm wearing."

"Now that the both of you are well fed, there's something Chance and I would like to discuss with you."

Both Marcus and Tiffany looked up from eating their ice cream. Marcus's smile faltered somewhat and Tiffany rolled her eyes heavenward. "I knew this day was going too good to last," she said. "What do you want to talk with us about, Mom?"

"Your relationship."

"What about it, Ms. Hagan?" Marcus asked her in a respectful tone.

Kylie glanced over at Chance, who nodded for her to continue. "Chance and I talked about the best way to approach the situation, especially since Tiffany isn't old enough to date yet."

"But I should be old enough, Mom. The other girls at my school began going out with boys when they were thirteen."

Kylie frowned. "I'm not going to discuss what the other girls are doing, Tiffany. You're my concern. And for me it's not a particular age but a maturity level. I personally don't think you're ready to begin dating."

"If you had your way I would never date!"

"That's not true. You're the one who has to prove to me that you're ready. But Chance and I do understand you and Marcus would like to spend some time together, so we came up with what we feel is a workable solution."

"And what solution is that?" Marcus asked when Tiffany refused to do so.

It was Chance who responded. "You and Tiffany can date only if the dates are chaperoned."

Tiffany glanced over at Marcus before looking back at their parents. "You mean that you'll be coming with us to the movies? Bowling? On picnics?"

"Yes," Kylie answered. "So what do you think?" She braced herself for her daughter's tirade.

"I think it's a wonderful idea," Tiffany said, smiling.

Kylie blinked. "You do?"

"Yes. Since Marcus and I will be getting married after college, I think it would be good that all four of us get to know each other." She smiled at Marcus. "Don't you agree, Marcus?"

He smiled back at Tiffany. "Right, and in the process we can prove to our parents just how responsible we are."

Kylie glanced over at Chance knowing he was just as confused as she was. Tiffany and Marcus were beaming. If anything, Kylie and Chance had thought their suggestion would be met with some pretty strong opposition.

"Well, if everyone agrees with our plan then that's great," he said.

"So how soon can we go someplace?" Tiffany asked excitedly.

"Where would you like to go?" Chance asked.

"Umm, I've never been camping and Marcus said you take him all the time."

Kylie rolled her eyes. "Tiffany, we're not talking about a family outing. We're talking about a date."

"I don't have a problem with Tiffany coming along the next time Marcus and I go camping," Chance said. "Of course that means that you'll have to come, too, Kylie."

"Yes, Mom. You've never been camping before, either."

"Yes, but that doesn't mean we can just invite ourselves on a camping trip, Tiffany."

"But Mr. Steele invited us."

"Yes, but only after you—"

"It's okay, Kylie, honest," Chance cut in to say. "Marcus and I would love for you and Tiffany to go camping with us. My family owns a cabin in the mountains so we're really not talking about roughing it too much. The cabin has two bedrooms, so you and Tiffany can take one and Marcus and I can take the other."

"I'm not sure that's a good idea," Kylie said as her gaze moved from one person to the next. "When Chance and I thought of supervised activities we didn't mean anything that involved staying anyplace overnight."

"Yes, but it would be fun and different, Mom, and you and I have never done anything fun and different."

Kylie leaned back in her chair. She thought the two of them had done several things that were fun and different. How about that train ride from New York to California a few years ago? And then there was that vacation to Disney World for Tiffany's twelfth birthday. Had it really been three years ago? Okay, so they hadn't actually done a lot of fun and different things together on a regular basis. But she really hadn't had the time since she'd been busy going to school and trying to move up the corporate ladder to provide for her and Tiffany.

"Please, Mom, just this once. Mr. Steele did say it would be okay."

Kylie glanced over at Chance. "Are you sure you don't mind?"

He smiled. "No, I don't mind. In fact I think it's a wonderful idea."

Chance's statement should have had a calming effect on her but it didn't. She was no longer concerned for Tiffany, but for herself. She didn't want to think about a weekend spent in a mountain cabin with Chance in such close quarters. With all the heat they could generate, the kids might think something was going on between them when it really wasn't.

"Well, Mom?"

The enthusiasm she heard in Tiffany's voice almost made her say yes, but a part of her held back. This was something she needed to really think about.

Instead of answering Tiffany, she looked over at Chance. "Let me think about it some more and I'll give you my answer within a week."

CHAPTER SIX

WITH A SIGH OF RESIGNATION, Chance walked into his office Monday morning and met his brothers' inquisitive gazes. He knew why they were there. Marcus had mentioned to them that they'd been invited to Kylie's for dinner and no doubt they wanted to know how things went. But he wouldn't make it easy for them. He would pretend that he hadn't a clue why they graced his office with their presence.

"Good morning. Is there any reason the three of you have taken over my office?" he asked, placing his briefcase down on his desk.

After a few moments, when no one replied, he exhaled a long sigh and said, "I don't recall us having a meeting this morning. I know I have a meeting with Bas later today, but what's up with you guys? Is anything wrong?"

Not surprisingly, it was Bas who stepped forward and said, "How about cutting the bull, Chance. You know why we're here. We want to know how things went yesterday."

Chance looked at him. "Was there a particular way they were supposed to go?"

"You tell us," Morgan said, frowning. "You were the one who was all bent out of shape last week when you found that note. Can we assume you blew things out of proportion and Tiffany Hagan isn't the threat to our nephew's future that you assumed she was?"

Chance leaned back in his chair. A part of him wanted to tell his brothers that Tiffany was no longer a threat but her mother definitely was. But there was no way he could do that and have a moment's peace from their inquisition. "No, Tiffany's not a threat and although I'm not going to say I overreacted, I will say that I think Kylie and I have everything under control."

Donovan quirked an eyebrow. "Kylie?"

"Yes, Kylie Hagan. Tiffany's mother."

Donovan smiled. "Oh, yeah, the one who's such a good-looker."

A dark scowl suddenly appeared on Chance's face and he leaned forward. "And how do you know that Kylie is good-looking?"

Donovan was taken aback by the bite in his brother's tone. "You told us, don't you remember? In fact, your exact words were, 'If the daughter looks anything like the mother then I'm in trouble.'"

"Oh." Too late, Chance recalled having said that. He leaned back in his chair again, ignoring the curious glances his brothers were now giving him.

"You know what, Chance?"

Chance glanced over at Morgan and frowned. "What?"

A smile curved Morgan Steele's lips. "I hate to tell you this, but I have a feeling that you've gotten yourself into some trouble."

"So THERE YOU HAVE IT, Chance," Bas was saying after handing him the written report. "I'm glad to say that considering everything, we're doing well. Although some of our competitors have gotten bruised by the severe trading conditions of the past few years, we've been successful because we're a company that sets the pace and doesn't just follow the trend. Still, whether we like it or not, sooner or later we're going to have to give some thought to the possibility of outsourcing in order to stay competitive. I don't like it any more than you, but that's the way things are going now and we need to continue to adapt to change, even change we don't particularly like."

Chance tossed the report on his desk. Bas was right. He didn't like the thought of outsourcing as a means to stay ahead of the game. With the new importance being placed on countries like India and China, for the past year he'd seen huge restructuring taking place in a number of manufacturing and production companies.

As the corporation's problem solver and trouble-shooter, Bas kept them in the know. He was an expert at tackling the company's complex problems. So far the Steele Corporation was not unionized because, during the twenty-five years of its existence, the employees had always been pleased with the fair treatment they'd received. Their salaries were more than competitive, and the Steele Corporation had a reputation of never having laid off an employee, even during some of the company's rough times.

However, according to Bas, there was talk in the production area that the Steele Corporation would be outsourcing to a foreign country.

"I'm still not ready to go that route, Bas. Our employees are loyal and we owe them for all the hard work they do. Our people are the reason this company is successful, not the products we produce and deliver. What we're going to have to do is to continue to focus on developing our employees and executing those manufacturing strategies that integrate people, processes and technologies to assure us tangible results. Until that stops happening, I refuse to entertain the thought of outsourcing to another country."

Bas smiled. "I fully agree with you. So what do we do about those rumors that we're headed that way the first of the year?"

"Before I leave for Dallas next week, how about setting up a meeting between me and the production department heads? I want to make sure they're delivering the same message to our employees. There's evidently a communication breakdown somewhere. And make sure you include Vanessa. She will be back in the office then," Chance said of his cousin Vanessa Steele who headed the PR Department and was presently vacationing in Europe.

"All right. Consider it done."

Chance studied his brother as Bas placed the items back into his briefcase. Bas was a hard worker—too dedicated at times since he lived, ate and breathed the Steele Corporation. That would make one wonder when he had time for a social life, which he evidently had since he was engaged to be married. "Seems to me that you need to chill more than I do, Bas."

Bas glanced up and his lips curved into a lethal half smile. "I beg to differ, Chance. You're the one who's tackling woman troubles. I'm not."

"It's hard to believe Cassandra is that understanding."

Bas shrugged. "Frankly, she's not but she knows how far to take her complaints."

A frown pulled at Chance's lips. Not for the first time he wondered what had possessed his brother to become engaged to Cassandra Tisdale, a staunch member of

Charlotte's elite social group. Cassandra and Bas were as different as day and night. The woman was so incredibly self-absorbed, it boggled Chance's mind that Bas had even given her the time of day, let alone become engaged to her. She had a tendency to think she was the most important thing that existed in this universe. And while she was shining and polished, it was known that Bas was more than a little rough around the edges and had a few tarnished spots on his reputation from a few years back. But Cassandra was determined to do something nobody had ever been able to do—make Sebastian Steele sparkle.

Chance and his two brothers wondered how in the hell she planned to accomplish such a feat. If nothing else, they would give her an A for trying. They knew, even if she didn't, that it would be a wasted effort. The woman who would eventually capture Bas's heart would be the one who accepted him as he was, and not try to make him into something that he wasn't.

"Dinner is at six tonight, if anyone is interested," Chance decided to say, since his brothers had a tendency to drop by for a meal unannounced.

Bas chuckled. "I'll pass the word on to Morgan and Donovan."

"What about you?"

"I'm invited to dinner at the Tisdales'. My guess is that Cassandra's mother will try to get me to finally commit to a June wedding."

Chance nodded. That was eight months away. "Will you?"

"There's no reason for me not to, I suppose. Being engaged for almost six months is long enough, don't you think? See you later."

When the door closed behind Bas, Chance stood and

walked over to the window and looked out. Deciding to rid Bas and his issues from his mind, he turned his thoughts to his own problem.

Kylie Hagan.

He couldn't help wondering whether she'd made a decision about the camping trip yet. Several times that day he'd been tempted to call her but had changed his mind.

He felt excited at the prospect of having her at the cabin for an entire weekend, even with the knowledge that their kids would be around to keep them company. It would be hard to keep his attraction to her at bay, but he would.

He figured the reason she was hesitating was because the thought of them spending the night under the same roof bothered her. She was well aware that the kids would have to go to sleep eventually, and when they did, it would be parents' time.

She was fighting the chemistry between them. He knew that just as he knew it was a fight she wouldn't win. But he would let her try, up to a certain point. He'd give her until the end of the week and if he didn't hear from her by then, he would take some necessary action.

"SO, HAVE YOU DECIDED whether or not you and Tiffy are going camping with Chance Steele and his son?"

Kylie glanced up from the meal she and Lena were sharing during their weekly lunch date at a popular restaurant in town. "Who told you about that?" she asked.

Lena smiled. "Who else? My goddaughter, of course. She's all excited at the thought of going camping."

Kylie rolled her eyes. "I'm beginning to wonder if

it's the camping trip that has her excited or the thought of being around Marcus an entire weekend. If it's the latter then she might as well get unexcited because if I do decide to go, I'll have my eyes on her and Marcus the entire time. Any time they spend together will definitely be supervised."

Lena couldn't help the small smile that tugged at her lips. "So you think she has an ulterior motive for wanting to go?"

"Hey, remember I was young and in love once, and when you are their age, you look for every opportunity to be together, whether you're under your parents' watchful eyes or not."

"Yes, that could very well be, but at some point you're going to have to start trusting her, Kylie. You can't continue to judge Tiffy by the way you behaved with Sam. The more you do, the more she's going to resent it."

There was anguish in Kylie's eyes and a wee hint of guilt. "It's so hard being a parent these days, Lena. You want the best for your kids and you go on the premise that experience is the best teacher, but then you're faced with the question of how you can be there to protect them without suffocating them."

Lena nodded, clearly understanding. "I think for you it's more difficult because Tiffy is all you have. Over the years she has become your life. Have you given thought to becoming involved in other things?"

"Other things like what? I have a florist shop to run, Lena. It's not like I don't have anything else to do with my time."

"Yes, but only when Tiffy is at school. Other than that you're a full-time mother who really doesn't have a life other than her child."

Kylie knew where this conversation was leading since

they had been down this road several times. It was the one topic she and Lena didn't agree on. Lena felt it was a crying shame that she didn't have a man in her life and hadn't had one since high school.

Her thoughts shifted to Chance Steele and how much she had enjoyed his company on Sunday. It had felt strange sharing her time with anyone other than Tiffany, but she had to admit it had felt good, too. Too good. After they'd eaten they'd played a game of volleyball, the young against what Marcus and Tiffany had considered as "the old."

Kylie had been surprised at how much energy Chance had. The kids had been surprised, too, and she and Chance had won the game, showing Tiffany and Marcus that age was nothing but a number. Afterward, they had eaten ice cream and the cake she had baked.

As much as she had enjoyed Chance's company, she knew it was out of the question for something to develop between them. There was no way she would start depending on him or any other man for her happiness. She had done so once and refused to go that route again.

"I don't want a man in my life, Lena, at least not now," she decided to say. "Maybe when Tiffany leaves for college I'll feel differently and I'll get involved with someone, but I'm not interested now." She then turned her attention back to her meal.

"Okay," Lena said, placing her glass of iced tea aside. "Tell me about Chance Steele."

Kylie looked up again, giving her friend an uncomfortable stare. "What do you want me to tell you about Chance that you don't already know?"

"Well, Tiffy couldn't stop singing his praises when I picked her up from school yesterday. He definitely made a positive impression on her. She thought he was cool and fun to be around."

Kylie smiled. "She's right. He was a lot of fun."

She quickly resumed eating her meal, afraid that Lena might see all the lust that filled her eyes. The last thing she wanted was to tell Lena that Chance was the cause of her surging hormones lately. Which was exactly why she didn't think going on a camping trip with him, Marcus and Tiffany was a good idea. The longings he stirred within her could be relentless at times, and it took all the will power she could muster to hold on to her sanity. Her needy libido and her out-of-control hormones confined in a cabin for the weekend with Chance Steele were way too much to ignore. Especially when she'd have to stay focused on Marcus and Tiffany.

"Chance is not a bad catch you know, Kylie. He's good-looking, wealthy, intelligent and generous to a fault."

Kylie glanced up. "Umm, sounds like someone you should be interested in, then."

A sad smile tugged at Lena's lips. "You know the story of my life. Because of Mom's failing health, the two of us are a package deal and not too many men want that. At least none I've met so far. The moment I mention that I'm my mother's caretaker, they conveniently drop out of the picture. However, I do believe Chance would be different, but he and I never connected that way. I can only see him as a friend and nothing more."

Unfortunately, Kylie could see Chance as a lot more than a friend but she blatantly refused to go there. But right now, at that moment, her main concern was not the issue of her and Chance. It was Lena. She silently searched her mind for something to say that would ease the raw pain she'd heard in her best friend's words.

Propping her chin in her hand, she gave Lena a serious smile. "There's a man out there for you, Lena, who will be more than happy to take you and whatever and whoever comes along with you. I've always known that if I got interested in someone, that person would have to love Tiffany as much as he loved me. For some men it's easy to accept a package deal. For others it's not. And those who can't are the ones that women like us do better leaving alone."

Lena reached across the table and took her hand. "And I believe that there's a man out there for you, too, and believe it or not, he can be depended on. I know Sam and your dad let you down but you can't continue to judge all men by their actions, Kylie. Every young girl needs a good male role model in her life. Because of Dad's death, I missed having that, and you're cheating Tiffy of having that, as well. I think as a single mom you've done an admirable job in raising her. But don't you think at some point she needs to see you in a loving relationship with a man?"

Kylie looked Lena squarely in the eye. Conversations like this tended to expose emotions that she would rather keep under wraps because along with the emotions came the memories of the hurt and pain that Sam and her father had caused.

"Even if I did, Lena, that man can't be Chance Steele. For heaven's sake, he's the father of the boy that my daughter thinks she's madly in love with."

Lena placed her elbows on the table and laced her fingers together. "And what does that have to do with anything? More specifically, what does it have to do with you and Chance?"

"I don't want to confuse her, nor do I want to send out a negative picture about anything."

Lena shook her head. "Your daughter, and my god-daughter, is a lot smarter and mature than you think, Kylie. Kids these days know the score. They aren't as naive as we want to think they are. If something is going on between you and Chance, she'll be able to pick up on it, and personally, I doubt if she'll see anything wrong with it."

"She might not see anything wrong with it but I will. How am I going to lecture her about the difference between love and lust when I'm having problems knowing the difference between the two myself?"

Lena smiled. "So you are attracted to Chance." It was a statement and not a question.

"Yes, more than I want to be," she said, deciding to finally be completely honest with her best friend. "Around him I feel things that I've never felt before, Lena. We've kissed. Twice. And I'm not talking about a little kiss, either. The man takes kissing to a level I've never experienced before. All he has to do is get close enough to breathe on my mouth and my lips automatically open. Isn't that pathetic? Now can you understand why I'm hesitating about going on that camping trip?"

"Yes and no."

At Kylie's confused expression, Lena explained, "Yes, I can see why you're hesitant about going, and no, I don't agree with your assessment of the situation. So what if you have the hots for Chance? You're both adults and should be able to do whatever you want to do. Your attraction to him shouldn't have any bearing on what's going on between Tiffany and Marcus and how you're handling their situation. I know you and no matter what you do, you will always set a good example in front of Tiffany. However, what you and Chance do in private is your business. But then, like I said earlier, I think it's important for Tiffy to see you in a loving relationship with a man, and I can't think of a better person for that man to be than Chance Steele."

"There are bound to be complications, Lena."

"Only those of your own making, Kylie. Take it from someone who knows. Good men are hard to find, so if you meet one who's interested, you better grab him, hold on tight and not let go."

LATER THAT NIGHT KYLIE got into bed, wrestling with the knowledge that the main reason she didn't want to go on that camping trip was because of her growing feelings for Chance. She had to finally admit those growing feelings to herself after having lunch with Lena.

Their discussion had made her realize two things. She found Chance attractive and sexy, and thought he had a body that was all that and a bag of chips. But there was more to him than that. He'd already proven that he was dependable, unlike Sam and her father. When Chance and his girlfriend had been faced with a teen pregnancy, instead of leaving her in a fix like Sam had done to her, Chance had done the noble, honorable and responsible thing. He'd made whatever changes the situation called for to make a home for his wife and child. She could tell by his relationship with Marcus that he was a good father and from what she read in the business section of the *Charlotte Observer,* he was also a highly respected businessman. And she wanted to believe if he had shown up at her shop that day to tell her that their kids were involved in an unplanned pregnancy versus a plot to cut school, he would be angry, true enough, but nothing would make him turn his back on his only child, as her father and mother had done to her.

She sighed. One of the problems she was having trouble coming to terms with was the knowledge that their relationship—if they could call it that—had developed because of their kids. She doubted they would have met any other way. There was a strong possibility that if they'd been in the same room together at any given function, he wouldn't have given her a second look. So in her mind their meeting was a twist of fate rather than by their own choosing.

She jerked her head off the pillow at the sound of the phone ringing. The last time she had gotten a call this late it had been Chance. Sensations raced through her at that possibility and she quickly reached over and picked up the phone. "Hello."

"Sorry to call so late," Lena was saying. "But I forgot to mention today that the American Cancer Society is sponsoring their annual ball and I'm on the committee. The price of the tickets is high but it's all for a worthy cause, of course. Would you like one?"

Before Kylie could answer, Lena quickly inserted, "In fact, you can get two if you like and bring a date."

"I'll take one ticket, Lena," Kylie said softly, hoping Lena didn't pick up the disappointment in her voice. A part of her had hoped the caller was Chance. She hadn't seen or talked to him since Sunday, which was three days ago.

"Sure you don't want two?"

Kylie rolled her eyes. "No, I only want *one* ticket, Lena. I won't have a date that night. Will that be a problem? I either come alone or not at all."

"No, that won't be a problem but I was hoping there

was someone you could ask. Someone like Chance, perhaps?"

Kylie sighed. She knew where this conversation was leading and wasn't in the mood. "No. Only one ticket, Lena. Good night." She then hung up the phone.

A few seconds later, before Kylie could reclaim her comfortable position in bed, the phone rang again. She frowned. There were times when Lena was worse than a dog with a bone. She didn't know when to let up.

Snatching the phone, not giving her best friend a chance to say anything, Kylie said, "Look, Lena, forget it. There's no way I'm going to ask Chance to go with me."

There was a brief pause and then…

"And just where is it that you won't ask me to go, Kylie?" Chance Steele asked in a deep, husky voice that bespoke more than mild curiosity.

KYLIE'S EYES WIDENED and hot color rushed into her face. If she'd been standing she would have melted to the floor in embarrassment. Instead she found solace in burying her face under the pillow.

But even that couldn't drown out the sound of Chance's voice when he said, "Okay, Kylie, tell me. What's going on and why won't you ask me to go wherever it is that you're going?"

She closed her eyes and moaned. Her only saving grace was that she'd heard the teasing in his voice and was glad he had such a good sense of humor, even if it was at her expense.

"Kylie?"

She pulled her head from beneath the pillow. "What?"

"Are you going to tell me voluntarily or do I have to come over and tickle it out of you?"

The thought of Chance actually tickling anything out of her had a stimulating effect on her rather than an amusing one. Yet she couldn't help but smile. "I doubt if you can tickle anything out of me, Chance."

"Don't let me come over there and prove you wrong," he warned in an even huskier tone of voice.

Kylie closed her eyes and in her mind she could envision him lying in bed saying what he'd just said. He would be propped back against the pillow with a sexy smile on his lips and a teasing glint in his dark eyes.

She allowed her mind to go a little further by envisioning him lying on top of the bedcovers completely naked. Her overactive imagination spread warmth through her as she envisioned her gaze moving down his muscular chest and firm stomach before coming to rest on his exposed groin. He was hard as steel.

She inhaled deeply and wondered what it would be like to touch him there, caress his body all over, bury her face in the curve of his neck, taste his skin and nibble him in a few places to brand him hers. She would let his musky scent fill her nostrils before pressing her mouth to his, getting the deep, tongue-tangling kiss she knew awaited her. She would let her hand reach down to touch him in his most private area, feeling the heat of him, hot, hard and thick. The mere thought of seducing him that way had blood racing recklessly through her veins.

"Kylie?"

She swallowed, trying to bring her thoughts back in check. "Yes?"

"Tell me."

The sensuous tone of his voice was playing havoc on her sensibilities. She leaned back in bed, letting her body cool from the heated thoughts that had flowed through her mind earlier. Her lids lowered and for a long second she didn't say anything, wondering if she should. But she knew he wouldn't let up until she told him.

"Lena mentioned that the American Cancer Society is having their annual ball and she's on the committee," she started off by saying. "So quite naturally she's trying to get rid of as many tickets as she can. I told her I'd get a ticket to support the cause and then she tried talking me into getting two, knowing full well I wouldn't have a date that night."

"And?" he asked when she paused briefly.

That single, softly uttered word stirred an area of her body that it shouldn't have. "And...Lena suggested that I invite you."

"So that's what you meant when you screamed in my ear."

Color rushed into Kylie's face again. "Yes, that's what I meant."

"I see. Don't I have a say in the matter?"

"No. The only reason we met, Chance, is because of the kids," she said, giving voice to her earlier thoughts. "If we had been at any function together you wouldn't have noticed me. I'm not the type of woman you would have been drawn to enough to show any real interest in."

"You think not?"

"Yes."

"What if I said you're wrong?"

"We'll never know, will we?"

When he had no comeback, she said, "Besides, I don't date. I mentioned that to you before."

"Yes, you did mention it. Is that also the reason you won't go camping, because you see that as a date?"

"No, that in itself is a whole other set of problems, Chance. I just think the two of us spending a weekend at a cabin isn't a good idea, even with the kids there. Especially with the kids there."

"Why?"

"I think you know the reason without me having to go into any great detail. For some reason, we're like magnets—we attract."

"And you see that as a bad thing?"

"Yes. Our focus should be on our kids. What would Marcus think if he thought you were attracted to me?"

Chance chuckled. "He would probably think the same thing I did when I finally got to meet Tiffany. That he has great taste. She's a nice girl and so is her mother."

Kylie couldn't help but smile, pleased with his compliment, but still… "Can't you see the problems it will cause if our kids think something is going on between us?"

"No."

"Chance," she said, moaning his name in frustration.

"Kylie. We've had this conversation before and my feelings on the matter haven't changed. We're adults and what we do is our business. In fact, I think Marcus will find it strange if I'm not attracted to you. He thinks you're beautiful, so quite naturally he'll assume that I'll think you're beautiful, too. And I do. I also think you're someone I'd like to get to know better. He would assume as much, as well. But you're right. The camping trip will be about Marcus and Tiffany and not about us. Our time will come later."

She wondered what he meant by that.

"Will it make you feel better if I promise to be on my best behavior when we go camping?"

Kylie shrugged. How could she explain to him that his behavior really had nothing to do with it? It was her own behavior she was concerned about. He didn't have to do anything in particular for her to get turned on. Her dilemma was the fact that just seeing him did that.

"If you don't go, you know what might happen, don't you?"

Chance's question recaptured her attention. "No, what?"

"The kids are going to feel that they can't depend on us to keep our end of the bargain. We did tell them that we would agree for them to take part in supervised activities."

"But we never said anything about overnight activities, Chance."

"Neither did we clarify they had to be only daytime activities. They won't understand what the big deal is since we will be there as chaperones. They will only see it as a cop-out on our part. I don't think it's fair to cancel out a weekend of fun for them just because we can't keep our hormones in check for forty-eight hours. It makes us sound pretty damn selfish, don't you think?"

Kylie sighed deeply. It hadn't before, but since he'd put it that way, yes, it did make them—her in particular— sound selfish. Tiffany had never gotten the chance to go camping. Kylie had been too overprotective to even let her go with the Girl Scouts that time when she was ten. And now all her daughter wanted was to experience her first camping trip, and her selfish mother, who couldn't keep her overactive hormones in line, was standing in her way.

"Okay, you've convinced me. I'll go."

"Great! The kids will be happy."

She laughed. "Yes, I'm sure they will be."

"I'll make the arrangements for next weekend. Will that work?"

"Yes, that will work."

"And, Kylie...?"

"Yes?"

"The kids aren't the only ones who'll be happy. I'm going to be happy, as well. Good night."

Before she could say anything, he hung up the phone.

CHAPTER SEVEN

A FEW DAYS LATER KYLIE was praying that at some point her life would resume a sense of normalcy. Since she'd told Tiffany of her decision to go camping, her daughter had been nothing but a bundle of mass excitement. So much, in fact, that Kylie had to wonder whether being with Marcus was the primary reason for her daughter's happiness or the camping trip itself.

With teenage exuberance, Tiffany had gone on and on about all the things she planned to do, like swimming in the lake, fishing in that same lake, having a picnic by that lake and taking oodles and oodles of pictures of that lake. And she intended to do a lot of bird-watching and had even checked out a library book on the various species. Of course that meant she would need a pair of binoculars, which her godmother had been quick to buy for her.

Kylie hadn't talked to Chance anymore until he'd called early Saturday morning saying he would drop off a list of items she might want to bring along. The cabin's kitchen was well-stocked with cooking utensils, but he thought it would be good if they cooked outside on the grill or a camp stove. He'd gone on to tell her that although the cabin had electricity, usually he and Marcus enjoyed faking it by using candles and lanterns.

Anticipating his visit, she had been a mass of nerves,

and once she opened the door not even the loud wail of a fire truck siren could intrude on her jolting awareness of him. She pulled in a deep breath. And then another. Neither did a thing to stop the pounding of her heart or the barrage of sensations that overwhelmed her.

Standing before her in jogging pants, a T-shirt and a pair of what appeared to have once been expensive tennis shoes, Chance Steele was the epitome of everything hot and spicy. He looked like a man capable of doing anything he pleased, whether it was in the boardroom or in the bedroom. Especially in the bedroom. However, at that very moment she had to concede that there was nothing sophisticated about Chance's appearance. He looked like a man ready for some playtime, and his darkly stubbled jaw, which meant he hadn't yet shaved that morning, only added to his sharply male features.

"Here's the camping checklist I told you about," he said, breaking into her heated thoughts.

She took the paper he handed her. "Thanks."

"The only things you'll need to bring for you and Tiffany are the items listed under the first-aid section."

She nodded and quickly scanned the list, okay with everything she saw on it until she noted the snake bite kit. She lifted her gaze back to his. The eyes that met hers were dark, sexy and full of sexual interest he wasn't trying to hide, which made her thankful for two things: that she was a woman and that she was decently dressed. "Snake bite kit?"

A smile touched his eyes. "Yes, just as an added precaution. But I have one if you have trouble finding it. It's a rather popular item this time of the year."

An uninvited shiver ran through her. That wasn't exactly what she wanted to hear. She cleared her throat.

"Would you like to come in? Tiffany and I were just sitting down to breakfast. You're welcome to join us."

"No, thanks. I'm on my way to the gym. It's tradition that my brothers and I play basketball every Saturday morning. It helps get rid of any competitive frustrations we might have before the start of a new week."

She lifted a brow. "Competitive frustrations? Does that happen often?"

"I guess with four adult males it can't help but happen occasionally, given the closeness of our ages and our competitive natures. Then of course there's Donovan, who often forgets that I'm the oldest and he's the youngest."

It wasn't the first time she felt that an extreme closeness existed between the Steele brothers. It was there in his tone whenever he spoke of them. "Well, enjoy your game."

"I will. And just so you'll know, I'm catching a flight out first thing Monday morning to Dallas. I'll be there until Thursday. Marcus will be spending time with my brothers until I return."

"All right, thanks for letting me know," she said, missing him already, although she didn't want to feel that way. "Have a safe trip."

By the way he was staring at her, she knew without a doubt that if Tiffany hadn't been home he would have come inside and kissed her goodbye. That knowledge caused an ache in certain parts of her body. Their connected gazes were holding just a little too long. She knew it and was fully aware that he knew it, as well.

"I'll call you," he finally whispered huskily.

Kylie nodded. A promise made and one she knew he intended to keep. "All right."

She wrapped her arms around her waist, hugging

herself so she wouldn't be tempted to reach out and hug him.

He took a step back and looked deeply into her eyes one last time before turning back to his truck.

DURING THE NEXT FOUR days Kylie spent her free time shopping for the items on the list Chance had given her. After that was done, Tiffany had convinced her that they needed to spruce up their wardrobes, with a collection of new outfits suitable for camping.

Kylie enjoyed this carefree, happy-go-lucky side of her daughter. It had been a long time since she'd seen it and she couldn't help but count her blessings now.

She and Tiffany returned home from one of their shopping trips rather late on Wednesday night and were in her bedroom unwrapping their numerous packages.

"Mom, can I ask you something?"

"Sure, honey, you can ask me anything."

"Why don't you have a boyfriend?"

Kylie's hand went still on the new blouse that she was about to place on the hanger. *You can ask me anything but that,* she wanted to say but decided it was a good question. If only she could give her daughter what she felt was a good answer. She decided to go for the truth…but only after she found out why Tiffany wanted to know.

"Why do you ask?"

"Because I think you're so pretty and all the other girls at school whose moms are single always talk about their mothers' boyfriends. In fact, Trisha Nobles's mom is getting married next month."

Good for Trisha Nobles's mom, Kylie wanted to say. But she knew the only reason Tiffany had asked the question was because the answer was important to her.

"I've been too busy to have a boyfriend," she said honestly. "Running the shop takes up a lot of my time."

"But even before we moved here and you worked for that marketing firm you never went out on a date or anything."

Kylie lifted an eyebrow. "And that bothered you?"

"I really never thought about it until recently."

Kylie sat on the bed next to her daughter. "And why recently?"

"Because now I know how it feels to care for someone and I think it's sad that you never cared for anyone before. It doesn't seem right."

Kylie pulled her daughter into her arms and was mildly surprised when she came willingly. "Oh, honey, but it's okay. Some things aren't just automatic. Another reason I never went out was because I'm a very selective person."

"Nitpicky?"

Kylie laughed. "Yeah, nitpicky. Only a certain type of man appeals to me."

Tiffany pulled back and glanced up at her. "Really? And what kind is that, Mom?"

Kylie immediately thought of Chance and forced him from her mind. "First and foremost he has to be willing to be a good father to you. Then he has to treat us both good, look good, be health-conscious, fun to be around, be someone I can always depend on even during my darkest hour, and someone who loves me unconditionally."

"Unconditionally?"

"Yes. Someone who would love me no matter what

and who would take me as I am—the good, the bad and the ugly."

Tiffany smiled. "You know that's funny."

"What is, honey?"

"Marcus said he recently asked his dad why he never remarried. And it seems that he's nitpicky, too."

"Really?"

"Yes. And he gave almost the same exact answers as you did." Tiffany chuckled. "Boy, adults sure are strange."

"Strange in what way?"

Tiffany gave her mother a beaming smile. "If all of you are looking for the same thing in a person, then why is it so hard to find someone?"

Before Kylie could answer her daughter's question— not that she thought she had an answer anyway—the phone rang. Tiffany quickly picked it up. "Hello?"

Kylie watched her daughter's dark eyebrows lift curiously. "I'm fine, and yes, sir, she's here. Just a moment, please."

Her daughter then stared at her with bright, penetrating eyes and whispered, "It's for you and it's Mr. Steele. He's probably calling to make sure that you got everything on that list for the camping trip this weekend."

Kylie took the phone her daughter handed her. "Yes, I'm sure that's why he's calling," she said, trying to keep her voice neutral but feeling she'd failed miserably. She hoped Tiffany hadn't picked up on anything.

"That's really nice of him to call us all the way from Texas, isn't it?"

"Yes, it is."

"Well, it's late and I have school tomorrow so I'm going to bed. Thanks for taking me shopping, Mom. Good night."

"You're welcome and good night, sweetheart."

With quiet gravity Kylie watched Tiffany leave the room, closing the door behind her. It was only then that she turned her attention back to the phone and the man waiting on the line to talk to her.

"Hello?"

"Sorry about that, Kylie. I assumed Tiffany would be in bed by now."

"Usually she is but that's okay. I took her shopping after school and we just got back a little over an hour ago."

Chance chuckled. "Must have been some shopping trip."

Kylie smiled. "Trust me, it was." She didn't want to sound too excited but she was glad to hear his voice. "How are things going?"

"Busy. This is one of those annual meetings where the CEOs of various corporations get together, leave egos at the door and work on something we all need to improve within our companies."

"And what's that?"

"Employee relations. But I didn't call to talk about that. I wanted to see how you and Tiffany were doing."

"We're fine." Actually, there was something concerning her. Maybe Chance could shed some light on it. "I know Tiffany talks to Marcus every day, but I'm a little concerned about something."

"What?"

"Although I told him on Sunday that it would be okay if he wanted to visit with Tiffany for a few hours after school on occasion, he hasn't done so."

"Umm, even with football practice I'm surprised he

hasn't jumped at the chance at least once. Does Tiffany seem bothered by it?" Chance asked.

"No, and I know for a fact that they aren't mad at each other." Kylie sighed. Maybe things were different with teenagers today. She and Sam had practically tried living out of each other's pockets. It had gotten so bad that he had become a regular fixture around her parents' house, although they had wished otherwise.

"Maybe I'm assuming too much here, Chance, but I thought with them being so 'madly in love' that once I gave the go-ahead for supervised visits that Marcus would become a constant visitor."

"That's strange, because I know that I would."

"You would what?"

"Become a constant visitor if you ever gave me the go-ahead."

Chance's voice was hardly more than a whisper but she heard the underlying meaning loud and clear. Kylie's breath hung in her throat for a brief second and then she took a deep, calming inhale, which was followed by a series of flutters in her stomach.

"Kylie?"

"Yes?" She was glad to say anything, even that one single word, to assure her that her vocal cords were still working and that they hadn't drowned in all those sensations overtaking her.

"May I ask a favor of you?" Chance asked.

"Sure," she said with a small shrug, certain he wouldn't ask her to do anything indecent or immoral.

"Would you pick me up from the airport tomorrow around lunchtime?"

Surprise flickered in the depths of her dark eyes. "You want me to pick you up?"

"Yes. My car is at the dealership getting serviced

while I'm away. I can get one of my brothers to pick me up but I would like for you to…if it won't be any problem."

"No, it won't be a problem. But can I ask you something?"

"Yes."

"Why do you want *me* to do it?"

"You'll find out when I see you."

The sound of his voice held promises she wasn't sure she wanted him to keep. She'd been having a lot of mixed emotions since meeting Chance. A part of her knew that getting involved with him was not a good idea, but then another part of her—the one that lately was constantly reminding her that she was a woman with needs—was egging her on to enjoy what he was offering. At least within reason.

"All right. Would you like to give me your flight information now?" For the next minute or so, she jotted down the information that he gave her.

"Well, I'll let you go now. I'm sure the shopping trip tired you out."

"Yes, it did somewhat. I appreciate you calling."

"I told you I would. I just hope my doing so hasn't raised Tiffany's suspicions. I know how much you don't want the kids to think anything is going on between us."

"No, I don't think your call did. In fact, she said she thought it was very considerate of you to call and make sure we were all set for this weekend."

"And are you all set for this weekend, Kylie?"

More than I need to be, she thought, thinking of all the new outfits she had purchased with the hopes that he'd like each and every one of them. "Yes, I found all the items on the list, including the snake bite kit."

"Good girl. Now do something tonight when you go to sleep."

"What?"

"Think of me."

CHANCE SETTLED BACK IN the bed after placing the phone back in the cradle. He hadn't been able to concentrate on the summit all week because Kylie was on his mind. Hell, for the past couple of nights, he hadn't been able to sleep a wink.

It had been during Horace Doubletree's speech that day when he'd suddenly came to the realization that it was a waste of time trying to fool himself any longer and that things for him had moved past him trying to get to know Kylie better. The truth of the matter was that he knew all he wanted to know. His heart had decided. He had fallen in love with her.

How such a thing was possible he wasn't sure; especially when the woman had been sending out conflicting signals since the day they met. She was attracted to him, although she was determined to fight that attraction every step of the way. Her independence, while a turn-on, had ironically become a major obstacle to the relationship. That meant he needed to probe deeper and somehow break through her defenses. He also needed to take one day at a time and wipe away the fifteen years of hurt and pain she'd endured and prove that with him there would only be happier days. Even without her realizing she'd been doing so, for the past couple of weeks she had been extracting an unusual type of strength from him.

A strength of will.

He'd been fighting an intense longing, a deep-rooted desire for her since that day he'd walked into her florist shop. He could now admit that the first time their eyes had connected his heart had slammed into fifth gear. No wonder lunch at the Racetrack Café had seemed fitting as a place for their first date. Even then he'd known that something special was within his grasp.

After Cyndi died he'd actually thought that he could never love another woman again. And even with the few affairs he'd indulged in over the years, he'd never allowed his emotions to go any deeper than affection or desire. Yet here he had fallen hard for a woman whom he had never actually taken out on a real date, had never slept with and had never really spent more than a few hours with at a given time. His brothers would say such a thing was utterly insane. They would call in the shrink to have his head examined, or they would take him out somewhere and beat some sense into him. But then they would one day realize that some things in life were not meant to be understood, just accepted. Today he had accepted the fact that he had fallen in love.

And he knew he had his work cut out for him.

There was more than gentle pride in every bone in Kylie's body. He knew just from the time he'd spent with her that she could be stubborn, willful and defiant. That was all well and good if she was dealing with any other man than him. But he refused to wait around for her to bolster her courage to take a chance and fall in love again—this time with a man who wouldn't let her down. He still wouldn't rush her into doing anything, but he definitely planned to show her how good things could be between them. He planned to jar her emotions, jump-start her heart and make her stare the truth in the face.

There were chances in life worth taking and he was one "Chance" she should definitely take. In high school

he and his brothers had been pegged as guys who were
forged of steel. It was time to prove to Kylie that no
matter what, he was a man with the endurance to withstand just about anything.

THE NEXT DAY AT NOON Kylie was at the airport waiting
for Chance to arrive. As usual, no matter what day of the
week it was, Douglas International Airport was busy.
People were scurrying to their connecting flights or to
their rendezvous with their loved ones.

When Chance's flight number was announced, she
turned and glued her eyes on the gate. Evidently he traveled in first class because it didn't take long for him to
exit the Jetway. He was dressed in an expensive suit, and
his stride was long and confident as he passed through
the gate. There appeared to be an aura of power and
authority surrounding him. Chance Steele was one dy-
namic, compelling and forceful man.

He looked so dependable, like the kind of man at
whose feet a woman could leave her worries knowing
he would take care of them and she wouldn't ever have
to carry them on her shoulders again. He also looked
like the kind of man who could drive a woman crazy
with desire. She could definitely attest to that.

Her breath caught the moment their gazes met and
she felt that immediate quiver of anticipation in her
middle. He was going to kiss her. Somehow she knew,
and heaven help her but she wanted that kiss more than
anything.

She watched his long, elegant stride eating the distance separating them. And with each step he made, a
delicious heat inched its way through her veins, making
her blood hot and leaving her wondering, not for the first
time, how this particular man could affect her so. He

was the type of man that fantasies were built on, and who made realities even more poignant. And with every step he took toward her, he was making anticipation that much sweeter.

When he was within five feet of her, she saw the undisguised longing on his face. She could actually feel his desperation. There was a lot she didn't understand, but at that moment the one thing she did accept was that in less than a minute, now more like a few seconds, she was going to be kissed senseless.

ALL THE WHILE HE'D BEEN walking toward Kylie, the one thought that kept churning in Chance's mind was that she was the woman he wanted and needed in his life.

She was the woman he loved.

Other than his mother, he had never kissed a woman at an airport, but that thought was pushed to the back of his mind when he pulled Kylie into his arms and captured her lips with his. And as their lips engaged in one hell of a lockdown, he wished she could feel all the emotions flowing through him at that very moment.

Knowing he had to get a grip before the kiss really turned raw and primitive, he reluctantly pulled back, but kept his arms around her waist, refusing to let her go anywhere. "Now that was worth coming back to," he whispered softly.

Kylie struggled for breath and then noted they had become the center of attention. "We've caused a scene."

He smiled. "Yes, but some scenes are worth causing."

She looked up at him. "Is this what you had in mind when you asked me to pick you up last night?"

He reached out and caressed her cheek. "Not entirely, but it's definitely a start. Come on, let's get my luggage so we can get the hell out of here."

CHAPTER EIGHT

KYLIE COULDN'T REMEMBER the last time she had a problem with keeping her eyes on the road while driving. But Chance's presence in her car was interfering with her concentration and wreaking havoc on her senses.

After claiming his luggage, he had taken her hand as they walked out of the terminal to her parked car. Once he had placed his bags in her trunk, his arms had clamped around her waist, pulled her to him and he'd sunk his mouth down on hers in another kiss. The moment their lips connected, heat had exploded through her and the heavy bulge of his erection pressed to her middle had caused her entire body to ache.

"We've got to stop doing this," she'd said the moment he had released her mouth.

"Why?" he had whispered hotly against her moist lips.

"Because it won't lead anywhere. It's a dead-end."

His gaze had pinned her with a measured look. "And what if I told you that I see things differently?"

"Then my response is that you need a new pair of eyes."

"I have very good vision, Kylie." He'd then strolled to the passenger side of her car and got inside.

Bringing her thoughts back to the present, she took another quick glance over at him. He was sprawled in the seat next to her. His muscular body fit nicely into her Altima, although his broad shoulders took up a lot of space. His legs were long and his seat was pushed as far back as it could go to accommodate his height. His head lay back against the headrest and his eyes were closed.

Evidently the trip had tired him out, but not enough to stop him from engaging in a little mouth exercise with her a couple of times. She had begun thinking of their kisses as TST—taste, stroke and tangle—because each time they kissed he tried a new technique on her mouth that centered around those three basic elements.

"You're tired," she decided to say when she came to a traffic light. "Are you sure you want me to take you to the dealership to pick up your truck instead of taking you home? It might be a good idea for you to go to bed."

He opened his eyes, titled his head and let his gaze fasten on hers. "If you were to take me home and I got into bed, would you get in there with me and keep me company?" he asked, his voice low and sexy.

She inhaled deeply. Although he had phrased the question in a roundabout way, technically he had just hinted at the possibility of her sleeping with him. "No. I'd take you home and put you to bed, but I wouldn't get in that bed with you."

He smiled. "Spoilsport."

She chuckled and turned her attention back to the road when the traffic light changed. "I might be at that, but it seems I'm the one destined to keep us out of trouble."

"Some trouble I might like," he murmured in a low voice leaden with exhaustion, before closing his eyes again.

"And what if Marcus had that same attitude?"

"When he gets to my age he's welcome to it, but while he's underage, I decide what he likes and doesn't like. And stop comparing us to our kids, Kylie. Like I told you before, we're adults. They aren't."

"Sorry, I keep forgetting," she said sarcastically.

"It will behoove you to remember. The next time you forget it will cost you."

She lifted an eyebrow. "Cost me what?"

"A kiss. Right then and there. Even if it's in front of those two kids of ours."

She frowned and took a quick glance at him and saw that his eyes were open and he was staring at her. His expression was serious. "You wouldn't dare."

"I wouldn't count on that if I were you."

And Kylie was smart enough to know not to. She pulled her car into the dealership, parked it and turned to him. "And just what would doing something like that prove?"

"It would prove that our kids wouldn't have a problem with anything developing between us."

"But I'd still have a problem with it. I won't let any man use me to slake his sexual cravings."

In a flash Chance snapped the seatbelt off his body and before she could get out her next breath he loomed over her. Blatant anger was carved in his features. "This isn't about me slaking any sexual cravings, Kylie. But you're so out of practice with men that you wouldn't know that, would you? Well, let me tell you something, not about men in general but about this man in particular," he said pointing to himself. "I won't ever use you just to slake any sexual cravings, so don't try making my wanting you as anything sullied or dirty.

"It's the most natural thing in the world for a man to

desire a woman and vice versa. I won't apologize for it. When we do make love, Kylie, it will be a mutual thing. You'll want it as much as I do, so don't kid yourself into believing otherwise. And when it comes to me there's something else you need to keep in mind."

"And what's that?" she asked softly.

"When there's something I want, I won't give up until I get it."

"WHEN WE DO MAKE LOVE, Kylie, it will be a mutual thing. You'll want it as much as I do, so don't kid yourself into believing otherwise..."

The words Chance had spoken earlier that day woke Kylie up more than once that night. This time she knew she had to deal with them before trying to go back to sleep.

Taking the pillow from the other side of the bed, she wrapped her arms around it and hugged it to her chest, wondering how in the world one man could be so utterly self-confident, so damn arrogant. The nerve of him making such a statement as if it was a foregone conclusion they'd go to bed together. Well, she had news for him, she thought bitterly.

After this camping trip was over she would put rules into place where their relationship was concerned. The only thing between them would be Marcus and Tiffany. As parents they would have some connection in order to keep their offspring on the right path, but that would be as far as things went. It wouldn't bother her in the least if she never saw the infuriating man again.

Turning over on her side, Kylie gazed despondently at the digital clock on the nightstand. It was almost midnight, way too late to be having this sort of conversation with herself. She should be resting peacefully in a sound sleep, but thanks to Chance she was wide-awake.

He had upset her so badly that afternoon that it had been a good ten minutes before she'd been able to pull herself together to drive away from that dealership. And twice during dinner Tiffany had asked her if anything was wrong.

And to think she would be spending an entire weekend in Chance's presence. If there were any way she could cancel their plans without disappointing Tiffany she would, but she knew better than anyone how much her daughter looked forward to this trip.

The phone on her nightstand rang and not for the first time she wished that like the phone in the living room this one had caller ID. But somehow she knew it was Chance and reached out and picked it up. "Hello?"

"I need to apologize, Kylie."

It was his deep, rich, husky voice, more than the words he had spoken, that sent a sensuous shiver through her. "Do you?"

"Not for everything—just for getting upset with you. I won't apologize for our kisses. But your words caught me off guard. Never in my wildest dream did I assume you'd think I would want to use you that way."

"Okay, Chance, maybe it was a bad choice of words, but what I was trying to say was that I'm being logical here. I don't see things as you see them, and when it comes to a lot of man-woman stuff, you're right, I'm way out of my league. You aren't. So I have to protect myself."

"You'll never have to protect yourself from me, Kylie. I'd never hurt you, take advantage of you or use you. I give you my word."

"Thank you."

"But I won't give you my word that I'll stop pursuing you, stop trying to make you want me as much as I want you, stop trying to—"

"Get me in your bed?"

"No, I won't stop trying to get you in my bed, Kylie, because I think that's where you belong. And once I get you there I intend to keep you there for a long time. But it will be for all the right reasons."

"When is an affair good for any reason?"

"When the two individuals agree that it is. You and I have a long way to go, Kylie. We haven't even gone on what I consider a real date. I want that but you don't."

She sighed deeply. "It's not that I don't want it, Chance, it's just that I don't think it's wise, considering the kids."

"So you prefer that we do things behind their backs?"

"No, I prefer that we don't do anything at all. Why is that so hard for you to understand?"

"And just what is it that you're afraid of?"

She was taken aback by his question. "I'm not afraid of anything."

"I think you are."

"Then think whatever you want."

"I will, and right now I think it's time that I show you something, Kylie Hagan."

She didn't like the way that sounded. "Show me what?"

"What this man-woman thing is all about. Like I said earlier today, you've been out of the game for so long you don't know what's acceptable between couples and what's not. Maybe it's time that I start teaching you a few things and—"

"Teach me a few things?" she interrupted shortly.

"Yes, then maybe you'll realize that you're not immune to me as you want to believe. Good night, Kylie."

The phone had already clicked in her ear before Kylie could recover her power of speech.

"MOM, ISN'T THIS PLACE simply beautiful?" Tiffany asked in a high-pitched voice that was filled with enthusiasm and wonder.

"Yes, it is," Kylie replied, trying to direct her gaze out of the cabin window and not on Chance and Marcus as they brought in the items out of the truck.

Especially on Chance.

Instinctively, she took one hand and checked her pulse at her wrist, not surprised to find the strong beat racing beneath her fingertips. Already Chance was having an effect on her. He had shown up at her place wearing a pair of faded jeans and a T-shirt. The moment she'd seen him those wacky hormones of hers began soaring. She wished there was some type of injection she could take to build an immunity against him.

"Mom, you don't sound excited about being here. Are you okay?"

Kylie turned to meet Tiffany's concerned gaze and suddenly felt guilty. The last thing she wanted was her daughter worrying about her needlessly, which would place a damper on all the fun she'd planned for the weekend. "Yes, sweetheart, I'm fine, and it's going to be a wonderful and fantastic weekend. Now let's put this stuff down and go outside to see if Marcus and Chance need our help."

Once they had stepped back outside, Kylie glanced around. The spacious log cabin that sat on the shore of a huge lake blended well with the surroundings. Trees of all kinds provided plenty of shade, as did a sprawling front porch that had several wooden rocking chairs and a rustic porch swing. Kylie had to agree with Tiffany's earlier assessment. The place was beautiful.

"The air is so crisp and clean here. I can't wait until Marcus teaches me how to fish, and Mr. Steele said he would help. Isn't that nice of him?"

"Yes, that is nice of him."

They walked back toward the truck while Tiffany excitedly rambled on about what fun she planned to have and what a nice man Chance was.

"Need us to help carry anything else inside?" Kylie asked Chance and Marcus when they reached them.

"No, Dad and I can handle things, Ms. Hagan," Marcus said, not giving Chance an opportunity to respond. "But remember we don't use electricity, so you and Tiffany might want to unpack and get familiar with the inside of the cabin. Right, Dad?"

Chance smiled. "Right."

Kylie could feel Chance's eyes on her but she refused to look at him. She was beginning to feel ridiculous and out of sorts because a part of her was still upset about yesterday. He, however, was acting like their conversation never took place. To her chagrin, he was in the best of moods.

"So what's for dinner?" Tiffany would have to be the one to ask.

"I thought it would be nice if we grilled something outside on the open fire," Chance said. "Any ideas?"

Kylie saw the opportunity to make peace and seized it. She glanced over at Chance. "Anything but hamburgers," she said softly, as a tentative smile touched her lips.

Chance met her gaze, immediately recognized their private joke and smiled back. "Okay, no hamburgers."

"What about a hot-dog roast?" was Tiffany's suggestion.

"That's a great idea and we have plenty of hot-dog sticks to use," Marcus chimed in.

"Okay, all that sounds good," Chance said, as an amused grin eased up the corner of his mouth. "But because I need something a little bit more filling, I'll throw a couple of steaks on the grill, too."

He lifted the last box into his strong arms. "Come on, let's go inside and get this show on the road."

KYLIE INHALED A DEEP breath as she stepped out of the bedroom she and Tiffany were sharing. More than a dozen candles were strategically scattered about and a couple of huge lanterns blazed in the corners of the living room.

She couldn't help but smile, thinking of all the fun they'd had so far. Chance had given both her and Tiffany a quick lesson on camping and had shown them how to assemble a tent in case they ever needed to use one. Roasting hot dogs on the stick had been fun but she'd appreciated Chance's idea of grilling the steaks when Marcus and Tiffany overcooked the weiners.

And then later, before it had gotten dark, Chance had taken her out in a canoe to the other side of the lake. The scenery there had been just as breathtaking with numerous trees, flowering plants and a catfish-filled stream. Kylie smiled and thought that a person could get spoiled by so much of nature's beauty.

"Marcus is out like a light."

Kylie's smile froze when she turned and saw Chance

coming out of the bedroom that he and Marcus were sharing. She thought he had turned in for the night.

"So is Tiffany." She gave him a curious look and said, "I thought you had gone to bed, too."

"Not without first putting out the candles and lanterns. Fire hazards, you know."

She nodded. "I never realized there was so much to know about camping."

"There is but it's an excellent way to get back to nature. My mom agreed up to a point, which is why my parents purchased this place. She didn't mind getting back to nature but wanted all the comforts of home while doing so."

He grinned as he moved around the room to put out the candles and lanterns. "I hate to say this but we had more fun when we left her at home. Dad was too laid back to worry about us turning over in the canoe or eating berries off the bushes without washing them first. And the only reason we have hot and cold running water is because she refused to let us bathe in the lake. Good old Mom always came with a strict set of rules."

Kylie chuckled. "Haven't you figured out yet that's one of the things we're best known for? Your mother sounds like my kind of woman. I would love meeting her one day."

And I intend for you to do just that, Chance thought as he glanced over at her. *Mom would be happy to know that her oldest son has found love again.*

All the candles were out but one, and the luminescent glow from that one candle seemed to focus on Kylie, making her skin shine with an ethereal radiance. Her hair had been up in a ponytail earlier but now she'd taken it down, and the mass of braids fell in soft waves around her shoulders.

"Well, I guess I'll call it a night and—"

"Will you sit on the porch with me for a while?" he asked.

Kylie looked at him then shook her head. "I don't think that's a good idea."

The corner of his mouth tipped upward into a smile. "Has anyone ever told you that you think too much?"

"Possibly," she said slowly. "But I won't absolutely admit to anything."

Chance chuckled. "I didn't think you would."

"Now who's thinking too much?"

"Oh, that's real rich," Chance said, laughing. "Come on. I think you'll get a kick out of watching the stars." He reached out and offered her his hand and, only after hesitating briefly, she took it.

CHANCE WAS RIGHT. She was getting a kick out of watching the stars. Sitting here on the porch and rocking in the chair made Kylie realize all the little things she hadn't taken time to do before.

"Sure you don't want to come over here and share this swing with me?" Chance asked.

She chuckled as she glanced over at him. "I'm positive."

"But you aren't sitting close to me."

"I'm close enough, Chance."

"I beg to differ."

She shook her head, grinning. "Tell me something. Are your brothers like you?"

"No, I'm one of a kind."

"Thank God."

"Hey," he said with affront. "What's that supposed to mean?"

"Let's just say I'm glad after you were born that they broke the mold. I can't imagine another one like you."

"I'll take that as a compliment."

"You would." After a brief moment of silence she said, "Tell me some more about your brothers."

"All right. Like I told you that day at the Racetrack Café, Bas is eighteen months younger than me and he's the troubleshooter for the company."

"He's also the one engaged to be married, right?"

"So we hear."

She stopped rocking and looked over at him, studied his features from the glow of the moon. "Why do I have a feeling that it's one of those 'I'll believe it when I see it' deals?"

"Because it is. Cassandra Tisdale and Bas are as different as day and night."

Kylie raised a brow. "Tisdale? As in Tisdale who owns a number of car dealerships around town? As well as those two restaurants?"

"Yes, the dealerships belong to her father and the restaurants to her uncle. Same family."

"Why do you think Ms. Tisdale and your brother aren't compatible?"

"Because they aren't."

"He evidently thinks they are."

"Remember you're the one who thinks too much. In this case, I don't believe Bas is thinking at all. But I have all the faith in the world that he'll come to his senses before doing something stupid."

Kylie frowned. "You're serious, aren't you?"

"Quite." After a brief moment he said, "But only because I know my brothers, and Bas in particular. All through his life he's been known as the 'not so stainless Steele.'"

"Meaning?"

Chance frowned at the memories. "He was considered the black sheep of the family because he used to get into so much trouble. I guess you can say he went through quite a rebellious stage while growing up. You name it, he probably did it. It was a good thing my father was good friends with Sheriff Blandford, since Bas had a penchant for straying to the wrong side of the law. Most of the time it wasn't him but the crowd he hung out with. But you know what they say about guilt by association."

Yes, she knew. "So when did his future change for the better?"

"When he was about twenty. He dropped out of college after deciding he wanted to see the world. He was gone for a year without us knowing where he was most of the time. All we know is that when he returned he had a new outlook on life. He went back to college, graduated with honors and then came to work at the Steele Corporation, starting from the bottom. He was determined to learn everything he could. Now he's a vital asset to the company. I depend on him to keep me in the know and to put out small fires."

"What about the other two?"

"Morgan is Morgan. He has this thing about finding the perfect woman and until he does he won't settle for less. Then there's Donovan, who thinks he was born to have fun. He's serious enough while at work but otherwise there's really never a serious moment with him. My mother predicts he'll probably be the one who lives the longest because he enjoys life too much to get stressed about anything."

"Does that also mean he's having too much fun to settle down and get married?"

"So he claims. He just hasn't met the one woman to tame his game."

"Quite an interesting bunch."

"Yes, they didn't refer to us as 'Forged of Steele' for nothing."

Kylie lifted a brow. "'Forged of Steele'?"

"Yes. We were known for our endurance. We thought we could outlast anything."

She decided not to ask their endurance in what. "The possibility that Marcus might be a chip off the old block now has me worried. Should I be?"

Chance chuckled. "No, he's a good kid."

"Yes, I noticed and I'm appreciative of that. I was prepared not to like him, you know."

"Yeah, I know, and it was likewise with me and Tiffany. But I like her. You did a good job raising her, Kylie."

"So did you with Marcus."

"Thanks."

Kylie stretched and then stood. "Well, I think I'm going to call it a night."

"Already?"

"It's probably close to two in the morning, Chance, and I still have to take a shower. That checker game you played with the kids lasted quite a while."

"Only because your daughter didn't know how to play. I've never heard of such a thing. That's un-American."

"Well, I hate to tell you but her mother doesn't know how to play checkers, either."

"Then I guess I'll add that to my list of all the other things I intend to teach you."

"Don't do me any favors."

"Trust me. It will be for my benefit as well as for

yours. The more you know and understand, the better off we'll both be."

Kylie knew they weren't talking about checkers but about the intricacies involving a male and female.

But was she willing to learn?

CHANCE LAY IN BED AND could only stare up at the ceiling as he heard the shower going, imagining Kylie, naked and standing beneath a full spray of water that flowed down her breasts, flat stomach, thighs…

He tried tuning out the sound and turning his attention to his snoring son, who was sleeping on the opposite bunk. Damn, he sounded just like Donovan. Chance chuckled as he remembered that while growing up no one wanted to share a bedroom with Donovan because he snored.

After a few moments he released a groan and decided listening to Kylie in the shower was a lot better than putting up with Marcus. He smiled, thinking he had really enjoyed their conversation on the porch tonight. She seemed interested in his family, which was just as well, since if he had his way the Steeles would be her family one day.

God, he loved her.

Heat sizzled along his nerve endings at the thought of just how much. A slow, sinful grin touched his lips when he thought about what he'd told her last night. There was a lot she didn't understand about man-woman relationships and he intended to teach her. Things had definitely changed since her last date, especially in the bedroom. If he remembered correctly, that was the year the Hubble Telescope was launched into space, Nelson Mandela was finally freed from prison and George Bush Senior was president.

Hell, she probably wasn't aware that these days men and women who were in a serious relationship openly discussed such things as foreplay and orgasms, or that trying different positions in the bedroom was now the norm and not the exception. And she'd probably be startled to know that oral sex was pretty popular these days.

A slow smile rolled around his lips. Yes, he would enjoy teaching her all the finer things in life with one goal in mind: to make her fall as deeply in love with him as he was with her.

CHAPTER NINE

"WELL, LENA, HOW DO I look?"

Lena stood with her hands on her hips and gave Kylie an assessing stare. The two of them had been shopping for gowns to wear to this weekend's ball and it seemed as if Kylie had hit the jackpot.

"Girl, that dress is gorgeous and it looks fabulous on you," Lena said. "But of course you have the figure for it. You have more curves than the Daytona Speedway. You'd be nuts not to buy it."

With her courage bolstered, Kylie looked down at herself. Lena was right. The dress was a sexy black formfitting georgette mini with a halter crisscross bodice and a low-cut back. She had to admit it did look rather flattering on her, though it showed more skin than she would like.

"You don't think it's too daring?" she asked Lena.

"Heck, no. Like I said you have the body for it. Everyone can't say that. I most certainly can't."

Kylie frowned at her friend. "Hey, there's nothing wrong with your figure."

"That losing fifteen more pounds won't hurt?"

"Don't complain. A lot of men like full-figured women. You have a small waist, nice size hips, a gorgeous pair of legs—"

"Strong bones and a good set of teeth," Lena tagged

on. They laughed, remembering other times they had gone shopping together when they were much younger and were faced with the same dilemma. Kylie always thought she was too thin and Lena had made up in her mind years ago that at size sixteen she was too thick.

"So, are you going to buy it?" Lena asked as she walked around Kylie, admiring how the dress fit.

"Probably not," Kylie said, still looking down at herself. She felt half-naked wearing it. "But it's gorgeous, though."

"And it has your name on it."

Kylie glanced up at Lena. "You think so?"

"I wouldn't have said it if I didn't. Besides, since you've decided to be my date for the ball what I say counts, right?"

"Right."

"So what are you going to do?"

Kylie grinned. "I'm going to take it."

AN HOUR OR SO LATER THEY were back in Lena's car and exiting the mall. "You never told me how things went last weekend with the camping trip," Lena said.

Kylie glanced over at her. "Didn't think I had to. I'm sure Tiffany told you everything you needed to know."

"Yeah, but she didn't mention anything about you and Chance."

"Was she supposed to?"

"I guess not, if the two of you are keeping your affair a secret."

Kylie gave her friend a direct stare, although Lena's eyes were glued to the road and didn't notice it. "Chance and I are not having an affair."

"Oh. The two of you just meet every so often to lock lips, right?"

Kylie rolled her eyes heavenward. "So we kissed a few times, no big deal."

"I would think after fifteen years of abstinence that for you it *was* a big deal. And you even admitted he was a good kisser."

"Oh, my gosh, he's the best," Kylie breathed and then regretted that she'd admitted it.

Lena laughed. "Bingo. So how did you manage to keep those overzealous hormones under control?"

"It was hard but I managed."

"And the two of you didn't kiss not even once?"

"No, not even once. Marcus and Tiffany kept us much too busy. They wanted to do everything and by the end of the day we were too tired to do anything but sleep."

"Oh, how sad."

Lena and Kylie looked at each other and burst out laughing again. A few moments later, Lena said, "You know he's coming to the ball, don't you?"

Kylie tried to keep her attention on an object outside of the car's window. "What Chance does is his business."

"And he's bringing a date."

Kylie jerked her head around. "What!"

Lena laughed out loud. "Gotcha!"

Kylie frowned. "That's not funny, Lena."

"It is, too. You should have seen the way your head snapped around. It's a wonder you didn't break your neck. For someone who claims what Chance Steele does is his business, you were definitely interested in that piece of news."

"Well, is it true? Is he bringing someone?"

Lena shrugged. "Don't know. Cassandra Tisdale

mentioned at the committee meeting yesterday that her cousin was going to be in town that night from D.C. and she was going to ask Chance to be the woman's date."

"Good for her."

"Umm, do I detect a little jealousy in your voice?"

"Not on your life."

Lena smiled. "Okay, if you say so."

LENA WAS RIGHT, KYLIE thought as she got ready for bed that night. She was jealous. Of all the nerve!

She had to admit that Chance had been on his best behavior last weekend, probably because she didn't give him the chance to be otherwise. After that first night when he had invited her to sit out on the porch with him, she had gotten smart and made sure the opportunity never presented itself again. She went to bed when Tiffany went to bed and she stayed there.

Still, she thought things had gone rather well that weekend and Marcus and Chance had been perfect hosts. They had seen to all of her and Tiffany's needs, and with Tiffany and Marcus carrying on more like siblings instead of a couple the majority of the time, it was as if the four of them were a family.

Chance had been wonderful with Tiffany when he showed her the proper way to use a rod and reel, after Marcus had thrown up his hands and given up. And then there was the time Chance taught Tiffany how to paddle the canoe, and how he was the only one who actually seemed interested in her obsession with bird-watching. Seeing them together actually made her wonder if perhaps Tiffany had lost out by not having a father figure in her life all these years. At least Tiffany would have the chance to spend time with her grandfather this weekend. Kylie's parents had called a few days ago and asked if

Tiffany could go with them to Disney World for the weekend.

Since both Friday and the following Monday were teachers' planning days, things worked out perfectly. Kylie would put her on the plane Friday morning and then pick her up from the airport on Monday evening. That meant she wouldn't have to worry about her daughter while she attended this weekend's ball.

The phone rang and Kylie glanced over at the clock, knowing it was Chance. How could he talk to her every night and not mention he was taking someone to the ball? It didn't matter to her one iota that she hadn't taken Lena's advice and invited him herself. It was the principle of the thing.

She frowned when she picked up the phone. "Hello."

"How did things go at work today?"

This was how they began their conversation each night. He would ask her how things went with her job and she would ask how things went with his. They would hold a pleasant conversation for a good forty-five minutes and then they would say good night. Sometimes she wondered about the real purpose of them talking, other than to hear the other's voice each day.

"Things at the shop went okay. Business has really picked up this week. I got a lot of pre-Thanksgiving orders." Then she said, "I closed early. Lena and I went shopping for gowns for the ball this weekend." She wondered if he would mention if he were going, or more specifically if he had a date.

"Did you find something you liked?"

"Yes."

"What color is it?"

"Black."

"I bet it looks good on you."

"Lena thought so."

"Did she?"

"Yes."

There was a pause and then he said, "Marcus is going away this weekend."

Kylie raised an eyebrow. This was news to her since Tiffany hadn't mentioned it. "He is?"

"Yes. Cyndi's parents are coming through on their way to—"

"Not Disney World?" she asked, immediately jumping to conclusions and hoping they were the wrong ones.

"No, Busch Gardens in Virginia."

Thank goodness. "Oh."

"Why did you think they were going to Disney World?"

"Because that's where Tiffany is headed this weekend."

"Ahh. And you thought that perhaps they had manipulated their grandparents so the two of them could be in the same place and at the same time."

"It's been known to happen."

"I'm sure it has but I doubt they would go that far."

"Hey, you never know," Kylie said.

There was another pause and then Chance said, "We're going to have to start trusting them at some point, Kylie."

Tucking a braid behind her ear, she took a deep, frustrating breath. "I know, but for me it's hard, Chance, because I remember all the tricks I used to pull to be with Sam."

"Yes, but is it fair to judge them by what you did?"

"No."

"All right, then."

Kylie tilted her lips in a smile. Even if he were bringing a date to the ball, she still enjoyed her nightly talks with him. Although she had decided that they could never be lovers, it seemed that he had made up his mind that they would be friends. And deep down she didn't have a problem with that.

She'd always had Lena as another female to bounce her ideas and thoughts off of, but there had never been a guy she felt close enough with to do the same. Lately she had asked Chance's opinions about a lot of things, including how she should handle situations that had arisen at work. Being the savvy businessman that he was, he had always given her good, sound advice.

"So, how are things going at the Steele Corporation?" she asked.

"There was a development today that I wished could have been avoided."

"Oh? What?"

"We had to let a man go who's been with us for over ten years."

She heard disappointment, as well as regret, in his voice. "Why?"

"We found out he'd been stealing from the company. He was padding figures and having the products delivered elsewhere. Bas had suspected him for a while but we only got the proof we needed today to do anything about it."

They talked for the next thirty minutes or so and that night Kylie slept with an inner peace that she hadn't known in a long time.

"SO YOU THINK THEY WILL have their first date this weekend?" Marcus asked before biting into his sandwich.

Tiffany smiled. "Yes. They're going to that ball, although they aren't going with each other. I can't see how it won't turn into a date with the both of us gone for the weekend. Didn't you see how they were looking at each other last weekend when they thought no one was noticing? I think we did the right thing by contacting our grandparents."

Marcus nodded. "I hope you're right."

Tiffany took another sip of her soda, smiled and said, "Just think, Marcus, if we actually pull this off, you'll be the big brother I've always wanted."

Marcus grinned. "Yeah, and then I can give Rhonda Denton my full attention. I think she likes me."

CHAPTER TEN

HE WANTED HER.

That thought rammed through Chance's mind the moment he saw Kylie enter the ballroom. His heart began hammering in his chest and he actually felt his pulse rate spike drastically. And if that wasn't bad enough, his body got hard as a rock.

At that moment he was grateful he was standing behind a waist-high plant that could shield the physical evidence of just how much he desired her. That, coupled with the knowledge of how much he loved her, was setting his loins on fire.

The minidress she was wearing was definitely a shocker he could sum up in three words—short, sassy and sexy. It fit her body to perfection, showing off all her curves and the luscious length of her long, shapely legs. And if the dress wasn't jaw-droppingly seductive enough, then there was the way she had her hair piled atop her head with a few swirling braids crowning her face.

"Who are they?" Morgan leaned over and whispered, while raising an impressive eyebrow. "I don't know either of them," he said as if it were his God-given right to be acquainted with every beautiful woman in Charlotte.

Chance studied his brother's face for a second and

noted his gaze wasn't as glued to Kylie as it was to Lena Spears. That was a good thing since it would have been of waste of Morgan's time to show any interest in Kylie. When it came to her he could get downright territorial. "The one in the black dress is Kylie Hagan, and she's mine," he said, deciding to state his claim here and now. "The woman in the fuchsia dress is her best friend, Lena Spears."

"Spears? Where have I heard that name before?" Morgan asked.

"I have no idea. She's a part of the committee that put on tonight's ball and owns a real estate office in town."

"A real estate office?"

"Yes."

Morgan glanced over at Chance after taking a sip from his wineglass. "You know her, then?"

"Yes."

Morgan's dark eyes sparkled in the glow of the huge chandelier that hung over their heads. "Good. I want an introduction." He then glanced back over at the two women. "So the one in black is Marcus's girlfriend's mother?"

At Chance's nod, he said, "Umm, definitely good-looking. But she doesn't look old enough to have a fifteen-year-old daughter."

"Well, she does," Chance answered, with no intention of going into any details as to how that had happened.

For a brief moment Morgan didn't say anything and then he spoke. "It seems she's caught Derek Peterson's eye. He didn't waste any time going over there to talk to her. If I were you I'd go claim what's mine."

Chance had noticed the man's flight across to the room to get all in Kylie's face. Derek Peterson, twice divorced, had a reputation as a skirt chaser and it seemed that he wasn't wasting any time making Kylie's acquaintance. "I think I will."

"AREN'T YOU GOING TO introduce me to your friend, Lena?" Derek Peterson asked.

"I'll think about it," Lena responded noncommittally.

Kylie raised an eyebrow. Lena was known for her friendly disposition. If she was giving this man the cold shoulder, there must be a good reason.

"Since Lena won't cooperate, I guess I have to introduce myself," the man said, capturing Kylie's hand in his. "I'm Dr. Derek Peterson."

Upon recognizing the name, Kylie understood her friend's less-than-friendly attitude. Derek was a doctor who had at one time shown interest in Lena until he discovered she was her elderly mother's caretaker. He'd told her there was no way the two of them could get serious since she came with "extra baggage."

"And I'm Kylie Hagan," Kylie said, in an attempt to be polite.

He gave her a smile that showed perfect white teeth. "Ms. Hagan, it is a pleasure to meet you. You must be new to town."

Kylie decided she didn't like him any more than Lena did, probably because his gaze was focused more on her chest than her face. "I've been living here for almost four months now."

"What section of town do you live in?"

"Myers Park."

"Myers Park?"

"Yes." She heard his impressed tone. Myers Park, one of the first suburbs of Charlotte, featured large stately

homes that were canopied in willow oaks. More than
any other neighborhood in the city, Myers Park had
preserved its true character over the years. The "front-
porch" neighborhoods had the traditional sidewalks,
funky shops and restaurants. The house she had purchased had cost a pretty penny but thanks to Lena's
negotiating skills, the owners, who'd needed a quick
sale, had readily agreed to her offer.

"Then I must definitely get to know you. We're neighbors," Dr. Peterson said, "though I don't ever remember
running into you while out and about."

Kylie was just about to tell him that she was both
a full-time mother and a working woman who didn't
have time to be "out and about," when she felt a sudden
quiver in her midsection. She knew without a doubt that
Chance was in close range.

She didn't want to seem too obvious when she
scanned the crowded ballroom, but knew from the way
her heart began hammering that she didn't have to look
far. He stood on a raised dais, staring directly at her.
The person standing by his side was a man and not a
woman, which gave her some relief. It was easy to tell
the man was one of his brothers, as the resemblance was
striking.

What was also obvious was the intensity in Chance's
eyes. She could almost drown in the look she saw there.
Male interest. Male appreciation. Male longing. Even a
novice like her could recognize the three. He was silently
sending her a message, one her body fully understood.
Her hormones were on ready, set, go. But she knew
there was something else involved here; something she
hadn't counted on happening. It was also something she
wasn't prepared for.

Emotional feelings of the deepest kind.

Now she understood why she'd been having all those vibrant and uncontrollable urges since meeting Chance. And why her body was so aware of him whether he was with her in person or was talking to her on the phone. The thought that he easily ignited her fire had always bothered her because she hadn't understood the why of it. Whenever he kissed her she got caught up in his special skill of tongue-play, as if his tongue was made for her and hers for him. She hadn't wanted to get in the same fix she'd been in with Sam; something she now thought of as forbidden obsession.

She was old enough now to know better. She was at that age of maturity where she no longer took things at face value. She didn't trust easily and had a tendency to expect the worst. But standing here being absorbed in Chance's heated gaze she knew at that moment that it wasn't about obsession, nor was it about lust. It was about love.

She had fallen head over heels in love with him.

"And what do you do for a living, Kylie?"

She tore her gaze away from Chance upon hearing Dr. Peterson's question. "I own a florist shop."

"Oh? Where?"

"In the newly developed section of town, Hazelwood."

"That's a nice area, but if you ever want to move to another location, a friend of mine owns a couple of buildings that he's leasing downtown and—"

"Good evening, everyone."

That deep, husky voice made the pounding of Kylie's heart increase. She glanced up and met Chance's direct gaze.

"Chance! It's good to see you," Lena said, deliberately showing a lot more enthusiasm upon seeing him than she had Dr. Peterson.

"Thanks, Lena, and it's good seeing you, as well."

He then gazed back at Kylie and held out his hand. "Hello, I'm Chance Steele. And you're…?"

Kylie wondered what game Chance was playing, but at the moment decided to go along with him. "Kylie Hagan."

"Well, Ms. Hagan, it's nice meeting you. And I'd like to introduce my brother, Morgan." He then proceeded to introduce Morgan Steele to both her and Lena. It was only then that she noted that he'd given Derek no more than a cursory glance. Kylie immediately felt the tension that surrounded the three men and was bewildered by it.

"Derek," Chance acknowledged.

"Chance. Morgan. I thought you guys ran in packs. Where're the other two?"

Chance's smile didn't quite reach his eyes. "Bas and Donovan are around here somewhere. Why? Are you looking for them?"

"No." Derek then turned his attention to Kylie. "It was nice meeting you, Ms. Hagan, but I'm being beckoned elsewhere."

"And it was nice meeting you, as well, Dr. Peterson." The man quickly left. Once he was no longer in sight, Kylie turned to Chance to inquire what that had been about, but found her hand enveloped in the warmth of his when the orchestra began playing.

She met his gaze and all thoughts of Derek Peterson were forgotten as she was immediately swept away by the intensity in Chance's dark eyes and the warmth of the smile that spread across his features. "Would you dance with me?" he asked quietly.

She wondered if he could sense her inner turmoil. Did he know the emotions she was feeling were real and far exceeded the ones she'd assumed she had felt for Sam all those years ago? What she'd felt then was the passion of a young, naive girl. What she was experiencing now was the passion of an adult woman who had discovered love for the first time and knew there was no place for her to run, and no place for her to hide. There was nothing she could do but accept her fate.

Love was staring her in the face in the form of Chance Marcus Steele.

"Yes, I'll dance with you." His hand on hers tightened gently and she felt the warm strength of his touch as he led her toward the dance floor.

Once there he pulled her into his arms, close to the solidity of his form, the heat of his body. She wondered how long she could continue to stand and not melt at his feet with all the sensations overtaking her. Finding out at thirty-one that you had the ability to love again was definitely a shocker.

"You look beautiful tonight, Kylie," Chance said, claiming her absolute attention. "Without a doubt you are the most gorgeous woman here."

Kylie lowered her gaze to study the Rolex watch on his wrist. "Your date might have a problem with you thinking that."

"I didn't bring a date."

She raised surprised eyes to his. "You didn't?"

"No. What made you think I did? Or even more important, what made you think I would?"

"Your brother's fiancée mentioned to Lena that some woman in her family was coming to town and that you would be bringing her to the ball."

He shrugged. "Cassandra did call and try convincing me to escort her cousin tonight but I refused."

"Why?" she asked swiftly, then regretted doing so. It was really none of her business.

"Because the only woman I want to be with tonight was going to be here, although she didn't ask me to be her date."

Kylie couldn't help but smile, elated he'd come alone. "Oh, what a pity," she commented teasingly.

"Yes, I thought so, as well. But now that she's here, right where I want her to be, which is in my arms, I'm declaring myself her date for the rest of the night."

Kylie didn't have a problem with that. "Are you?"

"Yes. That's one sure way to protect you from the Derek Petersons of the world."

The contempt she heard in his voice proved her earlier assumption had been correct. There was no love lost between Derek, Chance and Morgan. "You and Morgan don't like him," she said, stating what had been so obvious. "Why?"

"Let's just say we don't exactly appreciate the way he's been known to treat women."

Not wanting to talk about Derek Peterson any longer, Chance brought Kylie's body closer to his. He drank in her softness, her nearness, her scent—everything that was woman about her. After seven years of doing without a woman in his life, the one he was holding in his arms made him feel complete.

"Why did you pretend that the two of us hadn't met before?"

Kylie's question invaded Chance's thoughts. He gazed at her, thinking that her question was easy enough to answer. "Something you said a few weeks ago made me want to prove you wrong."

She arched an eyebrow. "And what did I say?"

"You said that we had only met because of our kids and chances were if we'd been at any function together that I would not have given you a second look. It was your opinion that you're not the type of woman I would have shown interest in."

Kylie nodded, remembering she *had* said that. "And?"

"And I've proven you wrong, Kylie," he drawled.

She gave him a bemused look. "How?"

"By being here with you tonight, seeing you walk through that door for the first time. Tonight has nothing to do with our kids. It's a function where we are both in attendance, and I did give you a second look. You are definitely a woman I would be interested in. And to go even further, you *are* a woman I *am* interested in, Kylie. The *only* one I'm interested in."

His words touched her more than he would ever know and Kylie didn't think she could feel more desired and more wanted than at that very moment. The way he was looking at her made her feel hot, feverish. The intensity in his eyes made her pulse flutter and a heat wave consumed her, sending blood thrumming through her veins. She felt her nipples puckering against his chest. What was passing between them was too arousing for a dance floor.

The music ended and she felt him curl his fingers around her upper arm to lead her toward the exit doors. "Where are we going?" she asked breathlessly, trying to keep up with his long strides.

"Outside to get some fresh air."

Kylie swallowed. She had a feeling that fresh air wasn't the only thing Chance intended to get.

WHEN CHANCE FINALLY CAME to a stop beneath a cascade of low-hanging branches, he turned to Kylie and gently pulled her to him. And when his lips creased into that sexy smile that could automatically turn her on, she didn't think twice about tilting her head back for his kiss.

Her breath escaped in a shallow sigh the moment he slanted his mouth across hers, causing her already heated body to become a blazing flame. And when the glide of his tongue across hers caused her stomach to clench, she reached up and wound her arms around his neck, bringing their bodies closer.

She felt his erection pressed so strongly against her, actually wedged between her thighs, and moaned in his mouth at the same time her body instinctively rocked against him. A part of her didn't know what to make of her actions. She had never been this loose, this free with any man. The couple of times she and Sam had made out, she'd been too busy worrying about whether they would get caught to fully enjoy the experience.

Now getting caught was the last thing on her mind. If an entire ballroom discovered her and Chance outside kissing beneath a bunch of willow branches, then so be it. Nothing, and she meant nothing, could make her stop being a participant in this. She'd needed his mouth on hers, his seductive taste mingling with her own tongue more than she had known. She had been hungry and now he was feeding her with a skill that only he possessed. He tasted, stroked and tangled his way around her mouth, pleasuring her as only he could do.

And then she felt him smooth a hand up her silken thigh. As it eased beneath her short dress and inched its way to her waist, she moaned deep within her throat.

The sensations his touch invoked overwhelmed her and instinctively she arched closer to him.

Slowly he released her mouth, raised his head and met her gaze, and she knew he saw the longing that was there in the dark depths of her eyes, mirroring what she saw in his. He reached up and skimmed a fingertip across her lips and she moaned against his finger. Heat shot down to the area between her legs.

"I want to leave here and take you somewhere to be alone with you, Kylie."

She knew what he was asking. She knew what he was saying. He might not love her but he wanted her. And at that moment it was all that mattered to her. What he'd tried telling her all along suddenly made perfect sense. They were adults and they could do whatever they wanted to do within reason. Would it be so awful to take what he was offering? A chance for the two of them to be alone? She had lived the past fifteen years without a man in her life, she didn't need promises of forever.

Right now the only thing she needed was him, the man she knew she loved. And for the first time in a very long time, she would be led by her heart and not her mind. Regrets, if there were any, could come later.

"I want to be alone with you, too, Chance."

"I'm glad to hear that," he whispered, smiling. "I think we should go back inside, mingle, dance a couple more times and then leave. What do you think of that?"

She smiled up at him. The thought of being alone with him later made her heart beat in an erratic rhythm, and the pure male desire shimmering in his eyes wasn't helping matters. "I think that's a wonderful idea."

The moment they stepped back into the ballroom a woman called out to Chance, claiming his attention.

They turned and watched two beautiful, and gorgeously dressed women head their way. Chance's hand on Kylie's arm tightened and when she glanced up at him she could detect a frown that he was trying to hide behind a forced smile.

"Chance, I've been looking for you."

"Hello, Cassandra. I'd like you to meet a friend of mine, Kylie Hagan."

Cassandra barely spared Kylie a glance, until she noticed Chance's hand possessively on her arm. Then, after a swift appraisal, she extended her hand. "Oh, hello. Have we met before?"

"I don't think so," Kylie said, noticing the woman's immediate dislike of her. The feeling was reciprocal.

Cassandra then turned her attention back to Chance and to the woman at her side. "This is my cousin, Jamie, the one I told you about who's visiting from Washington, D.C."

"Hello, Jamie. Welcome to Charlotte," Chance said politely. He then turned to Kylie. "And, Jamie, I'd like you to meet Kylie Hagan, a good friend."

After introductions were made Cassandra didn't waste time. "Chance, I think you and Jamie should spend time together while she's in town," she said, disregarding Kylie and Chance's hold on her arm.

"Really? And why would you think that?"

"Because her father is Senator Hollis."

Chance's expression became barely tolerant. It appeared he didn't appreciate Cassandra's lack of manners. "Sorry, but is that supposed to mean something to me?"

Cassandra tilted her head back to look at him. The glint in her eyes said she was annoyed. "Well, I thought it would since you're a businessman interested in world trade and he's on the Fair Trade Commission in Washington."

"Well, that's all rather nice," Chance said, irritation evident in his tone. "But I don't think I need Jamie to arrange a meeting with her father if I ever need to discuss business with him. After all, he is a paid politician representing *all* the people, right?"

Cassandra's hazel eyes narrowed. "Right."

"Okay, then." In an attempt to save face, he changed the subject. "The committee did a wonderful job with the ball tonight, Cassandra. Kylie and I were headed over to the buffet table."

"Well, enjoy," Cassandra said, clearly not happy that she hadn't gotten Chance to bend her way.

Chance gave Jamie a smile. "It was nice meeting you. Give your father my regards." Tightening his hold on Kylie's arm, they walked off.

When they reached the buffet table, Chance let out a long sigh. "That woman had a lot of nerve to suggest that I date her cousin while you were standing there. She was willing to use Jamie's father's political connection to set her up on a date. I've never seen anything so tacky. I'm sorry about that."

Kylie chuckled as she picked up a plate. "Don't be. I learned a long time ago that usually it's people with money who lack real manners."

"I hope you're not grouping everyone with money in that category."

She smiled up at him. "No, only some of them. The Cassandras and the Dereks of this world."

Chance grinned. "I agree."

They remained at the ball for an additional hour or so, long enough to mingle and for Kylie to meet Chance's three female cousins, and his other two brothers, whom she thought were as handsome and as well-mannered as Chance and Morgan. After meeting Sebastian Steele, she couldn't picture him married to someone like Cassandra Tisdale.

"We've hung around long enough," Chance whispered in her ear. "Ready to leave?"

She looked up at him, her smoldering eyes telling him she'd been anxiously counting the minutes. "Yes, I'm ready."

THEY LEFT THE BALL, THEN waited as a valet brought Chance's car to them. It was then that he asked, "Did you need to find Lena and let her know you've left with me?"

She shook her head. "I think she'll have an idea what happened when she doesn't see me anymore tonight."

He opened the passenger door on his car when it came. "Will her knowing bother you?"

"No. Will her knowing bother you?"

"No."

"What about your brothers and cousins?" she asked.

"It wouldn't bother me for anyone to know we're together, Kylie," he said, closing the door when she slid onto the smooth leather seat.

When he got inside the vehicle and slid beneath the steering wheel she said, "Nice car."

He grinned. "Thanks. I decided to leave the truck home and bring my toy."

She chuckled. A Mercedes sports car was some toy. "Where are we going?"

He glanced over at her. "Where do you want to go?"

They could go to either her place or his since there

weren't any kids at home. That thought made a girlish giggle escape her lips. He glanced over at her when he pulled out of the parking lot and headed toward the interstate. "Are you okay?"

She grinned. "Yes. I was just thinking that with the kids away the parents will play. I feel like being naughty tonight, Chance."

He surprised her when he braked and veered off to the shoulder of the road.

"Why are we stopping, Chance?"

"I feel like being naughty tonight, too, starting now," he replied simply, before leaning over and connecting her mouth with his again. Her lips parted without any hesitation and his aggressive tongue mingled diligently with hers. He tasted of the wine he had consumed earlier and it only raised her body's temperature. She returned his intensity with her own, and as their tongues mingled, her insides turned to molten liquid.

When he pulled back, they were both breathless. He captured her gaze, held it. "So, will it be my place or yours?"

She reached out and placed her palm against his cheek. "Mine. I want you in *my* bed, Chance Steele."

CHAPTER ELEVEN

LESS THAN A HALF HOUR later, they entered Kylie's home. As she closed the door, a warm, tingly, tantalizing sensation began building up inside of her in anticipation of what was to come.

There in the middle of the room stood Chance. The dark eyes looking at her were smoldering and, as always, he looked the embodiment of extreme male sexuality. And there was no doubt that he was the most tempting sight she'd ever seen.

Neither of them spoke.

He continued to look at her, long and hard, making her already heated body that much hotter, making her fully aroused. When she thought there was no way she could stand the intensity of his gaze any longer, he smiled, that slow, sexy smile that was meant to warm her. Instead it ignited everything woman within her, making her body respond to his physical presence in the most primitive way. When she thought she couldn't possibly take any more, he slowly closed the distance separating them.

"Are you sure about this, Kylie?" he whispered huskily, taking her hand in his and bringing her closer to him. So close that she felt his huge erection.

Kylie felt off balance and her mind became a mass of desire, of wanting, of need. "I've never been so sure of anything in my life, Chance," she whispered back. "But..."

"But what?"

"But I don't have any real experience at this and I don't want to disappoint you."

He wrapped his arms around her waist and pulled her closer still. "Trust me, sweetheart, you won't. There's no way you can."

He leaned down and took her lips, and seconds later she felt herself being lifted in his strong arms. He carried her up the stairs. "Which room is yours?" he asked when he'd reached the landing.

"The first door to your right."

She had left a low lamp burning in her bedroom and now it cast an intimate glow in the room.

"I love that dress you have on but it's coming off, Kylie," he said as he set her on her feet. Without hesitation he stripped off his tuxedo jacket and bow tie, and unbuttoned his white shirt.

She tilted her head back. "If you want it off, you'll have to take it off," she said with sass.

He accepted the sensuous challenge in her voice. "I have no problem doing that, because it *is* coming off. I have a lot of plans for you tonight."

She smiled. Whether he knew it or not, she had a lot of plans for him, as well. "I take it you're going to teach me a few things."

"Yes," he said, undoing the last of his buttons, exposing his muscular chest. She had seen his chest before, when they'd gone camping and he had taken a swim in the lake. And then, like now, she thought it was definitely a chest worth looking at, worth sliding her hands over, worth teasing with her tongue.

Her gaze followed Chance's fingers as he removed

his shirt and tossed it aside, but when those same fingers went to the fastener of his pants her breath caught. Still, she couldn't avert her eyes. They watched as he eased his zipper down. A heaviness settled in her stomach and every nerve ending within her came vibrantly alive when he pushed those same pants down his hips.

She had never seen a man undress before. At sixteen she had actually closed her eyes when Sam had done it. As an adult she was now seeing a male in the flesh for the first time. She'd always suspected Chance had a nice body, but now, she saw first hand just how nice it was. And she saw just how aroused he was since the black briefs he wore showed the large ridge of his erection. She couldn't help but stare when he proceeded to remove the last stitch of clothing.

"Now it's time for your clothes to come off."

Her gaze flew up to his face, fighting the panic of not knowing just how her body would be able to accommodate such a well-endowed man. But when her eyes met his, that sexy smile of his aroused her even more and she knew that she wouldn't worry. The two of them would fit perfectly.

With slow and precise steps, he covered the short distance separating them and his hand, as gentle as it could be, reached out and stroked her arm. "Do you know how often I've dreamed about undressing you?" he whispered huskily as he lifted her hand to his mouth and kissed her palm.

She took a deep breath to steady herself. The touch of his moist tongue on her hand only fueled the fire that was steadily burning inside of her. "No, how often?" she managed to get out in a raspy breath.

"Too often," he said, reaching behind her to undo the

clasp at the nape of her neck. "And seeing you in this dress tonight didn't help matters any."

He took a step back, loosened the straps away from her neck and the black georgette material slid down her legs. And when he offered her his hand for assistance, she took it and stepped out of the dress. Now she was naked except for her thong, thigh-high hose and shoes.

His gaze, she noticed, was fastened on her breasts and she watched, as if in slow motion, when he reached out and fondled them, caressing them, shaping them to the feel of his hands.

At his touch, her breathing became erratic, and she leaned into him to grip his shoulders, for fear she would melt to the floor. She clutched him when he leaned forward and took a nipple into his mouth, licking and sucking first one then the other. Each and every tug sent sensuous sensations all the way to her womb.

"Chance," she whispered, arching toward him even more. She gasped when he scooped her into his arms and carried her over to the bed, placed her on it. Gently he removed her shoes and then his hand slid up her legs to get rid of her hose. Taking off her thong was easy since there wasn't much to it but Kylie saw how dark his eyes got when the most intimate part of her body became exposed.

His smoldering gaze focused on the mound between her thighs, and Kylie began to feel nervous with all the attention. Chance was definitely enjoying the view, but if he only knew how fast her heart was beating, he wouldn't be looking at her this way.

"I want you, Kylie," he said silkily.

She met his gaze and replied softly, "I want you, too, Chance."

Her words, spoken honestly and seductively, zapped Chance of what little control he had. Placing a knee on the bed, he reached down and drew her naked body to his and kissed her with all the love he had in his heart. The moment he slipped his tongue inside her mouth she latched onto it, returning his kiss with an intensity he knew the both of them felt.

He reluctantly broke the kiss and began caressing her all over, becoming familiar with the soft feel of her body and the sexy scent of her arousal. He kissed her all over, starting with her breasts and moving down to her navel, but as he went lower still, he felt her tense. Knowing he was about to carry her through unchartered waters, he lifted his head and met her gaze. "Kylie?"

The eyes that met his were glazed with desire and shadowed in uncertainty. "Yes?"

"Do you trust me?"

"Yes," she responded in a breathy sound. "I trust you."

"How much?" he asked, giving her one of those sexy smiles again.

Her voice was soft and throaty when she said, "Considering all you know about me, I trust you a lot. I haven't been with anyone in fifteen years, Chance. That in itself should say something."

"It does. And your trust in me is special. I want to make not just tonight, but this entire weekend special for the both of us."

He must have read the question in her eyes, as he chuckled and said. "And no, I don't plan on keeping you in bed all weekend. There's going to be more to our relationship than sex, Kylie. I want to take you on our first official date tomorrow night. Will you let me do that?"

Kylie caught her bottom lip between her teeth. She still wasn't ready for their kids to know they were involved, but with Marcus and Tiffany away for the weekend, she and Chance were finally free to do whatever they wanted to do. "Yes, I'd like that," she said quietly.

He smiled. "Good. And another thing."

She quirked an eyebrow. "What?"

"I want to introduce you to various types of lovemaking but I promise to take things slow and easy. And I also promise not to do anything you're not comfortable with doing. I want to show you that making love is the most intimate act two people can share, as well as the most pleasurable. And I want to share every aspect of it with you." He reached out his hand and slowly traced it up her leg toward the center of her thighs.

The closer he got to a certain part of her, the harder it became for Kylie to concentrate and to breathe. "Every aspect?" she asked breathlessly.

"Yes. I want to take you to a place you've never been before. Pleasureland. I want us to go there together and participate in the kind of pleasure that only the two of us can generate." His voice went lower when he asked, "Will you go there with me?"

She swallowed when his knuckles nudged her thighs apart and his fingers touched her—right there in what had to be her hot spot. And she knew he'd found her not only hot but wet, as well. "Yes, I'll go there with you," she said, barely able to get the words out.

"Anyplace? At anytime…within reason?"

Chance was stroking her and she could feel pressure building inside of her. Pressure she needed to release. "Yes."

"My touching you this way is just the beginning," he

said as he continued to stroke her. "I want to take you on one hell of an adventure. Are you okay with that?"

Biting back a moan, she closed her eyes. "Yes, I'm okay with it." The feathery touch of his fingers was slowly driving her insane. It seemed as if he was touching every sensitive cell that was located between her legs.

"You sure?"

"Yes, I'm sure."

"And what if I replaced my fingers with my tongue?" he leaned over and whispered hotly in her ear.

Her eyes flew open. And she knew the flush that had suddenly appeared on her face told him everything. She took a deep breath as she melted inside with the thought of him doing that. "Why would you want to do that?" she somehow managed to ask.

"Because I want to satisfy my taste for you in a way that kissing won't do, Kylie."

"But no one has ever… I've never . . ."

"Yes, I know," he said silkily. "But I want to be your first. May I?"

Her heart pounded erratically in her chest. She had to swallow twice before she spoke. "Yes, if you're sure you want to do that."

"Oh, baby, more than anything, I do."

As soon as he had spoken those words, Chance slid off the bed, gently brought her body closer to the edge and knelt in front of her open legs. Then he leaned forward, inhaled her scent and took her into his mouth.

Kylie's body bucked at the first touch of his tongue. A deep groan escaped her throat when he proceeded to taste her with a hunger that appeared unquenched. She clutched the bedspread, needing something to hold on to.

His mouth was literally driving her insane and she had to clamp her lips closed to stop herself from screaming.

Chance lifted his mouth only long enough to say, "Just let go, baby, and come for me."

No sooner had he replaced his mouth on her, she did just what he had asked. The force of the climax hit her. And when it did she forgot everything except how all of her senses seemed to be gathered at this one particular spot, making it impossible to hold back. She screamed out his name when her body splintered into a thousand pieces. Waves and waves of pleasure washed over her and through her. She cried out several more times as her body, soul and mind were transported to a place where only pleasure resided.

Pleasureland.

It was a place that only Chance could take her.

CHANCE RELUCTANTLY PULLED his mouth away and sat back on his heels, watching the last contractions of Kylie's orgasm move through her. He had dreamed of taking her this way for so long, the only thing he could do for the moment was to sit there and inhale the womanly scent of her, savor her taste.

Hearing the woman he loved scream out his name had filled him with a joy he'd never felt before. But he knew for them, this was just the beginning of one hell of a weekend, one hell of a relationship and one hell of a future.

Driven by an intense need to become a part of her in yet another way, he reached for the pants he had discarded earlier. He pulled his wallet out of the back pocket to get one of the condoms he'd put there. He quickly slipped it on, wanting to join their bodies while she was still in the throes of lingering passion.

He eased her back to the center of the bed and joined her there. When his face was mere inches from hers she slowly opened her eyes and met his gaze. A satisfied curve touched the corners of her mouth. "Hi."

He smiled back. "Hi."

"I came," she said like it had been a miracle, a pleasure she would remember always.

He smiled. "Yes, you did and I'm going to make you come again."

She blinked at him as if such a thing wasn't possible. "You will," he assured her.

And then he kissed her, taking her mouth in a way that let her know just how intent he was on making it happen for her again. Moments later, his mouth left hers to skim down her jaw, past her neck, as it traced a damp trail toward her breasts, tasting them as he'd done earlier, while reaching down to sink his fingers in the flesh he had just tasted a while ago.

"Chance." She called out his name when she felt her body getting all heated again.

He eased over her. "Open your eyes, Kylie, and look at me." He wanted to be caught in her gaze the exact moment he joined with her. If she wasn't quite ready to hear about his love, he wanted her to at least feel it.

Desire and love pulsed through his veins, made his erection just that much harder, thicker, and when she opened her eyes he knew he needed to be inside of her, feel the length of him stroking her, claiming her as his, totally consuming her.

He raised her hands above her head and with their fingers laced together, their gazes locked, he slowly eased inside of her, finding her wet, ready, yet tight.

"Oh, Chance. I need this. I need you," she whispered.

His response was a hard thrust that shook him to the core, and as he went deeper inside of her, she moaned out her pleasure. "Yes!"

And then her body arched beneath him and he began moving inside of her, in and out, as her moans grew louder, more intense, more demanding and the eyes holding his looked at him with amazement and wonder. She began moving with him, their bodies in perfect rhythm.

Then she came again.

He felt the explosion of pleasure rip through her. Her fingers dug into his back and her legs locked around his waist, and he kept making love to her. Reality was better than any dream he could possibly have. He moved in and out of her, intensifying both their pleasure with every movement, feeling the urgency building up inside of her again.

Her next explosion triggered his and he screamed her name the exact moment she screamed his. He took her mouth in one final deep kiss, putting into it everything that he had, everything that was him. And moments later when the waves finally subsided, he was too weak, too satisfied, too far spent to move. But not wanting to crush her with his weight, he somehow managed to shift while keeping their bodies connected. He wasn't ready to sever the ties yet.

Feeling an aftermath of pleasure that he hadn't ever felt before, he buried his face in her breasts and wrapped his legs around her to lock her body in place with his, as they both closed their eyes in sheer exhaustion. The only word he could think of to describe what they had just shared was *incredible*.

As Chance's breathing began to slow, he knew that Kylie becoming a part of his life was a gift that he would cherish forever.

CHAPTER TWELVE

CHANCE LAY THERE AND watched as Kylie awakened.
Even before she fully opened her eyes, she covered her
yawn, and it was then that he leaned over and gently
pulled her hand away before capturing her mouth in
his. Seconds later the same desire that was raging
through him took over her. She sighed into his mouth
and wrapped her arms around his neck, surrendering to
the passion he evoked.

The mere memory of all the things they had done last
night sent heat escalating through his body and made it
harder not to take her again. The intensity of his love for
her went well beyond the scope of his understanding,
but as far as he was concerned it didn't really matter as
long as he was smart enough to accept it. And he did.

He couldn't imagine ever being without her and while
he'd watched her sleep, he had felt as if he couldn't
breathe unless he had kissed her again. Now he was
getting his fill, as he'd done last night while making
love to her. They had made love more times than he
could count, but he wasn't keeping numbers so it hadn't
mattered. The important thing was that each time he'd
opened his arms she had come into them willingly, without any hesitation or reservation, and that had meant a
lot to him.

When he slowly released her mouth he watched as

she dragged in a shaky breath. It was pretty obvious that she had never been awakened in such a manner before. "Wow," she said softly. "What was that for?"

He smiled and brought her body closer to him. He wished he could tell her it was for being the woman he loved, but there was no way he could do that. At least not yet. "That was for being the special person you are, and for allowing me to spend so much time with you last night."

A crooked smile claimed her lips as she remembered. "Yes, we did spend a lot of time together, didn't we?" Even now the rock-solid feel of him pressed against her belly was making her hot and achy all over again.

His lips formed into a half grin. "Sweetheart, we did more than that. I spent so much time inside of you that a certain part of my body actually thinks that's where it belongs. It wants another visit and is worse than a junkie in need of a fix."

"Really?" she said, arching her back and automatically pressing her pelvis against his hard erection.

"Yeah, and if you keep that up—"

"What are you going to do?"

She gasped when he quickly took hold of her hips and lifted her leg to cross over his, locking their position. Before she could gather her next breath he shifted his body and entered her.

Once inside her warm depth, he began thrusting back and forth inside of her, while his hands, wrapped tightly around her waist, held her immobile. His mouth feasted on hers with the same intensity as the lower part of his body was taking her. Mating with her.

She reluctantly tore her mouth from his. "Wh-what about protection?" she asked, barely able to get the words out.

He withdrew slowly and then sank back deep inside of her to the hilt. "I got it covered." And then he took her mouth again and her hips automatically bucked against his, reestablishing the rhythm they had created the night before.

After last night he should have been exhausted, but after sleeping with her nestled in his arms, his entire body was primed with more sexual energy than he'd ever had before. He could mate like this with her for hours. She was just that wet and he was just that needy.

She tore her mouth from his and dropped her head into his chest and moaned with each thrust he made into her body.

"Had enough?" he asked, refusing to stop or slow down. The sensations flowing through him were giving him added stamina, making him greedy.

She lifted her head and looked him in the eye. "No."

A single chuckle escaped him. "That's good," he said adjusting his angle. "Because I couldn't stop now even if you asked me to."

"What if I changed my mind and begged you to stop?"

"Forget it."

He started making little circles around her lips with his tongue. And then he began thrusting his tongue back and forth inside his mouth, mimicking the action going on below, using the same rhythm.

"Chance!"

He latched his gaze on her face, saw the intensity in her features and knew she was about ready to explode. "Let go, baby," he coaxed, knowing whenever she came he would, too.

She arched toward him, locked her body tighter to

his. It was obvious from the way she was digging her fingers into his shoulders that he'd hit gold again and zeroed in on her G-spot, that sexually sensitive area that he had discovered last night had made her have multiple orgasms back-to-back, several times over.

He grabbed hold of her butt and slowed down his strokes, although it tortured him to do so. But he was attuned to her pleasure. He stroked slowly in and out of her, hitting her in that very special spot that made her moans become louder and her breath deeper. When she glanced down and saw the way he was moving in and out of her, she began mumbling. "Oh, yes, that's the spot. Go deeper, Chance. Please. Deeper."

He did what she asked and she surprised him when she began flexing her inner muscles, milking him for all it was worth. He began feeling sensuous contractions inch all through his groin. "Aw, hell."

He began stroking her with an intensity that almost bordered on obsession, intent on pushing her over the edge, the same way she was pushing him. She dropped her head back against his chest again and he was getting turned on even more from the way their bodies were vigorously mating.

"Had enough yet?" he asked, his voice ragged. He hoped she hadn't.

She lifted her face and shook her head. Her eyes, glazed with desire, met his and she arched into him, letting him know her answer before she said the words. "Not enough. More."

"Be careful what you ask for, sweetheart," he said. "I'm a Steele, remember. I'm made to last."

And then he withdrew slowly, just long enough to adjust positions, and in a flash Kylie found herself on her back with her legs wrapped around the upper part of Chance's shoulders. And then he thrust inside of her to the hilt, harder and faster.

She screamed out his name, clung to him and succumbed to him as a rush of molten heat speared through her. When he screamed her name and pressed her hips she knew he had gotten caught up in the same exhilarating passion as she had.

She nipped at the corner of his lip and he leaned down and opened his mouth fully over hers, deepening the kiss to taste as much of her as he could. And at that moment, Kylie knew if another fifteen years went by without ever having taken part in something like this, she would survive, because in a mere twelve hours Chance had given her enough lovemaking to last a lifetime.

"YOU HAVE A BEAUTIFUL home, Chance," she called out to him.

"Thanks," he answered from the bedroom.

Kylie stood leaning against the marble counter in Chance's kitchen. After enjoying their early-morning delight, she had lain in bed, convinced that she couldn't move, and had wondered if she would ever be able to do so again. But he had gathered her into his arms like a newborn baby and had taken her into the bathroom to shower with him. It was a shower she doubted she would ever forget. She managed a smile and shook her head thinking that even now it was hard to believe that the woman who had made love to him beneath the spray of water had actually been her.

She had changed into her favorite capri pants after their shower, then she had fixed them a quick breakfast and he had talked her into going with him to the gym to watch him and his brothers play their regular Saturday morning game of basketball. But first he needed to swing by his place to change clothes. Showing up on the courts wearing his tux would definitely give his brothers something to talk about for a long time.

On the drive over to his place he had told her that he'd had the house built a few years after his wife died, because he felt he could not get on with his life while still living in the home they'd shared together. Now here she was, waiting patiently while he changed into a T-shirt and jogging pants.

"Sure I can't get you anything?" he asked, coming into the kitchen and setting his gym bag on the counter beside her.

A smile touched her lips. "No thanks. You've given me too much already."

"You haven't seen or felt everything yet," he said, as he smoothed his hand over the bare skin of her arm before grabbing her curvy bottom to bring her closer to the fit of him. He dipped his head, kissing her still-swollen lips thoroughly.

"You know we can skip that game with my brothers," he murmured softly against her lips.

"Hmm, and deny them the chance to work off their competitive frustrations? I wouldn't dare," she said, grinning.

He gave her one of his most charming smiles. "Forget my brothers. I promise if we were to stay here I'd make it worth your while."

Her grin broadened. "There's no doubt in my mind that you would, but I'm not sure I can keep up with you, Chance."

He bent his head and nipped gently at her neck. "Hey, you've been doing a pretty good job so far."

Her laughter was low and husky. "Thanks, but I have

only so much energy to spare. I may be younger than you but I'm definitely out of practice."

He took her hand, raised it to his lips and kissed her fingers. "If you're sure you're not ready to try the springs in my bed then I guess we'd better go."

While walking her out to the car, he said, "I've made reservations for us tonight at Cedar Keys."

She glanced up at him. "Cedar Keys?" She'd heard the place was rather expensive.

"Yes, Cedar Keys. My special lady deserves special treatment," he said, opening the car door for her.

My special lady. A part of Kylie wished that she was indeed his special lady and then immediately regretted the thought. Just because she was in love with him didn't mean he had to love her back. She had to remind herself that this weekend was about absolute pleasure. Love had nothing to do with it.

"Will your brothers wonder why I'm with you?"

Chance glanced over at her before starting the ignition. "They know we left the ball together last night, Kylie."

The insinuation of his statement gave her a moment's pause. "So chances are they know we spent the night together." It was a statement more so than a question.

"Not necessarily. For all they know I took you home and I went to my place after inviting you to join me this morning. But will it bother you if they've figured things out?"

"I know that it shouldn't," she said quietly. "But I am the mother of the girl their nephew has a crush on."

Chance lifted an eyebrow. "So?"

"So they might figure that I should be setting a better example."

Chance frowned. He reached over and took her hand

in his. "Hey, we're spending time in Pleasureland this weekend, remember? We don't have time to take any guilt trips. Besides, there's no need for one," he said gently. "One day you're going to have to accept that what we do is our business, Kylie. And we don't have to answer to anyone."

She drew in a long, unsteady breath. "I wish it was that easy for me to think that way, Chance. But after I got pregnant with Tiffany, my parents made sure that all their friends knew they had nothing to do with the way I turned out. I heard them call me a bad seed once. Since then I've tried so hard to be good and to raise Tiffany the right way."

He reached over and pulled her into his arms, hugging her close. "Oh, baby, you have. You're being too hard on yourself. No one is perfect, not even your parents. And they had no right to lay something that heavy on you. We all make mistakes. I bet if you were to clean out their closets you'll find something they'd rather leave hidden."

She shook her head. "I doubt it. You don't know my parents."

"Yes, I think I do. They aren't one of a kind, you know. There are others out there just like them."

A smile she couldn't contain curved her lips. "Yes, I know."

"Then remember that. Always keep that thought in mind."

He released her and Kylie thought she fell in love with him even more at that moment. "You're good at that, you know."

He glanced over at her as he began backing the car out the driveway. "Good at what?"

"Soothing my ruffled feathers."

He smiled. "Glad I could help."

"HEY, MAN, DID YOU HAVE to bring your own personal cheerleader?" Bas whispered as he set a screen for Chance to shoot.

Chance laughed as he made yet another shot and Kylie stood and cheered again. "Jealousy won't get you any points, Bas. You could have brought Cassandra."

Bas frowned. "Are you kidding? Can any of you imagine her sitting over there on the bleachers watching me get hot and sweaty?"

Donovan chuckled. "No, I don't think we can."

"Hey, will the three of you cut the crap and let's get some playtime?" Morgan growled, pushing Bas out of the way and getting the ball from Chance.

"Hey, that's a foul, Morgan," Chance called out, watching Morgan dribble the ball down the court to make a shot. He then turned to Bas. "What's his problem?"

"Seems like some lady he was interested in last night at the ball wasn't all that receptive," Bas said as they ran down the court to retrieve the stolen ball.

"Who?"

"The woman who could be Queen Latifah's twin, Helena Spears. He asked her out and she declined. She's probably the first woman who's ever turned down a dinner date with him. He evidently doesn't handle rejection well."

Chance grinned. "Evidently."

The game ended an hour or so later with Bas and Chance winning. Morgan, who'd made six fouls, would have gotten thrown out of the game had they been playing by real basketball rules.

Kylie sat patiently on the bleachers waiting for the men to come out of the locker room, where they had gone to shower and change. When Bas came out first, he crossed the gym to come over to talk to her.

"So," he asked dropping in the seat next to her, "what did you think of our game?"

She couldn't help but smile. "Interesting. A lot of rules were broken."

Bas chuckled. "Yeah, better broken rules than broken noses. We need this game every week to work off frustrations. Otherwise, we'd be at each other's throats at some point during the week."

"So I heard."

After a few moments of silence, Bas, who had a habit of shooting straight from the hip, said, "Chance has never brought a woman to watch us play before, so I figure you must be special."

Kylie gave him a wry glance. "Do you?"

"Yes, I do."

"That's good to know because I think he's special, too."

Bas shook his head and chuckled softly. "You don't seem too happy about it."

Kylie let out a sigh. "We should be concentrating on our kids."

"Hey, Marcus is a smart guy and from what I hear your Tiffany is a smart girl."

"Yes, but trouble has a way of finding even smart people."

"You're talking to someone who knows. Trouble used to be my middle name."

Kylie caught her bottom lip between her teeth. "Chance is a nice guy," she said quietly. "Marcus is lucky to have him for a father."

"That's the same thing Chance said about you."

Kylie glanced over at Bas. "What?"

"That you were a nice person and that Tiffany was lucky to have you as a mother." Bas then leaned forward. "Hey, do me a favor, will you?"

"And what favor is that?"

"You've made him happy and—"

"Me?"

"Yes, you. I've never seen him in such a good mood. Sometimes I think that smile is plastered to his face."

Kylie shook her head. "I have nothing to do with it."

"Yes, you do. At first he was all bent out of shape at the thought that Marcus's attention had gotten off his books and shifted to a girl, but once he met you then he saw why."

Kylie's eyebrows pulled together in a frown. "What do you mean?"

Bas smiled. "He was so taken with you that he could see how Marcus could be taken with Tiffany." When Kylie didn't say anything, Bas said, "Now getting back to that favor…"

"Yes?"

"Keep making Chance happy. He's had a lot of sadness in his life and if there's anyone who deserves to be happy, it's him. I think he's a pretty great guy."

Before Kylie could say anything, Bas stood, jumped off the bleachers to the court and called over his shoulder, "I'll go see what's keeping him."

Kylie leaned back and thought about what Bas had said. Before she could give it too much thought, every nerve ending in her body came instantly alive when Chance walked out of the locker room. He had changed into a pair of jeans and another T-shirt. He crossed the gym to her with a heart-stopping smile on his face.

Catching her breath, she decided to go down to meet him. As soon as she got close he leaned down and brushed his lips over hers. "Sorry for the delay. I had to talk to Morgan about something."

She nodded as he took her hand in his and led her out of the gym. "That's okay. I enjoyed chatting with Bas while I waited. Is Morgan okay? He was playing a mean game today. He committed a lot of fouls."

Chance's smile curved into a full grin. "Yes, they were intentional. He had a lot of frustrations to work off."

"Oh."

Snaking his arm around her waist, Chance snuggled her closer to his side as they walked to the car. "What were your plans for today?"

"I was going grocery shopping."

He laughed. "Hey, so was I. Do you want to go together?"

When Chance opened the car door and she slid inside, she glanced up at him and smiled. "Why not? It just might be fun."

LATER THAT EVENING AS Kylie finished getting dressed for dinner she thought that grocery shopping with Chance had not only been fun, it had been educational, as well.

He had known what fruits were in season, he made sure she checked the expiration date on everything she purchased and he advised her to stay away from the generic brands, claiming there was a difference in taste.

And she had discovered that they liked the same foods, and the same flavor ice cream. In fact, they had almost argued about who would get the last half gallon of chocolate-chip cookie dough until one of the store clerks assured them there was a case in the back.

After their shopping adventure he had brought her home to unload her groceries and indicated he would return around seven to take her to dinner. It was almost seven now and she was ready.

Kylie smiled as she glanced at herself in the mirror. She was wearing a dress she had purchased earlier that year when she had attended her father's retirement party. Her mother had complimented her on how good she'd looked in it, and now she hoped Chance shared that same opinion. She was just about to add strawberry lip color to her lips when the phone rang. She quickly picked it up. "Hello."

"Hi, Mom."

"Tiffany! I'm glad you called. How's Disney World?"

"Disney World is fine but I think Gramma had too much of Mickey and Minnie for one day. Me and Gramps are going to leave her at the hotel and go to Epcot later. How was the ball last night?"

Kylie was surprised her daughter remembered anything about the ball. "It was nice. Your godmother's committee did an excellent job."

"Was Marcus's father there?"

Kylie raised an eyebrow, wondering why Tiffany wanted to know. "Yes, he was there."

"So you saw him?"

"Yes, I saw him."

"Was he with someone?"

Kylie refused to answer that. "Tiffany, why are you asking me questions about Marcus's father?"

"Oh, just curious. Marcus and I talked before I left and he's concerned that his dad doesn't date much."

"It's not the end of the world for a person not to date, Tiffany."

"I know and that's what I told Marcus since you don't date, either. Okay, Mom, I got to go, Gramps is waiting for me. Talk to you later."

"Okay, sweetheart, have fun and tell Mom and Dad hello."

After she hung up the phone Kylie decided to cover all her bases in case Tiffany hit up her godmother for answers about the ball. She quickly picked up the phone and dialed Lena's number. "Don't be surprised if you receive a call from Tiffany asking questions about last night's ball," she told her friend.

"What kind of questions?"

"Like who Chance was with."

Lena chuckled. "He was with you."

"Yes, but I prefer her not knowing that, Lena."

"Sure, if that's the way you want it."

"It is." Something in Lena's voice made Kylie wonder if her friend was all right and she decided to ask.

"No, not really. I met this gorgeous man last night at the ball. He asked me out and I turned him down."

"Why?"

"Kylie, you know the score. Do you know how many times I've been dropped, sometimes even before the first date, when the guy finds out Mom and I come as a pair?"

"Not all guys will make a big deal out of it, Lena."

"Yes, but I'm tired of trying to figure out those who will and those who won't. I don't plan on dating for a while."

Kylie frowned. "I don't know if that's a good idea."

Lena chuckled. "Looks who's talking."

"My situation is different and you know it. I don't

date because I prefer not to. You want to date but you're afraid to."

"I am not."

"You are, too."

"Okay, so maybe I am. What's wrong with me protecting myself against heartbreak?"

"You don't know that will happen for sure. And if a man doesn't want you because you care enough to see to your mother's welfare, then screw him."

"Umm, speaking of screw…where did you and Chance disappear to last night?"

Silence pulsed over the line for a brief second and then Kylie said, "He took me home."

"And?"

"And what?"

"And why do I think there's more to this story?"

"There is, but I'd rather not discuss it now."

"Okay, just know that I'll be all ears at lunch on Wednesday."

"I doubt if you'll let me forget. Goodbye, and remember what to say if Tiffany calls asking questions."

As soon as Kylie hung up the phone she thought about her conversation with Lena. Lena was her very best friend, but there was no way Kylie would confess to her all she'd done with Chance last night and this morning. Just thinking about it made her feel mortified on one hand and giddy with pleasure on the other. Still, some things had to be kept from even your best friend. She could just imagine the look on Lena's face if she told her what had happened in the shower this morning, and how Chance had taken her against the wall while water sprayed down on them.

She glanced at the overnight bag on her bed. Chance

had asked her to spend the night at his place and she'd agreed. Since this weekend was the only one they would share, she planned on making the most of it.

CHAPTER THIRTEEN

"I HOPE YOU ENJOYED tonight, Kylie."

She glanced up from studying the wine in her glass, locked gazes with Chance and smiled. "How could I not? Everything was wonderful. The food, the service, the location…my dinner date. Thanks for bringing me here, Chance."

A smile touched the corners of his lips. "I wanted our first real date to be special, somewhere that didn't serve hamburgers."

Kylie grinned. "And it was special." She was suddenly filled with regret knowing this had been their first real date and also their last. There was no way they could continue seeing each other after Marcus and Tiffany returned, but she didn't want to think about that now. They still had tonight and all day tomorrow.

"Do you want any dessert?" he asked, and she thought his voice had a kind of husky purr to it. The expression in his eyes wasn't helping matters any, either. She'd have dessert later, she thought. Chance wanted the same thing she wanted. A bed with both of them in it.

"None for me tonight, but thanks for asking. What about you? Do you have a sweet tooth?"

He shook his head and grinned. "No, not exactly. I think I'll pass, too."

He leaned over the table to make sure she was the

only one who would hear his next words. "What I really want is to take you to my place, strip you naked and make love to you. All night long."

Only the flicker of her eyelids told him she had been shocked by such honesty. But then the heated look in her eyes told him how much she wanted what he wanted.

With self-control, she neatly folded her napkin and placed it on the table. Then she looked up and shot him a sexy grin. "Then I guess we should leave now, don't you?"

KYLIE FOUND HERSELF glancing around Chance's home for the second time that day. She had given him her overnight bag and he had taken it to the bedroom.

He had surprised her. With the heated looks he'd been giving her all evening, she'd figured he would have pounced on her the first chance he got. She'd even expected him to pull the car to the side of the road like he'd done last night and kiss her senseless. If nothing else, she had fully expected him to strip her naked the moment she had stepped inside his home.

But he hadn't done any of those things and she thought he was controlling himself admirably. So much so that she was tempted to see just how far that control could go.

"Would you like a cup of coffee or anything?"

She turned when he reentered the room. He had removed his dinner jacket and tie, and now her gaze lingered on his white shirt as she thought about the chest it covered and remembered how she had smothered her face in that chest while he'd rocked back and forth inside her body, making her moan, groan and scream.

"No, I don't want any coffee. Thanks for asking. But there is something I want."

"What?"

"A kiss. It seems I've gotten addicted to them."

"Kisses?" he asked, slowly crossing the room to her.

"Yes, but only yours."

When he came to a stop in front of her, he reached out and wrapped his arms around her waist. In response, her arms wound around his neck. She raised her chin and looked him dead in the eyes and almost melted at the heat she saw there. When he leaned forward, she lifted her lips up for the kiss she knew she would get.

As soon as his mouth touched hers, she let out a deep, satisfied moan that she felt all the way to the pit of her stomach. And when he began stroking her tongue, with all the mastery that he possessed, she moaned some more. He tasted of the wine they'd had at dinner and of the peppermint he had popped into his mouth while walking her to the car. She enjoyed the flavor of both. When he deepened the kiss she forgot everything except for the way he was making her feel.

His arms were no longer around her waist. At some point in time they had moved and his hands were now cupping her bottom, pressing her closer to him, letting her feel the strength of his growing arousal.

He released her mouth long enough for her to draw in a breath. The same breath that hitched when his lips trailed to her throat and he branded her neck again.

"Chance," she whispered.

"Yes, sweetheart?"

She tilted her head back and met his gaze. "I thought you wanted to strip my clothes off."

"I do."

"What's stopping you?"

"You never said that I could."

Kylie stared at him, remembering that last night he had asked if it was okay to undress her. It seemed that Chance Steele operated with a code of honor and that endeared him to her even more. "All right, then, I'm giving you my permission."

He took a step back and she watched his gaze travel slowly over her body, from head to toe. When he looked up, his eyes lingered on the curves of her breasts visible in the low V-neckline. He realized she wasn't wearing a bra. She could tell by the look in his eyes. That same look made her nipples harden, become sensitive to the point where she could actually feel desire roll around in her stomach.

His gaze then moved to the hemline of her dress. It was longer than the one she'd worn last night, but he seemed mesmerized by the front split, probably wondering what she had or didn't have on underneath.

"Last night I thought you looked simply gorgeous in black. But tonight I think you look sexy as hell in red," he said in a husky voice.

She blinked when she watched him back up a few steps, and then walk over to the sofa and sat down. "Come here, Kylie," he said in a voice that sounded strained even to her ears.

She stared at him, confused. How was he going to strip her bare while sitting down?

"Kylie?"

Deciding she would soon find out, she crossed the room to him.

"Lift your leg in my lap so I can take off your shoes."

She did what he asked and he took off her shoes one at a time. When she was about ready to place her foot back on the floor, he kept it in his lap, resting against his hard erection while he slid his hand up her leg a little farther, going underneath her dress to touch the center of her thighs, only to discover her panty hose was a barrier.

Apparently deciding a pair of Hanes wouldn't stop him from doing what he wanted, he placed her foot on the floor then eased to the edge of the sofa and reached both hands under her dress to work the panty hose down her hips. She stepped out of them and then kicked them aside.

"Now put your right leg back in my lap."

Again she did as he requested and this time he was able to slide his hand a little farther up her leg than before. She moaned out loud when his finger touched her center and slowly stroked her.

"Ahh, just as I thought," he leaned in closer to say. "You aren't wearing any panties."

His words hardly registered. All she could think about was the feel of his fingers inside of her, making her even wetter.

"Let me see just what else you aren't wearing tonight, Kylie."

Before she could gather her next breath, he reached up with his free hand and yanked the top part of her dress down. Her breasts spilled free right in his face.

"Place your hands on my shoulders, bend your knee a little more and lean toward me."

The moment she did so, he captured a breast in his mouth and his tongue stroked it, just like his fingers were stroking her.

She clutched at his shoulders, unable to hold back just how his mouth and fingers were making her feel. Chance definitely knew how to work both ends at the same time. She was melting from the inside out. If he continued doing this for much longer she doubted even his shoulders would be able to support her.

He let go of her breast and leaned forward. "Are you ready for me, Kylie?" he whispered hotly in her ear.

Unable to answer, she nodded.

"That's good because I've been ready for you all day. And tonight at dinner it was hard for me not to spread you out on the table and make you the only entrée I wanted to feast on."

At his words an all-consuming need raced through her body and she cried out his name when she felt the first sign of an explosion on the horizon. "Chance, I need you."

"And where do you need me, baby?"

"Inside of me," she whispered.

He suddenly lifted her in strong arms, and she closed her eyes and pressed her face against his chest.

Her eyes opened when she felt herself being placed on a hard, solid surface. He had sat her on his kitchen counter. "Chance?"

He smiled as he began taking off his shirt and removing his pants. "When I saw you in here today, standing in this very spot, I knew I had to do this. I want to take you right here. Right now," he said, quickly putting on a condom.

"Here? Now? Are you serious?"

"Oh, yes."

He then pulled her dress over her head and tossed it to the floor to join his own discarded clothing. Before she could say another word, or let out another breath, he took hold of her hips, opened her thighs and guided his shaft inside of her.

And then the thrusting began. She wrapped her arms around his neck as delicious sensations began engulfing her. "This is insane," she said, leaning forward and nipping the corner of his mouth.

"No," he said in a husky voice as his body continued to mate with hers. "This is a dream come true. A fantasy in the making. So enjoy."

And she did. He drew her closer and she spread her legs wider to accommodate him. He kissed her deeply. Then he released her mouth to pay homage to her breasts again, flicking his tongue across each nipple, sucking one and then the other, causing a sensuous tension to coil deep within her womb.

"Chance!"

The explosion hit and she cried out, dug her fingers deep in his shoulders as sensation after sensation engulfed her. She thought she would die then and there from consuming so much pleasure.

And then she felt his body jerk and knew he was experiencing one hell of an orgasm, as well. She reached out and held him as he shuddered uncontrollably with his release.

It was a while before either could catch their breaths, and when they did, neither seemed inclined to move. So she inched closer, and with as much strength as she could muster, she tightened her legs around him, enjoying the feel of him still buried inside of her. When he was finally able to lift his head to meet her eyes, she gave him a sated smile. "I've heard that things can get pretty hot in a kitchen, but this is a bit much, don't you think?" she whispered with barely enough breath.

He reached out and caressed her cheek. "And this isn't as hot as it will get for us."

That bit of news made her inch even closer to him. "It's not?"

"No, it's not. You haven't seen or experienced anything yet."

Kylie wondered what else there was. They had made love in a bed, in the shower, on the kitchen counter…

"You ever do it in a hot tub?"

His question got her immediate attention. "No."

He smiled. "Good. Then this ought to be fun."

LATE SUNDAY AFTERNOON after returning home, Kylie stood in front of her bedroom mirror and gazed at her reflection. With her messed up hair, kiss-swollen lips and hickeys on both sides of her neck, she definitely looked like a woman who had let go and indulged in her sensuous side. *Naughty* was too mild a word to describe how she had acted this weekend. *Wanton* and *loose* were probably better.

"Hey, what are you doing? Looking for a spot that I missed?" Chance asked, entering the room. He walked up behind her, wrapped his arms around her and settled her body back against his.

Kylie thought him missing a spot was impossible. It had started out very innocent with them enjoying a bowl of ice cream after lunch. Then for no reason at all he had squirted caramel topping all over her, and moments later began licking every inch of her skin to get it off. And she had reciprocated, squirted him and licked every inch of him. She had to admit that for once in her life she had thrown caution to the wind and yielded to temptation.

"What are you thinking about, sweetheart?"

She met his gaze in the mirror and leaned back against him when he tightened his arms around her. "You. Me. And what a wonderful weekend we had. I wish it didn't have to end."

"It doesn't."

She shook her head and grinned. "Yes, it does. Have you forgotten the kids will be back tomorrow?"

"No, I didn't forget, but that shouldn't have any bearing on us."

She turned around to face him. "Of course it does. Surely you don't expect us to still swap beds with the kids around?"

He frowned. "No, but I do expect us to continue to see each other. And if we have to be discreet whenever we do share a bed, then we will."

"And what about the kids?"

"Tomorrow we can tell them that we've decided to start seeing each other."

She took a step back. "No, I don't think that's a good idea."

Chance rubbed his hand down his face. "Don't tell me we're back to that again."

"As far as I'm concerned we never left it."

"Then what was this weekend about, Kylie?"

"It was about us indulging in our fantasies. But now it's time to return to the real world, Chance, and there's no way I can let Tiffany know that I was involved in a weekend affair with you."

Angrily, he reached out and gripped her shoulders. "A weekend affair? That's all this was to you?"

She yanked away from him. "Why? Was it supposed to be something else?"

"I had hoped so," he said quietly, trying to get his anger and frustrations under control. "The start of a committed relationship was how I saw things."

"But I can't become involved with anyone until Tiffany leaves home."

"Why?"

"Because I can't!"

"Then let me tell you what I think is your reason, which in my opinion is a damn poor excuse. Your parents have convinced you that getting pregnant at sixteen was a bad thing, and every since then you have worked your ass off trying to be a good girl in their eyes. So much so that you won't allow a man in your life. At first I thought it was all about the men in your life letting you down and not being dependable, and that still may be a part of it. But since you claim you trust me, why are you so afraid of letting me into your life?"

"I have to set an example for my daughter. Why can't you understand that?"

He frowned. "And not having a real life, not having a man around to show her how two people can share a loving relationship is setting an example for her?"

"There's more to life than people getting involved, Chance."

"What about people falling in love? Would it mean anything if I were to tell you that I love you? That I fell in love with you probably the first time I saw you that day?"

Kylie's eyes widened and then she shook her head and felt the tears that stung her eyes. "No, it wouldn't matter because I could tell you the same thing, Chance. I love you, too. And I probably fell in love with you that day, as well."

"But then—"

"No. You loving me and me loving you won't make it okay. We still have to put our kids first. They think they're in love, too, and we can't downplay their feelings just because we've discovered ours. Just think of how it will look. The father loves the mother and the daughter loves the son. How dysfunctional can that be?"

His frown deepened. "So what are you suggesting? That we wait to see what becomes of our kids' romance before seeking our own? Well, I don't plan to do that. If you love me, and I mean truly love me, you'll know that we'll work things out together. But you have to be willing to step out on love and believe it."

She bowed her head and took a deep breath and then she looked back at him. "No, it won't work, Chance. Please try to understand. There are times in life when sacrifices have to be made."

"Well, if you're willing to let your love for me be the sacrificial lamb then it must not be the real thing, Kylie, because I can't think of anything that will ever stop me from loving you and wanting a committed relationship with you."

Without saying anything else he walked out of the room, and moments later Kylie heard the door slam shut behind him.

CHAPTER FOURTEEN

"MOM?"

"Hmm?"

"Are you sure you're okay?"

Kylie pulled two bottles of apple juice out of the refrigerator before turning to her daughter. "I'm okay, sweetheart. What makes you think I'm not?"

Tiffany lifted one shoulder in a dainty shrug. "I don't know. It's just a feeling I have. Every since you picked me up from the airport yesterday you've been quiet."

"Well, I guess I have a lot on my mind, but I'm okay."

"Why are you still wearing that scarf? You usually don't wear scarves."

Kylie's hand automatically went to the scarf around her neck, the one she was wearing to hide the two hickeys that Chance had placed there. "My throat had gotten sort of scratchy with the changing of the weather, I guess. I thought I'd take all precautions. The last thing I need to catch is a cold."

"But you're wearing it in the house."

Kylie gave Tiffany a pointed look. "I'm aware of where I am Tiffany. Is wearing a scarf in the house a crime?"

"No, ma'am."

"Okay, then."

The kitchen got silent and Kylie regretted having gotten upset with Tiffany when she was only showing her concern. With a mantle of guilt on her shoulders, Kylie crossed the room and sat down at the table opposite her daughter. "Hey, how about you and I go to a movie this weekend?" she asked, trying to reclaim the easy camaraderie they'd started recently, at least before this past weekend.

Tiffany smiled. "Oh, that'll be neat. Will it be okay to invite Marcus and his dad?"

Kylie's body tensed with her daughter's question. The last person she wanted to be around this weekend was Chance. "I was hoping we could make it a girls' thing. We could even invite Lena to come with us."

"That sounds like fun, Mom, but I was hoping I could get to see Marcus this weekend."

"Didn't you see him at school today?"

"Yes."

"And won't you see him again tomorrow?"

"Yes."

"And the next day and the day after?"

"Yes, Mom, but you and Mr. Steele promised that we could have supervised outings and it's been almost three weeks since we went camping."

Kylie sighed. A part of her regretted having made that promise but at the time both she and Chance had known it was the best thing to keep the budding romance between their offspring under control. "Okay, then I'll take the both of you. There's no need to bother Chance this weekend and—"

"Mom, if you take us, it'll seem as if you're babysitting us. If both you and Mr. Steele go then it will be a foursome and it won't be so obvious that you're there to spy on us."

Kylie rolled her eyes. "I'd be there as a chaperone, Tiffany."

"Same difference."

Not wanting to get into an argument with her daughter, Kylie stood and said, "Have Marcus check to see if his father is free this weekend. Chance is a busy man and might have made other plans."

Later that night Kylie lay in bed and every so often she would glance over at the phone. Chance had made it a habit to call her around this time every night, but she knew after Sunday chances were that he wouldn't be calling anytime soon, if ever. And a part of her thought maybe it was for the best. He thought he had all the answers, but he would never understand the guilt trip her parents had placed on her shoulders after she'd gotten pregnant.

As she cuddled under the covers she thought about the weekend she had spent with Chance. There was no denying that it had been a fantasy come true, and heat flooded through her just thinking about all they had done. In fact, today at the florist when she'd been alone her body actually trembled with the memories that were so vivid in her mind.

Their first date had been everything a first date should be, and what he probably hadn't even realized was, although it had been their first date, it had been her *first* date period. She and Sam had been too young to actually date and she hadn't gone out to dinner with any other man. So in reality, Chance had been her first in a lot of ways.

Tears blurring her eyes, she glanced over at the phone. She might as well get used to him not calling her ever again.

CHANCE THREW ONTO HIS desk the document he'd been reading and glanced at the clock. Not that he was counting, but it had been three days, sixteen hours and forty-five minutes since he had last seen and talked to Kylie.

After what she had said to him on Sunday evening, she should have been the last person on his mind. She had decided that love or no love, there would not be a future for them.

Chance leaned back in his chair and hooked his hands behind his head. Dammit, he didn't want that. He wanted a life with her, a life that included marriage. Kylie was being more than stubborn. She was being downright difficult.

He couldn't help but remember their weekend together, and the days and nights they had shared. Those memories would sustain him in the coming months. He would need them.

He walked over to the window and stared out at Charlotte's skyline. It was almost two in the afternoon. Kylie would be at her shop. Was she thinking about him the way he was thinking about her? Probably not.

But she had admitted that she loved him.

He should have known that when a woman gave herself as completely to a man as Kylie had done to him this past weekend that love was involved. One thing was for certain: there was still Marcus and Tiffany to deal with, and because of their kids, Kylie couldn't put distance between them, regardless of how much she might want to.

Whether she liked it or not, she hadn't seen the last of him.

"I DON'T KNOW WHAT, but something happened this weekend between our parents, Marcus," Tiffany whispered.

Marcus, who was sitting across from her in the library, glanced around to make sure Mrs. Kennard, the librarian who had a strict no-talking policy, wasn't anywhere close by. "Yes, I know," he whispered back. "This weekend was supposed to get them to together, not pull them apart. What do you think happened?"

Tiffany shook her head. "I don't know but I do know they spent time together this weekend."

Marcus lifted a brow. "And how do you know that?"

"Because Carly Owens said she saw them together at the grocery store."

"The grocery store? What were they doing at the grocery store?"

"Carly said they were actually shopping together. They didn't see her but she saw them. She said my mom had her cart and your dad had his, but they had come together in the same car."

"And she's sure it was *our* parents?"

"Yes, she's sure. She's met the both of them before but at different times."

"Umm, I find that interesting. If they were friendly enough to go grocery shopping together then what happened?"

Tiffany sighed. "I don't know. And there's also something else." She leaned in closer to make sure the students sitting at the other table didn't hear her. "My mom had a hickey on her neck and I think your dad put it there."

Disbelief flickered in Marcus's eyes. "You're kidding."

"No. She's been wearing a scarf to hide it, but I saw it anyway when she took the scarf off thinking I wasn't around."

Marcus nodded. "That means they had to have kissed."

"Right."

"Then what happened to make them start acting funny?"

Tiffany shook her head. "Who knows? Adults can be weird that way. Did your dad say that he would be available to go to the movies with us on Saturday?" Tiffany asked.

"I haven't asked him yet. He hasn't been in the best of moods since I got back."

"Neither has my mom. If after this weekend at the movies they're still not getting along, then we have to do something. I know they really like each other, but now I'm worried because your dad hasn't been calling at night like he used to do. I've been checking the caller ID every morning but your phone number isn't showing up."

"So what do you think we should do?"

Tiffany scrunched her forehead and then moments later a smile touched her features. "I have an idea but we may have to get an adult to help us pull it off."

Marcus glanced around again for Mrs. Kennard, and then turned back to Tiffany. "An adult like who?"

Tiffany thought about her godmother and decided it wouldn't be a good idea to solicit her help. "How about one of your uncles? The one you said who likes to have fun."

Marcus sighed. "That's Uncle Donovan, and this sounds serious."

"It is. We'll see how things go with them this

weekend, but if they still aren't on the best of terms, we go to Plan B."

"What's Plan B?" Marcus asked.

Tiffany leaned in closer. "Here it is, so listen up."

KYLIE CHEWED THE CORNER of her lip as she watched Chance and Marcus get out of the SUV and begin walking toward her front door. That deep fluttering in her heart and the sensations that rolled around in her stomach whenever she saw Chance made her release the breath she'd been holding. She could only stand at the window and stare out at him, providing irrefutable proof of just how much she had missed seeing him these past few days, missed talking with him…making love with him.

A part of her questioned the sanity in not giving in to the love she felt for him. Even Lena had raked her over the coals during their lunch meeting that week when she'd told her best friend that Chance had admitted his love and she had admitted hers. Lena staunchly refused to agree with Kylie that this was one of those no-win situations where love wasn't enough.

"Mom, are Marcus and Mr. Steele here?"

Kylie turned away from the window upon hearing the excitement in her daughter's voice. "Yes, they just arrived."

"Good. I'll go open the door for them." And then Tiffany raced off.

A few moments later Kylie could hear the deep sexiness of Chance's voice all the way from the foyer, and the sound sent sizzling heat all through her body. Taking a deep breath, she grabbed her coat off the back of the sofa and left the living room to join everyone in the foyer.

The moment she rounded the corner she felt Chance's gaze on her. And the moment her eyes locked with his dark brown ones, she almost forgot to breathe. For some reason she couldn't look away.

"Hi, Kylie."

"Chance."

"You look nice."

"Thanks." Kylie inwardly sighed. Holding a conversation with him used to be so easy and now she was finding it too hard.

"Hi, Ms. Hagan."

Her gaze moved from Chance to Marcus and for a second she thought she saw a worried glint in his eyes. She smiled affectionately. "Hello, Marcus. How was your trip to Busch Gardens?"

"It was fun. I was telling Tiffany about it. Maybe the four of us could go there this summer."

Kylie nodded, although she doubted it.

"Is everyone ready to go?" Chance asked. "We don't want to be late for the movie."

Marcus and Tiffany rushed out the door leaving their parents alone in the foyer. Chance turned to her. "I meant what I said earlier, Kylie. You look nice in that pantsuit. That color looks good on you. But I think any color looks good on you."

"Thanks." She had decided to wear a lime-green linen pantsuit and instead of pinning her braids up she let them tumble about her shoulders.

She stared at the floor for a second and then glanced back up at him. "You look nice, too." She decided not to tell him that she'd always thought he looked suave in a suit, but sexy as hell in a pair of jeans.

"Thanks. Are you ready to go?"

"Yes."

"And, Kylie, no matter what's going on with us, let's make sure the kids have a good time tonight, all right?"

"All right."

They then walked out the door to join their kids in the SUV.

THEY SAW THE NEW HARRY Potter movie.

Kylie was certain it had been a good movie but she hadn't fully concentrated on what was happening on the big screen. Instead her concentration had been on the man who had sat next to her. They had barely exchanged a single word but all during the movie she could feel the weight of his heavy stare. More than once she had glanced his way in the semidarkened theater to find him watching her.

Too often she had been tempted to reach out and slip her hand in his, filled with an intense desire to touch him, to feel his heat. It didn't take much for her to remember that heat, how he had consumed her with it whenever he touched her, kissed her or made love to her.

"Wasn't the movie awesome, Mom?" Tiffany said with enthusiasm in her voice as they left the theater and walked through the parking lot back to Chance's truck.

"Yes, it was nice."

Then Marcus and Tiffany got into conversations about all their favorite scenes and left Kylie and Chance to do nothing but remain silent. He didn't seem inclined to make idle chatter and neither did she. He opened the truck door for her and when their hands brushed she felt him tense the exact moment she did.

"Can we stop for ice cream?" Tiffany asked when everyone was inside the truck and buckled up.

"No," Kylie and Chance called out simultaneously, and then glanced over at each other. Chance cleared his throat and said in a more subdued voice. "I'm going out of town on Monday and there's a lot I need to do to get prepared for the trip."

"And I need to look over my accounting books tonight," Kylie added.

Both Chance and Kylie heard the disappointment in Tiffany's and Marcus's voices but decided that a movie had been enough. There was no way they could sit across from each other and eat ice cream without remembering what had happened the last time they'd done so. It had been the cause of their "lick me all over" party.

All it took was a memory—of Chance stripping her naked in her kitchen, licking sticky caramel sauce off her body—and Kylie's palms started to tingle. Her breasts suddenly felt heavy, her nipples tight, and erotic sensations built up inside of her, settling right smack between her legs. She forced a deep breath of air into her lungs thinking that this was definitely not the time nor the place for arousal.

She glanced over at Chance, and as if he felt her gaze on him, he turned to her. From the heated look in his eyes she could tell he, too, was remembering what they'd done that Sunday afternoon in her kitchen.

Kylie settled back in her seat. This was going to be one long and extremely hot ride home.

IT WAS TIME FOR PLAN B.

Marcus and Tiffany wasted no time putting it into

action. On Tuesday they had Donovan Steele's full attention as they filled him in on the failure of Plan A. "So as you can see, Uncle Donovan, we need your help."

Donovan leaned back and looked at the both of them. Marcus had contacted him on his cell phone asking that he meet them after school on the football bleachers.

Donovan shook his head. "Let me get this straight. The two of you aren't girlfriend and boyfriend? You aren't madly in love? And you only pretended you were to get your parents together?" he asked incredulously.

Both Tiffany and Marcus nodded. "That's right," Marcus said. "Tiffany and I are best friends and we thought it was a good plan. Things were going along smoothly but something happened that weekend the two of us left town."

Donovan lifted a brow. "And what do you think happened?"

"We don't know but before we left they were beginning to like each other a lot, but now we're not sure how they feel."

Donovan had heard the story from Bas and Morgan but he wasn't about to share the information with these two. "So what do you need for me to do?"

"Help us," Tiffany said.

Donovan was confused. "Help you do what?"

It was Marcus who answered. "Carry out our plan to get our parents together."

Donovan crossed his arms over his chest, not believing what they were asking of him. He loved his nephew but was he willing to incur his oldest brother's wrath? "I think you had better tell me about this plan first."

Marcus nodded. "I'll let Tiffany explain things since it's her idea. But I think it's a good one."

Donovan doubted it was all that good but decided

to listen anyway. Twenty minutes later a smile touched his lips. He hated to admit it but he liked their idea, although it could use a little tweaking here and there to make sure neither Chance nor Kylie panicked and got the police involved. There was no doubt that Chance would be mad in the beginning, but in the end odds were he would be a very happy man. "Okay, count me in. I'll help but only on one condition."

"What?" Marcus asked.

"That you modify your plan somewhat."

Marcus and Tiffany quickly agreed.

Donovan then smiled and said, "Now, I think that this is the way we should handle things...."

CHAPTER FIFTEEN

LATE FRIDAY NIGHT KYLIE glanced over at the clock on her nightstand the moment the telephone rang. It was almost midnight. She suddenly got a funny feeling in her stomach. Was it Chance? The last time she had seen him was Sunday night when they had all gone to the movies.

Deciding that answering was the only way to determine who her caller was, she reached out and picked up the phone. "Hello?"

"Mom?"

Kylie shot straight up in bed. The voice sounded like Tiffany's, but there was no way her daughter could be calling her when she was down the hall in her bed sleeping.

"Mom? Are you there? It's me."

Kylie jumped out of bed to her feet. "Tiffany! Where are you?"

"Mom, I'm fine."

Kylie angrily began pacing her bedroom. "Fine, nothing! Where are you, young lady? No one gave you permission to leave this house. How dare you pull something like that!"

"Mom, please calm down. I'm fine. Marcus and I are together."

"What?" Kylie screamed at the top of her lungs,

before collapsing in the wingback chair in her room. "What do you mean you and Marcus are together? It's after midnight. No one gave you permission to—"

"Mom, Marcus and I have been thinking."

Kylie gripped the phone tightly in her hand. "Thinking? The two of you have been thinking? Fine, then think at your own houses. I want you home immediately!"

"Not until you and Mr. Steele promise to become friends again."

Kylie frowned. What was Tiffany talking about? "Listen, honey, Chance and I are friends. You need to come home."

"The two of you didn't act like it Sunday night. You barely said two words to each other. If Mr. Steele is going to be our in-law one day, then the two of you are going to have to get along."

Kylie threw her head back and began silently counting to ten, not believing the conversation she and her daughter were having. "Look, Tiffany, I don't know where you are but I want you to end this call right now and come home. Better yet, tell me where you are and I'll come and get you."

"No, Mom, I can't do that. Marcus and I aren't going to do anything we shouldn't, so don't worry about that."

"But I am worried about that! You're only fifteen, it's after midnight and you're out somewhere with a boy when you should be home sleeping in your bed. How dare you tell me not to worry!"

"Then maybe I should ask you to trust me, and to also trust Marcus. We're in a safe location and we won't do anything that you and Mr. Steele will be ashamed of."

"That's not the point!"

"It is the point, Mom. You and Mr. Steele are going

to have to trust us. Marcus and I figured the reason the two of you can't get along is because you don't trust each other and you don't trust us."

Kylie struggled to keep her voice calm. "I do trust Chance and I've tried to stop being so uptight and to start trusting you more, but I see doing so was a mistake. You either come home within the next thirty minutes or I'm calling the police."

"Mom, please don't. All it will do is cause unnecessary embarrassment for me and Marcus."

"Tough! The two of you should have thought of that sooner."

"Mom, I'm serious. If you call the police then we won't come back. All we need is time to talk."

"And just what do the two of you have to talk about that you had to sneak out in the middle of the night to do it?"

"We need to talk about you and Mr. Steele and your inability to get along."

"We can get along!"

"Then you sure fooled us. You *were* getting along, then something happened. We don't know what but the two of you sure acted like you were avoiding each other on Sunday."

"Tiffany, I—"

"Good night, Mom. We'll call you in the morning and tell you our decision."

Kylie's stomach dropped to the floor. "Your decision about what?"

"About whatever we decide. Marcus has to call his father now. Goodbye, Mom. I'll talk to you in the morning, and I promise Marcus and I won't do anything."

Before Kylie could open her mouth to say another word, there was a resounding click in her ear.

KYLIE QUICKLY SNATCHED up the phone the moment it rang again five minutes later knowing it was Chance.

"Kylie, you okay?"

His deep, husky voice had a comforting effect on her. "Oh, Chance, what are we going to do?"

"You didn't call the police, did you?"

"No."

"Good. I got a chance to talk to the both of them and—"

"Can you believe what they've done? Just wait until I see them. I'm going to—"

"Calm down, Kylie."

"Calm down? My child is out somewhere after midnight and you want me to calm down?"

"Yes. My child is out there, too. One good thing is that they're together."

"You think that's a good thing?"

"I trust Marcus, Kylie. He won't let anything happen to Tiffany. And he gave me his word that they won't do anything they aren't supposed to do."

Kylie glanced out her bedroom window. A fist tightened around her heart knowing her little girl was out there somewhere. "Yes, that's the same thing Tiffany said," she murmured quietly. "And you're right, we're going to have to trust them."

Kylie was quiet for a long while, then she said, "Did Marcus tell you why they did it?"

"Yes, he told me."

"I thought we acted pretty normal on Sunday night," she said.

"Yeah, but I guess they still picked up on something."

"Well, even if they thought we weren't on the best of terms, it wasn't any of their business!"

"Oh? You finally agree with me about that?"

Kylie frowned. "I'm serious, Chance."

"I've always been serious about that." He then asked, "Where are you now?"

"In my bedroom."

"How about going downstairs and putting some coffee on. I doubt if either of us will get much sleep tonight and if we're going to worry, we might as well do it together. I'm on my way over."

"All right. I'll have the coffee ready when you get here."

CHANCE MADE IT TO KYLIE'S house in less than ten minutes. She met him at the door with a cup of steaming hot coffee.

As if it was the most natural thing to do, he leaned over and kissed her lips. "You okay?" he asked quietly, after taking the cup from her hand and following her into her living room, where he sat down on the leather sofa beside her.

"Yes, I'm okay. But I'm still worried about them, Chance. I didn't think to ask how they were getting around. I assumed Marcus took his car."

Chance nodded after taking a sip of his coffee. "Yes, he has it. Boy, he's going to be grounded for life."

"So is Tiffany and she hasn't started driving yet. And just to think I had considered surprising her with a car for her sixteenth birthday. She might as well kiss that surprise goodbye."

"And they pulled this just to make a statement that they didn't like the way we acted on Sunday. If that doesn't beat all," Chance said.

"Yeah, I guess it means a lot to them for us to get along."

"But it's not like we argued or anything, Kylie."

She inhaled deeply. "I know, but I guess they were watching us more closely then we thought. You have to admit we were rather distant to each other."

"Yes, we were," he readily admitted. "And I didn't like it."

She met his gaze and said, "Neither did I."

After a few moments of silence she added, "Do you think we're doing the right thing by not calling the police?"

"Yes. But I did contact my brothers. There was no way I could not let them know. At least I was able to reach Bas and Morgan. Evidently Donovan is still somewhere out on the town and he isn't answering his cell. But I'll talk to him tomorrow. And I notified my cousins, as well, in case Marcus contacts them."

Kylie nodded. "I forgot about your basketball game in the morning."

Chance shook his head. "Yeah, but there's no way I'm going to go anyplace until the kids come home."

"They will come home, won't they, Chance?"

When he heard the trembling in her voice, he set his cup on the table and wrapped his arms around her shoulders. It felt good to hold her again. "Yes, they'll come home. When they get hungry, they'll be back."

His words made Kylie smile. "Yeah, Tiffany definitely likes to eat."

"And so does Marcus."

Kylie cuddled deeper into Chance's warm embrace. It felt good to be held by a man who cared about her. A man who'd told her he loved her. A man she knew she could depend on. "Where do you think they'll sleep tonight?"

Chance shrugged. "Either in the car or at a hotel."

Kylie pulled back and looked at Chance. "Are they old enough to get a hotel room on their own?"

"It depends on where they go. To some hotel owners, money and not age is the determining factor."

Kylie really hadn't wanted to hear that. More than anything she had to remember that Tiffany said she and Marcus wouldn't do anything. She had promised.

"Come here and lay beside me. You must be tired."

She automatically did what he suggested without thinking twice about it. He stretched out his legs on the sofa to accommodate her and gently held her as they lay side by side. Before he had arrived, she had changed out of her nightgown into a pair of silk lounging pants and top. Heat curled through her when he wrapped his arms around her. It felt good knowing she wasn't alone now.

"Try to get some sleep."

"I don't think I can, Chance. I want my baby home." A few moments later, sleepily she said, "Did I ever tell you about the first time I let Tiffany sleep somewhere other than her own bed?"

"No, I don't think that you did."

"She was two and my parents had finally acknowledged that they had a grandchild and wanted some bonding time. At first I wasn't going to let her go but then Lena convinced me that I should. I barely slept that entire night knowing she wasn't in the house. I finally was able to sleep only after going into her room and stretching out on the floor beside her little bed. Now isn't that pathetic?"

"No, it sounds to me like you were a mother who had missed her child and needed the connection." After a few moments he added, "It works like that for adults, too, you know."

She lifted her head and met his gaze. "Does it?"

"Yes." He reached out and stroked her cheek with one finger. "You slept in my bed that one night but that's all it took for me to get used to your presence. All this week I found myself reaching out, as if you were still there, wanting that connection."

Kylie's stomach knotted when her gaze slipped to his mouth and she remembered how that mouth had driven her crazy in so many different ways. She remembered the taste of it, the feel of it. She also remembered something else. The amount of love she had in her heart for this one particular man.

"Oh, Chance." She reached up and tightened her arms around his neck at the same time she leaned up for his kiss.

With agonizing slowness he took her mouth, claimed it, branded it. His tongue made love to her mouth. The more it did, the more she became fully aware of the steady, strong arms holding her. They were protective arms. They were arms that would shield her from any storm, whether raging or mild. They were arms that would always be there to hold her when she needed to be held. It had been late in coming but she realized that now.

Moments later when he lifted his mouth she let out a satisfied sigh. "Thanks. I needed that."

He looked at her and smiled. "So did I."

Determined to maintain control of the situation he then said, "Now let's try to get some rest so we can be well-rested to give our kids hell when they come back home."

"Yes, *our* kids." Kylie said the words as if they suddenly had new meaning to her.

As he pulled her closer she settled against his

comforting muscular form and believed that from this time forward somehow everything was going to be all right.

"Mom?"

"Dad?"

Chance slowly opened his eyes. Had he been dreaming or had he actually heard Tiffany's and Marcus's voices? The first thing he noticed was that he was stretched out on the sofa with Kylie lying beside him, her head resting on his chest. That would not have been so bad if his hand wasn't possessively cupping her bottom or one of her legs wasn't entwined with his. Even her hand was resting pretty darn close to the fly on his jeans.

He sucked in a deep breath, letting the scent of her fill his nostrils. She was still asleep, but he could remember a time that weekend when he had patiently waited for her to wake up so that he could—

"Dad?"

"Mom?"

Chance swallowed as he slowly glanced across the room and his gaze lit on two pairs of curious eyes. He blinked. No, make that three.

He quickly sat up and the movement startled Kylie out of a sound sleep. "Chance, what's wrong?" she asked sluggishly, slowly coming awake.

He shifted his gaze from the three sets of eyes to her still-drowsy ones. "Wake up, sweetheart, the kids are back," he whispered.

She blinked. "What?"

"The kids are home."

She was off the sofa in a flash. He had to catch her to keep her from stumbling. "Tiffany! Marcus! We've been so worried about you," she said, hugging them so tight Chance wondered how they were able to breathe.

Then as if it finally hit her what they had done, she stepped back, placed her hands on her hips and gave them one hell of a fierce frown. "The two of you have a lot of explaining to do."

"Seems they aren't the only ones," Donovan Steele said in a low voice, after clearing his throat.

Kylie jumped and jerked her head around. She hadn't seen Chance's youngest brother standing at the edge of the foyer. "Where did you find them?" she asked, tossing her mussed-up braids over her shoulders.

Before Donovan could answer, Tiffany said, "He didn't find us. We were with him the entire time. We spent the night over at his house."

"What?" That loud exclamation came from both Kylie and Chance at the same time.

"And we had so much fun," Marcus said, smiling. "The three of us played video games until—"

"What the hell do you mean you were with him the entire time?" Chance shouted, coming to his feet beside Kylie.

"Dad, don't get mad at Uncle Donovan," Marcus said, rushing in. "I can explain."

Donovan smiled as he leaned against the wall. "Yes, Chance, let him explain. And trust me, it's a doozy. And I think you and Kylie might want to be sitting down when you hear it."

CHAPTER SIXTEEN

"LET ME MAKE SURE I have this right," Chance said as he paced back and forth in front of the two teenagers, who were now the ones sitting on Kylie's sofa. To say they were in the hot seat was an understatement. "Are the two of you saying you aren't madly in love and that you never were?"

It had taken the kids twenty minutes to explain to their parents what it had only taken ten to confess to Donovan a few days ago. But Kylie and Chance had stopped them periodically to ask questions.

"Yes, Mr. Steele, that's what we're saying. Marcus and I are good friends and have been since the first day I started at Myers Park High. One day while talking we decided that neither you nor my mom had a life that didn't center around us, so we decided to give you one," Tiffany said, smiling.

Chance frowned. "You decided? Just like that?"

"Yes, sir, we decided just like that. Wasn't that cool?"

Kylie came to stand next to Chance. "No, that wasn't cool. Did it ever occur to either of you that we liked the life we had?"

"Yes, it did occur to me, but then I wondered what you would do when I left for college in a few years, Mom," Tiffany said quietly. "Just the thought of you being here all alone almost made me give up the idea of leaving home and going off to school. But then I figured it wouldn't be fair for me to give up my life just because you didn't have one. So I decided to help you find one. And when Marcus mentioned how handsome his dad was, and I told him how beautiful you are, we decided the two of you would make the perfect solid soul."

Chance lifted a confused brow. "Solid soul?"

"Yes, it's where two souls combine into one. A very solid one that can withstand anything."

Kylie crossed her arms over her chest and glared at them. "The two of you deceived us. You had us almost pulling our hair out by pretending you were so much in love."

"We kept asking you to trust us, Ms. Hagan," Marcus spoke up and said. "Even if we were in love, Tiffany and I have been raised right. You and Dad have done a good job. We know right from wrong and we know what to do and what not to do. We kept telling you and Dad that, but you wouldn't listen."

"That's besides the point. What the two of you did last night was—"

"Necessary, Mom," Tiffany cut in and said. "I'm not a child. I knew you were beginning to really like Mr. Steele. I could tell. And I could also tell that you wouldn't let yourself like him fully because you probably thought I wouldn't go along with it when all I ever wanted was someone to come into your life and treat you nice, take you places and make you smile. And Mr. Steele made you smile, Mom. I've never seen you smile so much as when you were around him or talked to him every night on the phone. And I knew our plan was working because Marcus said his dad was smiling, too."

Marcus picked up their defense. "But we also knew something happened, Dad, that weekend Tiffany and I went out of town. When I got back to town the smile was gone and you were acting like you had lost your best friend. Tiffany told me that her mom was acting the same way so we figured the two of you had had an argument. We knew we needed to do something."

Chance sighed deeply. "Is that the reason for the stunt the two of you pulled last night?"

"Yes," Tiffany said softly. "I figured if you cared for my mom that you would come over and make sure she was okay. And you did just what I knew you would do, Mr. Steele."

"In other words, we played right into your hands," Chance said, frowning.

"No, you played right into each other's hearts," Donovan said, coming to stand next to Chance. "I think you've drilled them long enough, and yes, I let them talk me into being a part of their shenanigans because I saw the same thing they did. The two of you cared for each other and you *were* smiling a lot, Chance, when you were together." Donovan grinned. "You were even smiling when you weren't together. You don't know how many times when we were in your office for a meeting that Bas, Morgan and I were tempted to slap that smile off your face. The two of you were meant to be together."

"That's not the point," Kylie snapped.

"Then what is the point?" Donovan asked crossing his arms over his chest. "Your kids cared enough about the two of you to do something. I admit their plan might have needed a little polishing but what the hell. It worked, didn't it?"

The room got quiet. Chance met Kylie's gaze and

held it for a long moment. Then he said, "Yes, it worked. Only thing, Marcus and Tiffany, I really don't *like* Kylie. And the reason I don't like her is because I'm deeply in love with her. There's a difference."

Both Tiffany and Marcus smiled and pumped their fists in triumph. "Yes!"

"And how do you feel about my dad, Ms. Hagan?" Marcus asked a few moments later. Kylie knew all eyes were on her, especially Chance's. He knew she loved him. She had admitted as much—but she had also declared that she wouldn't act on that love. Now he was waiting to see if she would reconsider.

What he didn't know was that she had reconsidered the exact moment she had opened the door to him last night. He had come to her when she had needed him most. He had been there with her and had shown her just what a dependable man he was.

And something else. What he'd told her was true. For the past fifteen years she had been trying to be a good girl for her parents. But even her daughter had been able to see something that she hadn't. She needed a life that didn't revolve around Tiffany or her parents. She was a grown woman and if she made mistakes they were hers to make.

She slowly took the couple of steps that brought her in front of Chance. "And I love your dad, too, Marcus. I discovered just how much I cared for him that weekend and it scared me because I didn't think I was ready to take such a big step as that."

"And are you ready now?" Chance asked her quietly, taking her hand in his.

She held his gaze and said softly, "Yes, I'm ready."

Again Marcus and Tiffany grinned.

"Okay, time for me to take the two of you out for

breakfast," Donovan said, sensing his brother and Kylie needed to be alone. "And since we won't be playing our basketball game today, I'll go pick up Bas and Morgan and we can work out our competitive frustrations on the video games."

"That's a wonderful idea," Marcus said, rushing for the door. "And now that Dad knows there's nothing going on with me and Tiffany, I can give Rhonda Denton my phone number."

"And I can give Brad Reagan mine," Tiffany added, following right on Marcus's heels.

Donovan turned to his brother and chuckled. "Boy, the two of you will have a lot to deal with after you get married, with two dating-age teens in the house." He then patted Chance on the back. "We're leaving so the two of you can settle things."

Chance gave his brother an appreciative nod. "And give us a courtesy call before you come back."

Understanding completely, Donovan laughed before he walked out the door, closing and locking it behind him.

"You admitted that you love me in front of them," Chance said huskily, still holding Kylie's hand in his. "I didn't think that you would."

She nodded. "I had to because it's the truth and I couldn't pretend otherwise."

"You know what this means, don't you?"

Yes, she knew what this meant. Chance had told her once that if there was something that he wanted, he wouldn't give up until he got it. "Yes, I know and now, since you have me, what are you going to do with me?"

He smiled that sexy smile that could make her heart race and make her dizzy. "My long-term goal is to marry you by next summer, if not before. But my short-term goal is to make love to you, right here and now."

And with that said he captured her mouth in a soul-searing kiss that left her trembling. And then he began removing her clothes as well as his own.

"No visitors and no kids for a while," she whispered when he had gotten her completely naked and stretched out on the sofa.

He smiled. "I would go get the caramel topping but that would be too messy, so I'm just going to have to use my imagination."

He did and enjoyed taking the long, lazy swipes of his tongue over every inch of her body, liking the sound of her moaning and groaning while he did so. By the time he had slid back up her body he knew he was about to take her in a way he had never taken her before. He had already slipped on the condom and the moment he was poised between her thighs, he looked down at her and remembered the term Tiffany had used.

Solid soul.

And as he began sinking deep within her silken heat, he knew that the love the two of them shared was solid soul. It was also something else. It was a love meant to be. A love destined to last a lifetime. A love forged in steel.

He lifted his head and looked into her eyes, then whispered a heartfelt request. "Marry me, baby."

Kylie smiled at him and when he hit her G-spot at an angle that made her moan deep in her throat, he smiled and asked softly, "Was that a yes?"

Her darkened eyes took on a positive gleam when she tightened her arms around his neck and groaned a resounding, "Yes."

EPILOGUE

CHANCE COULDN'T WAIT until the summer. He and Kylie were married on Christmas Day in the presence of family and friends. Considering how they had met, it seemed very fitting for Marcus to be his best man and Tiffany to be Kylie's maid of honor.

The deafening sounds of cheers, catcalls, whistles and applause shook the room when Chance pulled Kylie into his arms and kissed his bride. It was evident to anyone looking on that the two of them were in love and extremely happy.

At least it was evident to everyone but Cassandra Tisdale. She leaned in and angrily whispered to Bas, "I can't believe he married her when he had a chance with my cousin Jamie. Jamie is a lot prettier and has a lot more class. Kylie works at a florist for heaven's sakes! Chance is the CEO of one of the largest corporations in Charlotte. He needs a wife that will complement him."

Bas stared at her, not believing anyone could be that rude or snobbish. But he was seeing a side of Cassandra that he'd always seen. For some reason he'd convinced himself that he could live with it, but now he knew there was no way in hell he could. He wanted to one day have the same thing his brother had—a marriage built on love and mutual respect.

"So you don't think them loving each other is enough?" he asked after taking a sip of his wine.

She gave a ladylike snort. "Of course not. Love is never enough and no one should foolishly think otherwise. According to my mother, who as you know is an expert on social decorum, a good wife, one with the proper breeding like I have, is to be seen and not heard. Her manners and refinements are so ingrained that her husband knows her job is to keep the household running smoothly and make sure they establish the perfect family tree."

Bas lifted a brow. "The perfect family tree?"

"Yes, when they have children. Everything has to be skillfully planned."

Bas thought he'd heard enough. He really didn't give a damn for manners and refinements. Hell, he would settle for a woman oozing in scandal and sin to one who was nothing but a boring social trophy. And he would definitely prefer to come home every night to a wife who would be wearing sexy lace nighties than to one in a starched, buttoned-up-to-her-neck gown.

He shook his head knowing that later, when he took Cassandra home, he would give her the ultimate blow. There was no way in hell he would marry her. "Come on, they're about ready to cut the cake."

"It's not much of a cake if you ask me."

He had heard enough. "I don't recall anyone asking you, Cassandra. If all you're going to do is find fault and be negative, then I'd rather you keep your damn refined and proper mouth closed."

Bas smiled, certain his statement had pretty much shut her up for a while.

Across the room Chance pulled Kylie into his arms. "I love you, Mrs. Steele."

She smiled up at him. "And I love you, Mr. Steele." She then leaned over and whispered, "So what do you think of my parents?"

He smiled. "I can deal with them. They might have preferred you as their good little girl, but frankly I'd rather have you as my bad one. In fact, I plan for the two of us to get downright naughty tonight."

"You plan on teaching me some more moves?" she asked saucily.

"Yeah, among other things."

Kylie's gaze tangled intimately with his. After this small reception they would catch a plane for Hawaii. Chance's parents had returned for the wedding and volunteered to watch Marcus and their newest grandchild Tiffany, who they were anxious to get to know.

"We are going to make one big happy family," Chance said, leading Kylie over to the cake they would be cutting together.

"Yes," she agreed as she paused to place a kiss on her husband's lips. "One big happy family."

* * * * *

COMING NEXT MONTH

Available July 12, 2011

#2095 CAUGHT IN THE BILLIONAIRE'S EMBRACE
Elizabeth Bevarly

#2096 ONE NIGHT, TWO HEIRS
Maureen Child
Texas Cattleman's Club: The Showdown

#2097 THE TYCOON'S TEMPORARY BABY
Emily McKay
Billionaires and Babies

#2098 A LONE STAR LOVE AFFAIR
Sara Orwig
Stetsons & CEOs

#2099 ONE MONTH WITH THE MAGNATE
Michelle Celmer
Black Gold Billionaires

#2100 FALLING FOR THE PRINCESS
Sandra Hyatt

You can find more information on upcoming
Harlequin® titles, free excerpts and more at
www.HarlequinInsideRomance.com.

HDCNM0611

USA TODAY *bestselling author B.J. Daniels takes you on a trip to Whitehorse, Montana, and the Chisholm Cattle Company.*

RUSTLED

Available July 2011 from Harlequin Intrigue.

As the dust settled, Dawson got his first good look at the rustler. A pair of big Montana sky-blue eyes glared up at him from a face framed by blond curls.

A woman rustler?

"You have to let me go," she hollered as the roar of the stampeding cattle died off in the distance.

"So you can finish stealing my cattle? I don't think so." Dawson jerked the woman to her feet.

She reached for the gun strapped to her hip hidden under her long barn jacket.

He grabbed the weapon before she could, his eyes narrowing as he assessed her. "How many others are there?" he demanded, grabbing a fistful of her jacket. "I think you'd better start talking before I tear into you."

She tried to fight him off, but he was on to her tricks and pinned her to the ground. He was suddenly aware of the soft curves beneath the jean jacket she wore under her coat.

"You have to listen to me." She ground out the words from between her gritted teeth. "You have to let me go. If you don't they will come back for me and they will kill you. There are too many of them for you to fight off alone. You won't stand a chance and I don't want your blood on my hands."

"I'm touched by your concern for me. Especially after you just tried to pull a gun on me."

"I wasn't going to shoot you."

Dawson hauled her to her feet and walked her the rest of the way to his horse. Reaching into his saddlebag, he pulled out a length of rope.

"You can't tie me up."

He pulled her hands behind her back and began to tie her wrists together.

"If you let me go, I can keep them from coming back," she said. "You have my word." She let out an unladylike curse. "I'm just trying to save your sorry neck."

"And I'm just going after my cattle."

"Don't you mean your boss's cattle?"

"Those cattle are mine."

"*You're* a Chisholm?"

"Dawson Chisholm. And you are…?"

"Everyone calls me Jinx."

He chuckled. "I can see why."

Bronco busting, falling in love…it's all in a day's work.
Look for the rest of their story in

RUSTLED

Available July 2011 from Harlequin Intrigue
wherever books are sold.